Sanity & Tallulah
Field Trip

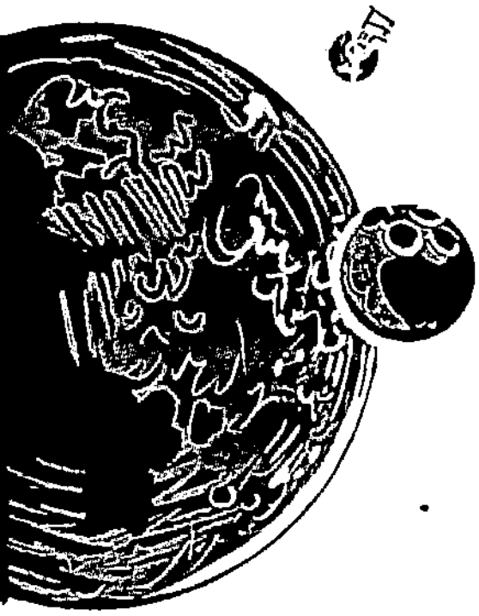

Sanity &

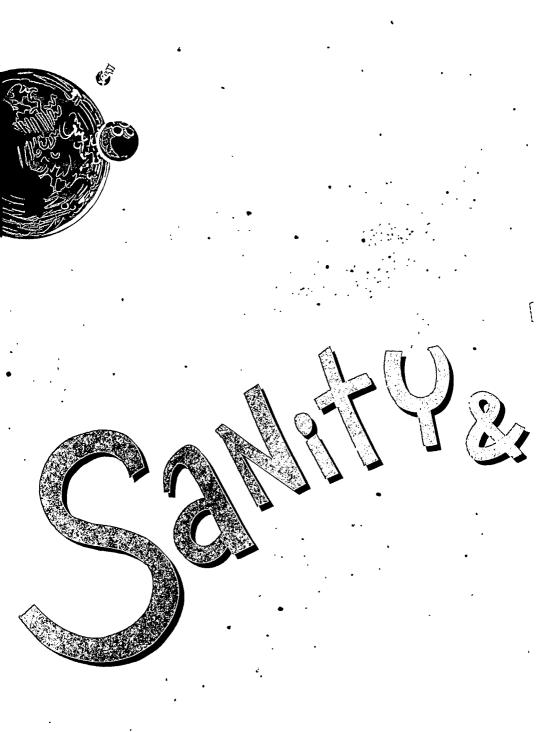

TALLULAH
FiELDTRiP

MOLLY BROOKS

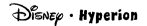

LOS ANGELES   NEW YORK

First Edition, October 2019

10 9 8 7 6 5 4 3 2 1

FAC-020093-19249

Printed in the United States of America

This book is set in 9-pt Gargle/Fontspring
Designed by Phil Buchanan

Library of Congress Cataloging-in-Publication Data

Names: Brooks, Molly (Molly Grayson), author, illustrator.
Title: Field trip / Molly Brooks.
Description: First edition. • Los Angeles ; New York : Disney-Hyperion, 2019 •
    Series: Sanity & Tallulah ; [2] • Summary: When Sanity and Tallulah are
    separated from their classmates during a disastrous field trip to a mining
    planet, they must rely on their creativity and problem-solving skills to
    save the day.
Identifiers: LCCN 2018057040 • ISBN 9781368009782 (hardcover) •
    ISBN 1368009786 (hardcover) • ISBN 9781368023771 (pbk.) • ISBN 1368023770 (pbk.)
Subjects: LCSH: Graphic novels. • CYAC: Graphic novels. • School field
    trips—Fiction. • Planets—Fiction. • Science fiction.
Classification: LCC PZ7.7.B765 Fie 2019 • DDC 741.5/973—dc23
LC record available at https://lccn.loc.gov/2018057040

Reinforced binding

Visit www.DisneyBooks.com

SUSTAINABLE FORESTRY INITIATIVE   Certified Sourcing
www.sfiprogram.org
SFI-00993
Logo Applies to Text Stock Only

for my brother, Eric.
I feel so lucky to be your friend. <3

SANITY & TALLULAH
FIELD TRIP

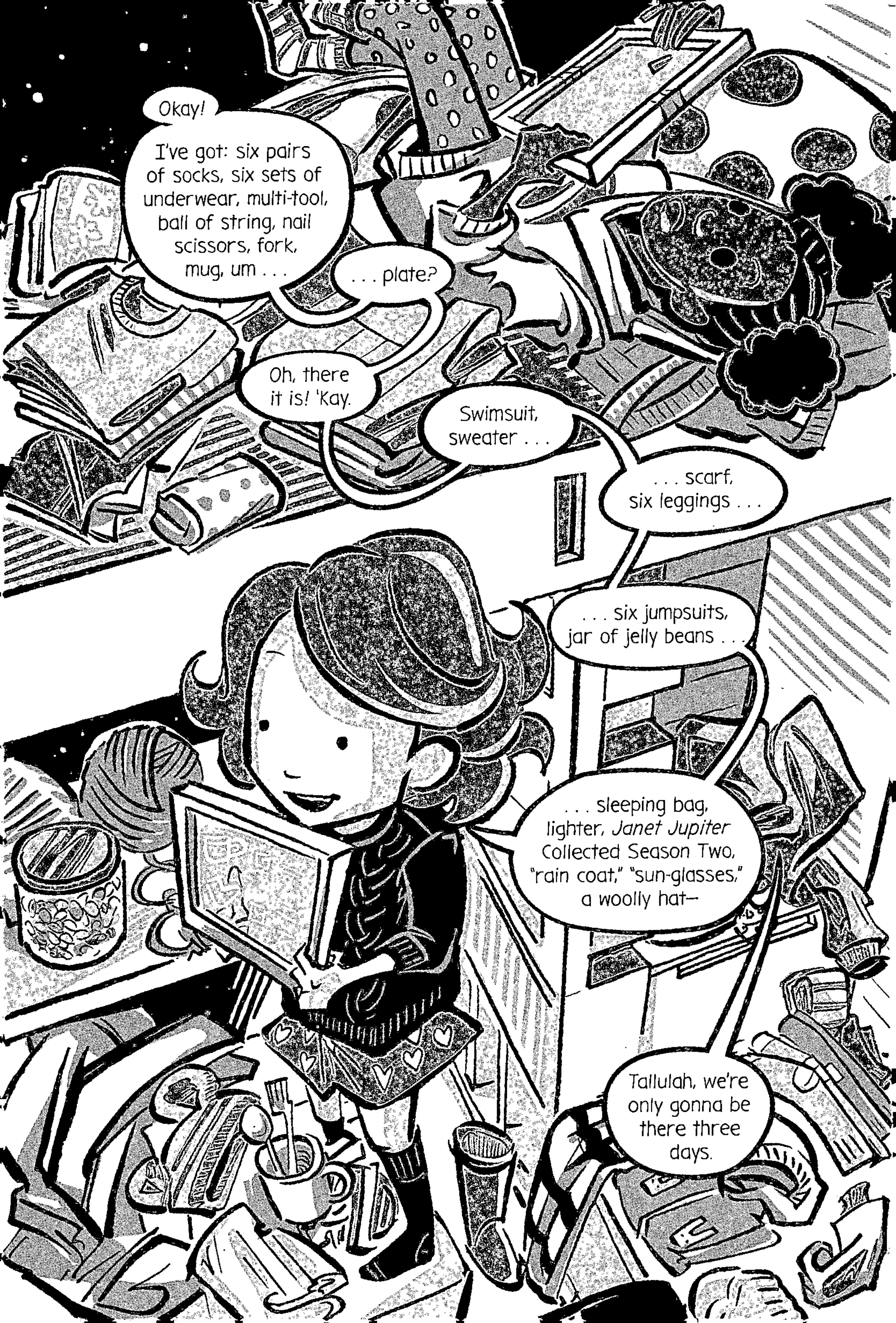
Okay!
I've got: six pairs of socks, six sets of underwear, multi-tool, ball of string, nail scissors, fork, mug, um . . .
. . . plate?
Oh, there it is! 'Kay.
Swimsuit, sweater . . .
. . . scarf, six leggings . . .
. . . six jumpsuits, jar of jelly beans . . .
. . . sleeping bag, lighter, *Janet Jupiter* Collected Season Two, "rain coat," "sun-glasses," a woolly hat—
Tallulah, we're only gonna be there three days.

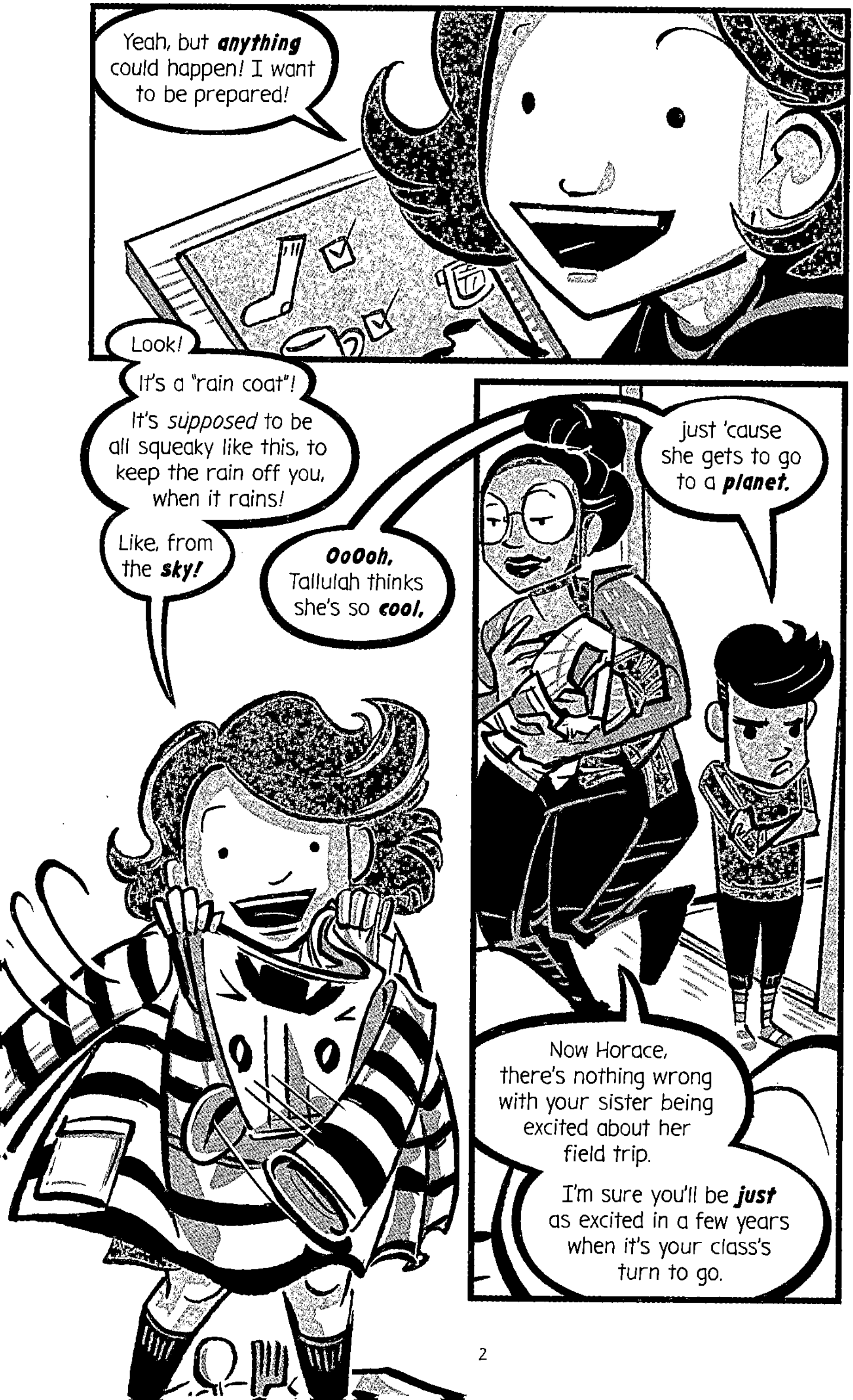
Yeah, but anything could happen! I want to be prepared!
Look!
It's a "rain coat"!
It's supposed to be all squeaky like this, to keep the rain off you, when it rains!
Like, from the sky!
OoOoh, Tallulah thinks she's so cool,
just 'cause she gets to go to a planet.
Now Horace, there's nothing wrong with your sister being excited about her field trip.
I'm sure you'll be just as excited in a few years when it's your class's turn to go.

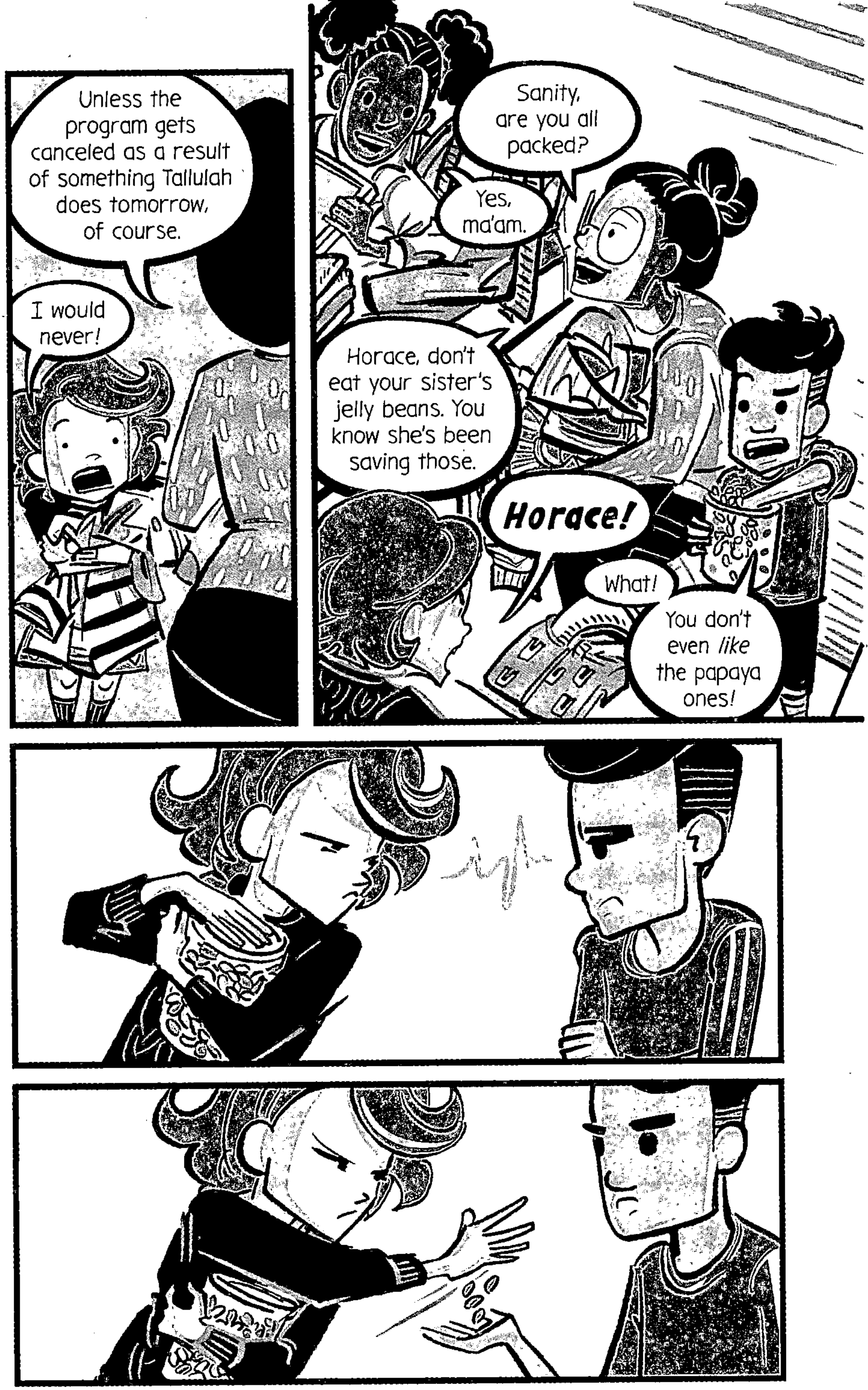
Unless the program gets canceled as a result of something Tallulah does tomorrow, of course.
I would never!
Sanity, are you all packed?
Yes, ma'am.
Horace, don't eat your sister's jelly beans. You know she's been saving those.
Horace!
What!
You don't even *like* the papaya ones!

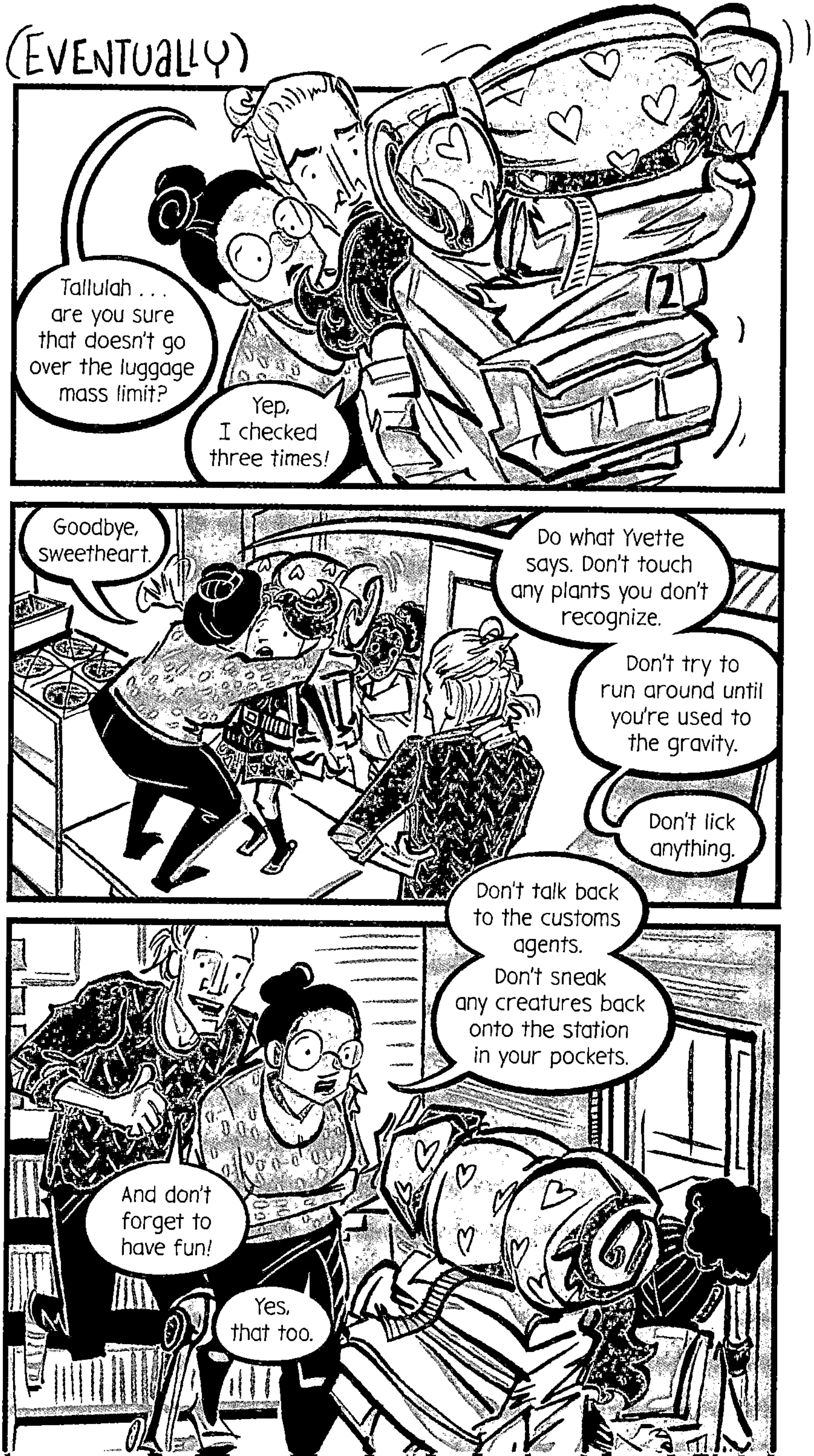
(Eventually)
Tallulah . . . are you sure that doesn't go over the luggage mass limit?
Yep, I checked three times!
Goodbye, sweetheart.
Do what Yvette says. Don't touch any plants you don't recognize.
Don't try to run around until you're used to the gravity.
Don't lick anything.
Don't talk back to the customs agents.
Don't sneak any creatures back onto the station in your pockets.
And don't forget to have fun!
Yes, that too.

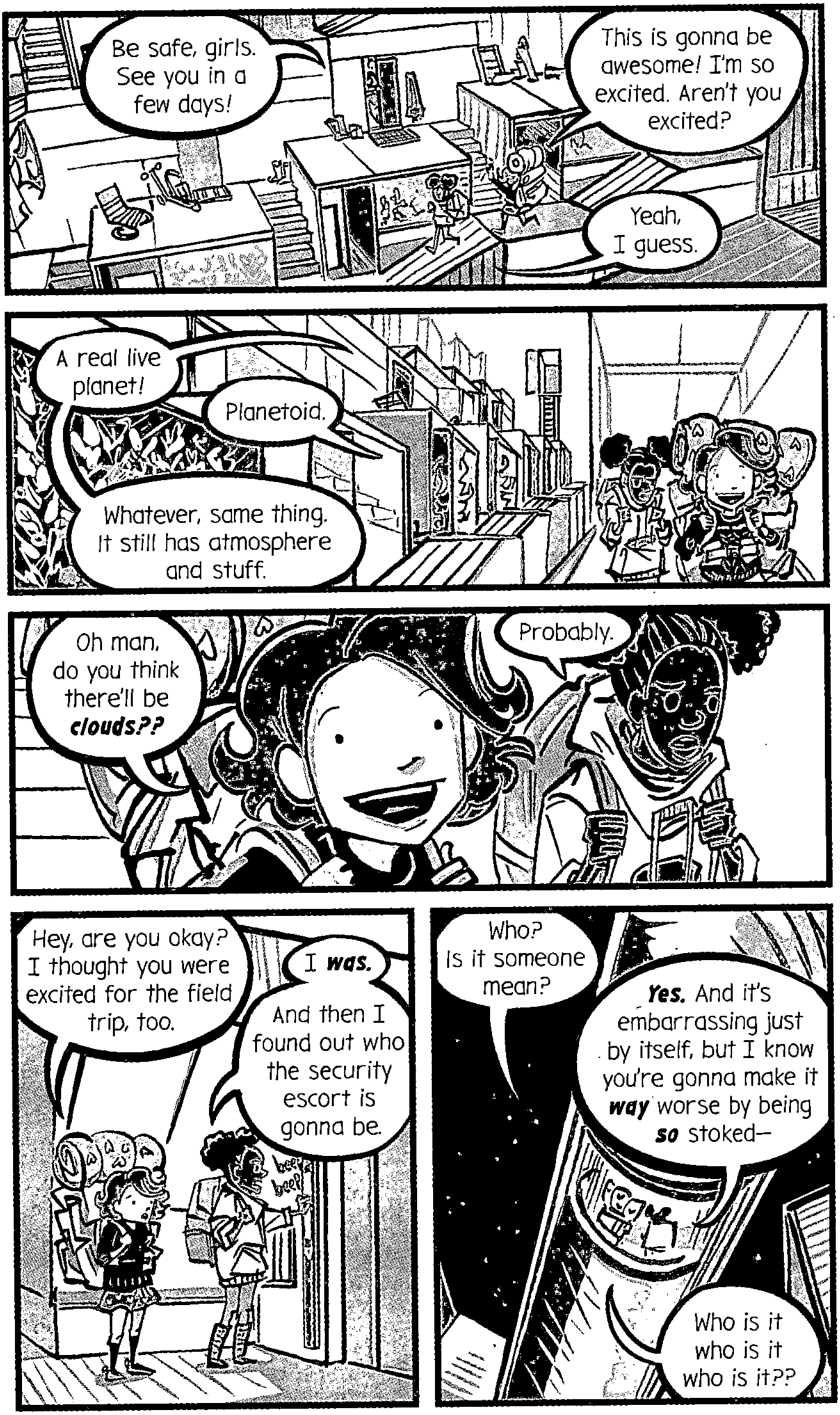
Be safe, girls. See you in a few days!
This is gonna be awesome! I'm so excited. Aren't you excited?
Yeah, I guess.
A real live planet!
Planetoid.
Whatever, same thing. It still has atmosphere and stuff.
Oh man, do you think there'll be **clouds??**
Probably.
Hey, are you okay? I thought you were excited for the field trip, too.
I ***was.***
And then I found out who the security escort is gonna be.
Who? Is it someone mean?
Yes. And it's embarrassing just by itself, but I know you're gonna make it ***way*** worse by being ***so*** stoked—
Who is it who is it who is it??

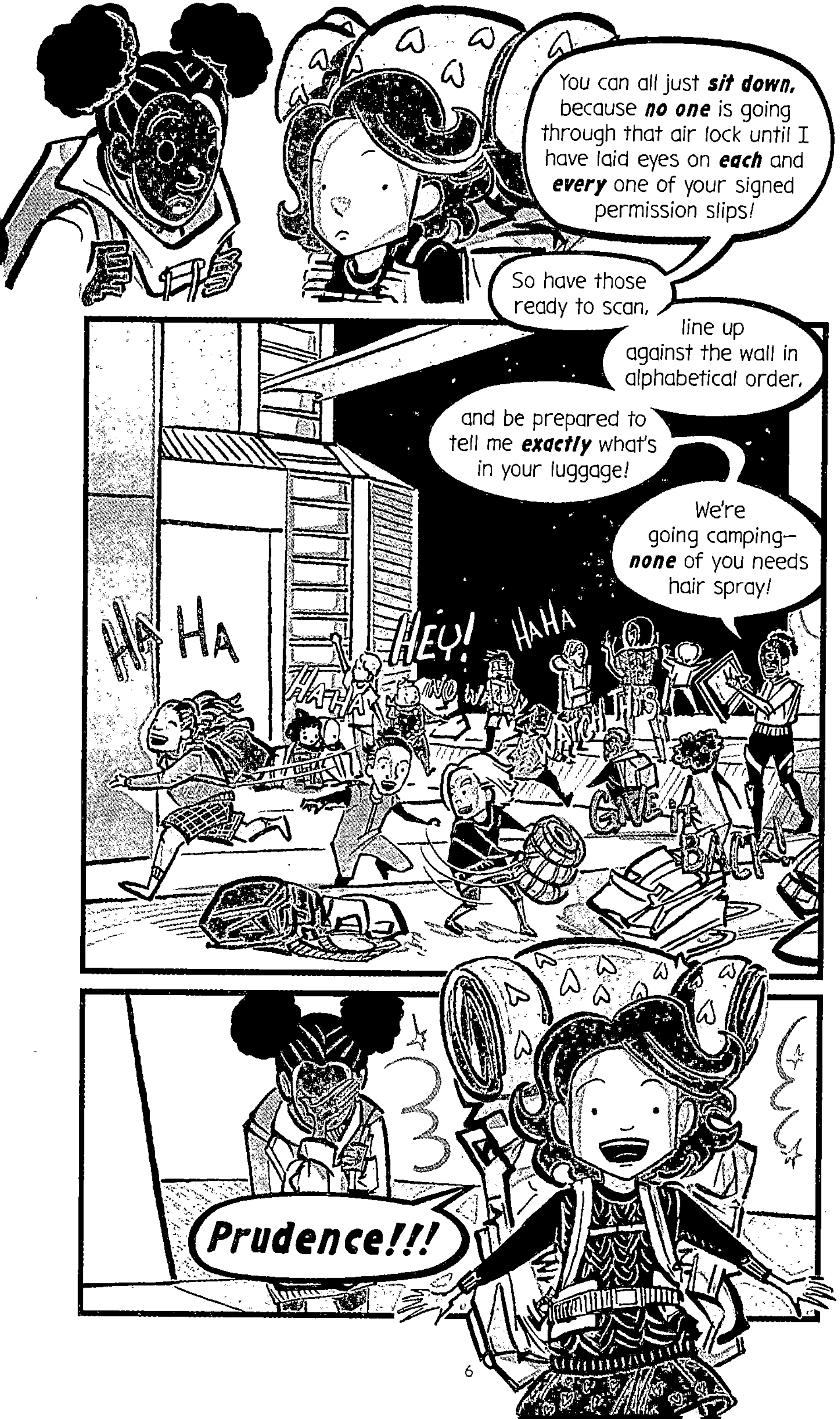
You can all just ***sit down,*** because ***no one*** is going through that air lock until I have laid eyes on ***each*** and ***every*** one of your signed permission slips!
So have those ready to scan,
line up against the wall in alphabetical order,
and be prepared to tell me ***exactly*** what's in your luggage!
We're going camping—***none*** of you needs hair spray!
HA HA
HEY!
HAHA
WATCH THIS
GIVE IT BACK
Prudence!!!

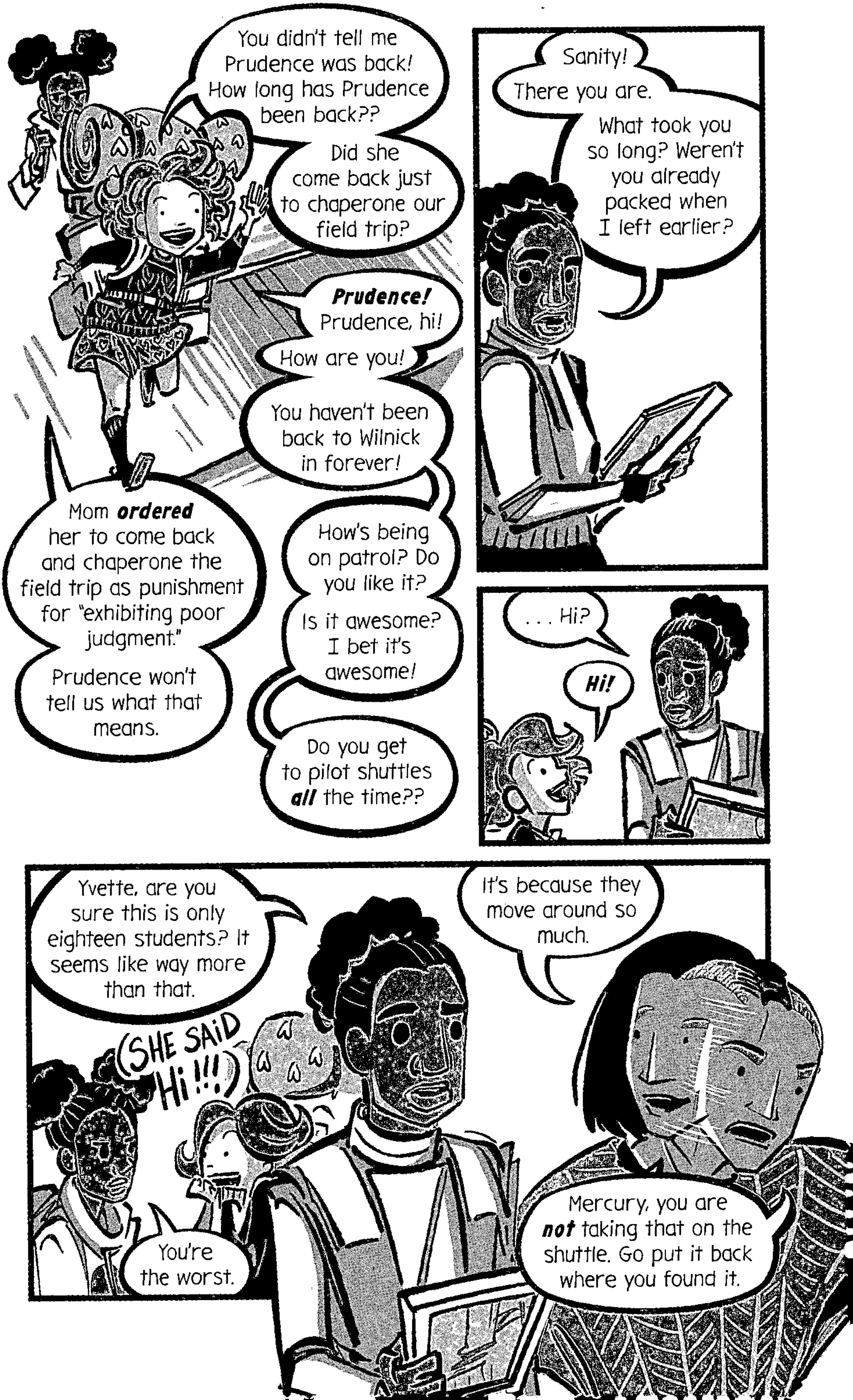
You didn't tell me Prudence was back! How long has Prudence been back??
Did she come back just to chaperone our field trip?
Prudence! Prudence, hi!
How are you!
You haven't been back to Wilnick in forever!
Mom ordered her to come back and chaperone the field trip as punishment for "exhibiting poor judgment."
Prudence won't tell us what that means.
How's being on patrol? Do you like it?
Is it awesome? I bet it's awesome!
Do you get to pilot shuttles all the time??
Sanity! There you are.
What took you so long? Weren't you already packed when I left earlier?
. . . Hi?
Hi!
Yvette, are you sure this is only eighteen students? It seems like way more than that.
It's because they move around so much.
(SHE SAID Hi!!!)
You're the worst.
Mercury, you are not taking that on the shuttle. Go put it back where you found it.

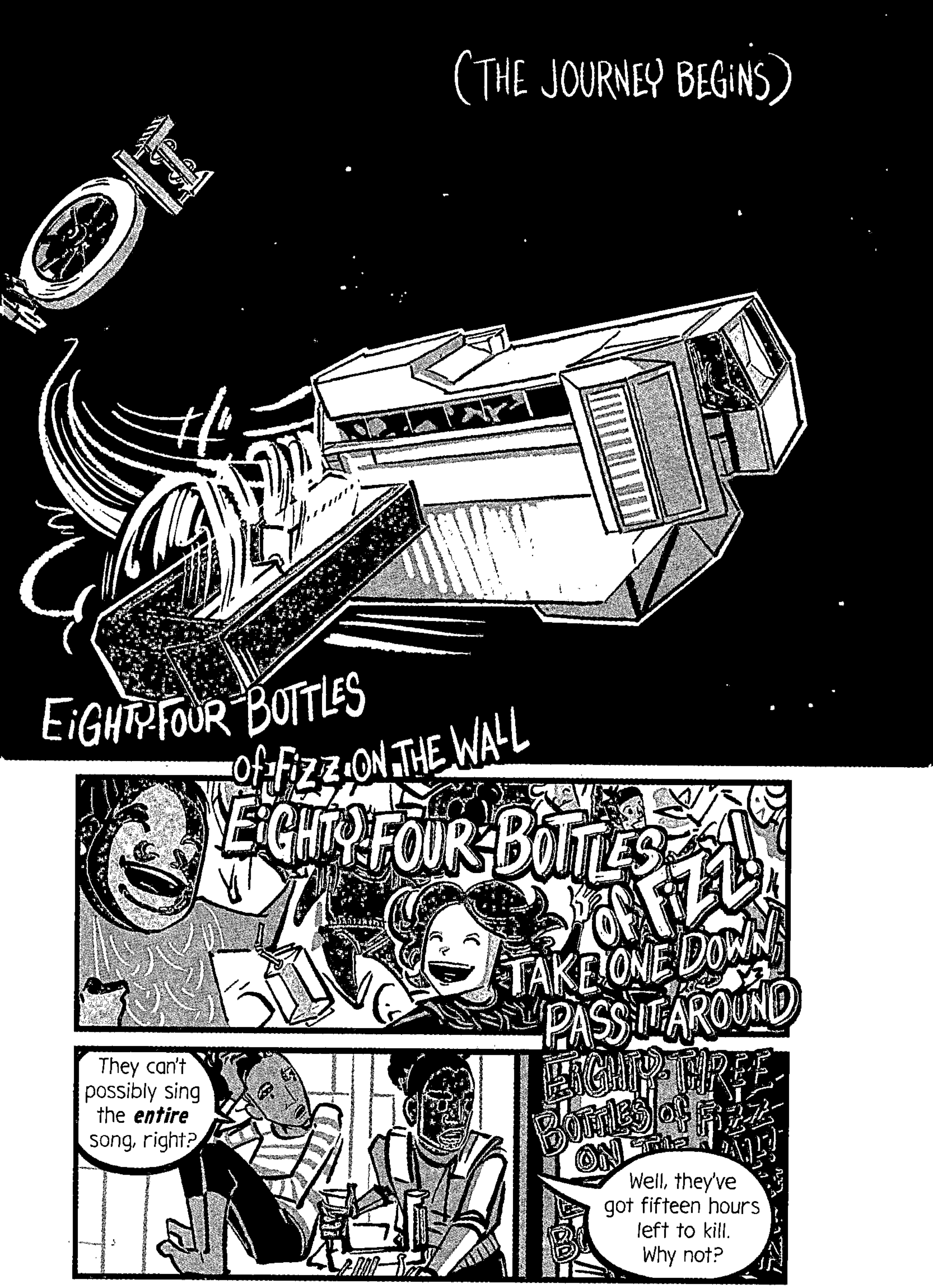
(THE JOURNEY BEGINS)
EIGHTY-FOUR BOTTLES
of FIZZ ON THE WALL
EIGHTY-FOUR BOTTLES of FIZZ!
TAKE ONE DOWN
PASS IT AROUND
EIGHTY-THREE BOTTLES of FIZZ
ON
They can't possibly sing the ***entire*** song, right?
Well, they've got fifteen hours left to kill. Why not?

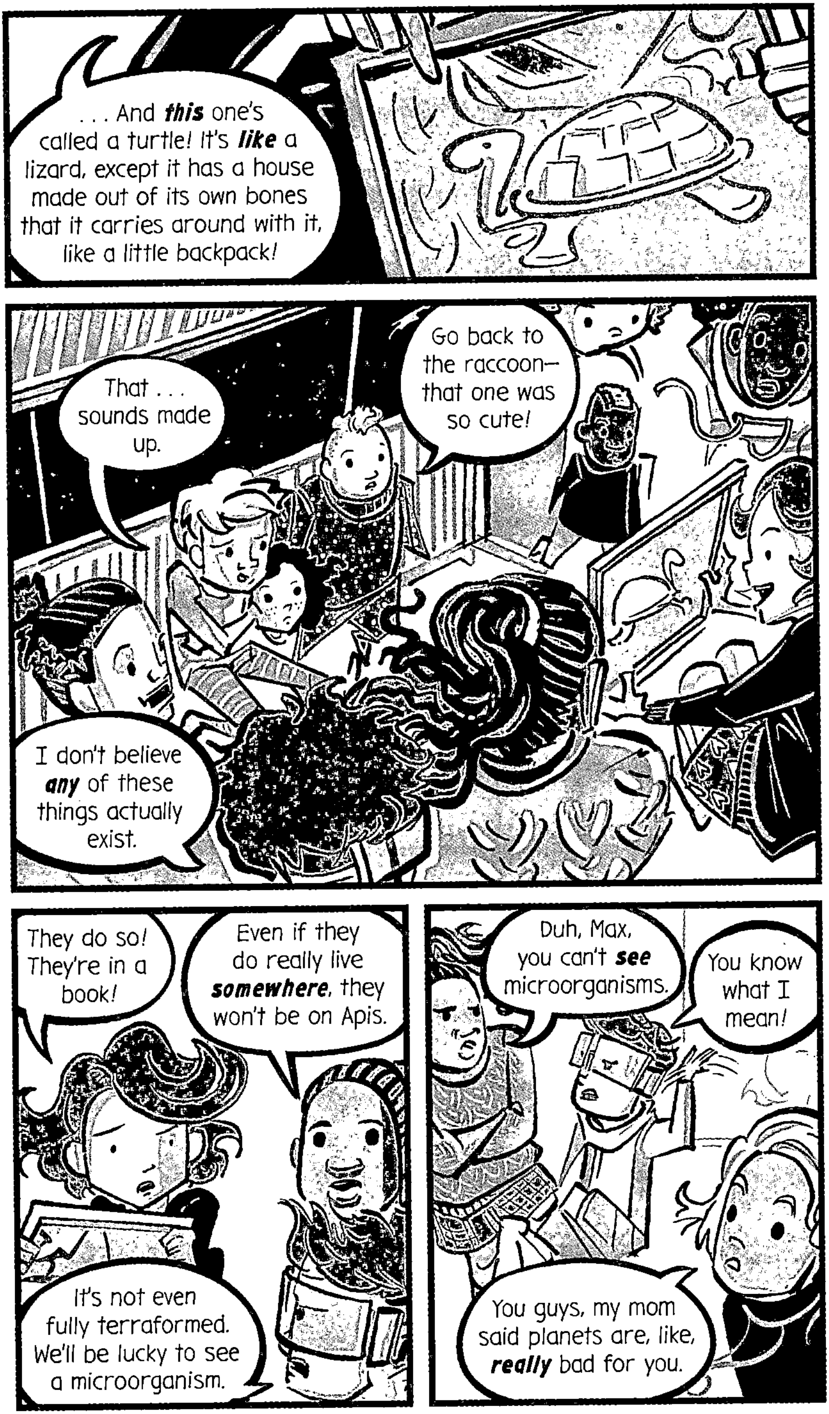

. . . And ***this*** one's called a turtle! It's ***like*** a lizard, except it has a house made out of its own bones that it carries around with it, like a little backpack!
That . . . sounds made up.
Go back to the raccoon—that one was so cute!
I don't believe ***any*** of these things actually exist.
They do so! They're in a book!
Even if they do really live ***somewhere***, they won't be on Apis.
It's not even fully terraformed. We'll be lucky to see a microorganism.
Duh, Max, you can't ***see*** microorganisms.
You know what I mean!
You guys, my mom said planets are, like, ***really*** bad for you.

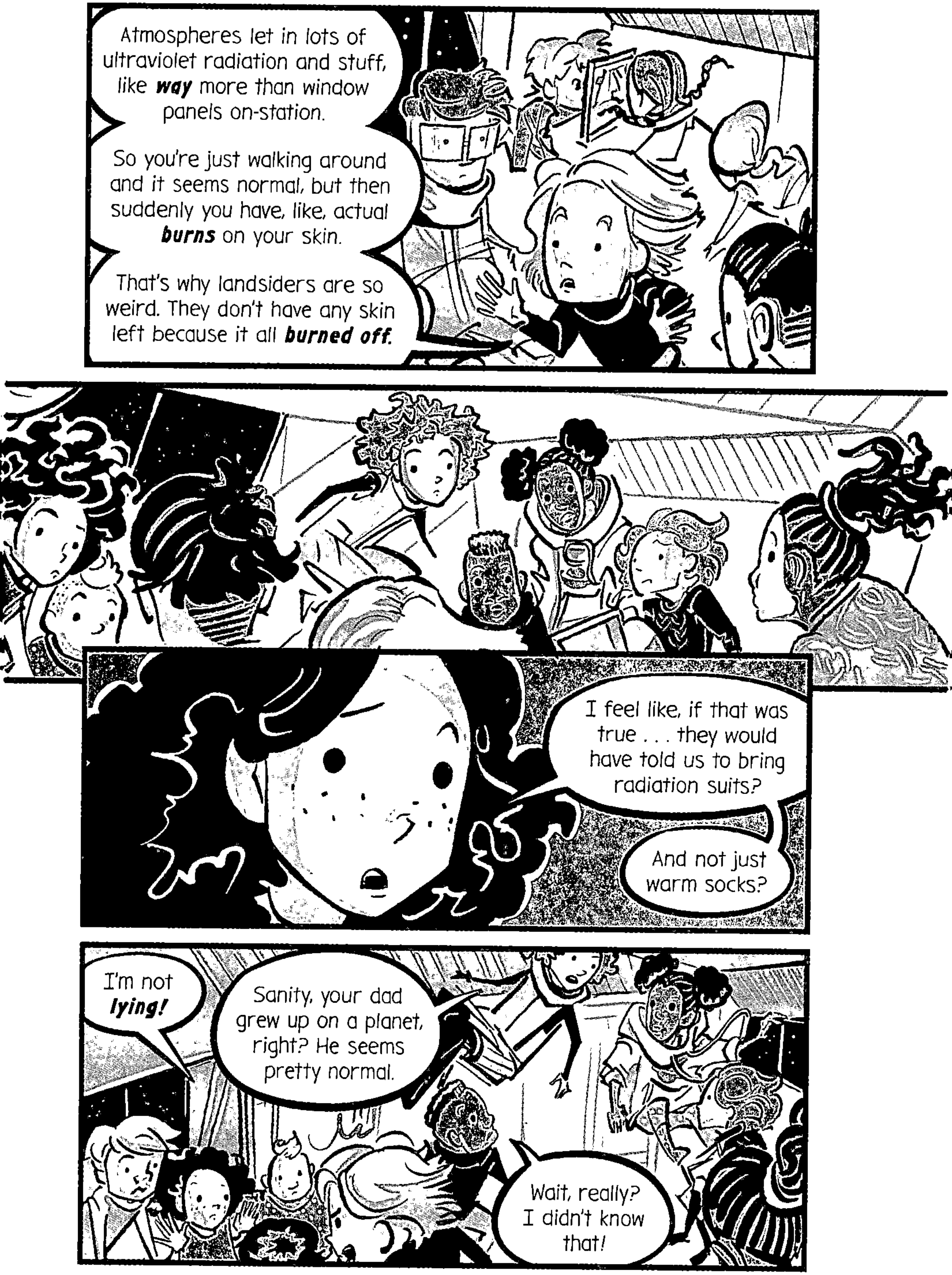
Atmospheres let in lots of ultraviolet radiation and stuff, like **way** more than window panels on-station.
So you're just walking around and it seems normal, but then suddenly you have, like, actual **burns** on your skin.
That's why landsiders are so weird. They don't have any skin left because it all **burned off.**
I feel like, if that was true . . . they would have told us to bring radiation suits?
And not just warm socks?
I'm not **lying!**
Sanity, your dad grew up on a planet, right? He seems pretty normal.
Wait, really? I didn't know that!

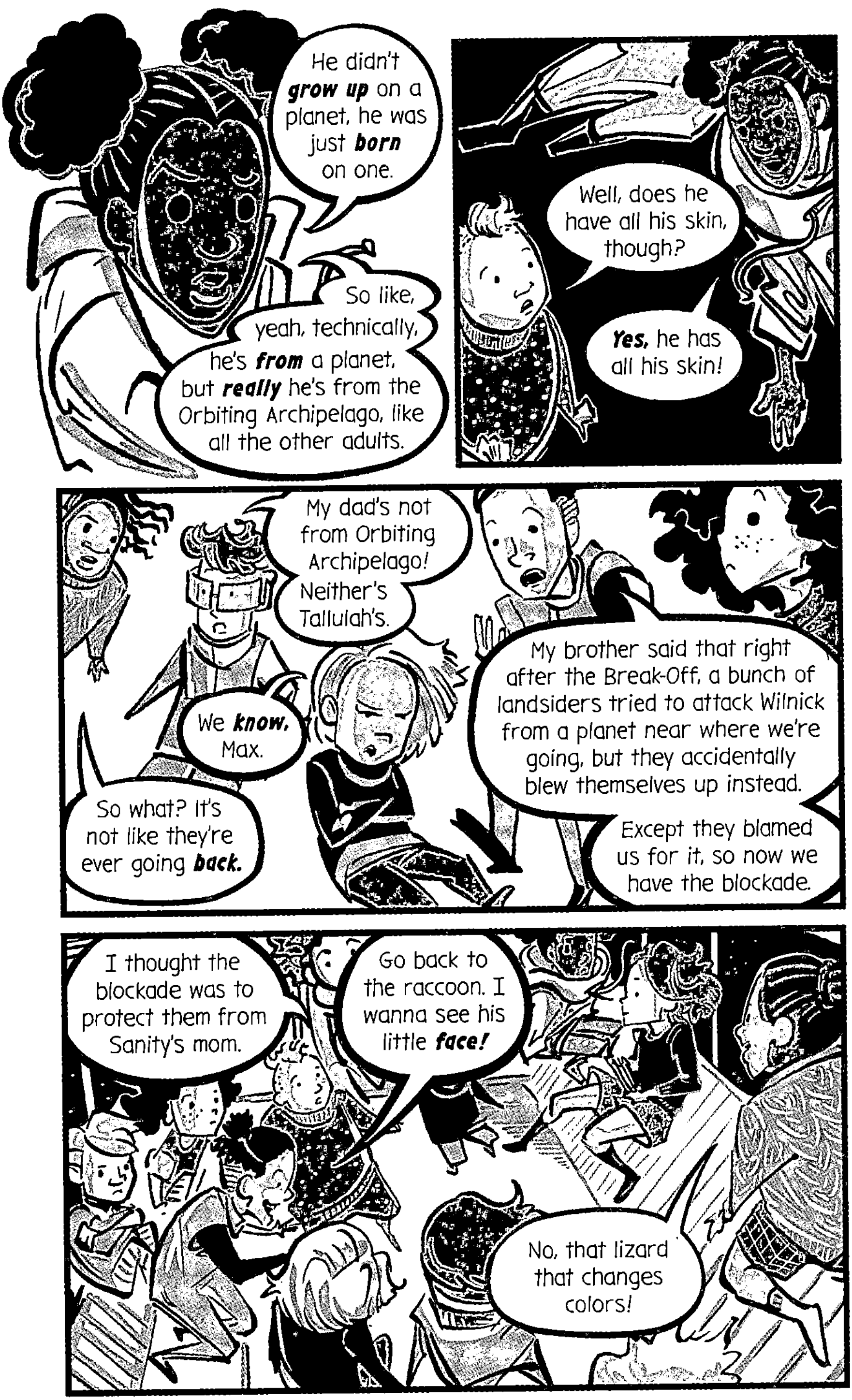
He didn't **grow up** on a planet, he was just **born** on one.
So like, yeah, technically, he's **from** a planet, but **really** he's from the Orbiting Archipelago, like all the other adults.
Well, does he have all his skin, though?
Yes, he has all his skin!
My dad's not from Orbiting Archipelago! Neither's Tallulah's.
We **know,** Max.
So what? It's not like they're ever going **back.**
My brother said that right after the Break-Off, a bunch of landsiders tried to attack Wilnick from a planet near where we're going, but they accidentally blew themselves up instead.
Except they blamed us for it, so now we have the blockade.
I thought the blockade was to protect them from Sanity's mom.
Go back to the raccoon. I wanna see his little **face!**
No, that lizard that changes colors!

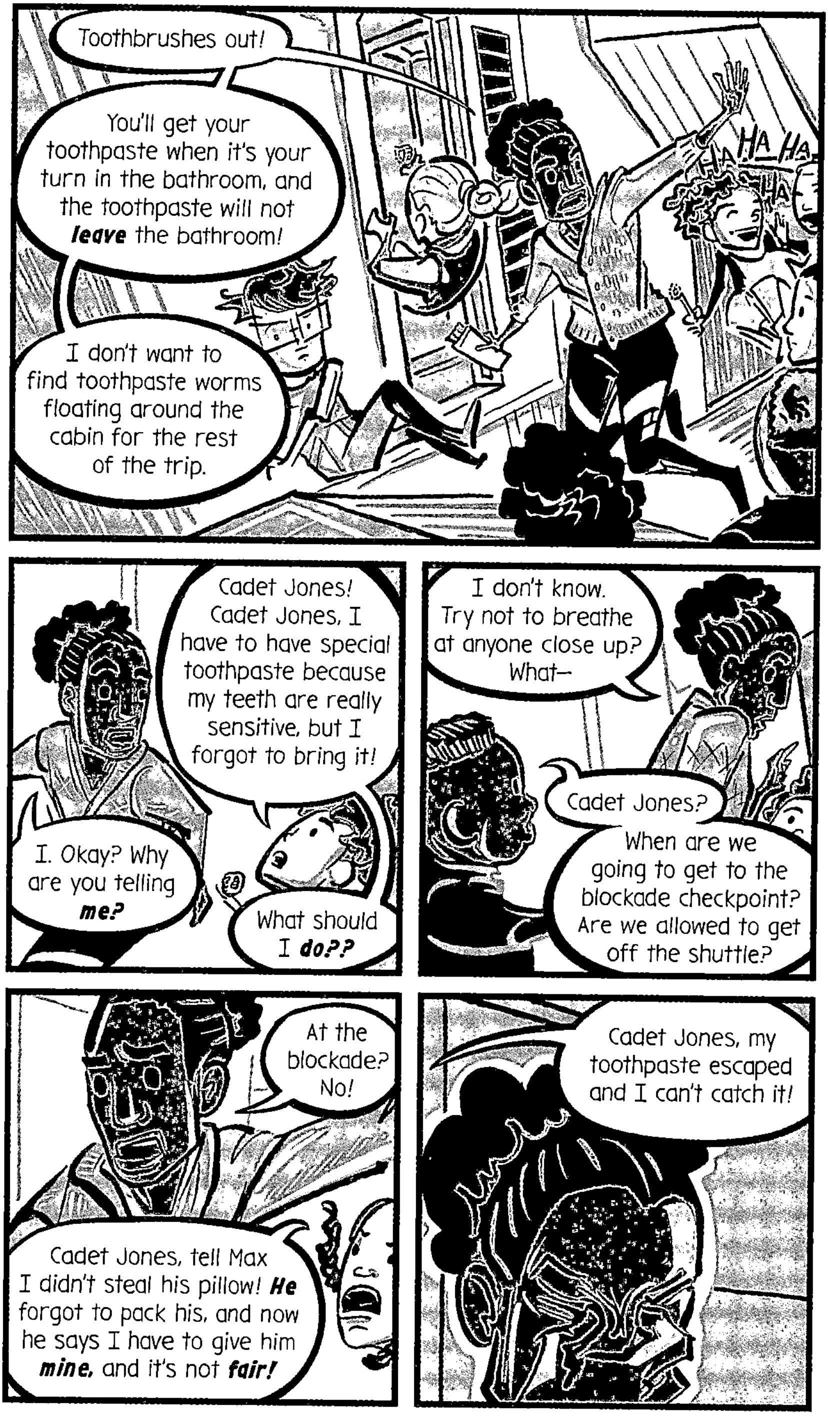
Toothbrushes out!
You'll get your toothpaste when it's your turn in the bathroom, and the toothpaste will not ***leave*** the bathroom!
I don't want to find toothpaste worms floating around the cabin for the rest of the trip.
HA HA HA HA
Cadet Jones! Cadet Jones, I have to have special toothpaste because my teeth are really sensitive, but I forgot to bring it!
I. Okay? Why are you telling ***me?***
What should I ***do??***
I don't know. Try not to breathe at anyone close up? What–
Cadet Jones?
When are we going to get to the blockade checkpoint? Are we allowed to get off the shuttle?
At the blockade? No!
Cadet Jones, tell Max I didn't steal his pillow! ***He*** forgot to pack his, and now he says I have to give him ***mine,*** and it's not ***fair!***
Cadet Jones, my toothpaste escaped and I can't catch it!

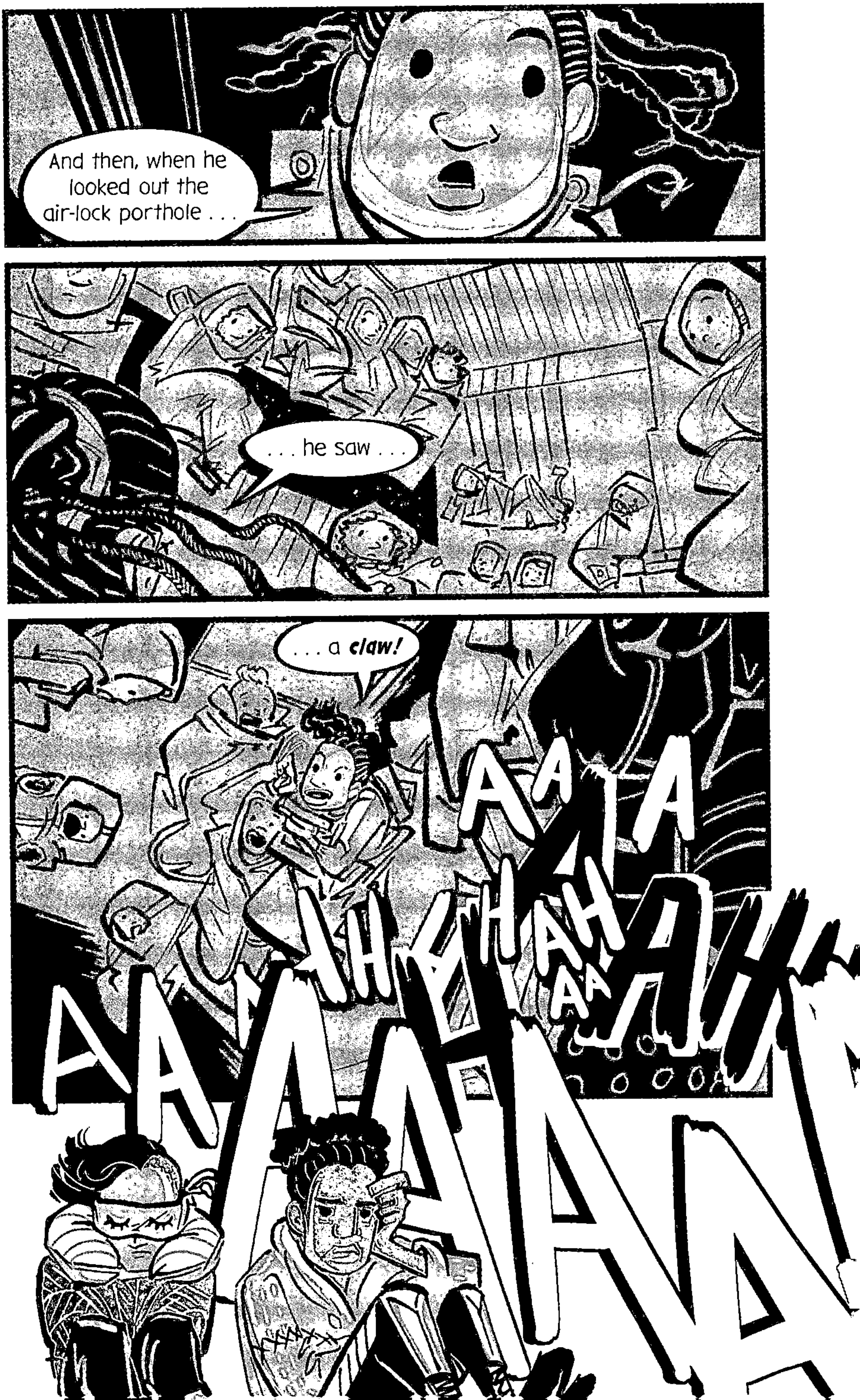
And then, when he looked out the air-lock porthole . . .
. . . he saw . . .
. . . a *claw!*
AAAHHHAAAAHAHAAAAA

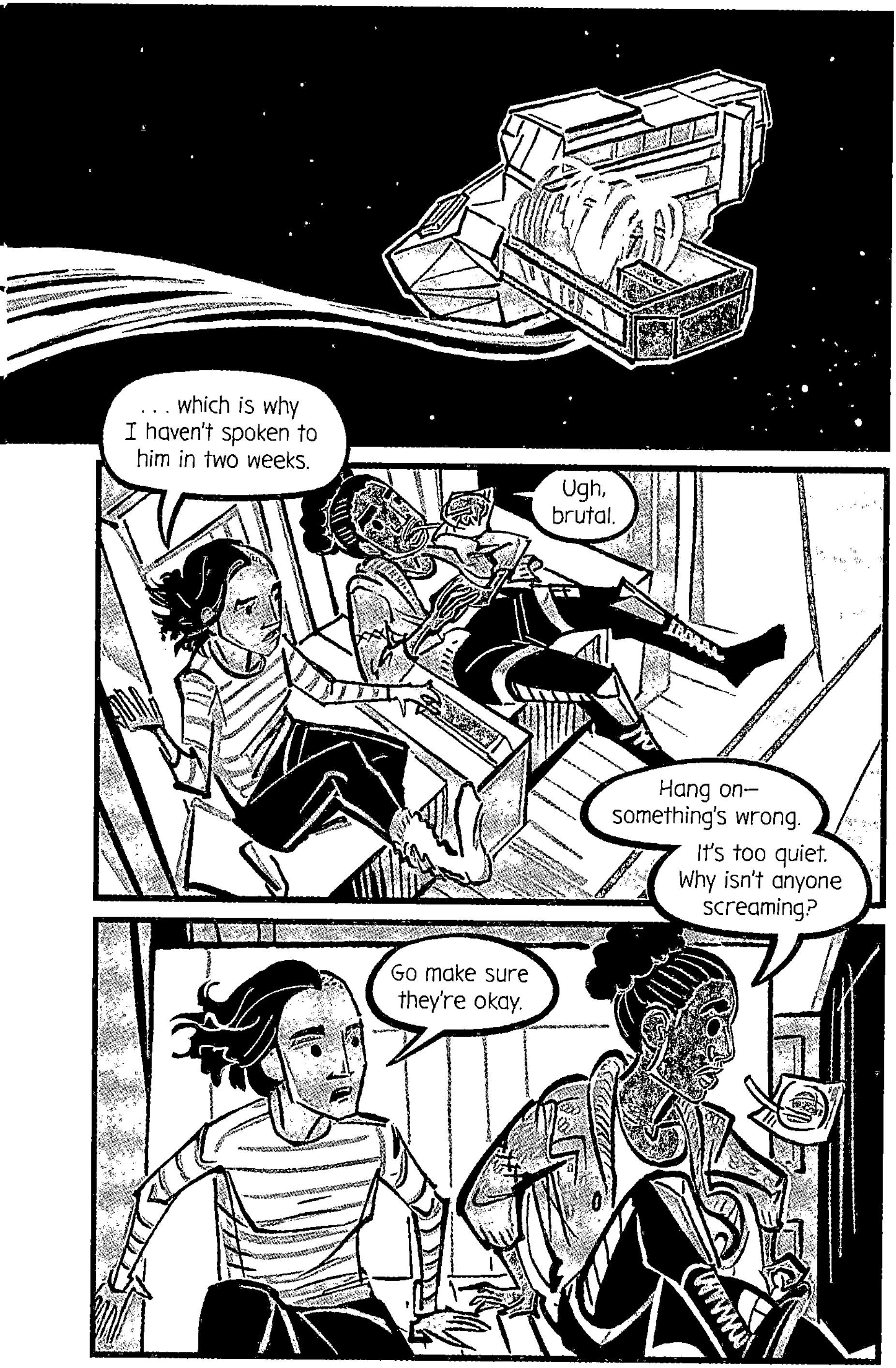
. . . which is why I haven't spoken to him in two weeks.
Ugh, brutal.
Hang on— something's wrong.
It's too quiet. Why isn't anyone screaming?
Go make sure they're okay.

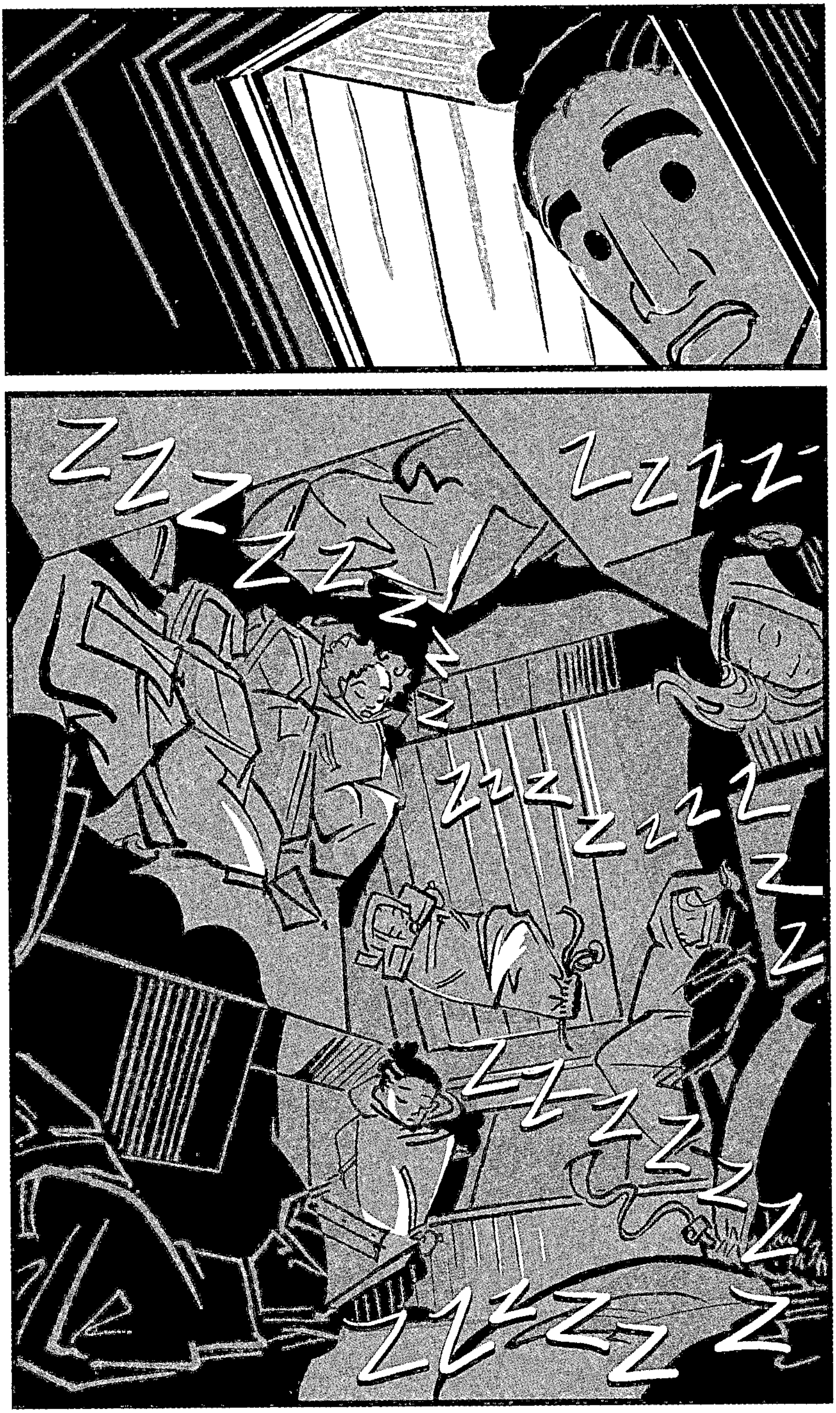
ZZZ
ZZZZZ
ZZZZZ
ZZZ
ZZZZZ
ZZZ
ZZZZZZ
ZZZZZZZ

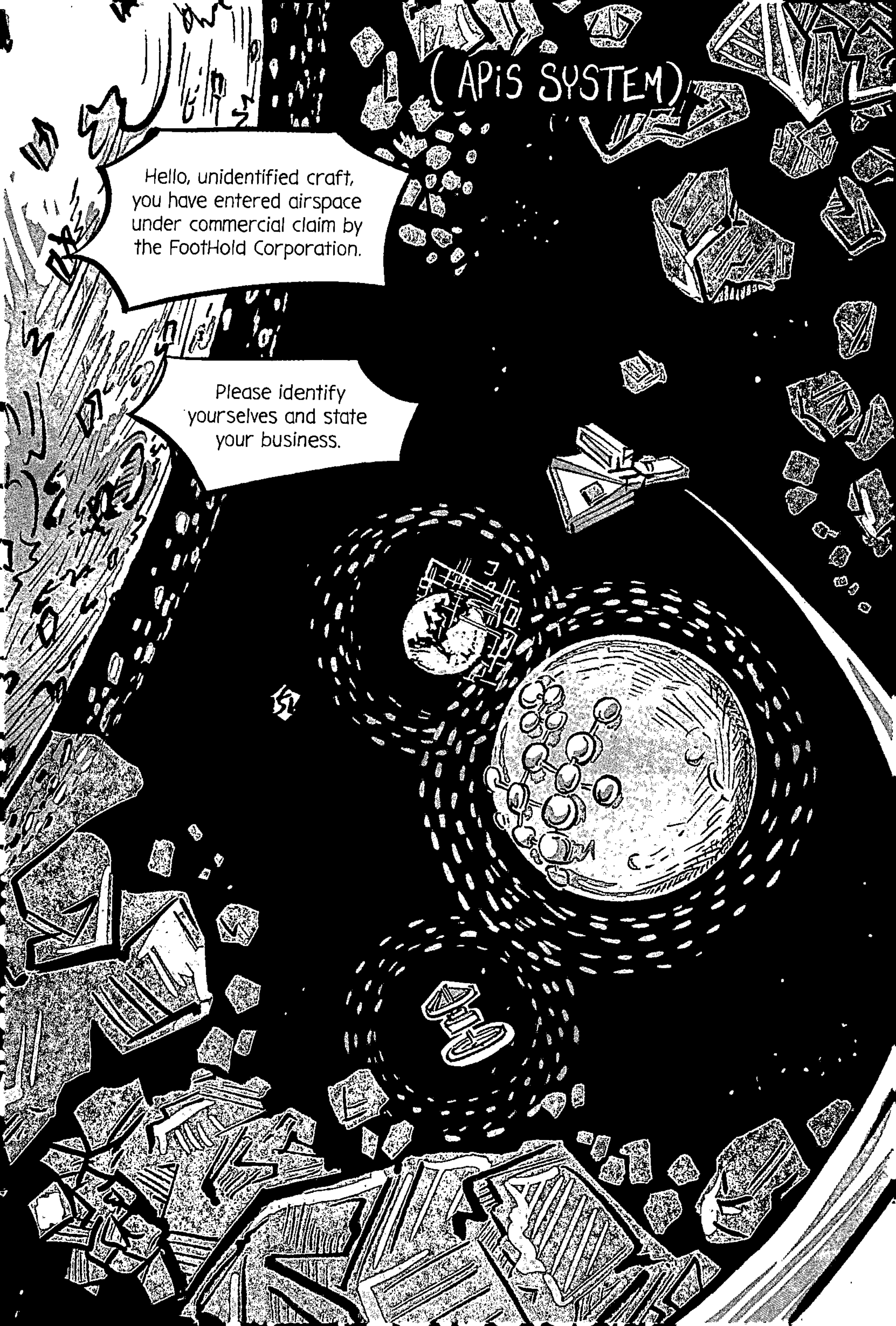
(APIS SYSTEM)
Hello, unidentified craft, you have entered airspace under commercial claim by the FootHold Corporation.
Please identify yourselves and state your business.

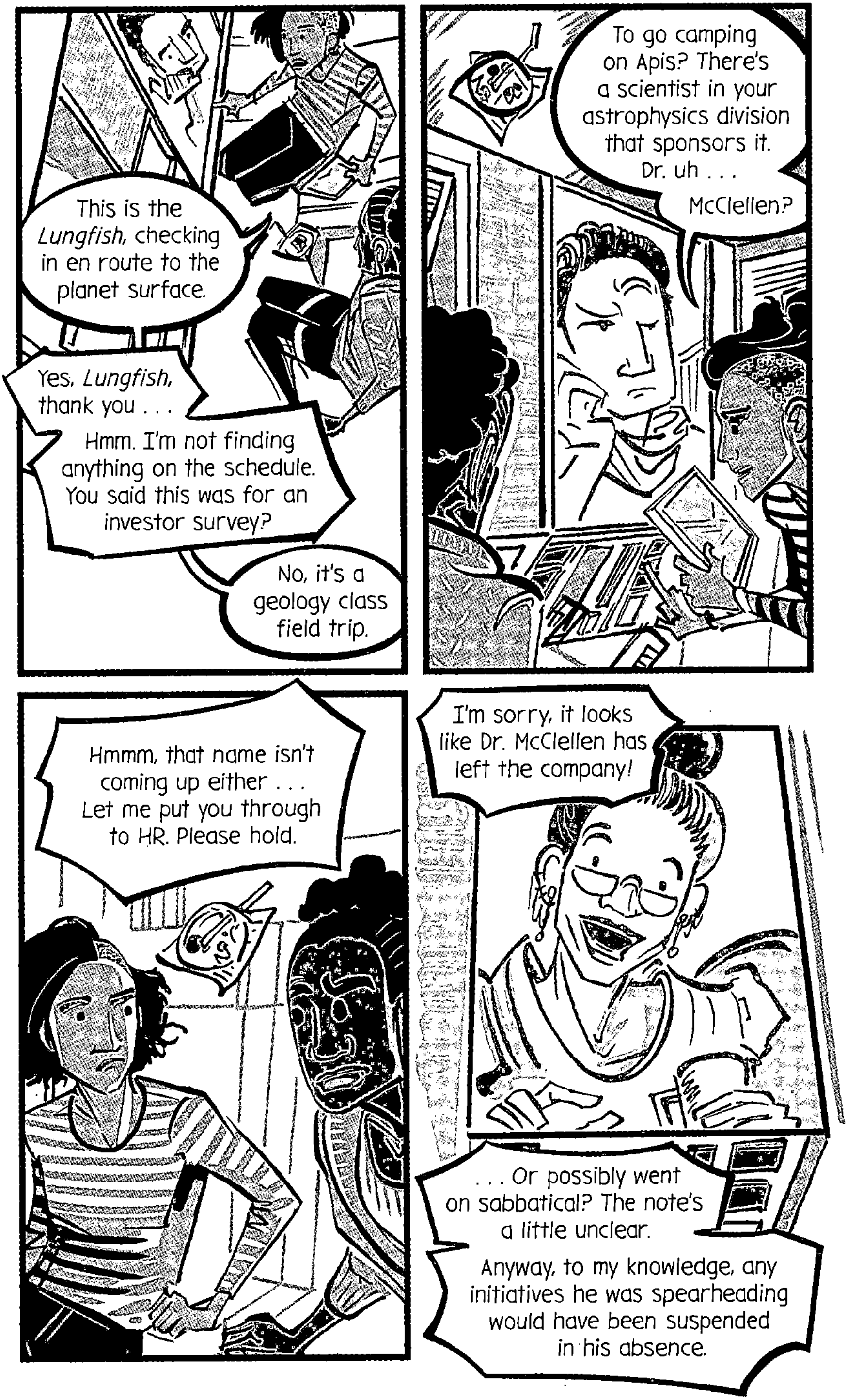
This is the *Lungfish,* checking in en route to the planet surface.
Yes, *Lungfish,* thank you . . .
Hmm. I'm not finding anything on the schedule. You said this was for an investor survey?
No, it's a geology class field trip.
To go camping on Apis? There's a scientist in your astrophysics division that sponsors it. Dr. uh . . .
McClellen?
Hmmm, that name isn't coming up either . . . Let me put you through to HR. Please hold.
I'm sorry, it looks like Dr. McClellen has left the company!
. . . Or possibly went on sabbatical? The note's a little unclear.
Anyway, to my knowledge, any initiatives he was spearheading would have been suspended in his absence.

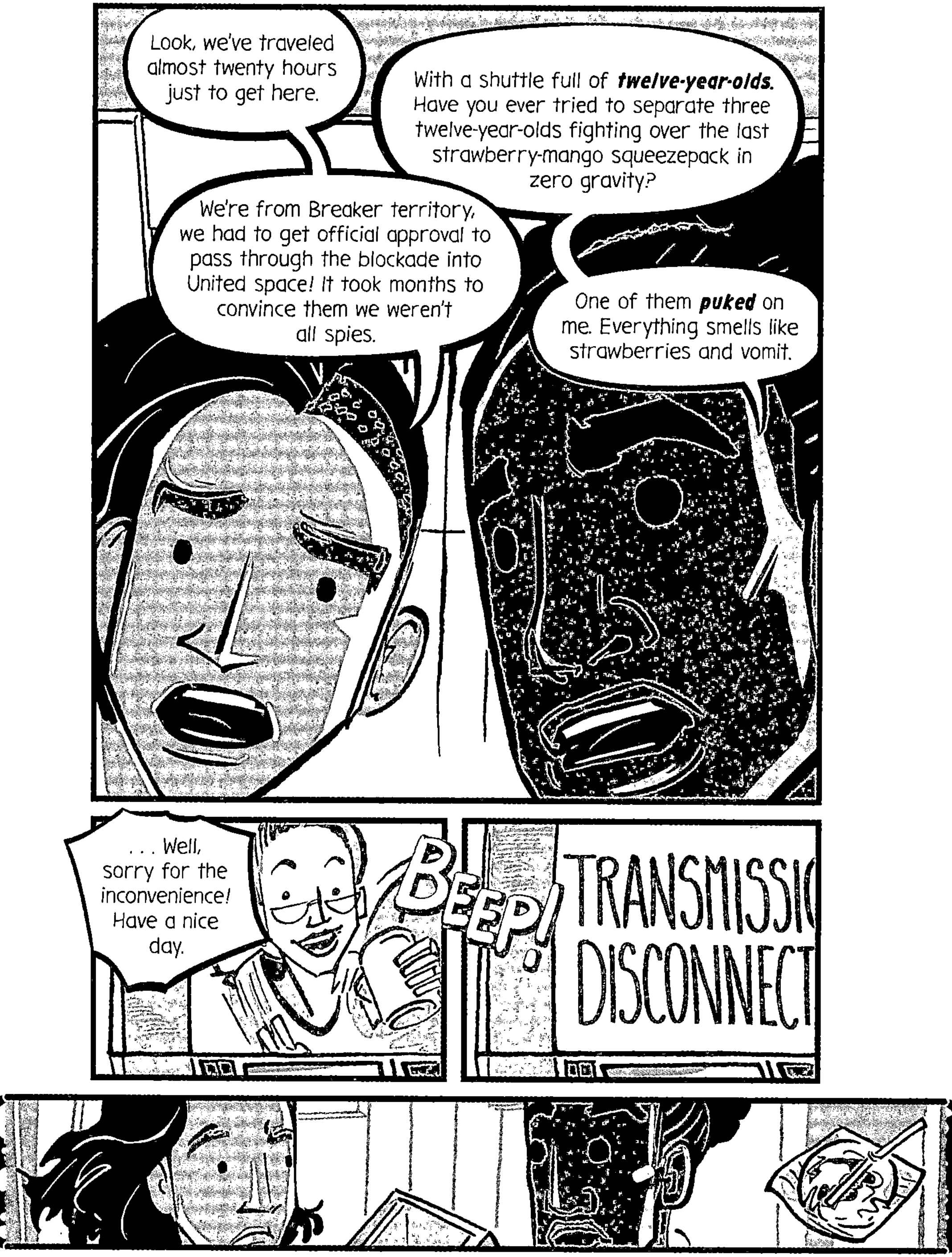
Look, we've traveled almost twenty hours just to get here.
With a shuttle full of **twelve-year-olds.** Have you ever tried to separate three twelve-year-olds fighting over the last strawberry-mango squeezepack in zero gravity?
We're from Breaker territory, we had to get official approval to pass through the blockade into United space! It took months to convince them we weren't all spies.
One of them **puked** on me. Everything smells like strawberries and vomit.
. . . Well, sorry for the inconvenience! Have a nice day.
BEEP!
TRANSMISSI
DISCONNECT

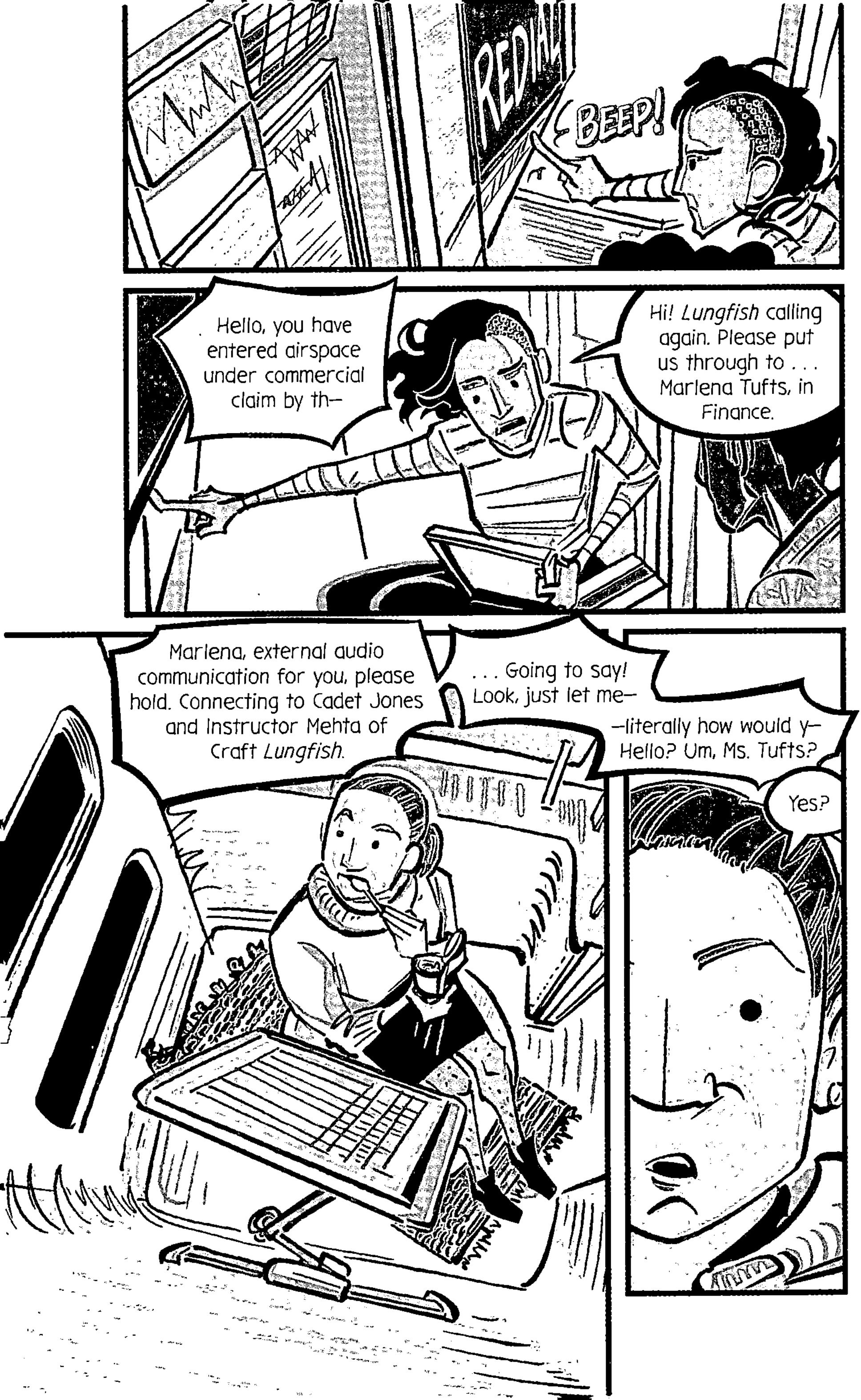

REDH
BEEP!
Hello, you have entered airspace under commercial claim by th–
Hi! *Lungfish* calling again. Please put us through to . . . Marlena Tufts, in Finance.
Marlena, external audio communication for you, please hold. Connecting to Cadet Jones and Instructor Mehta of Craft *Lungfish*.
. . . Going to say! Look, just let me–
–literally how would y– Hello? Um, Ms. Tufts?
Yes?

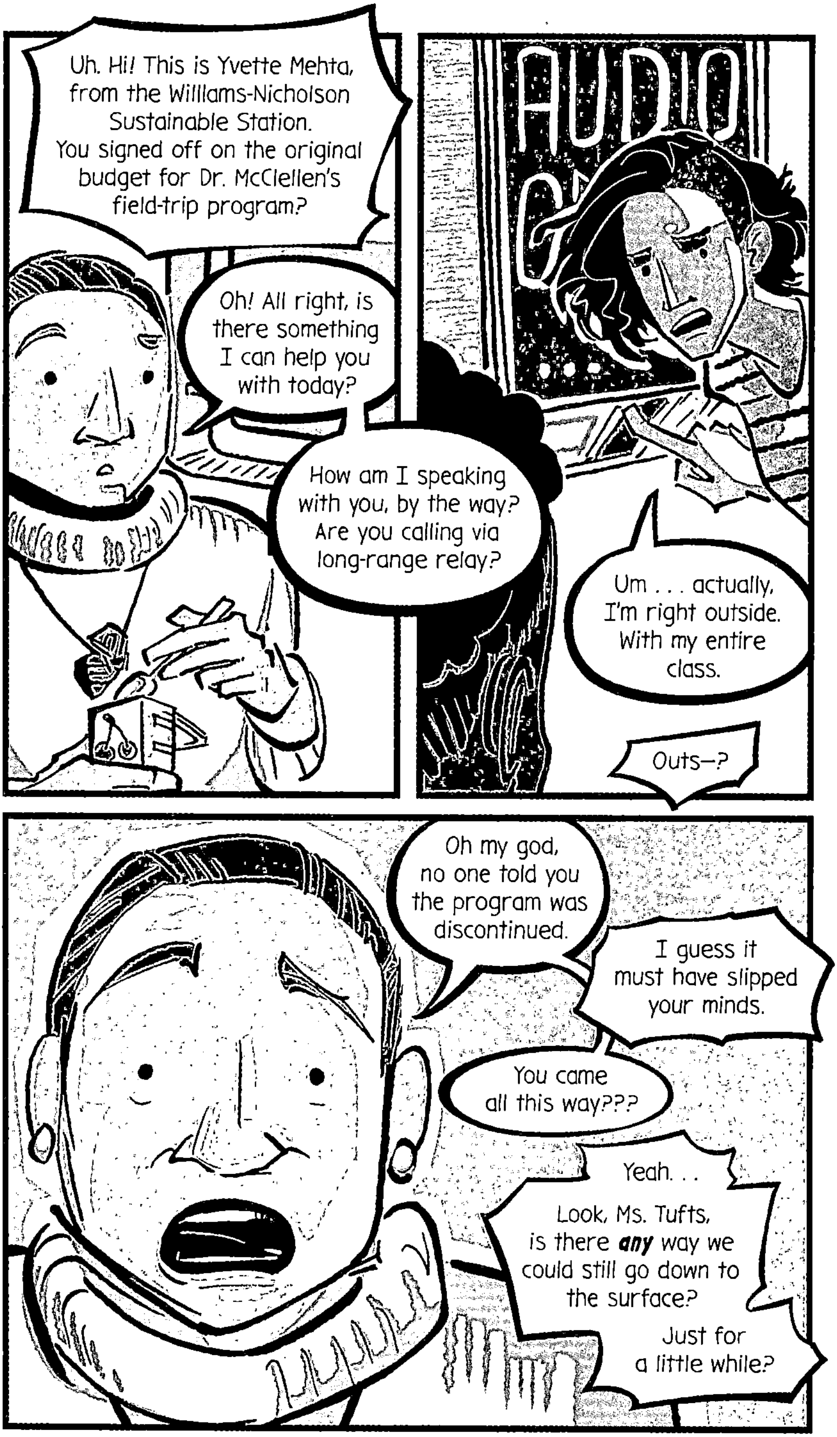
Uh. Hi! This is Yvette Mehta, from the Williams-Nicholson Sustainable Station. You signed off on the original budget for Dr. McClellen's field-trip program?
Oh! All right, is there something I can help you with today?
How am I speaking with you, by the way? Are you calling via long-range relay?
AUDIO
Um . . . actually, I'm right outside. With my entire class.
Outs–?
Oh my god, no one told you the program was discontinued.
I guess it must have slipped your minds.
You came all this way???
Yeah. . .
Look, Ms. Tufts, is there **any** way we could still go down to the surface?
Just for a little while?

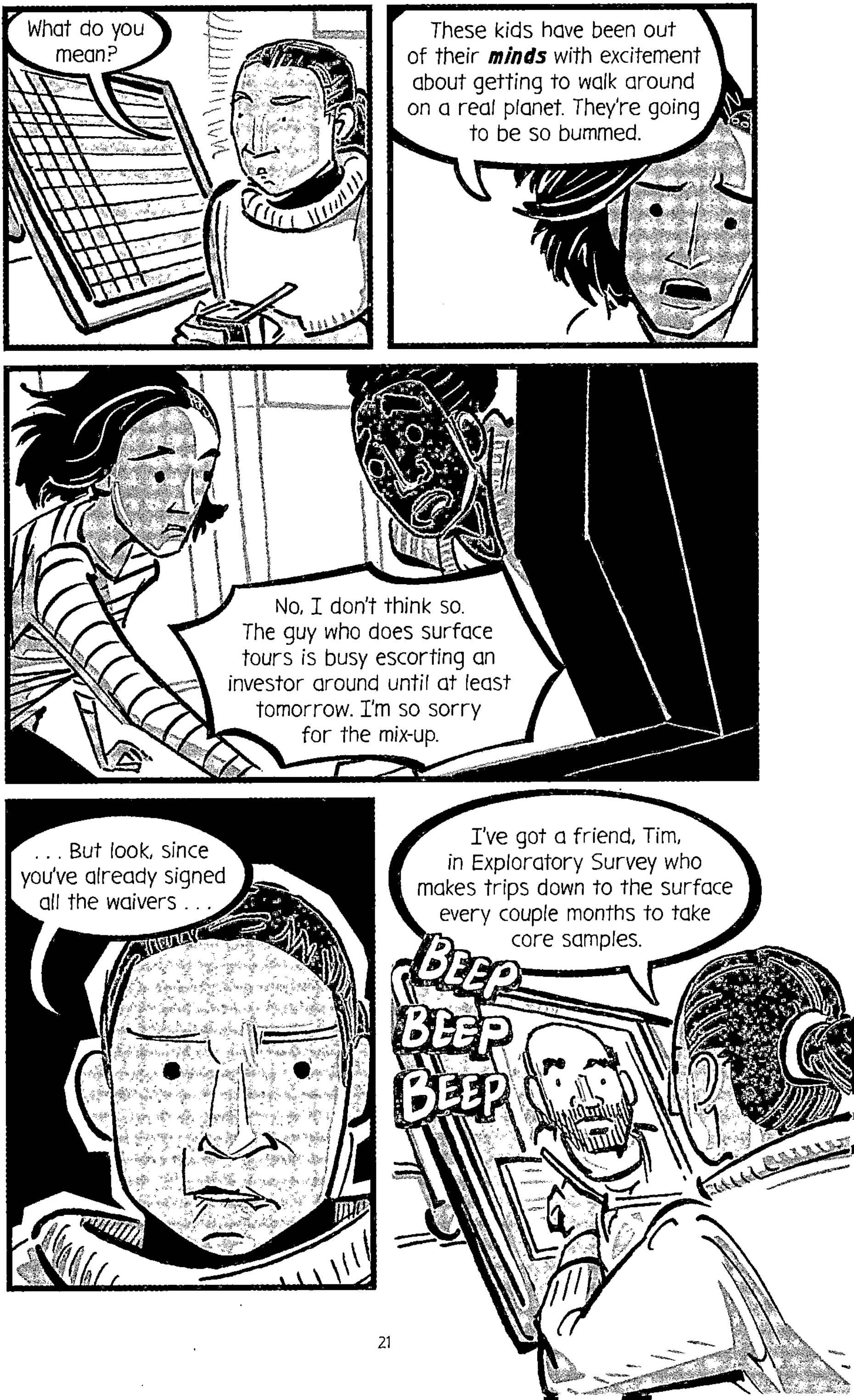
What do you mean?
These kids have been out of their **minds** with excitement about getting to walk around on a real planet. They're going to be so bummed.
No, I don't think so. The guy who does surface tours is busy escorting an investor around until at least tomorrow. I'm so sorry for the mix-up.
. . . But look, since you've already signed all the waivers . . .
I've got a friend, Tim, in Exploratory Survey who makes trips down to the surface every couple months to take core samples.
BEEP
BEEP
BEEP

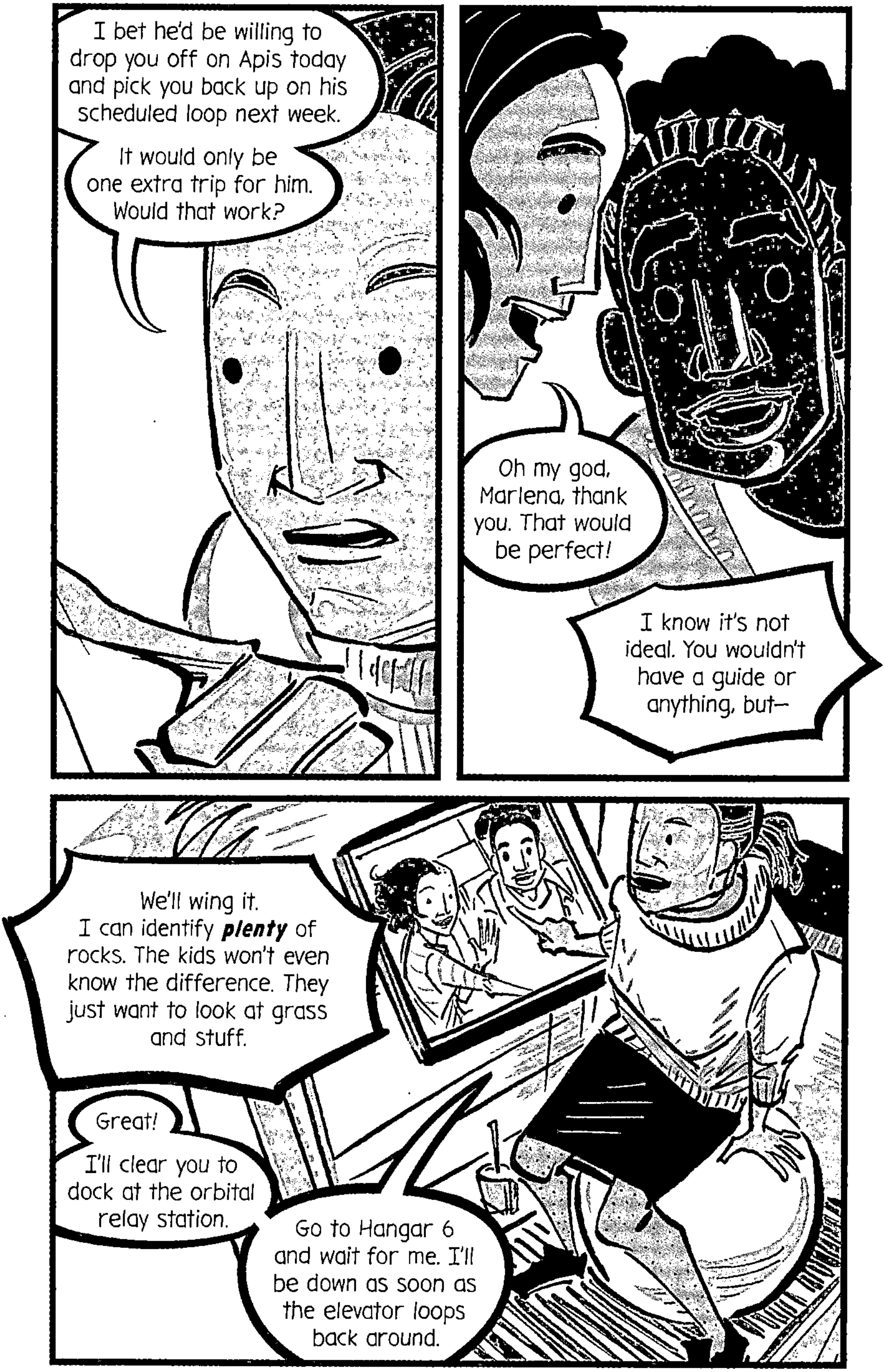
I bet he'd be willing to drop you off on Apis today and pick you back up on his scheduled loop next week.
It would only be one extra trip for him. Would that work?
Oh my god, Marlena, thank you. That would be perfect!
I know it's not ideal. You wouldn't have a guide or anything, but—
We'll wing it. I can identify **plenty** of rocks. The kids won't even know the difference. They just want to look at grass and stuff.
Great!
I'll clear you to dock at the orbital relay station.
Go to Hangar 6 and wait for me. I'll be down as soon as the elevator loops back around.

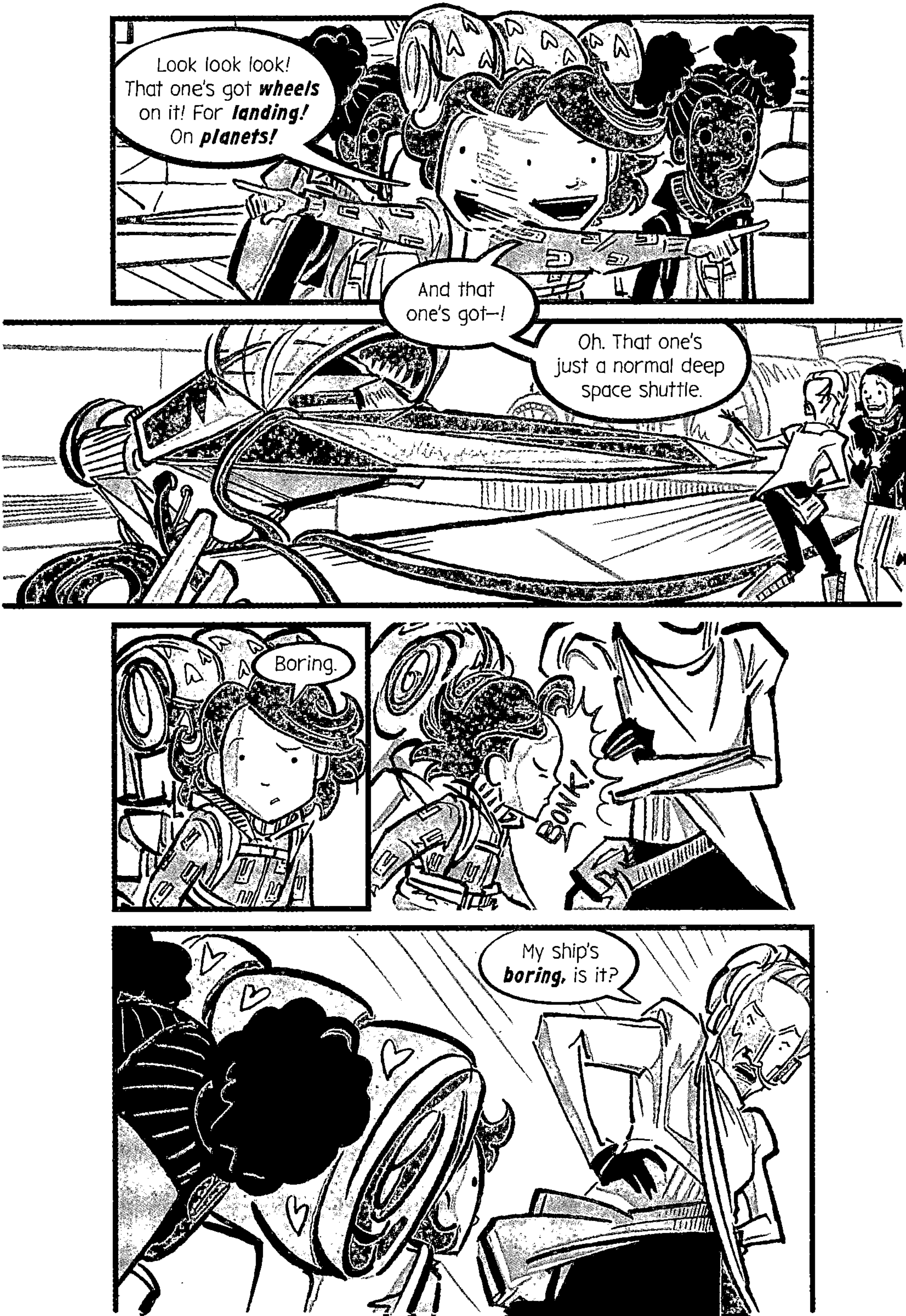

Look look look! That one's got **wheels** on it! For **landing!** On **planets!**
And that one's got—!
Oh. That one's just a normal deep space shuttle.
Boring.
BONK!
My ship's **boring,** is it?

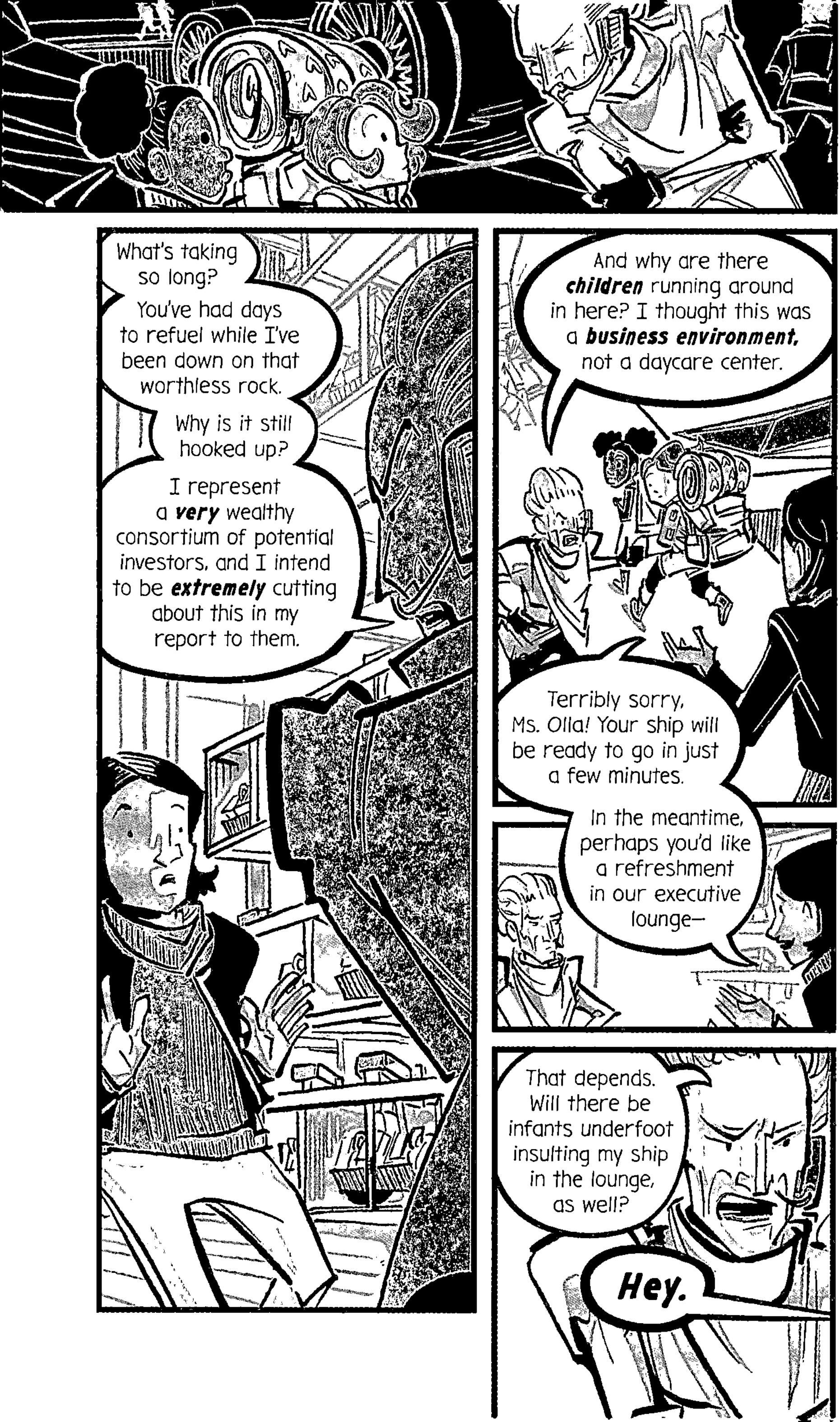

What's taking so long?
You've had days to refuel while I've been down on that worthless rock.
Why is it still hooked up?
I represent a **very** wealthy consortium of potential investors, and I intend to be **extremely** cutting about this in my report to them.
And why are there **children** running around in here? I thought this was a **business environment,** not a daycare center.
Terribly sorry, Ms. Olla! Your ship will be ready to go in just a few minutes.
In the meantime, perhaps you'd like a refreshment in our executive lounge—
That depends. Will there be infants underfoot insulting my ship in the lounge, as well?
Hey.

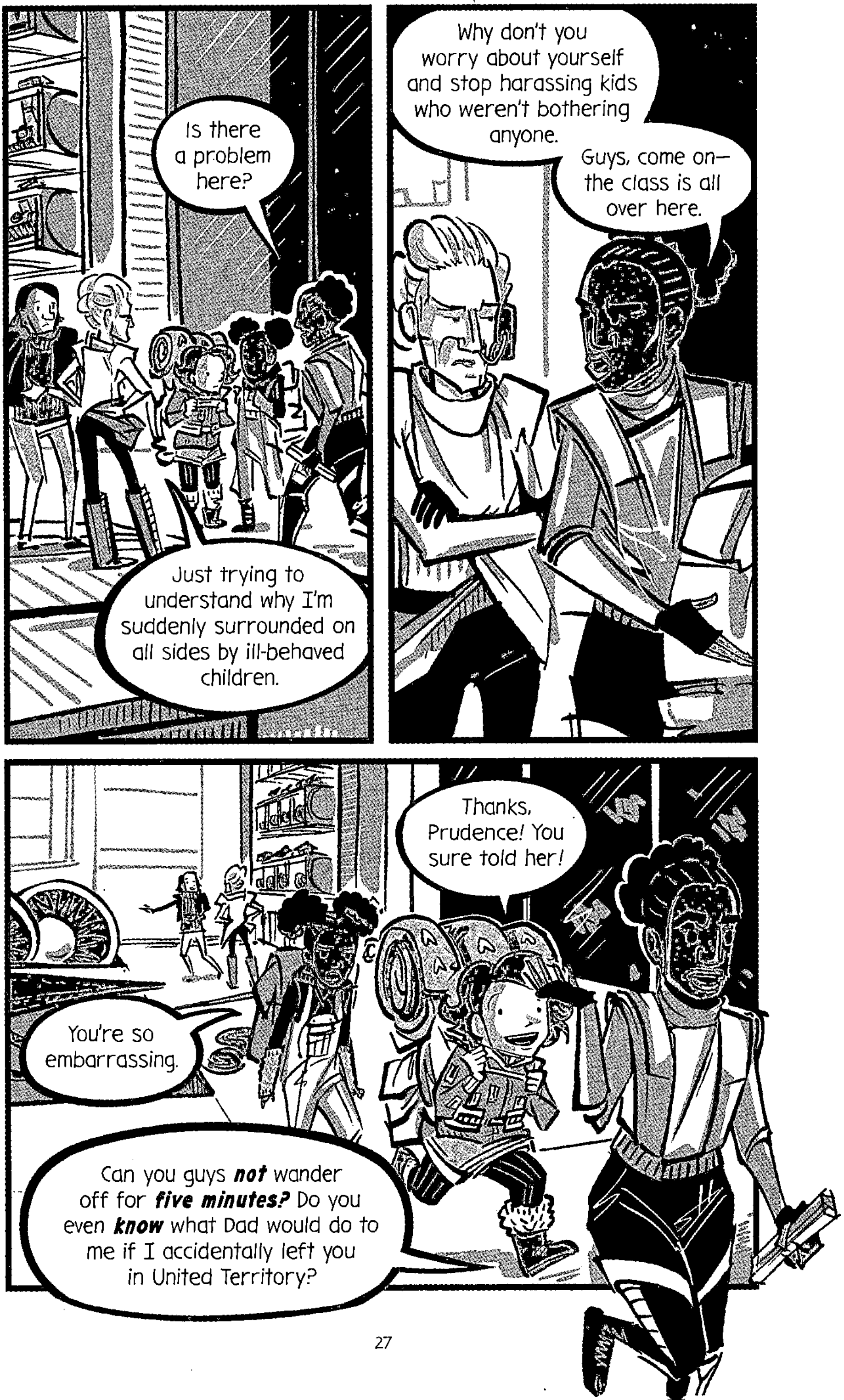
Is there a problem here?
Just trying to understand why I'm suddenly surrounded on all sides by ill-behaved children.
Why don't you worry about yourself and stop harassing kids who weren't bothering anyone.
Guys, come on— the class is all over here.
Thanks, Prudence! You sure told her!
You're so embarrassing.
Can you guys ***not*** wander off for ***five minutes?*** Do you even ***know*** what Dad would do to me if I accidentally left you in United Territory?

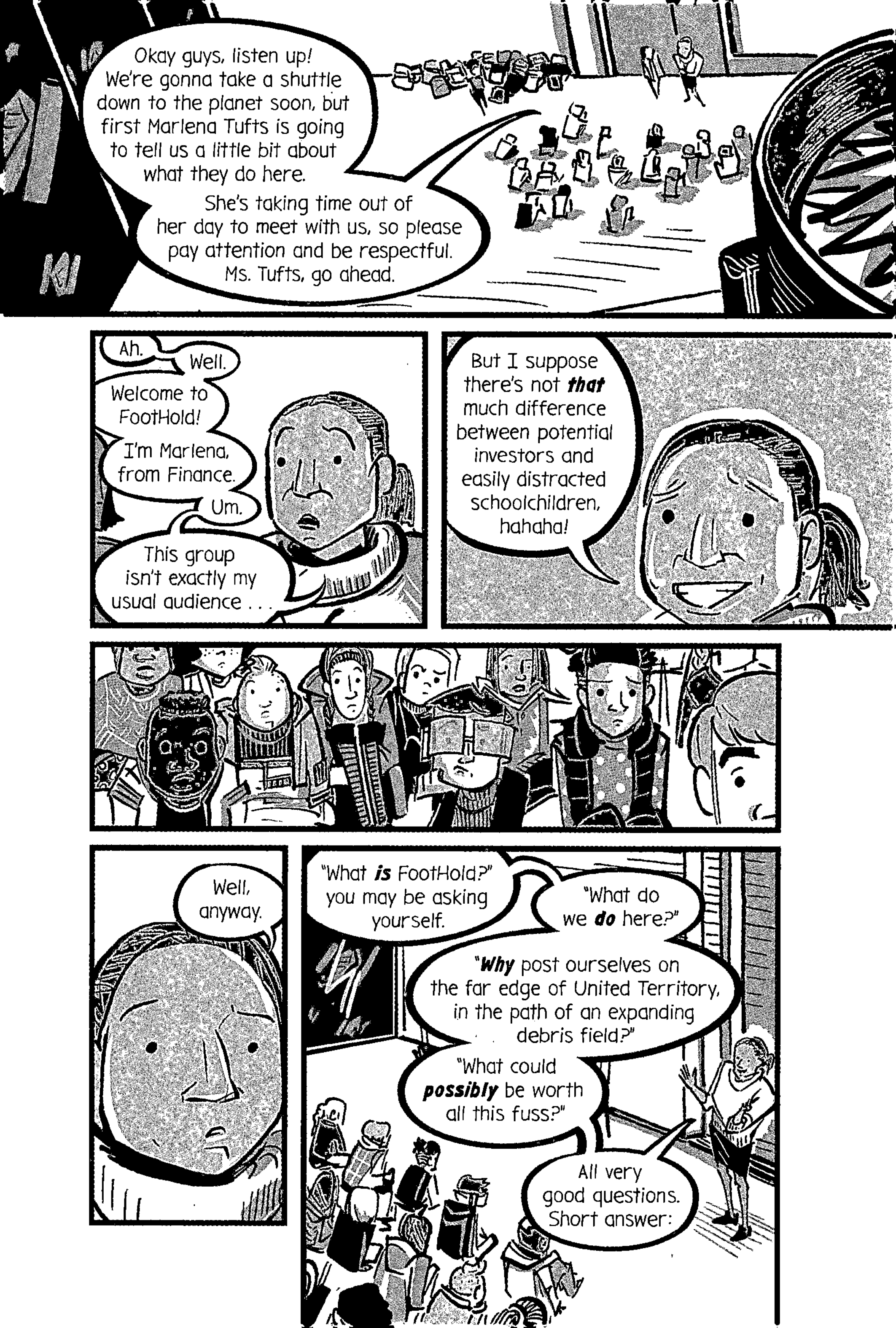
Okay guys, listen up! We're gonna take a shuttle down to the planet soon, but first Marlena Tufts is going to tell us a little bit about what they do here.
She's taking time out of her day to meet with us, so please pay attention and be respectful. Ms. Tufts, go ahead.
Ah.
Well.
Welcome to FootHold!
I'm Marlena, from Finance.
Um.
This group isn't exactly my usual audience . . .
But I suppose there's not *that* much difference between potential investors and easily distracted schoolchildren, hahaha!
Well, anyway.
"What *is* FootHold?" you may be asking yourself.
"What do we *do* here?"
"*Why* post ourselves on the far edge of United Territory, in the path of an expanding debris field?"
"What could *possibly* be worth all this fuss?"
All very good questions. Short answer:

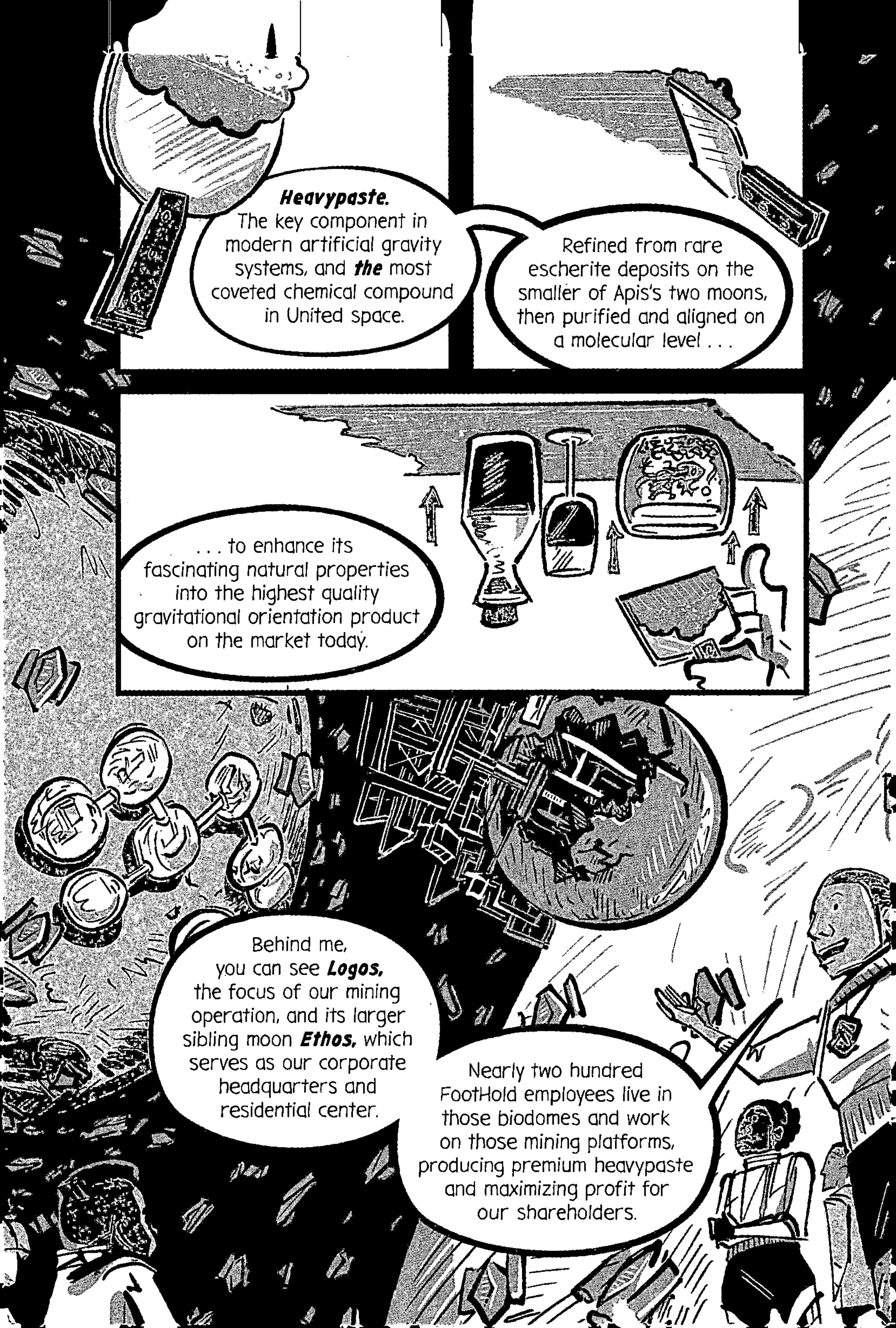

Heavypaste. The key component in modern artificial gravity systems, and the most coveted chemical compound in United space.
Refined from rare escherite deposits on the smaller of Apis's two moons, then purified and aligned on a molecular level . . .
. . . to enhance its fascinating natural properties into the highest quality gravitational orientation product on the market today.
Behind me, you can see Logos, the focus of our mining operation, and its larger sibling moon Ethos, which serves as our corporate headquarters and residential center.
Nearly two hundred FootHold employees live in those biodomes and work on those mining platforms, producing premium heavypaste and maximizing profit for our shareholders.

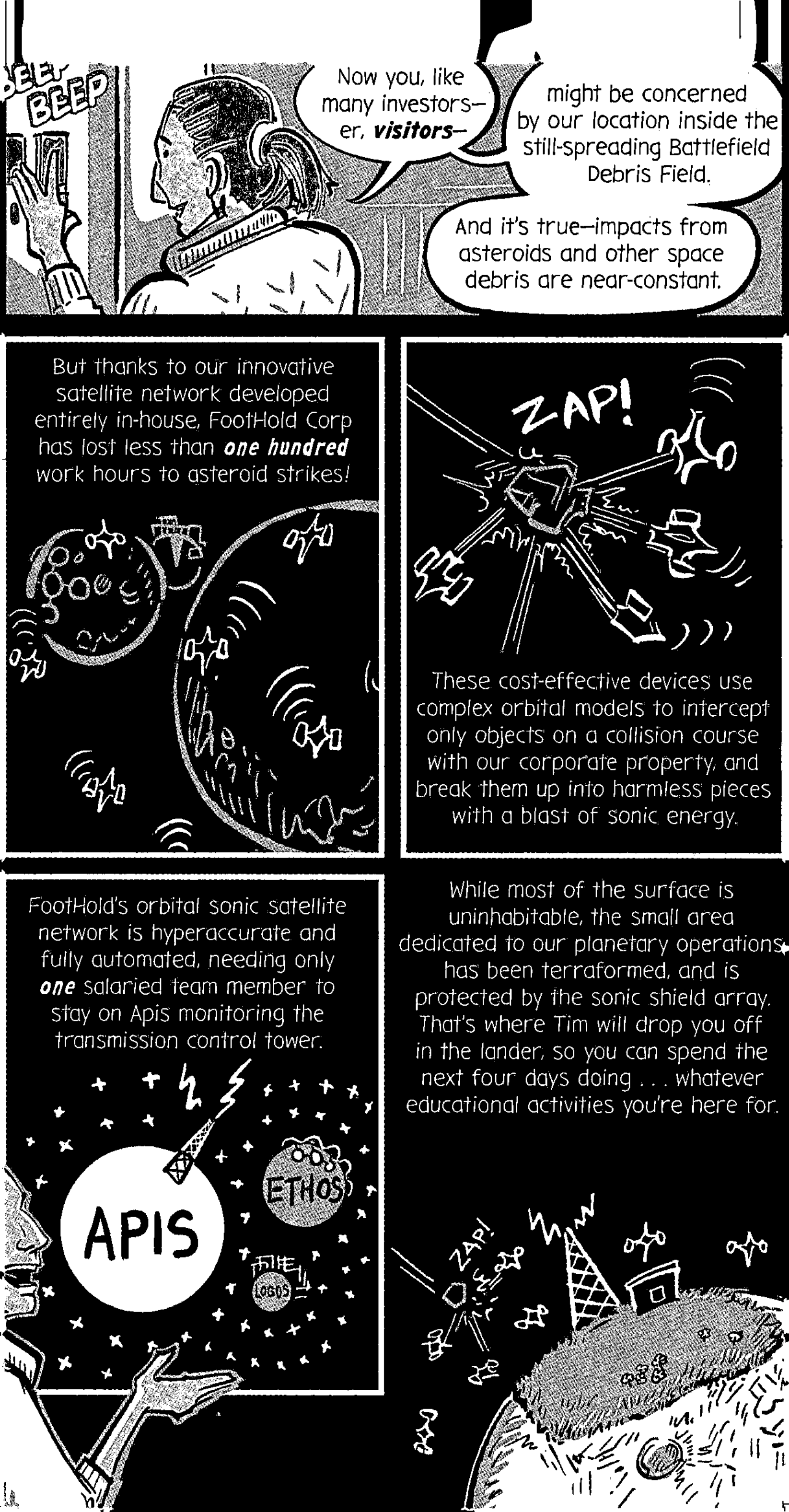
BEEP BEEP
Now you, like many investors— er, *visitors*—
might be concerned by our location inside the still-spreading Battlefield Debris Field.
And it's true—impacts from asteroids and other space debris are near-constant.
But thanks to our innovative satellite network developed entirely in-house, FootHold Corp has lost less than ***one hundred*** work hours to asteroid strikes!
ZAP!
These cost-effective devices use complex orbital models to intercept only objects on a collision course with our corporate property, and break them up into harmless pieces with a blast of sonic energy.
FootHold's orbital sonic satellite network is hyperaccurate and fully automated, needing only ***one*** salaried team member to stay on Apis monitoring the transmission control tower.
APIS
ETHOS
LOGOS
While most of the surface is uninhabitable, the small area dedicated to our planetary operations has been terraformed, and is protected by the sonic shield array. That's where Tim will drop you off in the lander, so you can spend the next four days doing . . . whatever educational activities you're here for.
ZAP!

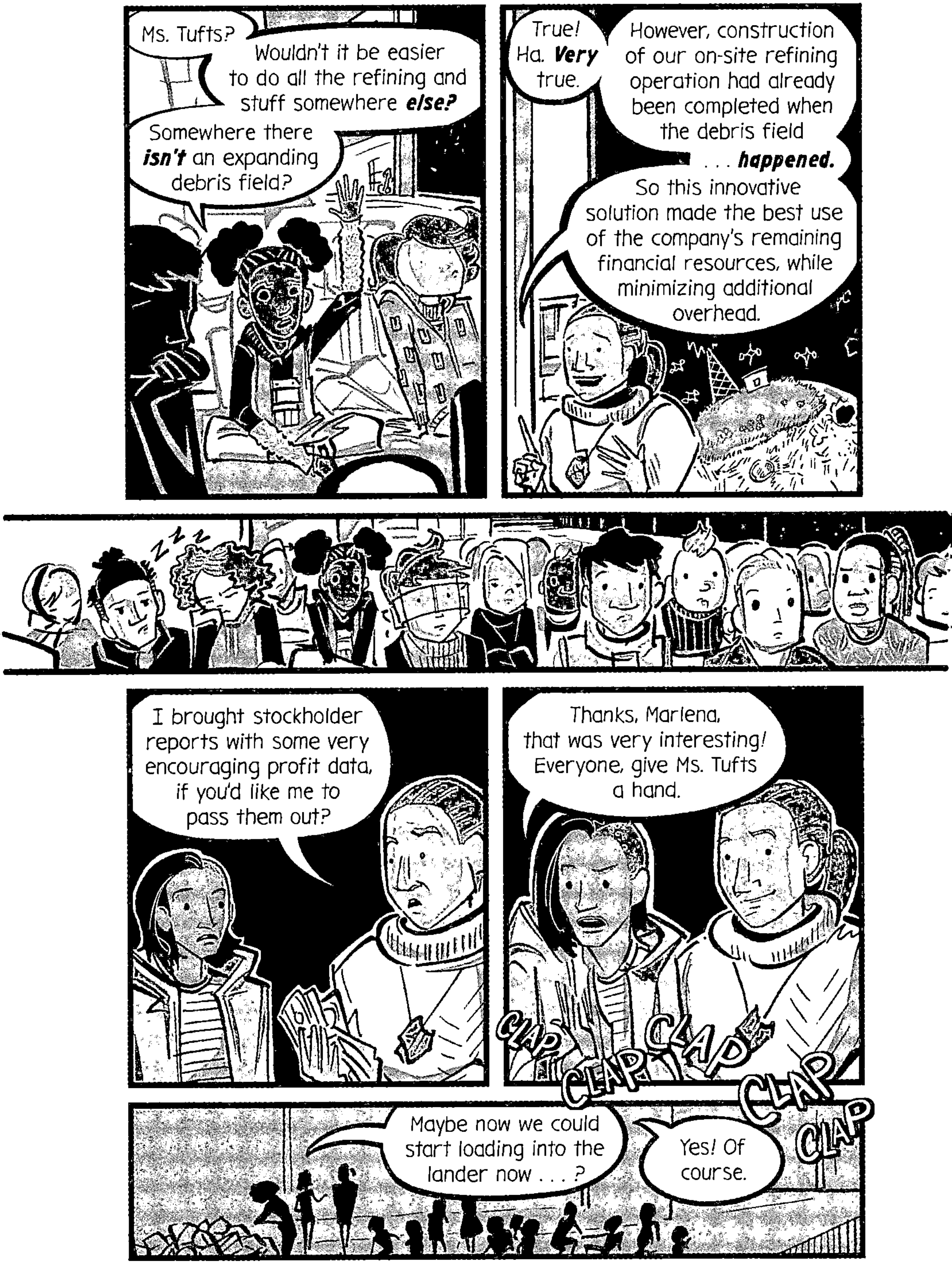
Ms. Tufts?
Wouldn't it be easier to do all the refining and stuff somewhere *else?*
Somewhere there *isn't* an expanding debris field?
True! Ha. *Very* true.
However, construction of our on-site refining operation had already been completed when the debris field . . . *happened.*
So this innovative solution made the best use of the company's remaining financial resources, while minimizing additional overhead.
I brought stockholder reports with some very encouraging profit data, if you'd like me to pass them out?
Thanks, Marlena, that was very interesting! Everyone, give Ms. Tufts a hand.
CLAP CLAP CLAP CLAP CLAP CLAP
Maybe now we could start loading into the lander now . . . ?
Yes! Of course.

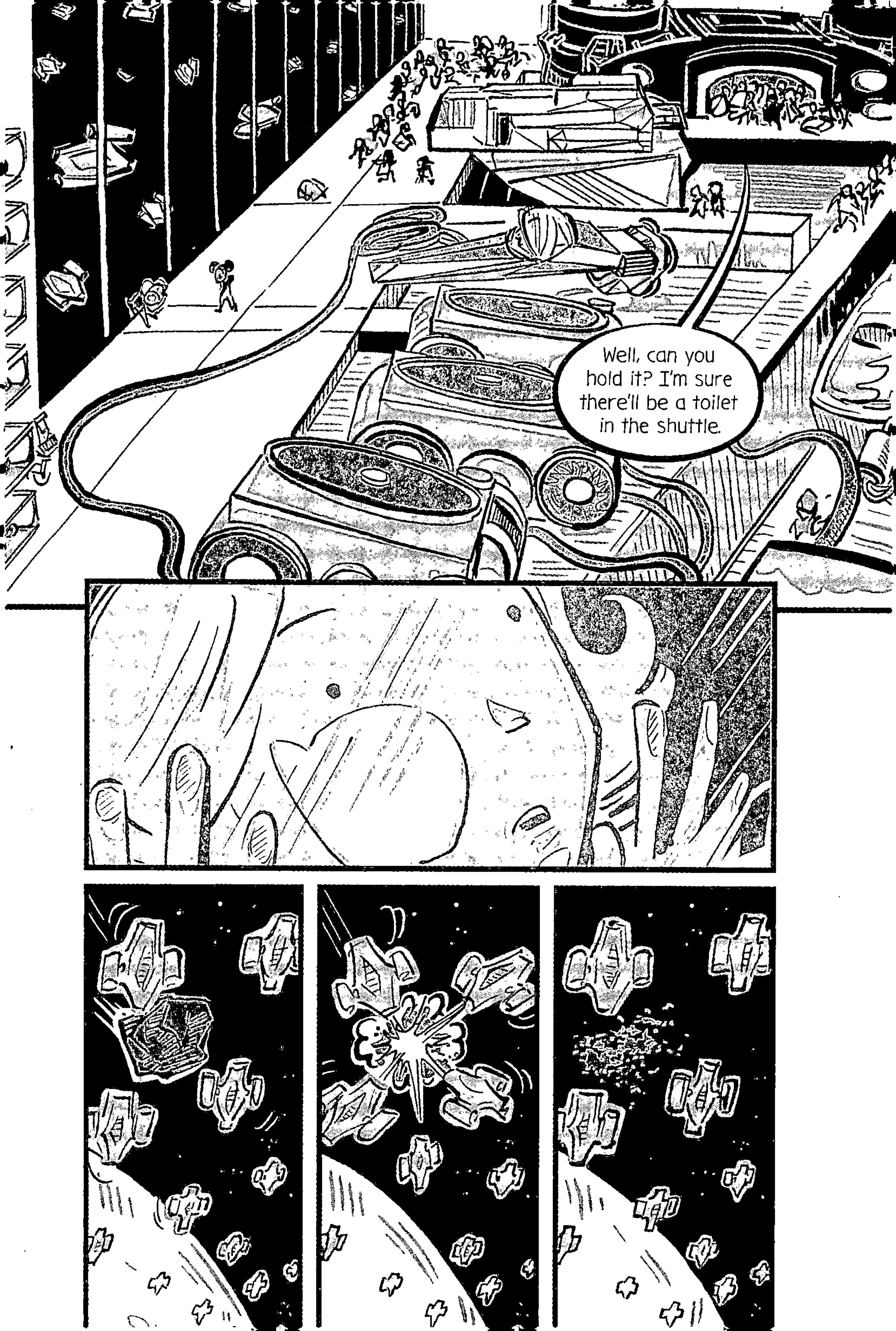
Well, can you hold it? I'm sure there'll be a toilet in the shuttle.

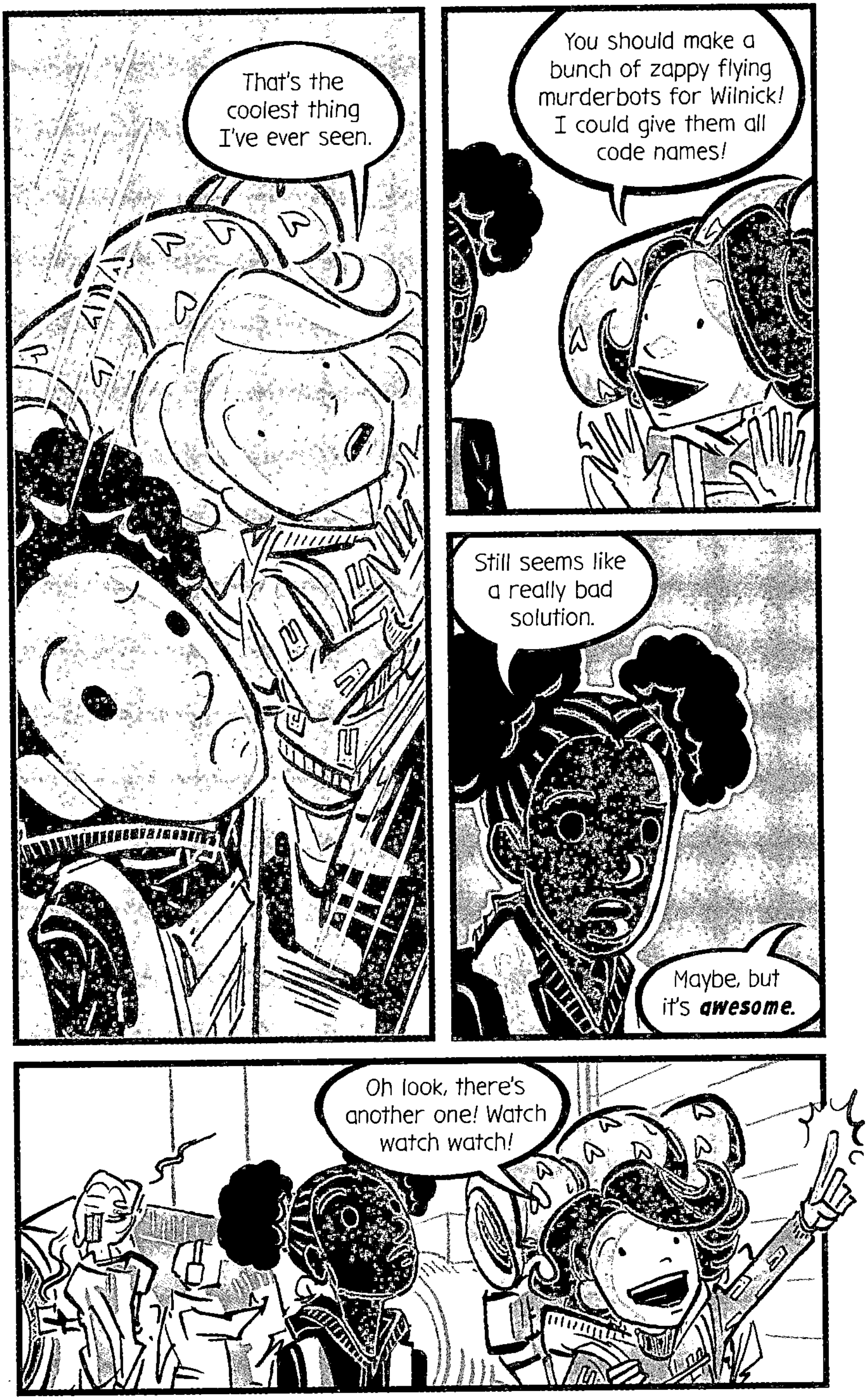
That's the coolest thing I've ever seen.
You should make a bunch of zappy flying murderbots for Wilnick! I could give them all code names!
Still seems like a really bad solution.
Maybe, but it's ***awesome.***
Oh look, there's another one! Watch watch watch!

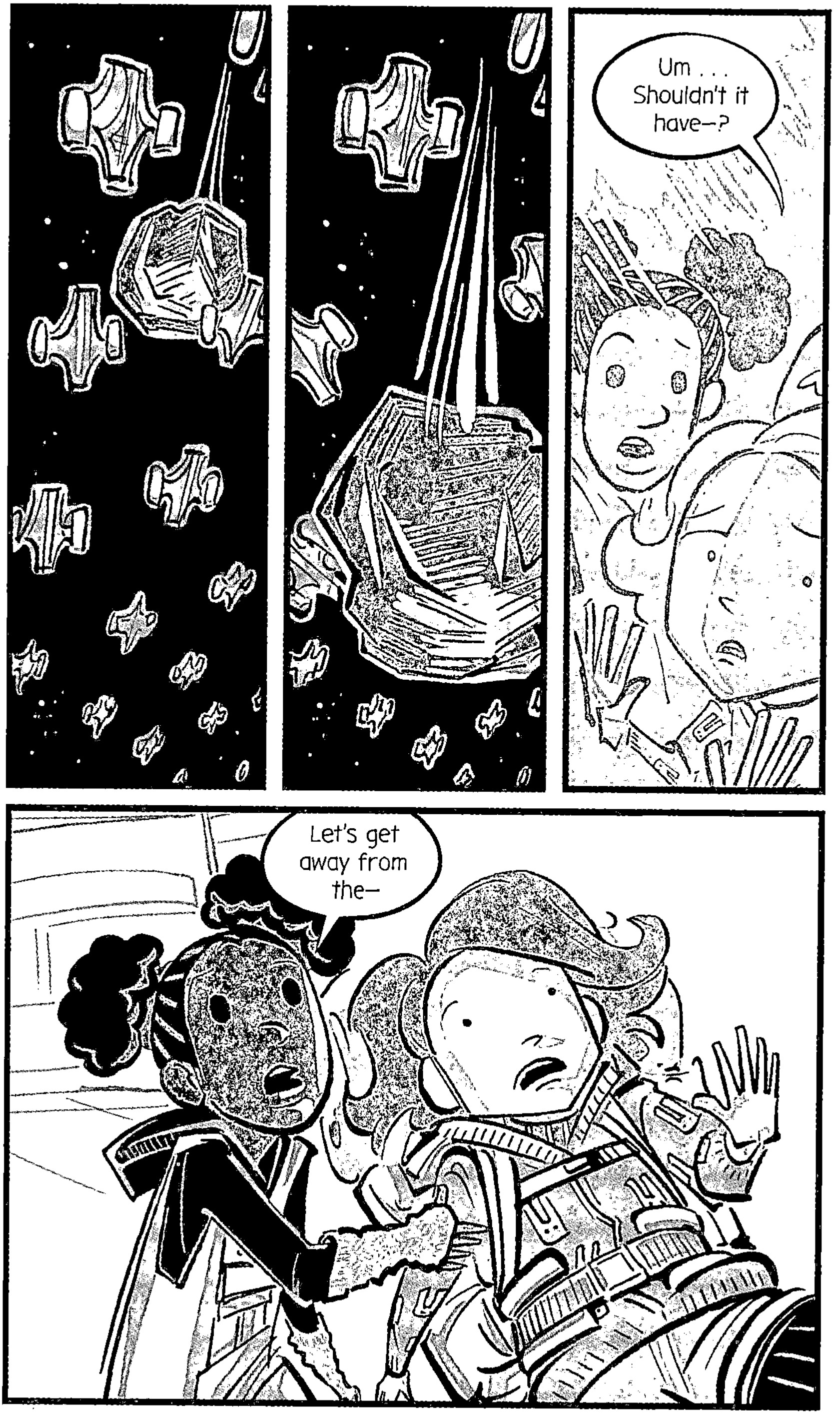
Um . . . Shouldn't it have—?
Let's get away from the—

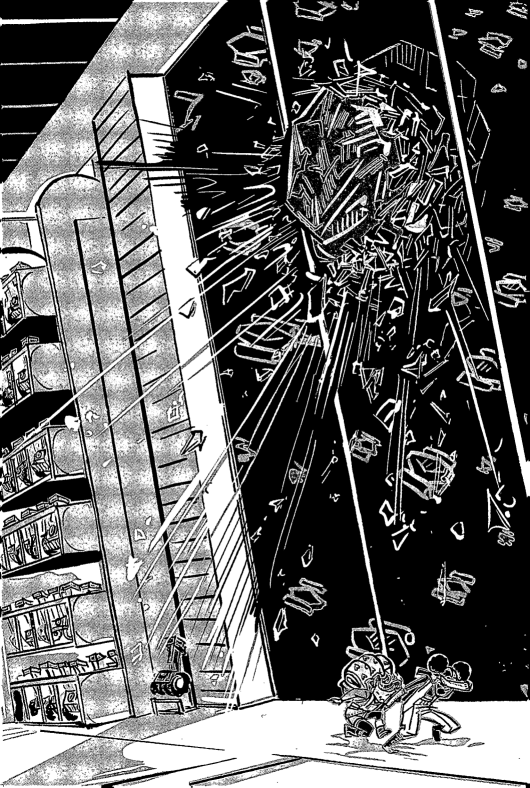

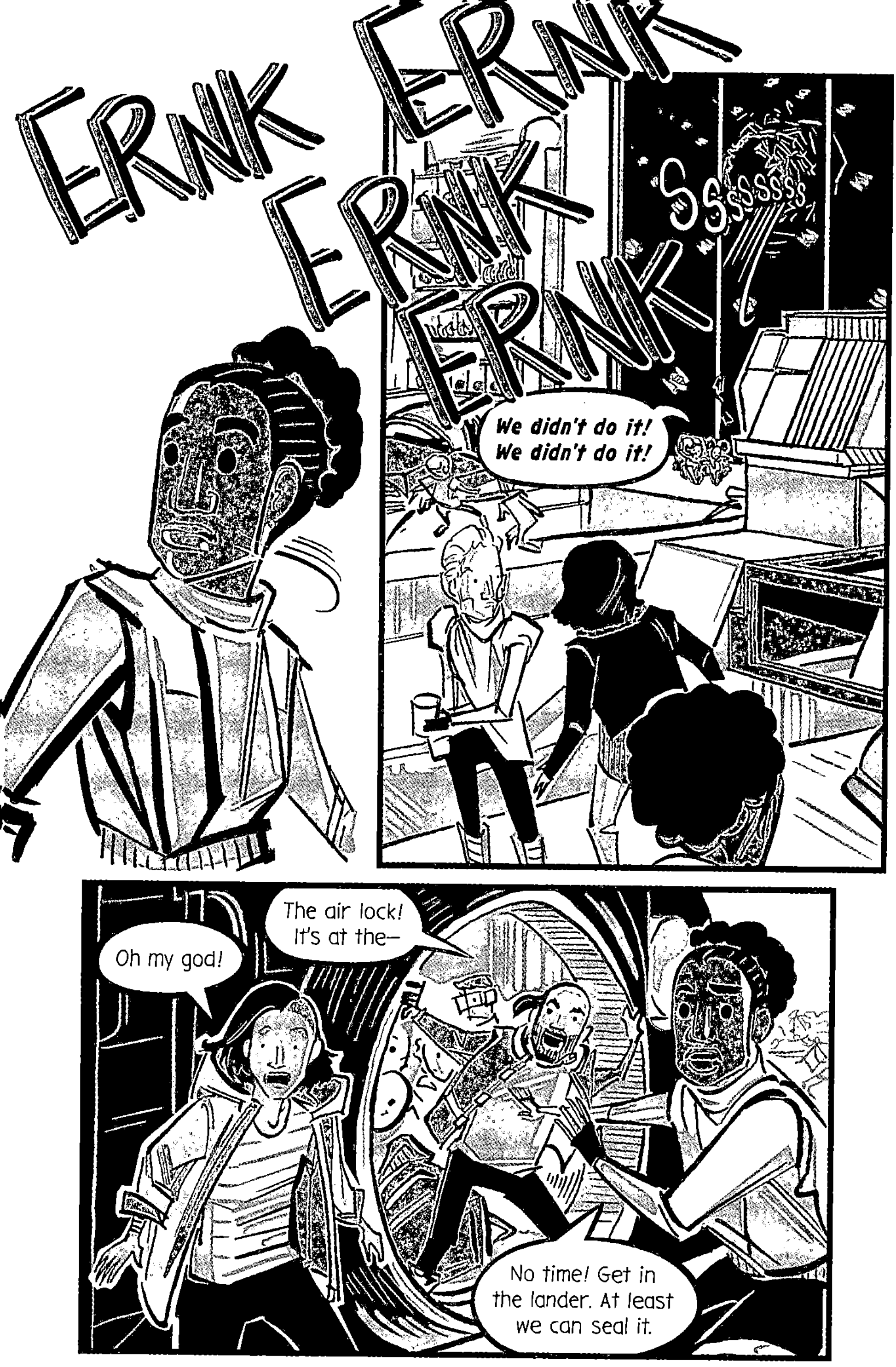
ERNK ERNK ERNK
ERNK ERNK
Ssssssss
We didn't do it! We didn't do it!
Oh my god!
The air lock! It's at the—
No time! Get in the lander. At least we can seal it.

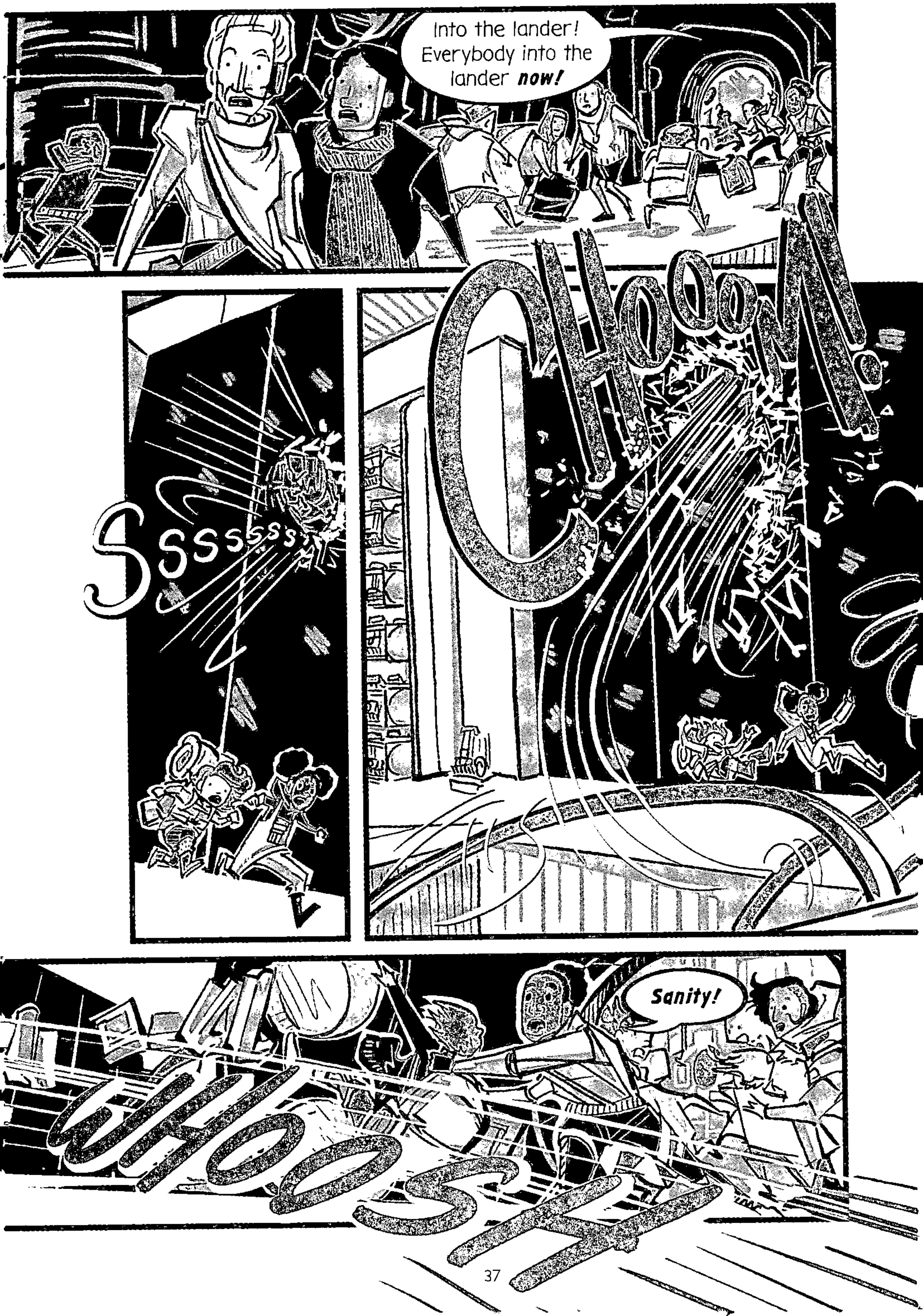
Into the lander! Everybody into the lander **now!**
SSSSSSS
CHOOOM!
Sanity!
WHOOSH!

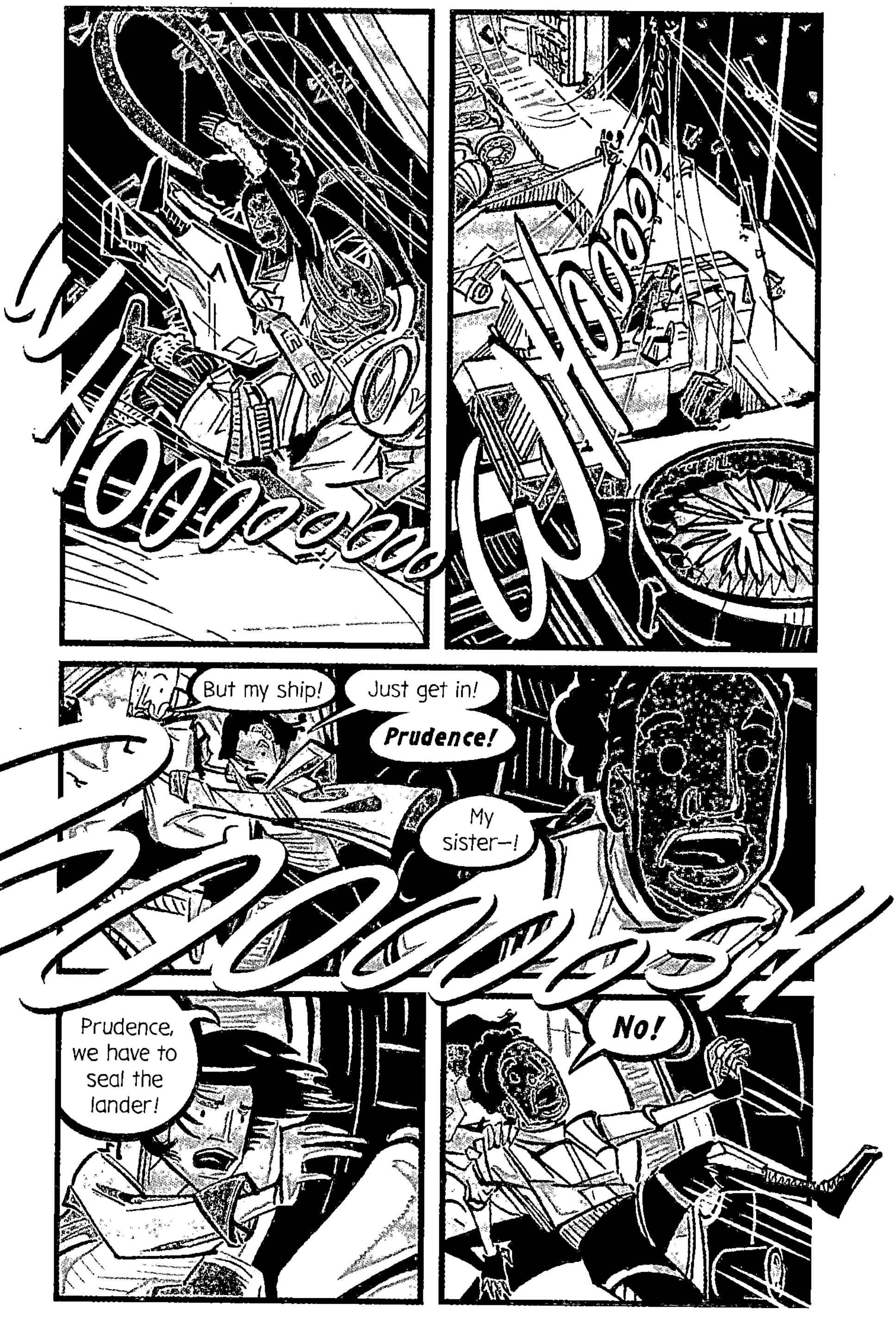
But my ship!
Just get in!
Prudence!
My sister—!
Prudence, we have to seal the lander!
No!

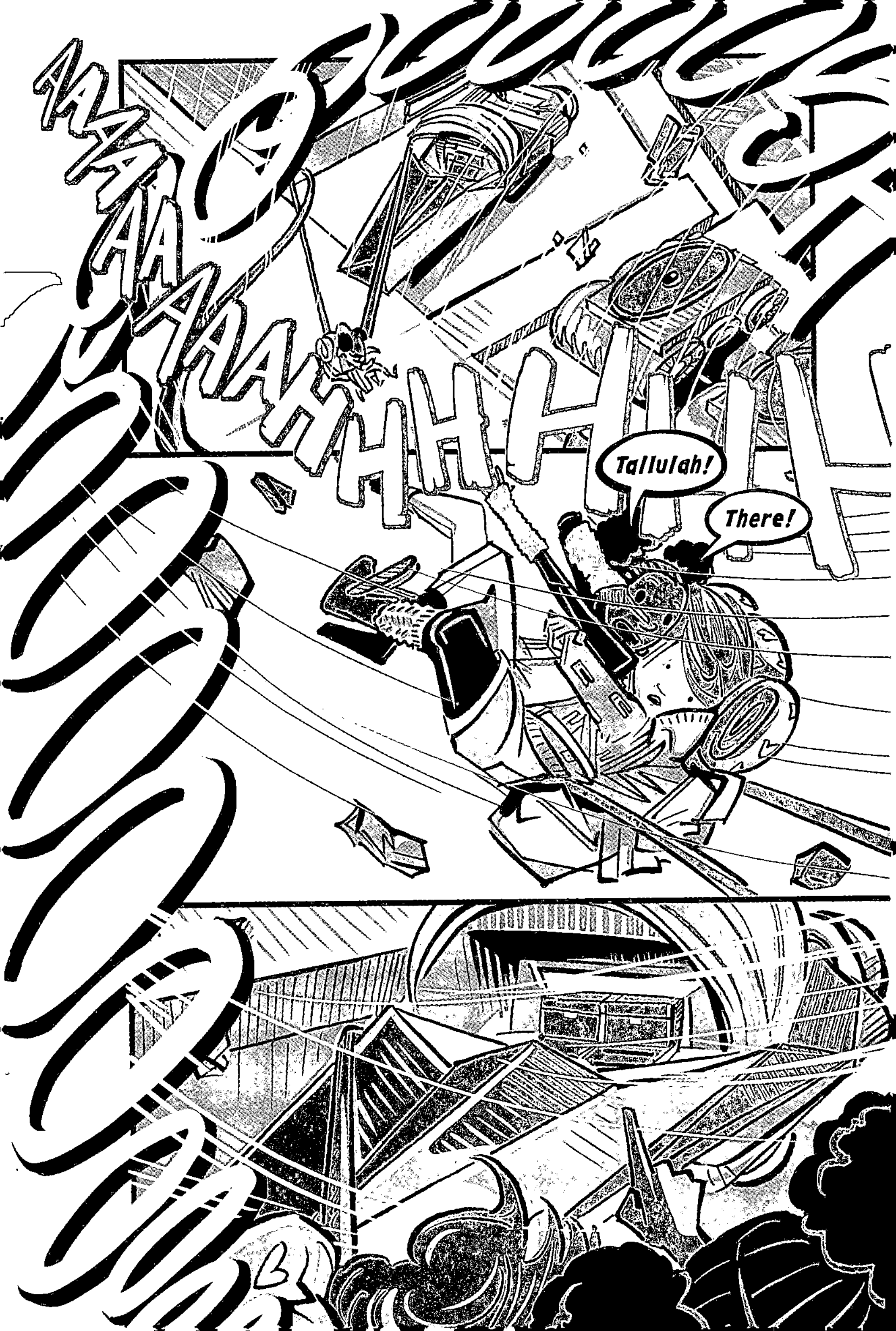
Tallulah!
There!

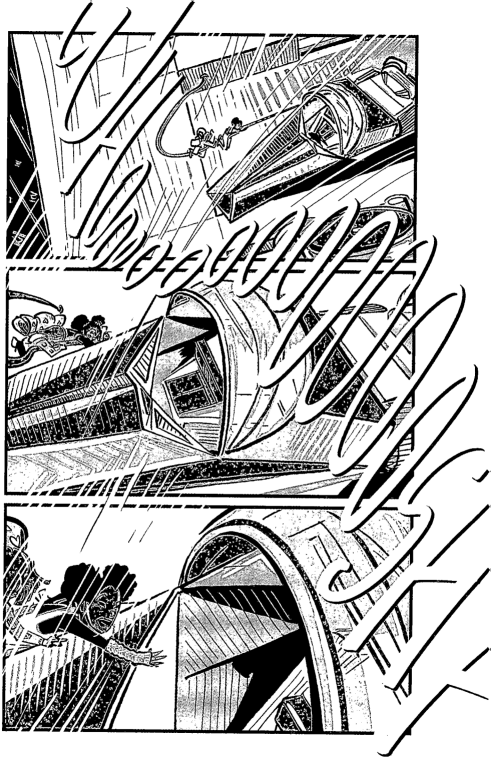

40

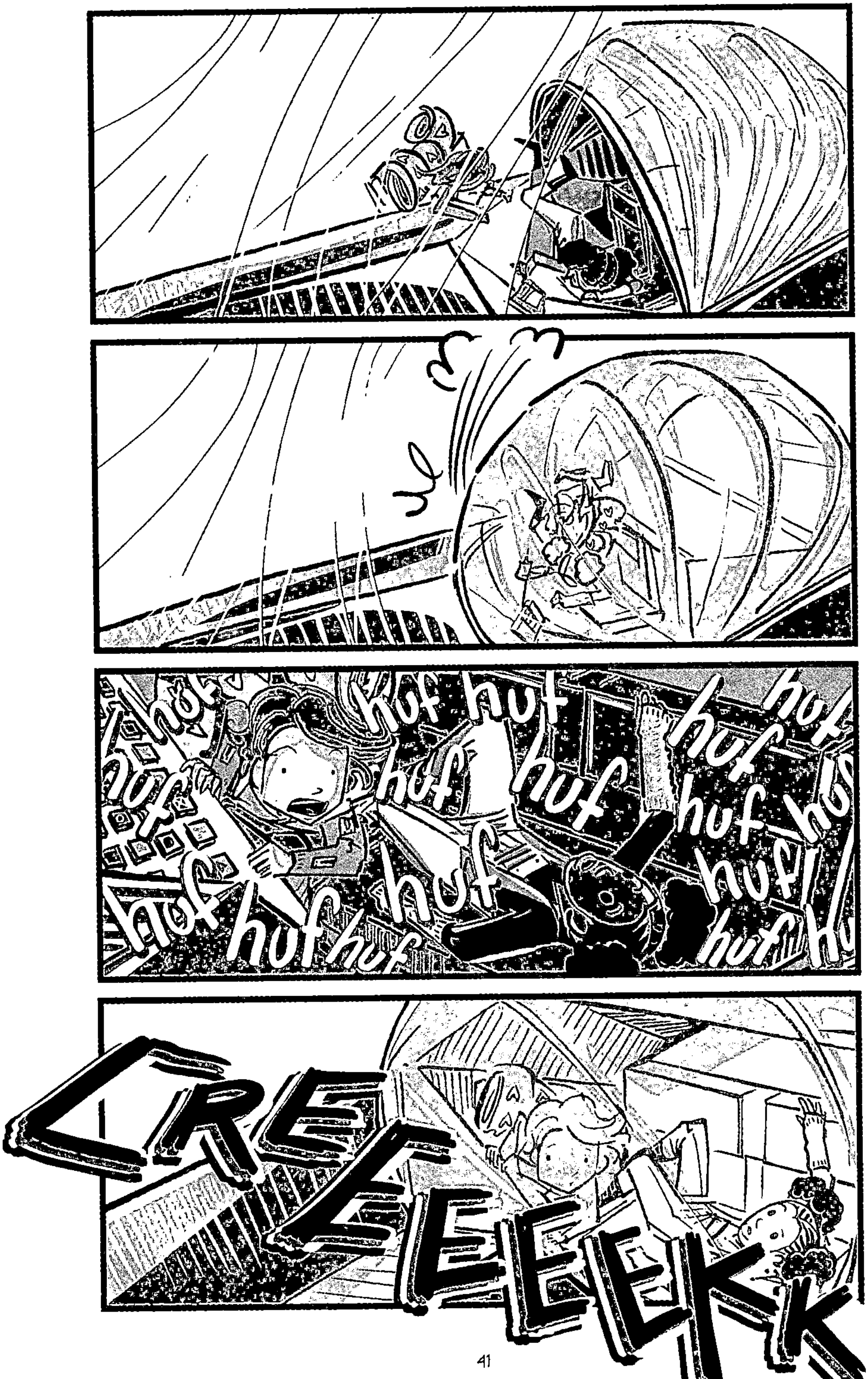
huf huf huf huf huf huf huf huf huf huf huf huf huf huf huf huf huf
CREEEEEKK

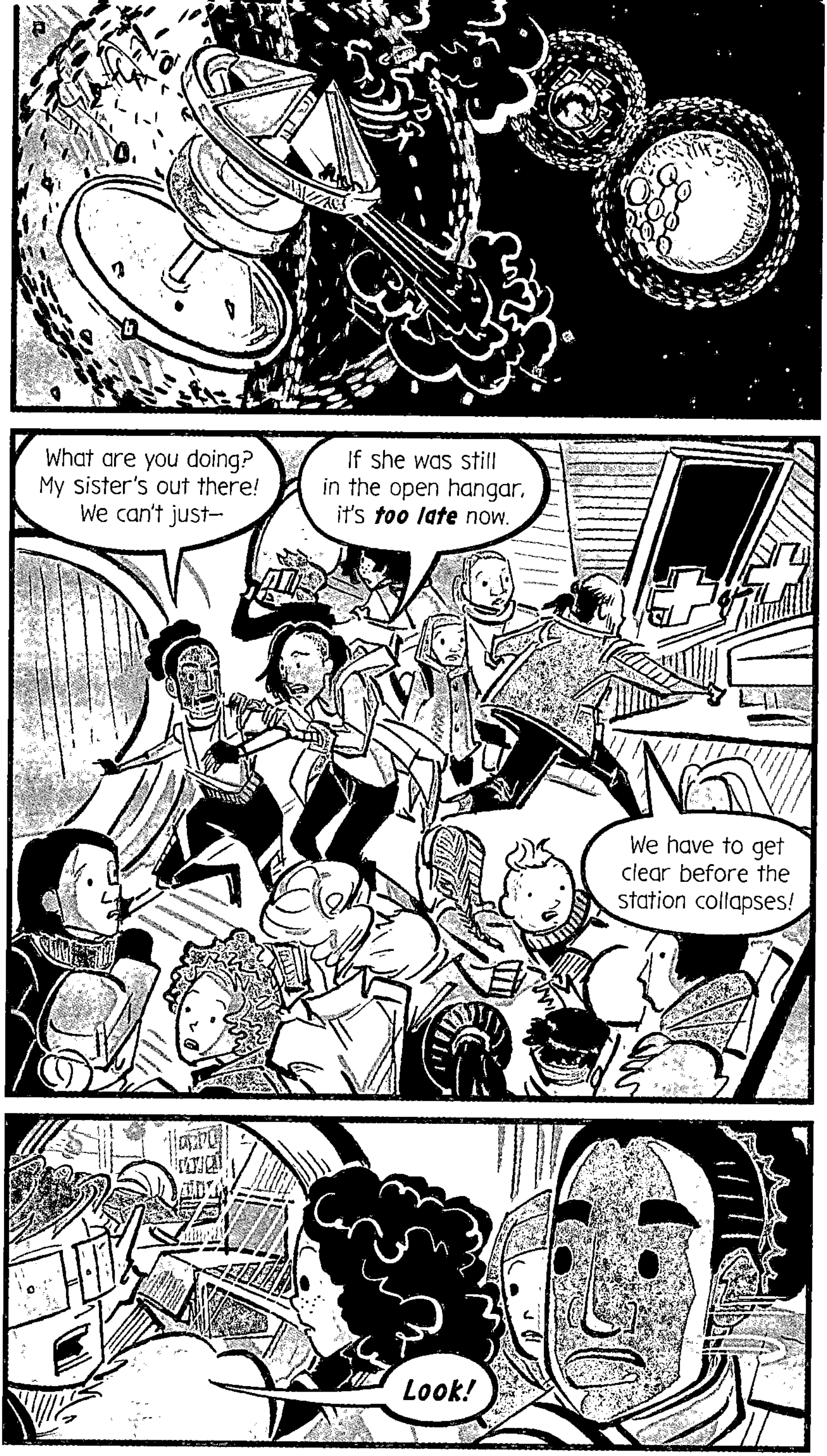
What are you doing? My sister's out there! We can't just–
If she was still in the open hangar, it's ***too late*** now.
We have to get clear before the station collapses!
Look!

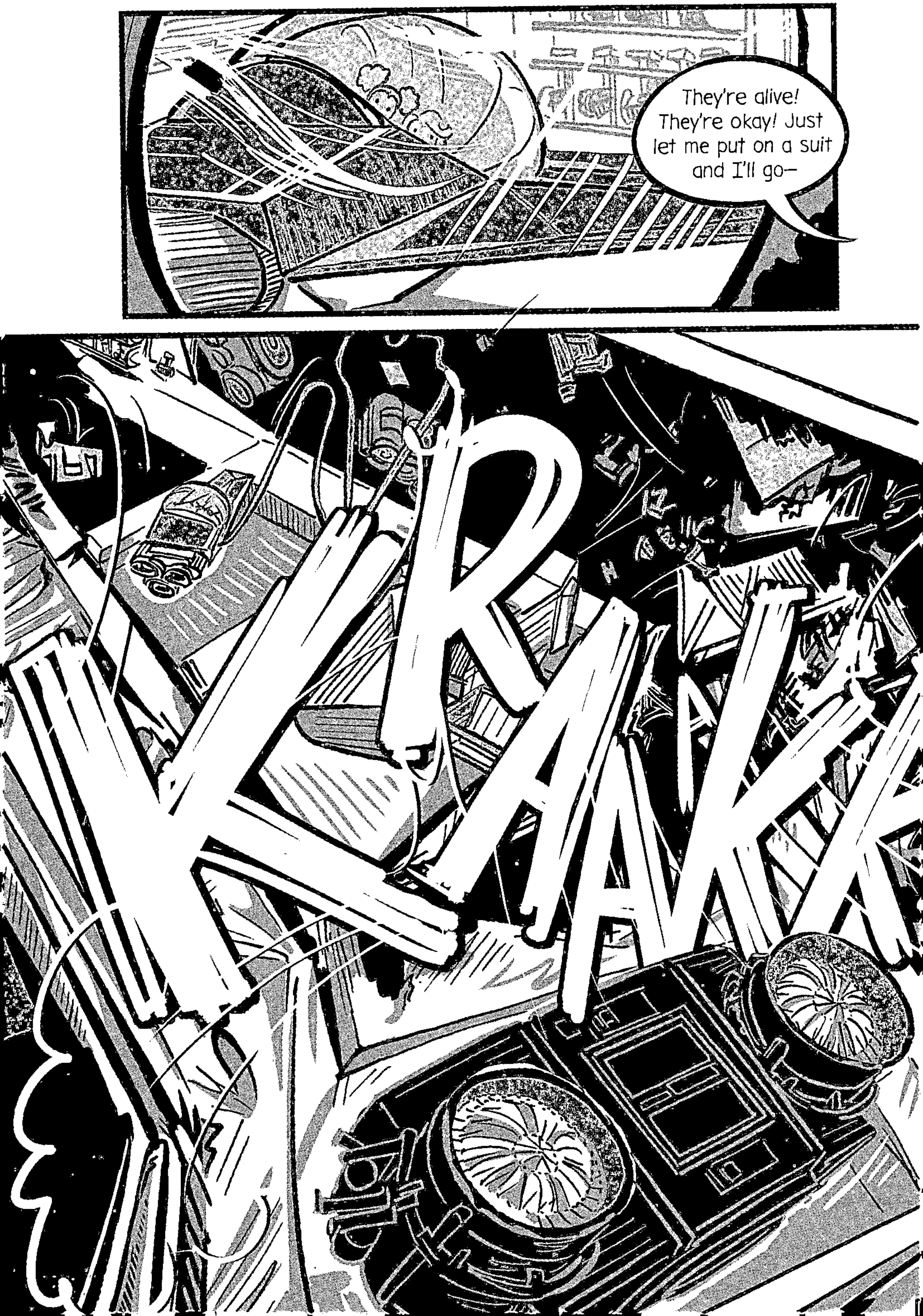
They're alive! They're okay! Just let me put on a suit and I'll go—
KRAKK

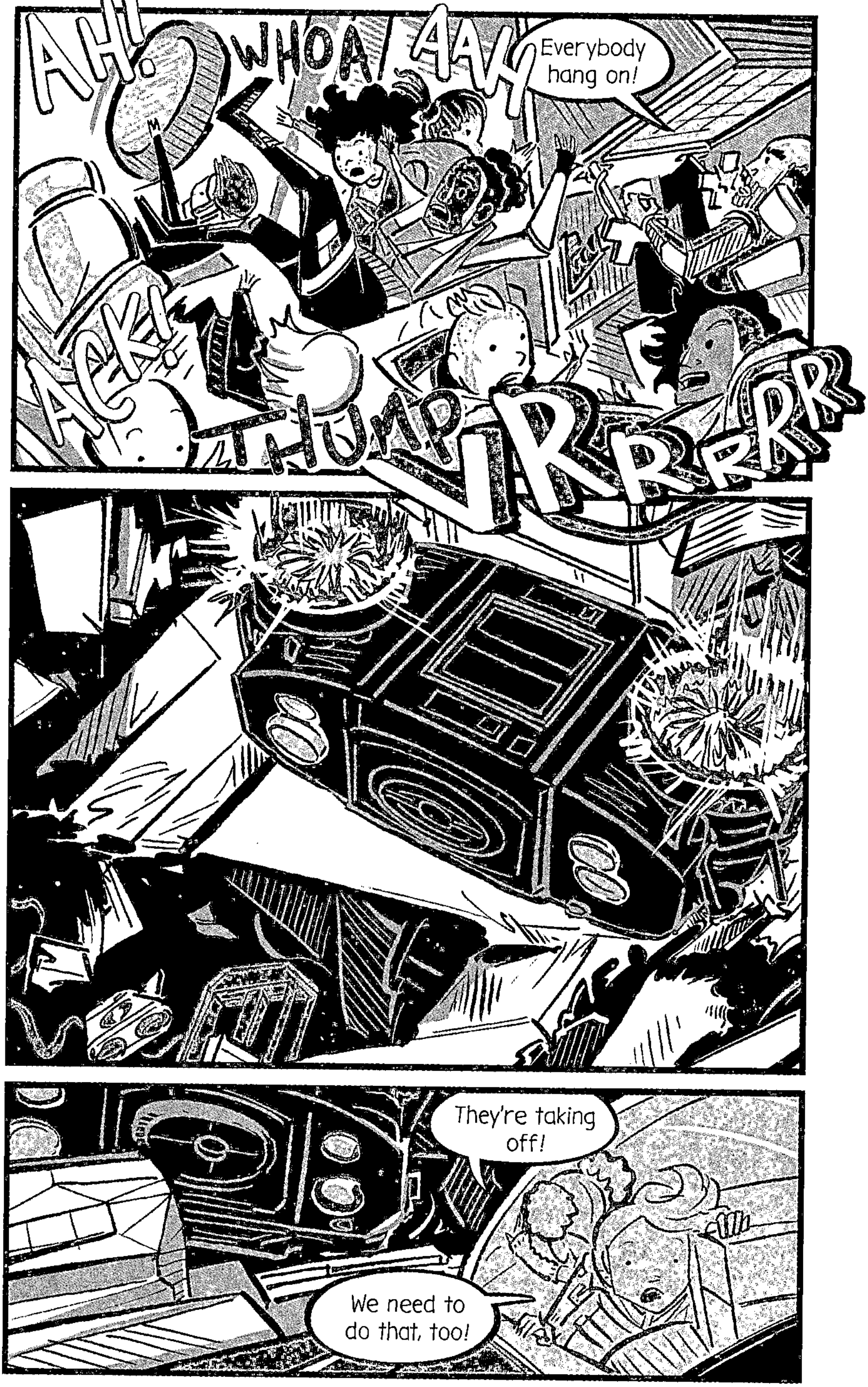
AH!
WHOA!
AAH
Everybody hang on!
ACK!
THUMP
VRRRRR
They're taking off!
We need to do that, too!

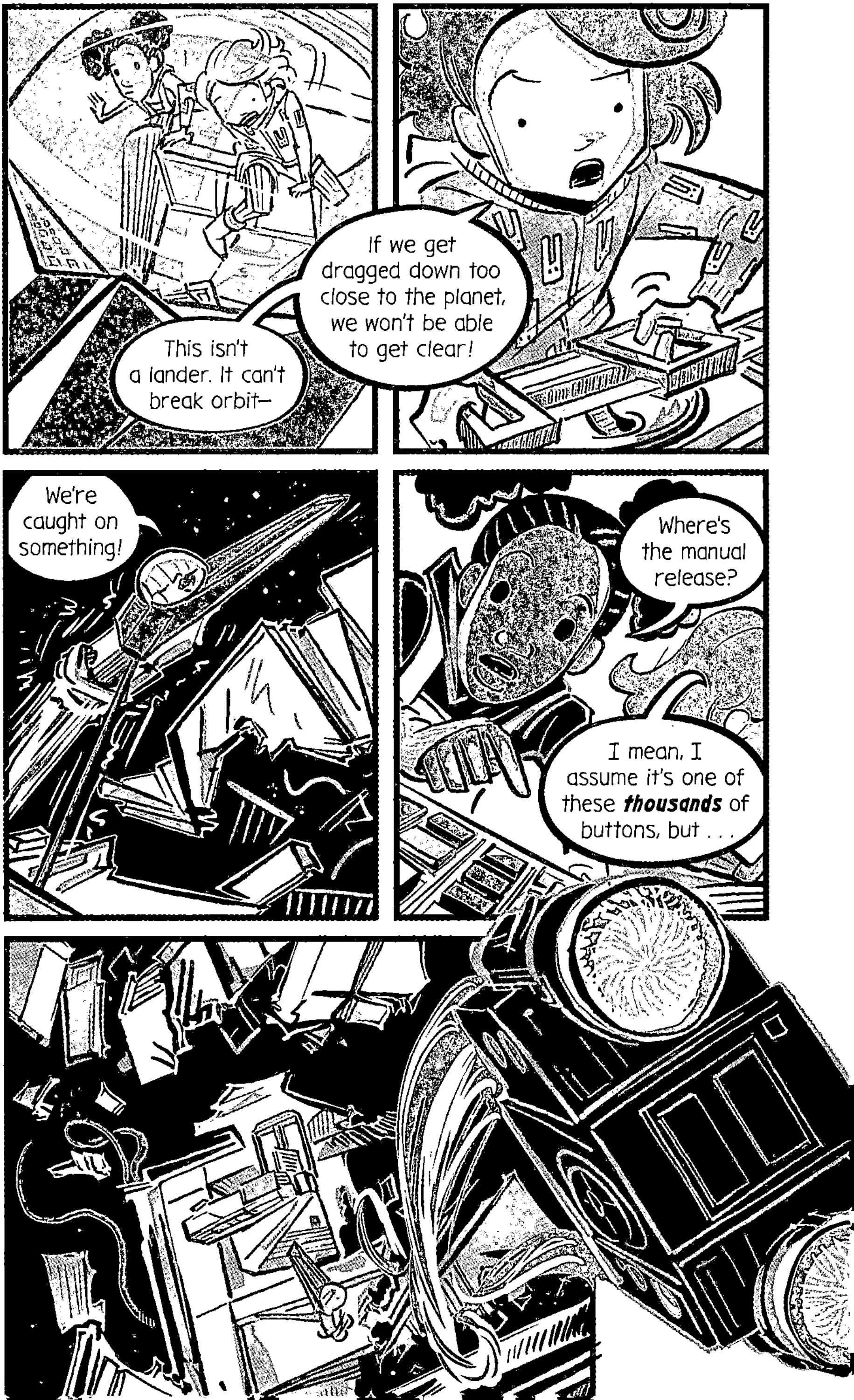

This isn't a lander. It can't break orbit—
If we get dragged down too close to the planet, we won't be able to get clear!
We're caught on something!
Where's the manual release?
I mean, I assume it's one of these ***thousands*** of buttons, but . . .

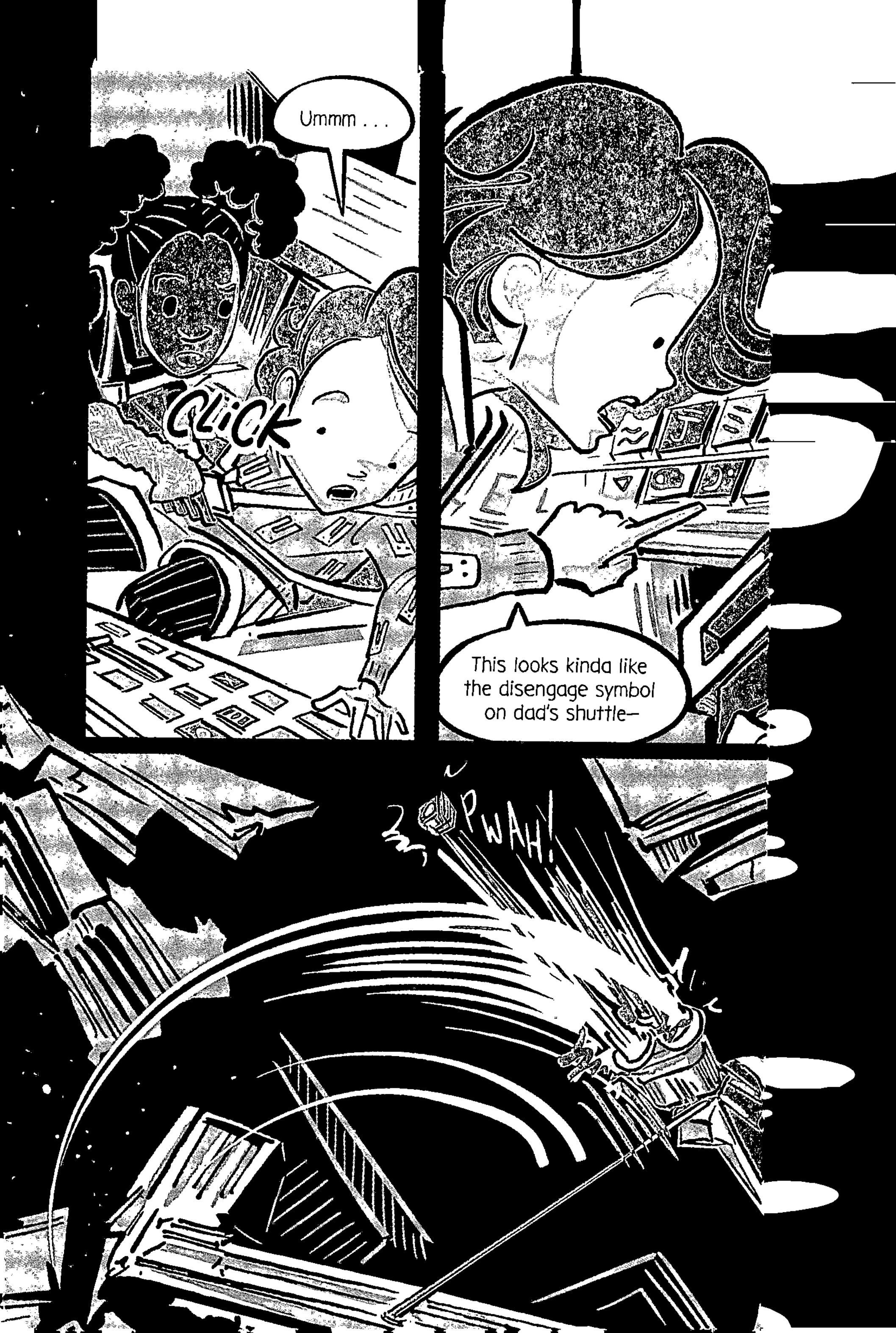
Ummm . . .
CLICK
This looks kinda like the disengage symbol on dad's shuttle—
PWAH!

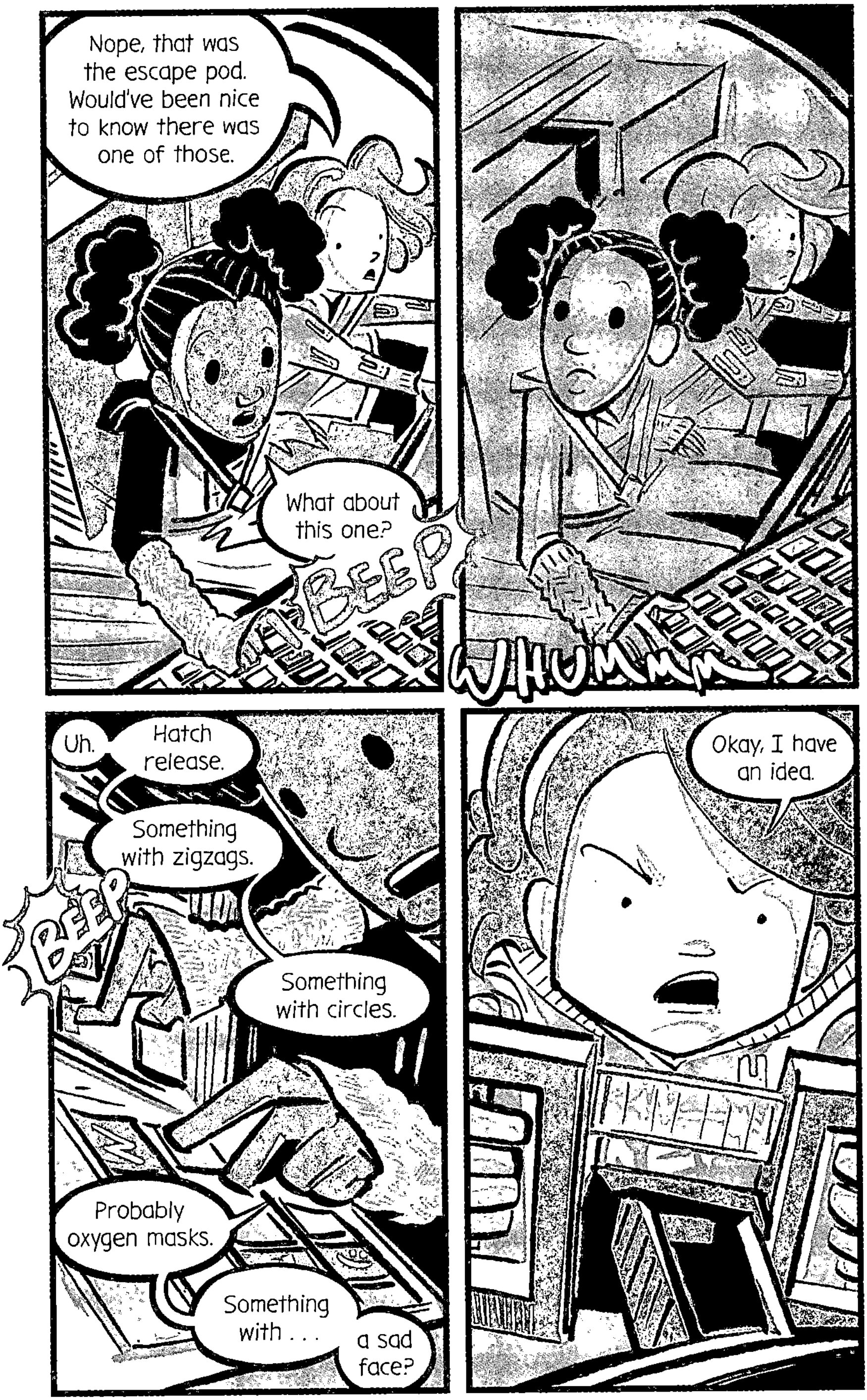
Nope, that was the escape pod. Would've been nice to know there was one of those.
What about this one?
BEEP
WHUMMM
Uh.
Hatch release.
Something with zigzags.
BEEP
Something with circles.
Probably oxygen masks.
Something with . . .
a sad face?
Okay, I have an idea.

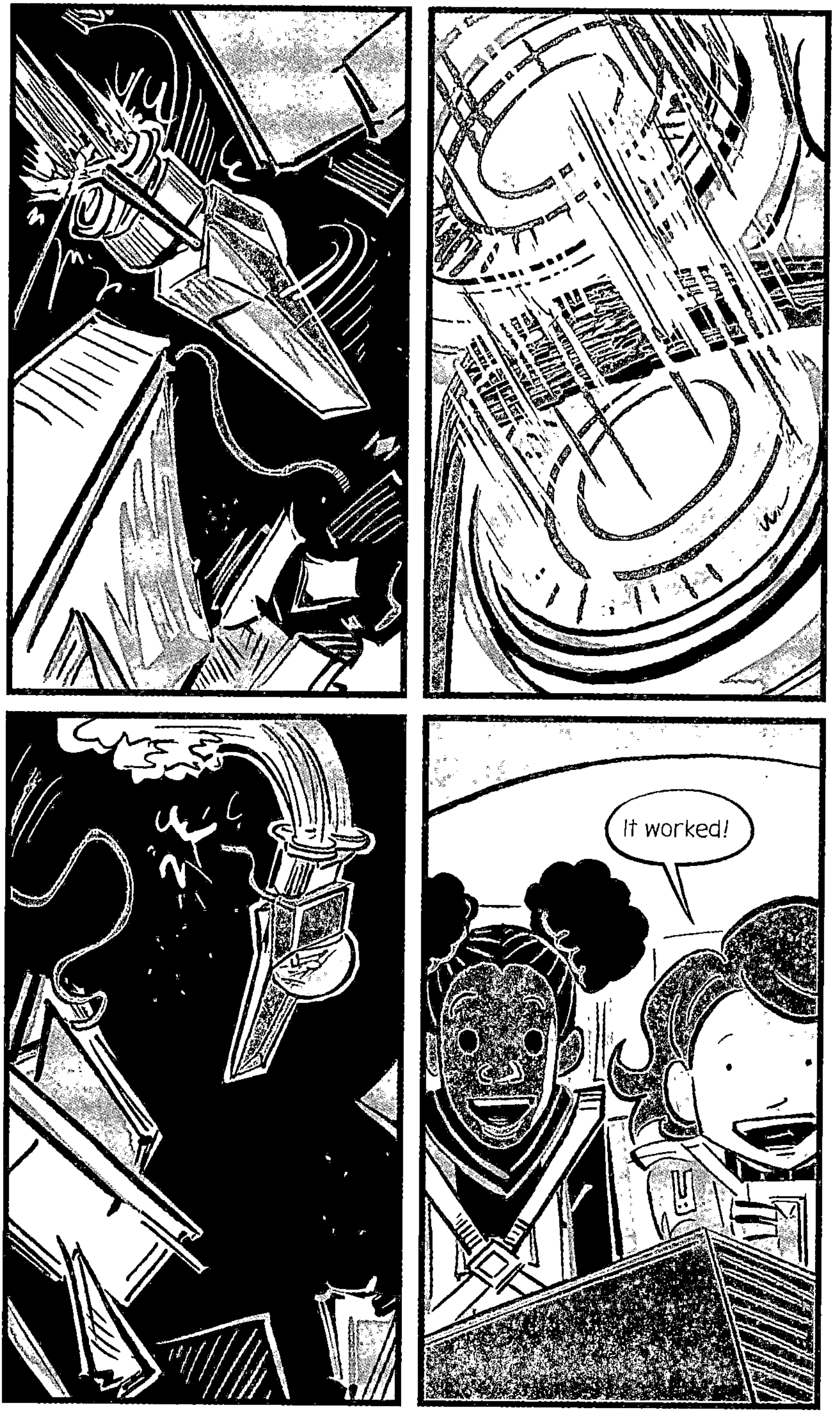
It worked!

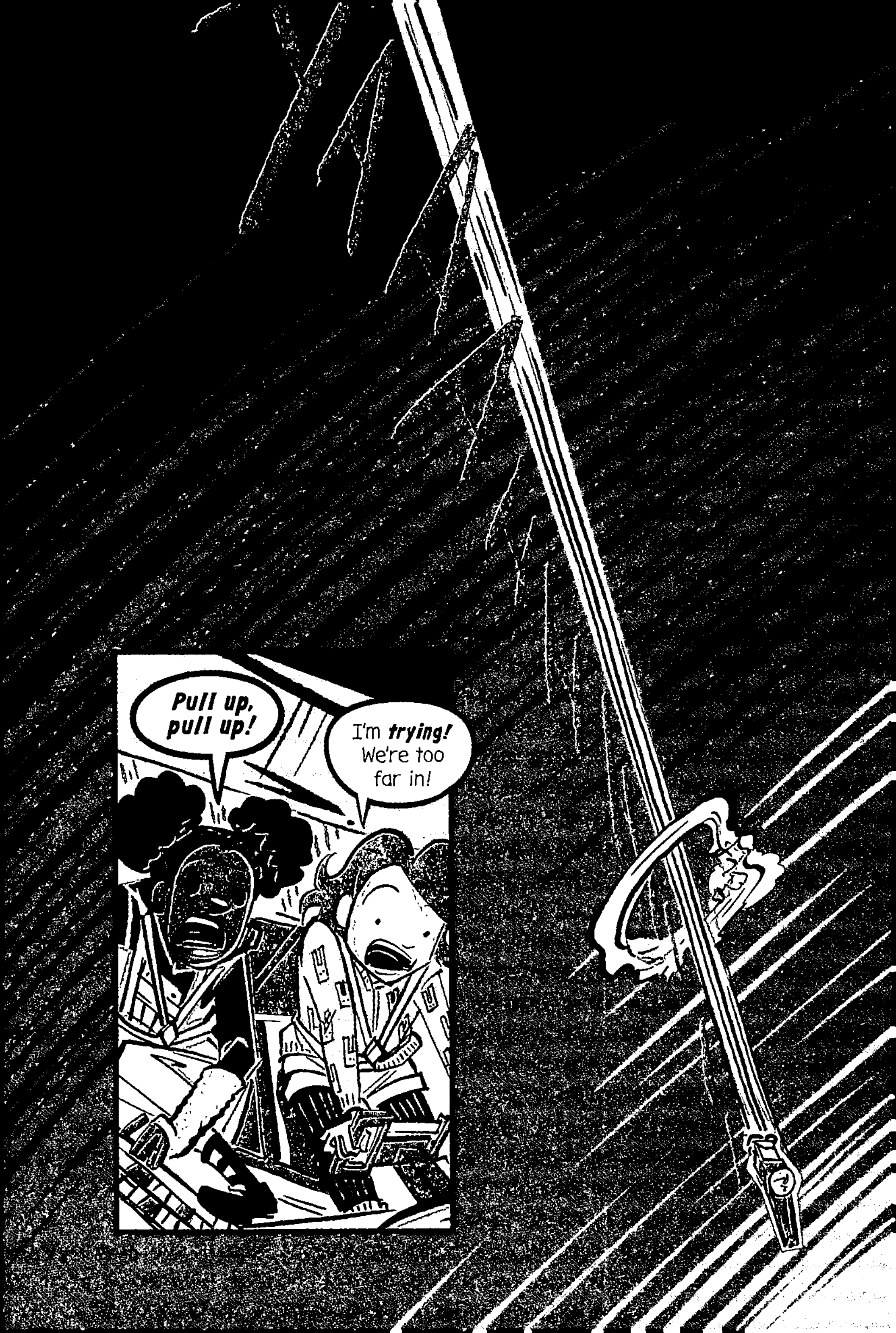
Pull up, pull up!
I'm trying! We're too far in!

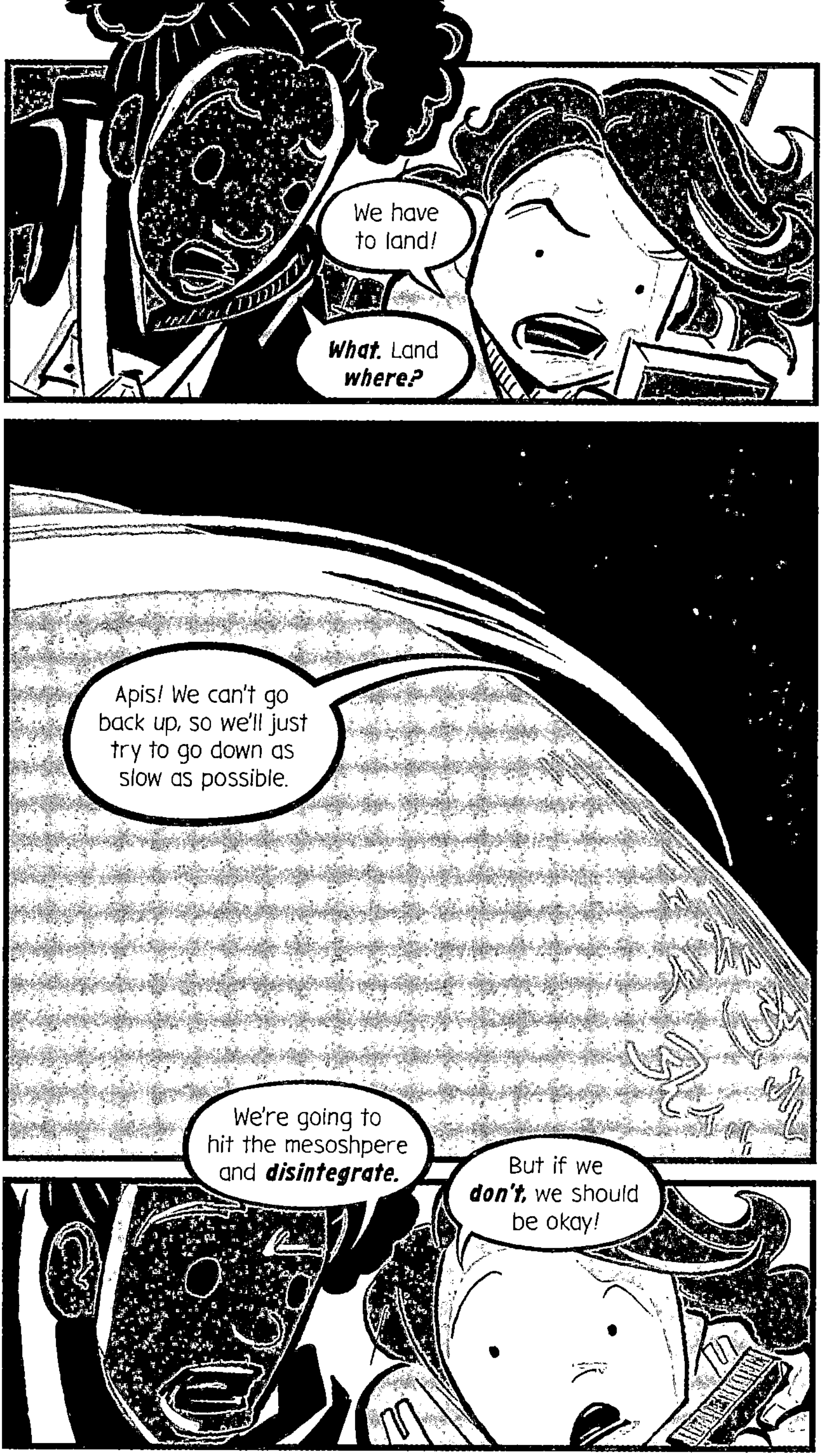

We have to land!
What. Land where?
Apis! We can't go back up, so we'll just try to go down as slow as possible.
We're going to hit the mesoshpere and disintegrate.
But if we don't, we should be okay!

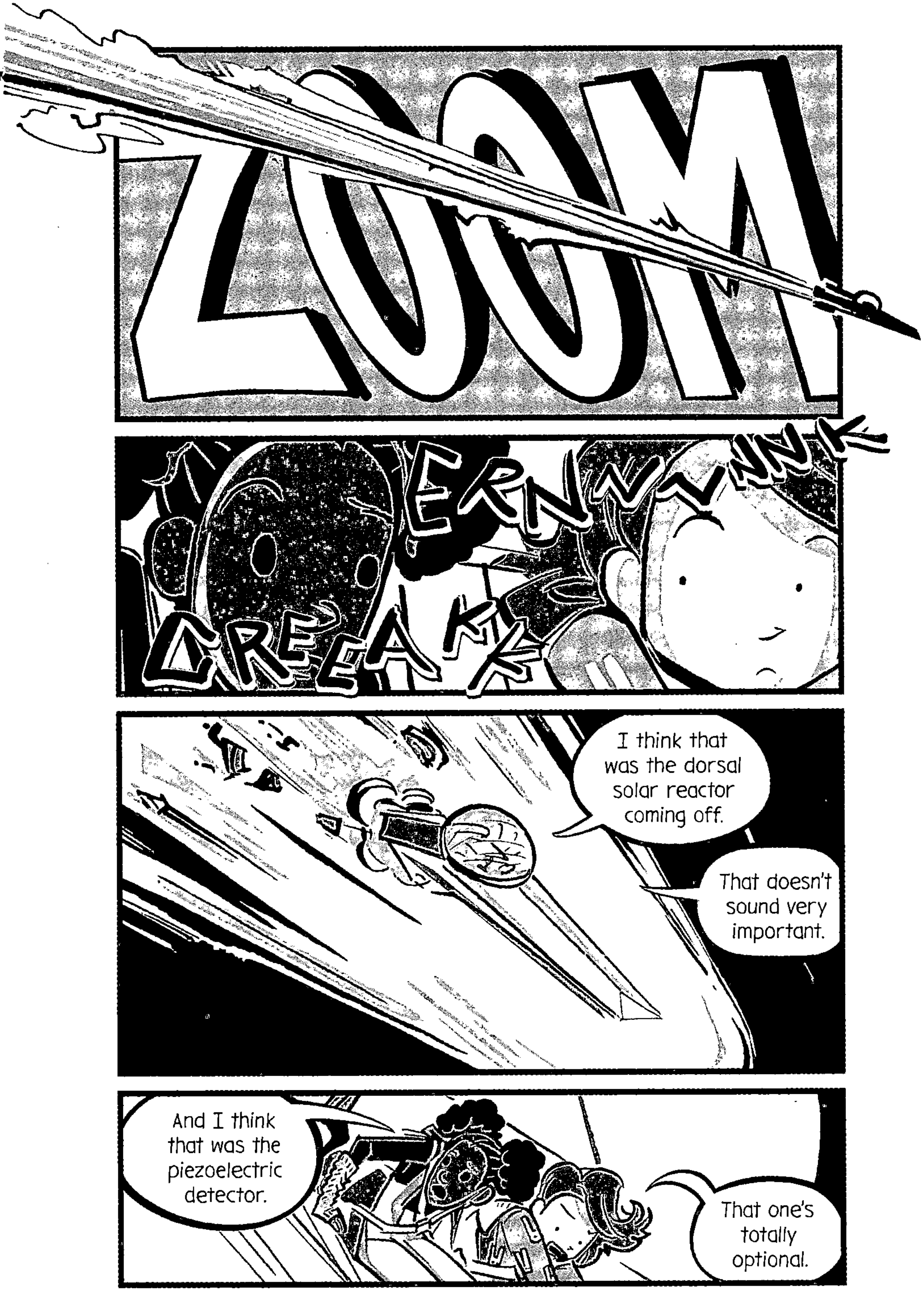
ZOOM
ERNNNNNK
CREEAKK
I think that was the dorsal solar reactor coming off.
That doesn't sound very important.
And I think that was the piezoelectric detector.
That one's totally optional.

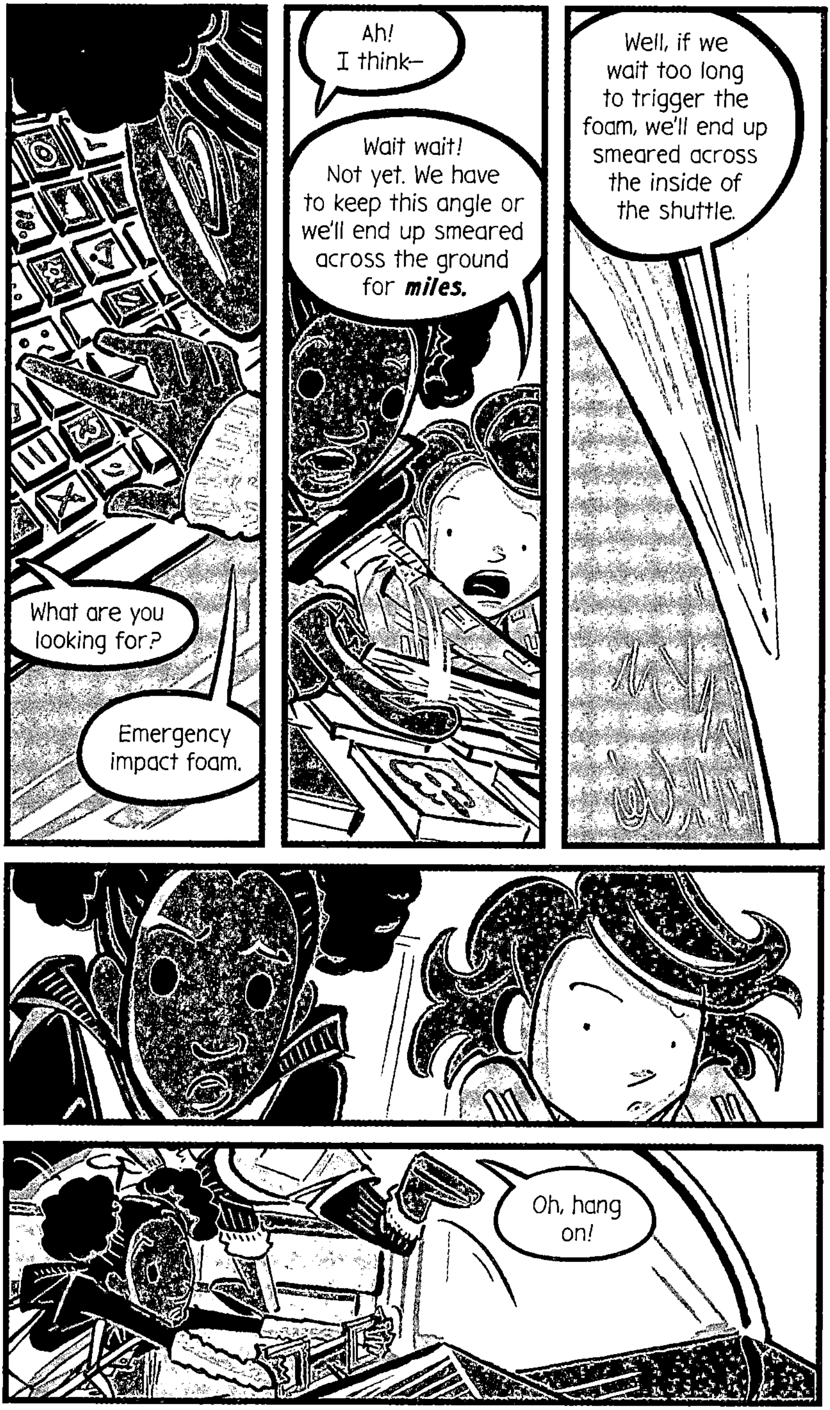
What are you looking for?
Emergency impact foam.
Ah! I think–
Wait wait! Not yet. We have to keep this angle or we'll end up smeared across the ground for ***miles.***
Well, if we wait too long to trigger the foam, we'll end up smeared across the *inside* of the shuttle.
Oh, hang on!

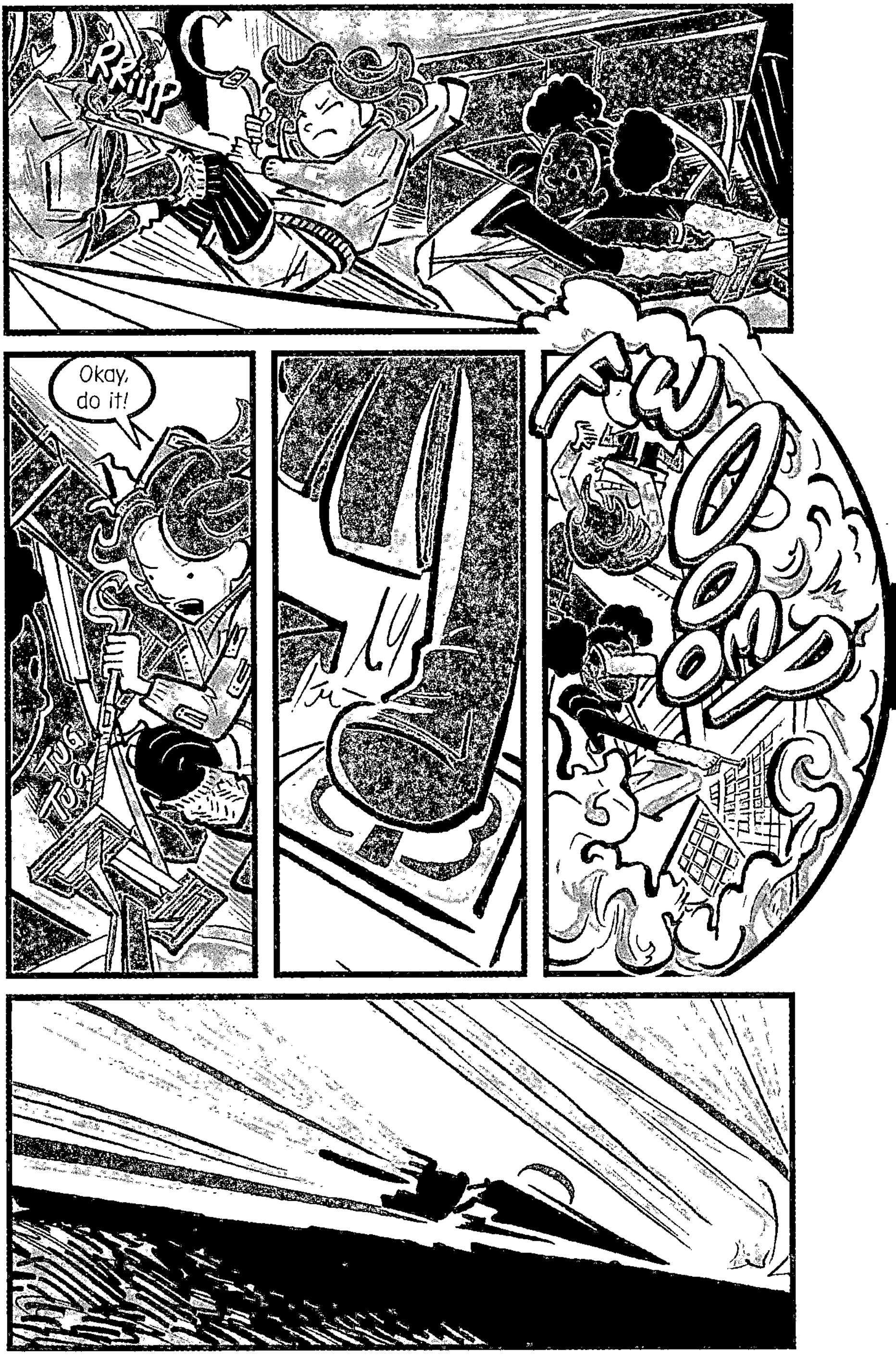
RRIIIP
Okay, do it!
TUG TUG
FWOOOOMP

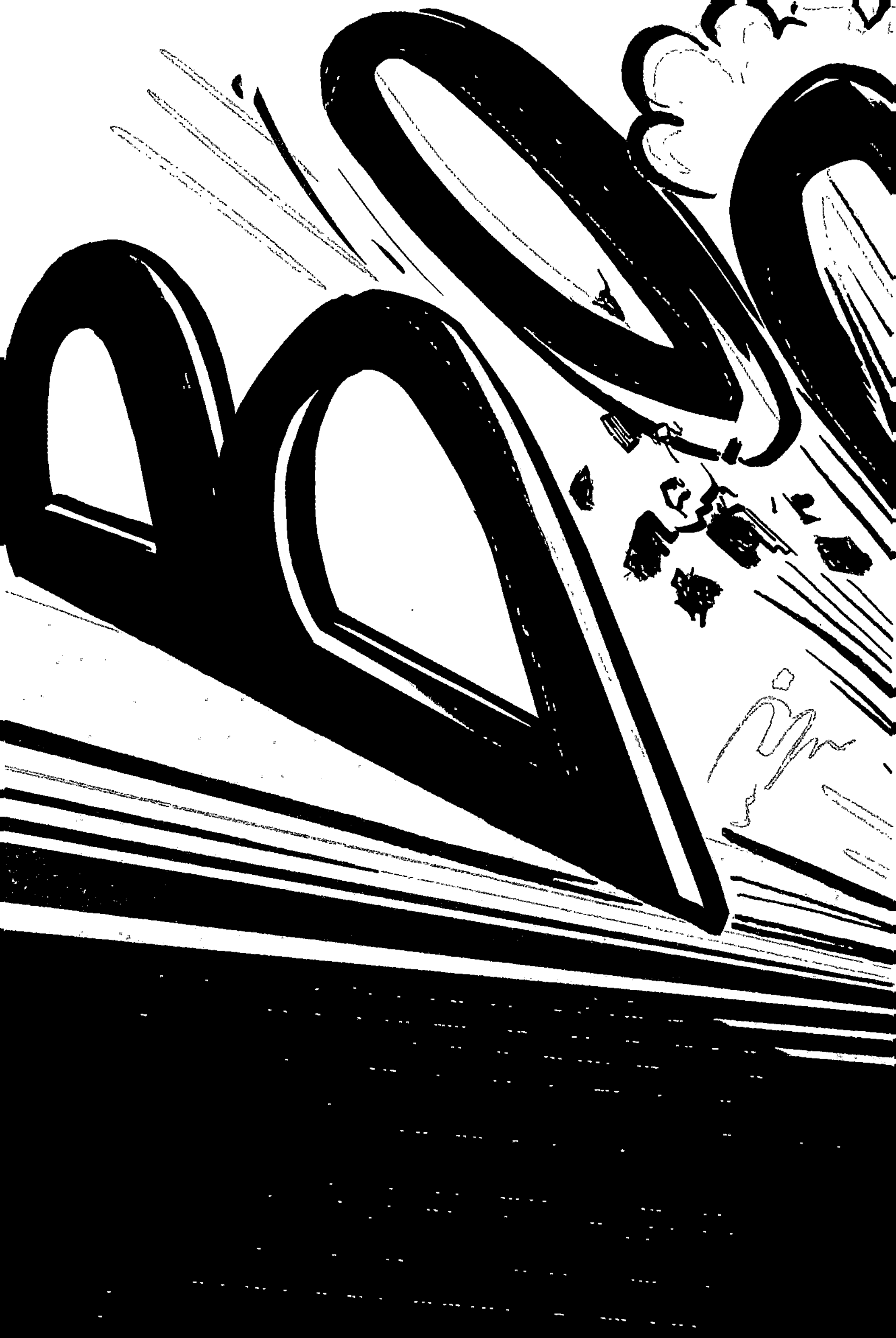

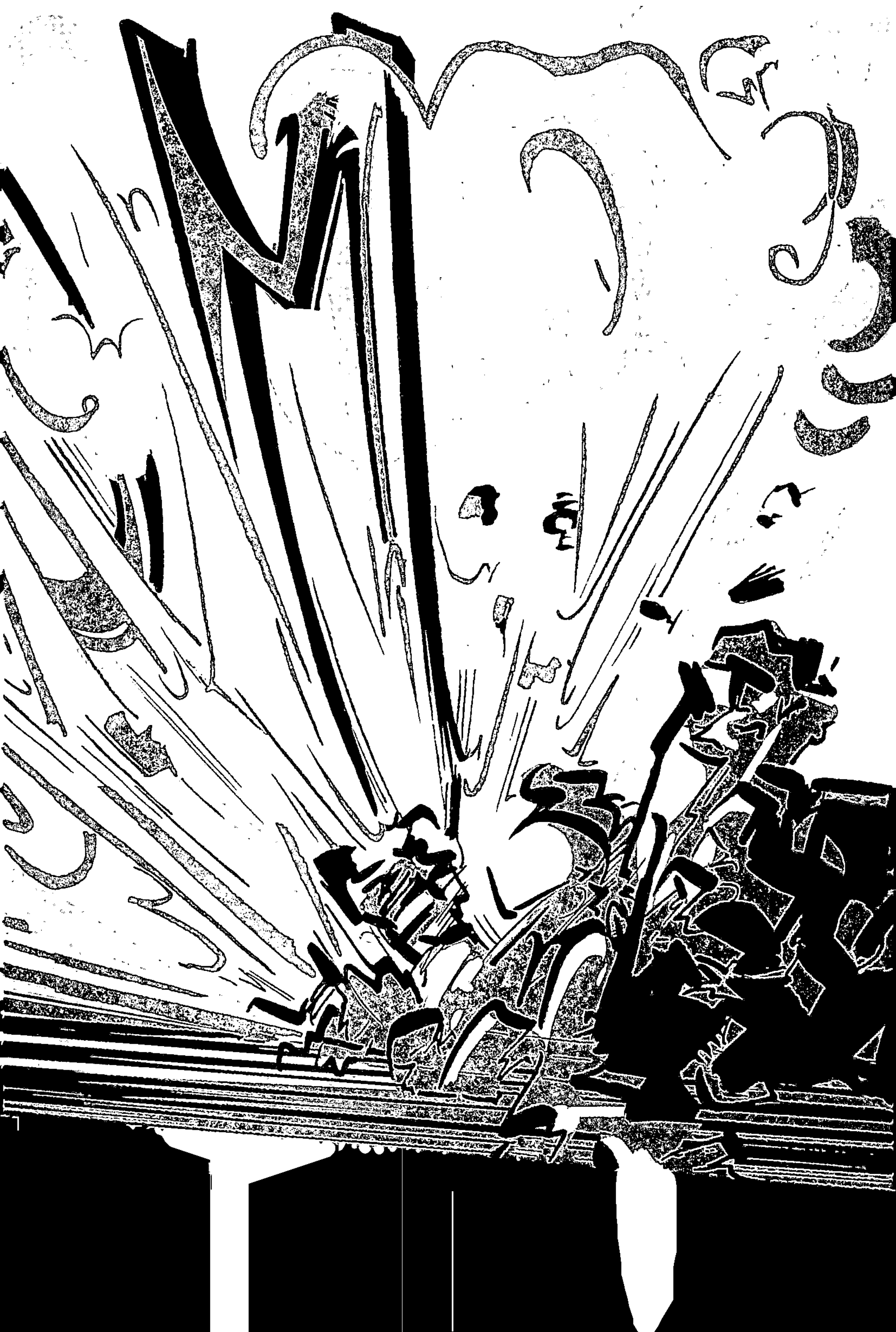

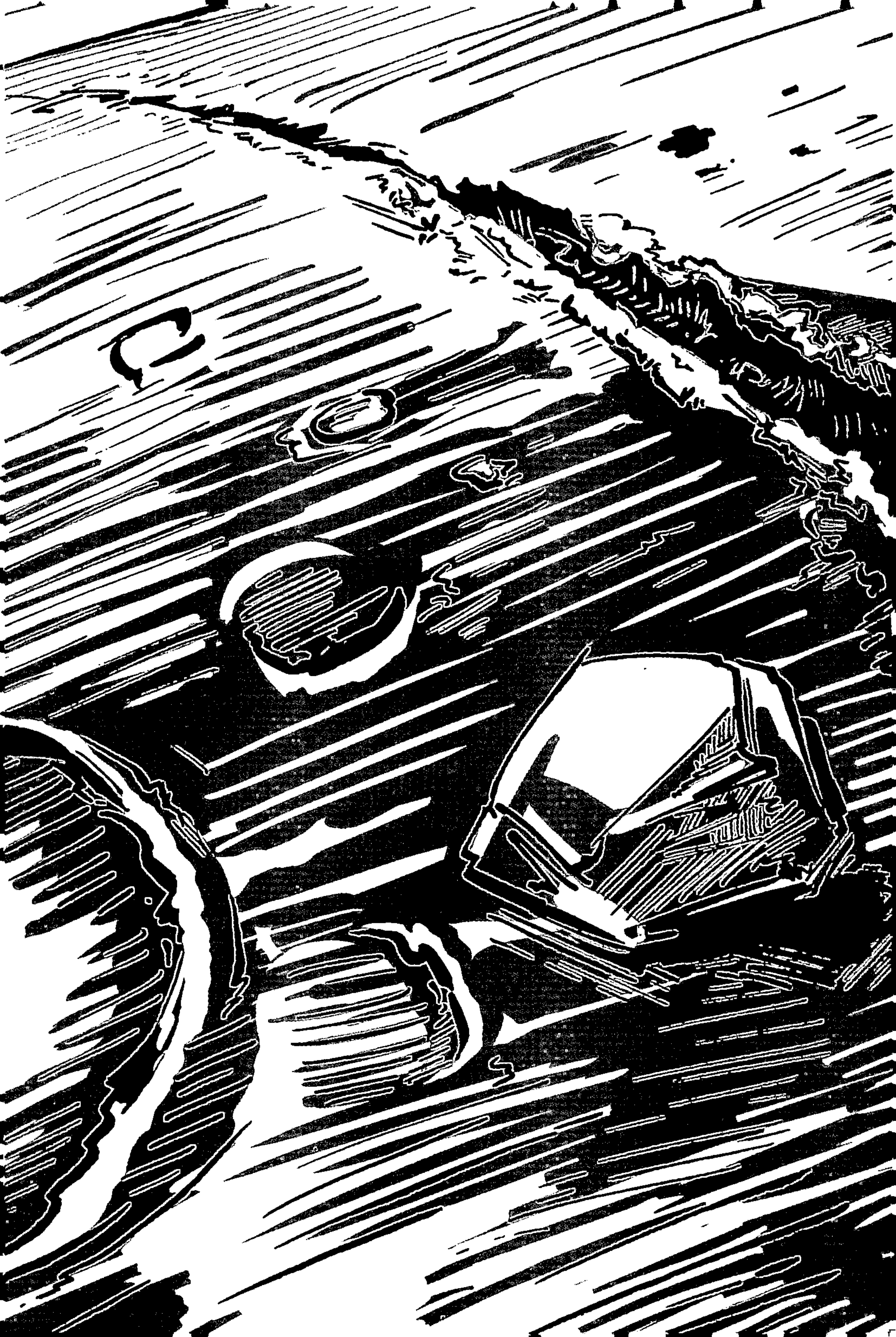

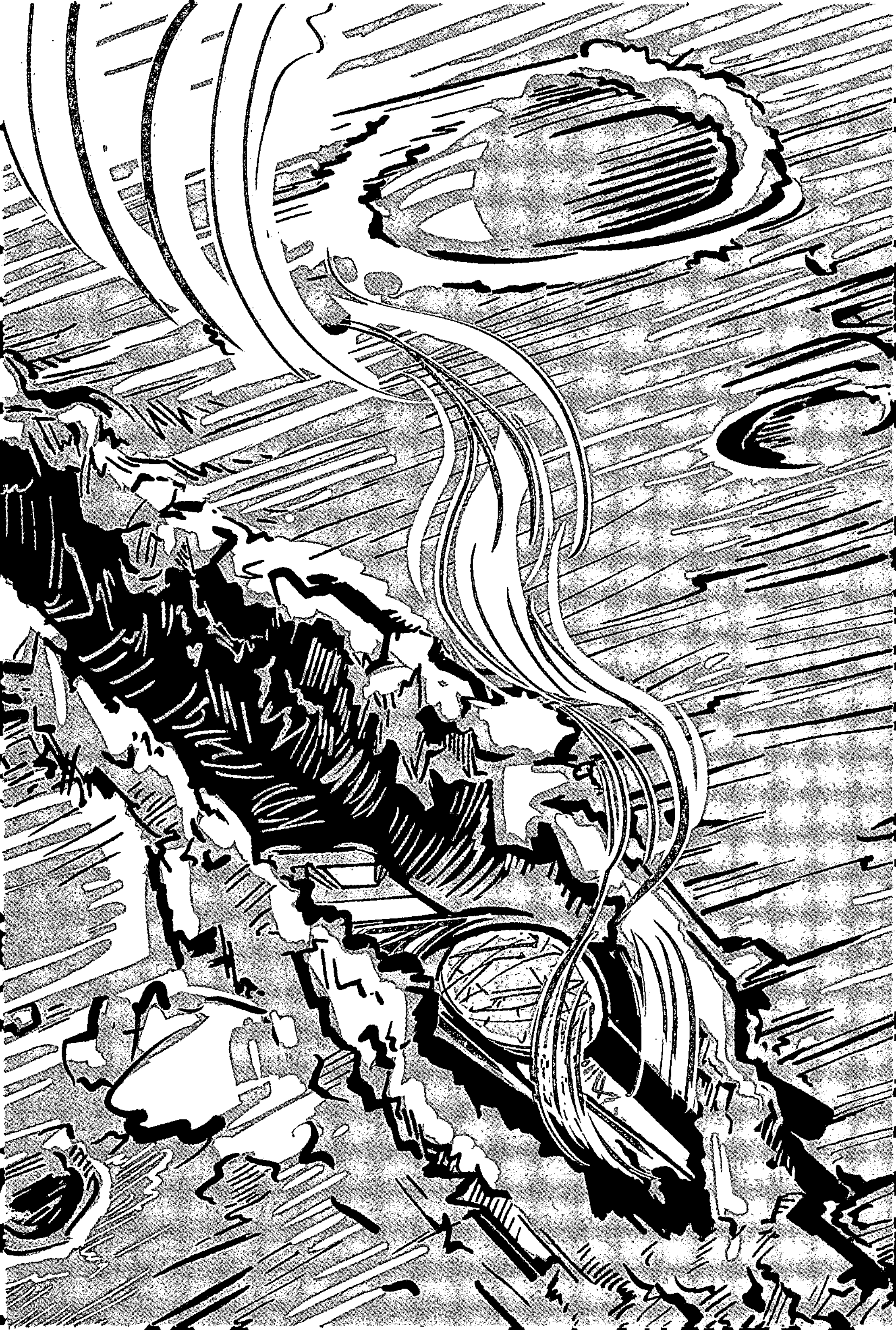

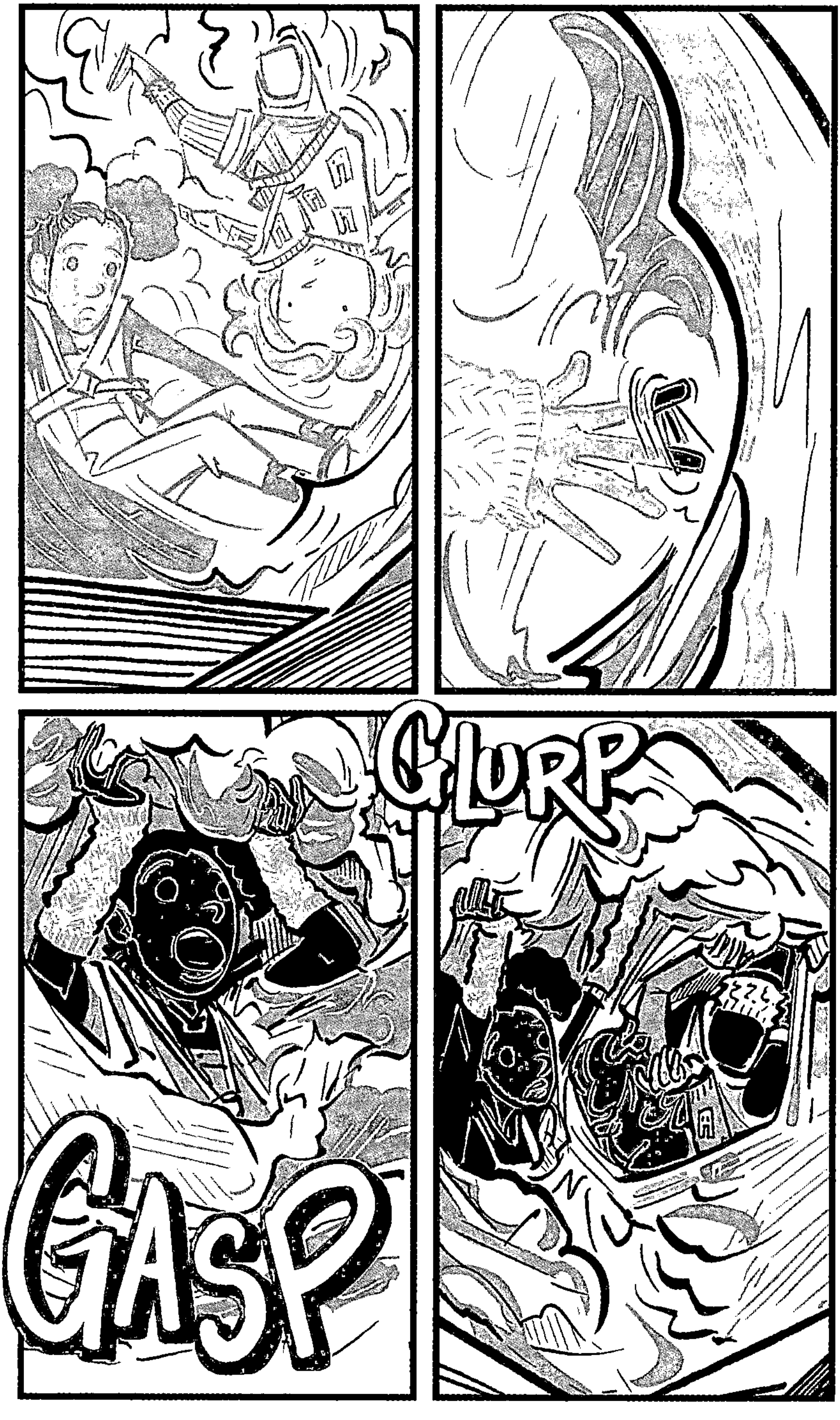
GLURP
GASP

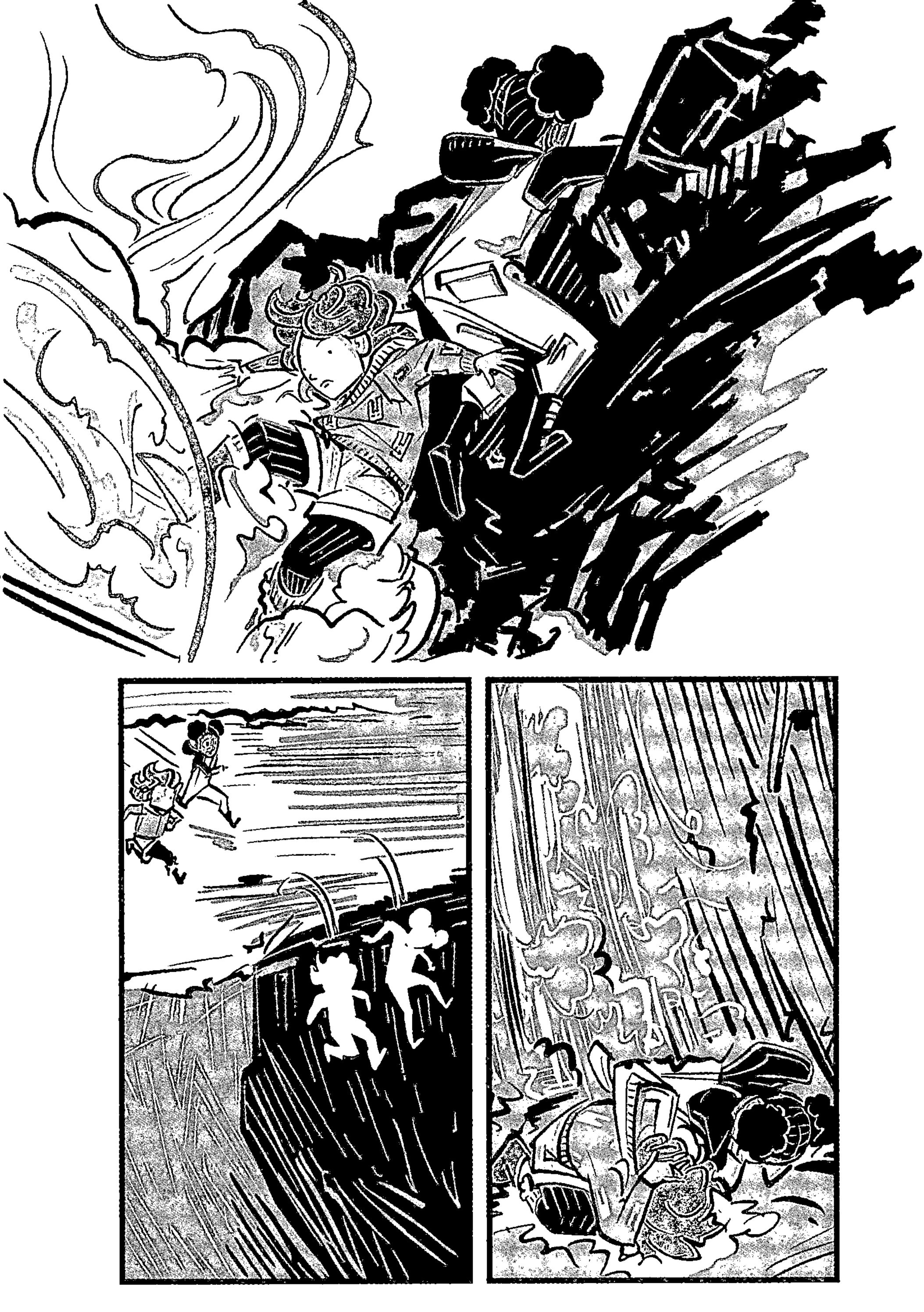

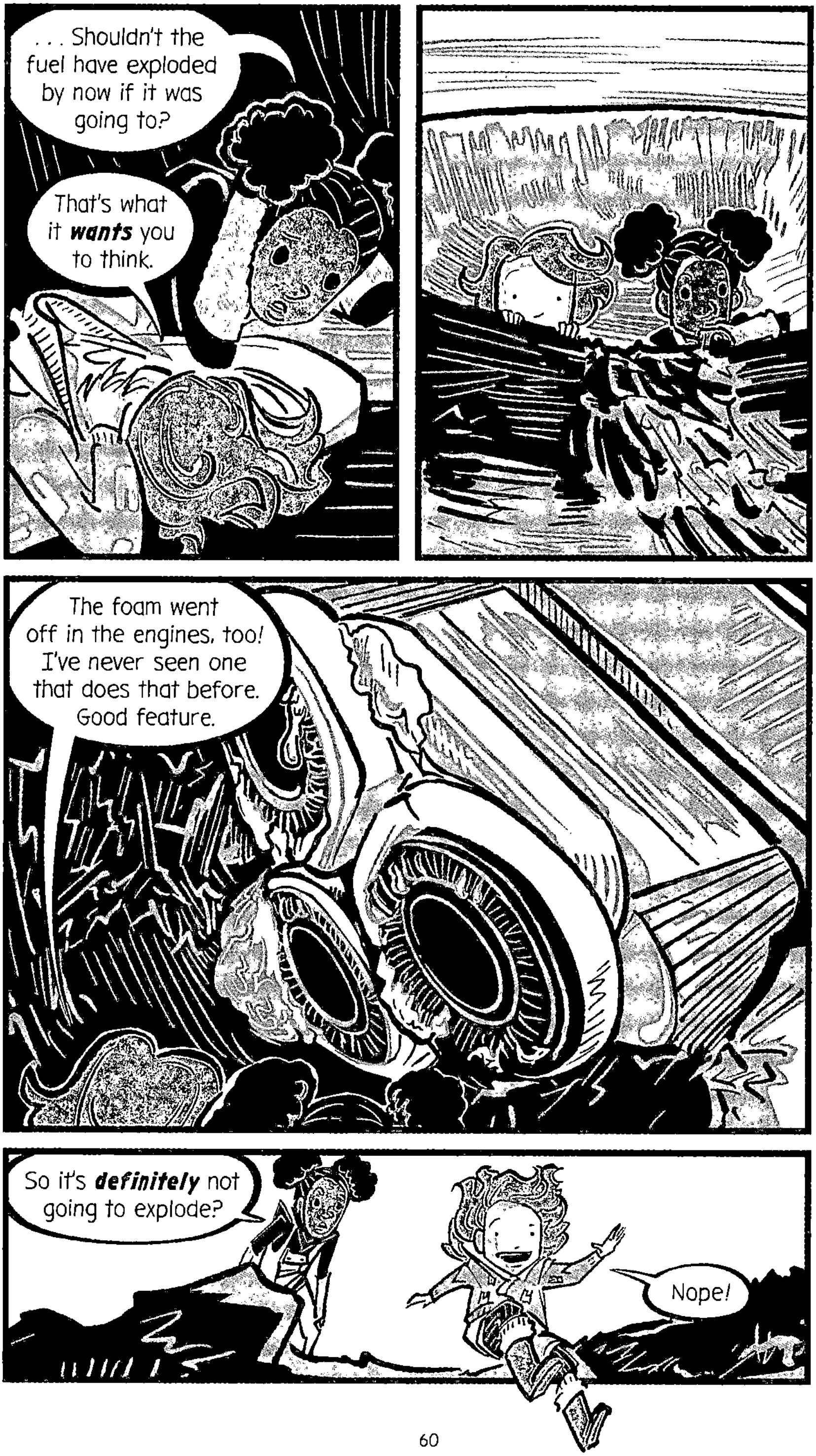
. . . Shouldn't the fuel have exploded by now if it was going to?
That's what it **wants** you to think.
The foam went off in the engines, too! I've never seen one that does that before. Good feature.
So it's **definitely** not going to explode?
Nope!

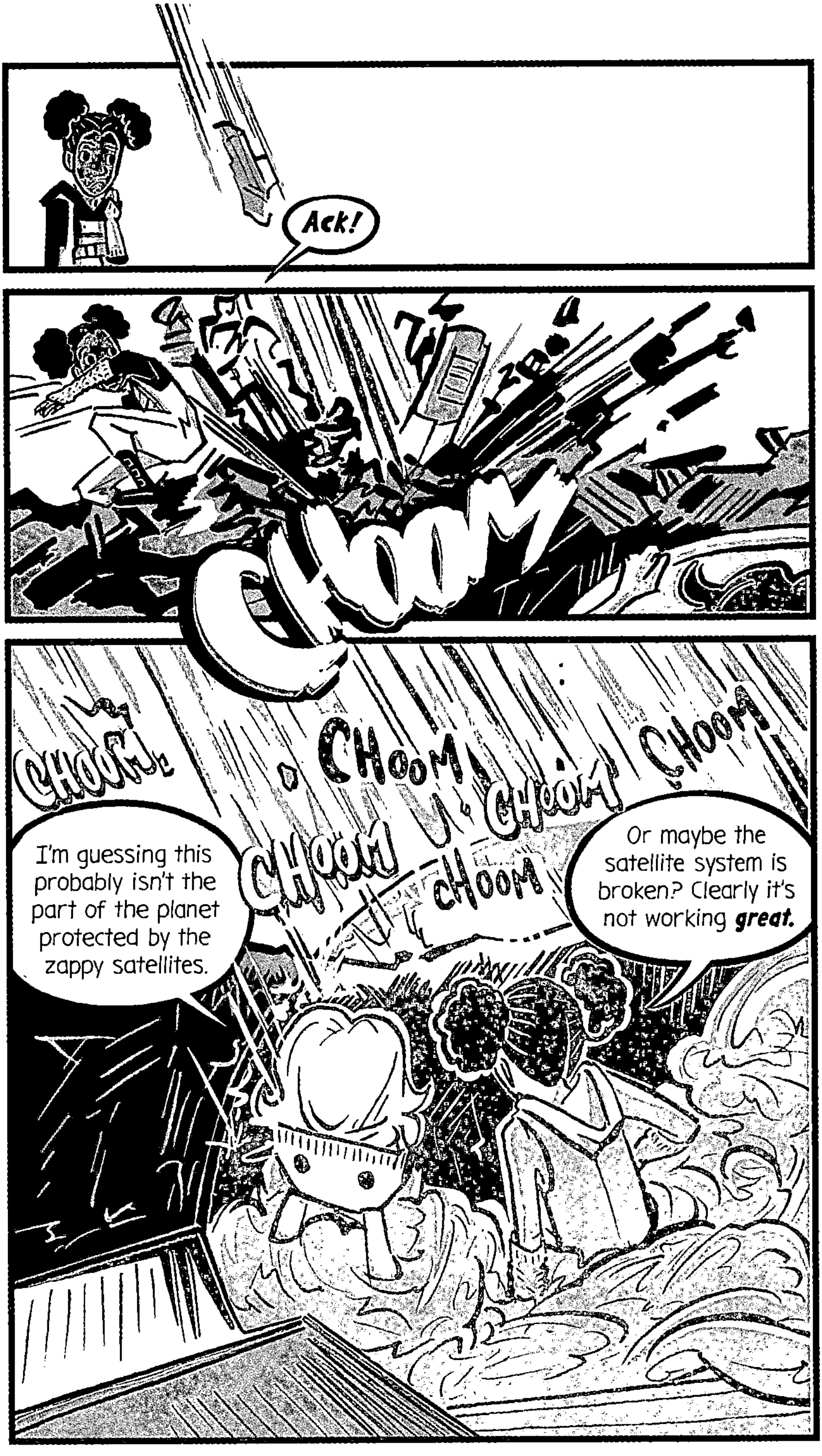
Ack!
CHOOM
CHOOM
CHOOM
CHOOM
CHOOM
CHOOM
CHOOM
I'm guessing this probably isn't the part of the planet protected by the zappy satellites.
Or maybe the satellite system is broken? Clearly it's not working ***great.***

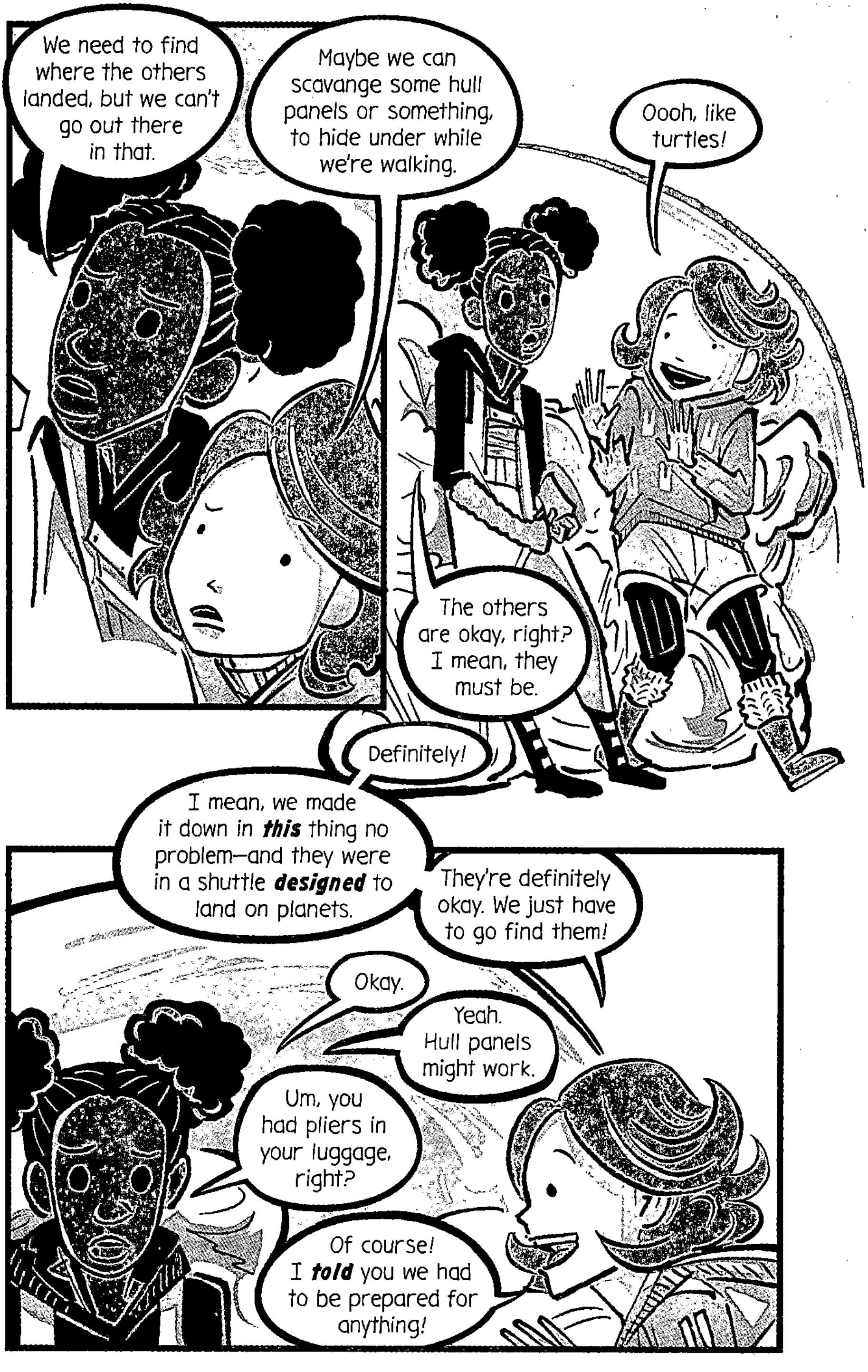

We need to find where the others landed, but we can't go out there in that.
Maybe we can scavange some hull panels or something, to hide under while we're walking.
Oooh, like turtles!
The others are okay, right? I mean, they must be.
Definitely!
I mean, we made it down in **this** thing no problem—and they were in a shuttle **designed** to land on planets.
They're definitely okay. We just have to go find them!
Okay.
Yeah. Hull panels might work.
Um, you had pliers in your luggage, right?
Of course! I **told** you we had to be prepared for anything!

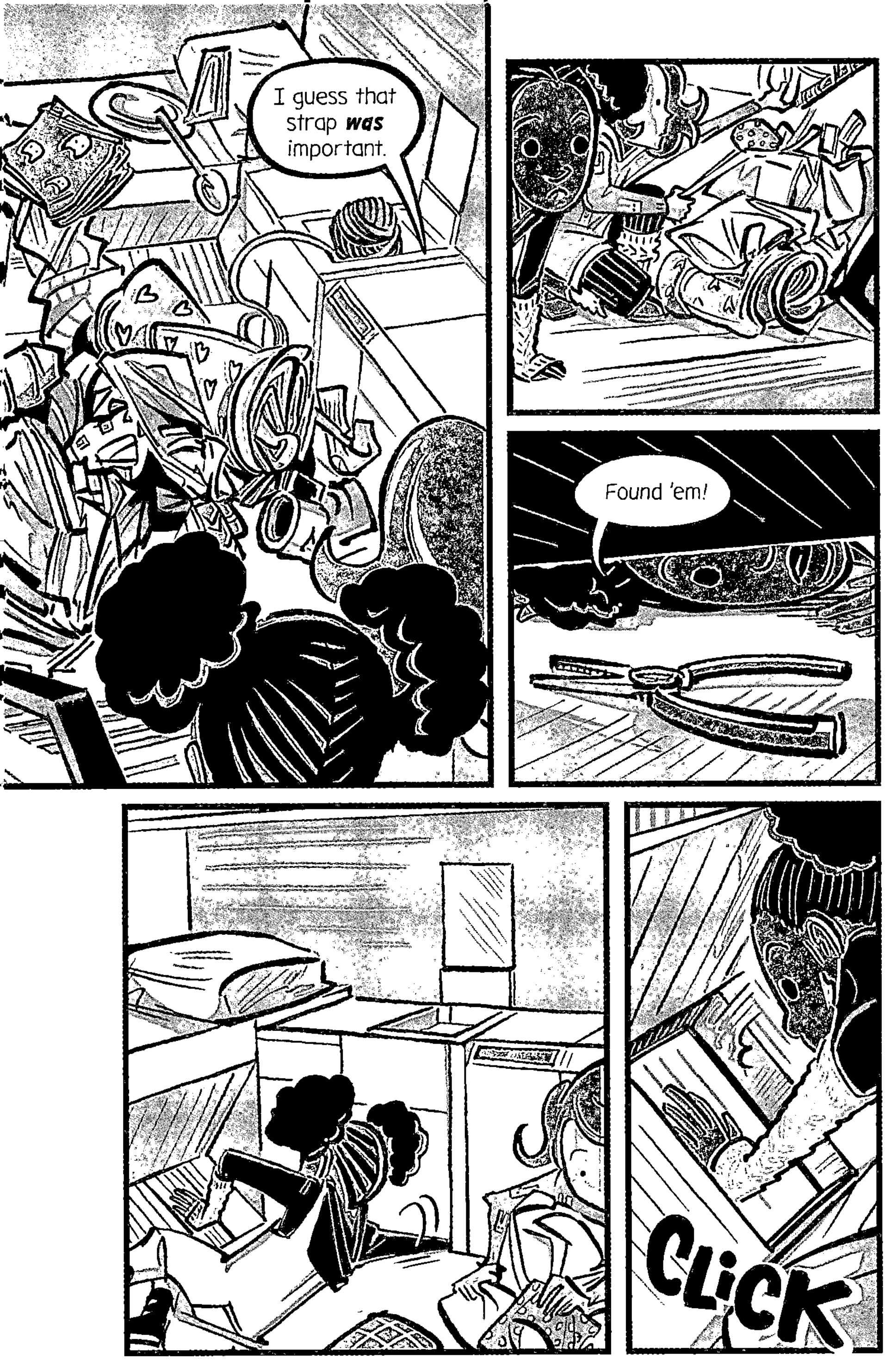
I guess that strap ***was*** important.
Found 'em!
CLICK

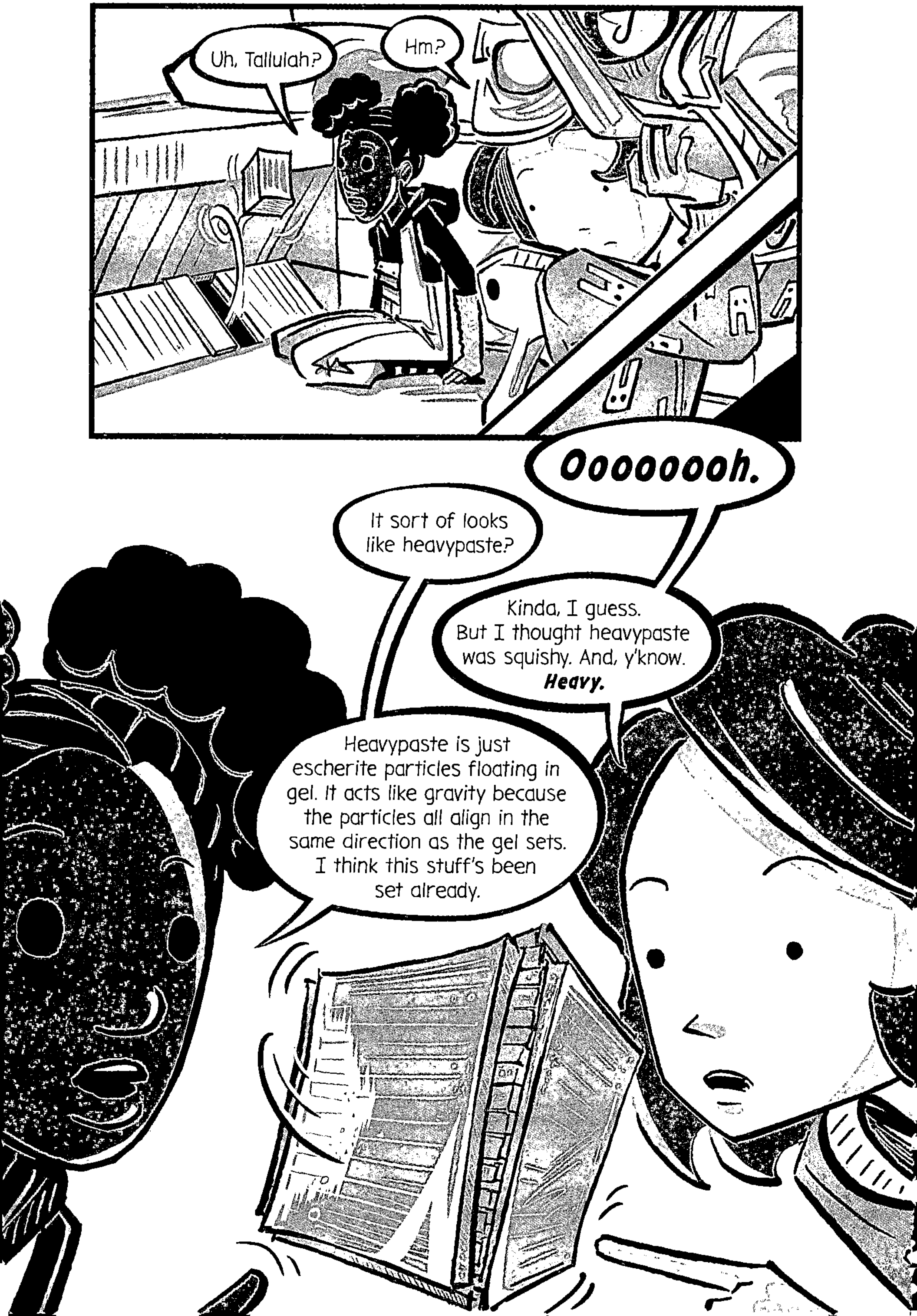
Uh, Tallulah?
Hm?
Ooooooh.
It sort of looks like heavypaste?
Kinda, I guess. But I thought heavypaste was squishy. And, y'know. ***Heavy.***
Heavypaste is just escherite particles floating in gel. It acts like gravity because the particles all align in the same direction as the gel sets. I think this stuff's been set already.

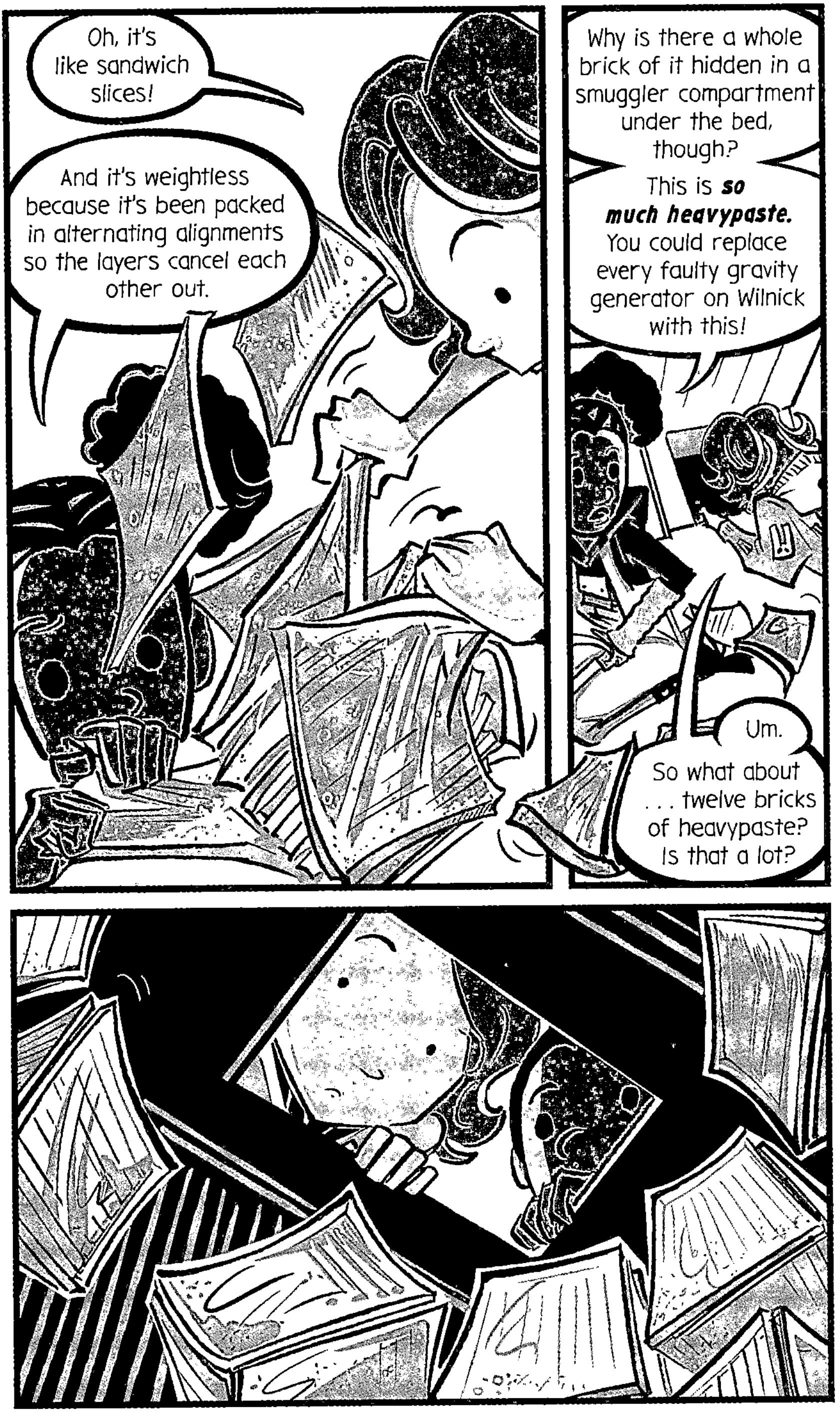
Oh, it's like sandwich slices!
And it's weightless because it's been packed in alternating alignments so the layers cancel each other out.
Why is there a whole brick of it hidden in a smuggler compartment under the bed, though?
This is **so much heavypaste.** You could replace every faulty gravity generator on Wilnick with this!
Um.
So what about . . . twelve bricks of heavypaste? Is that a lot?

(MEANWHILE, ON THE OTHER SIDE of the PLANET)

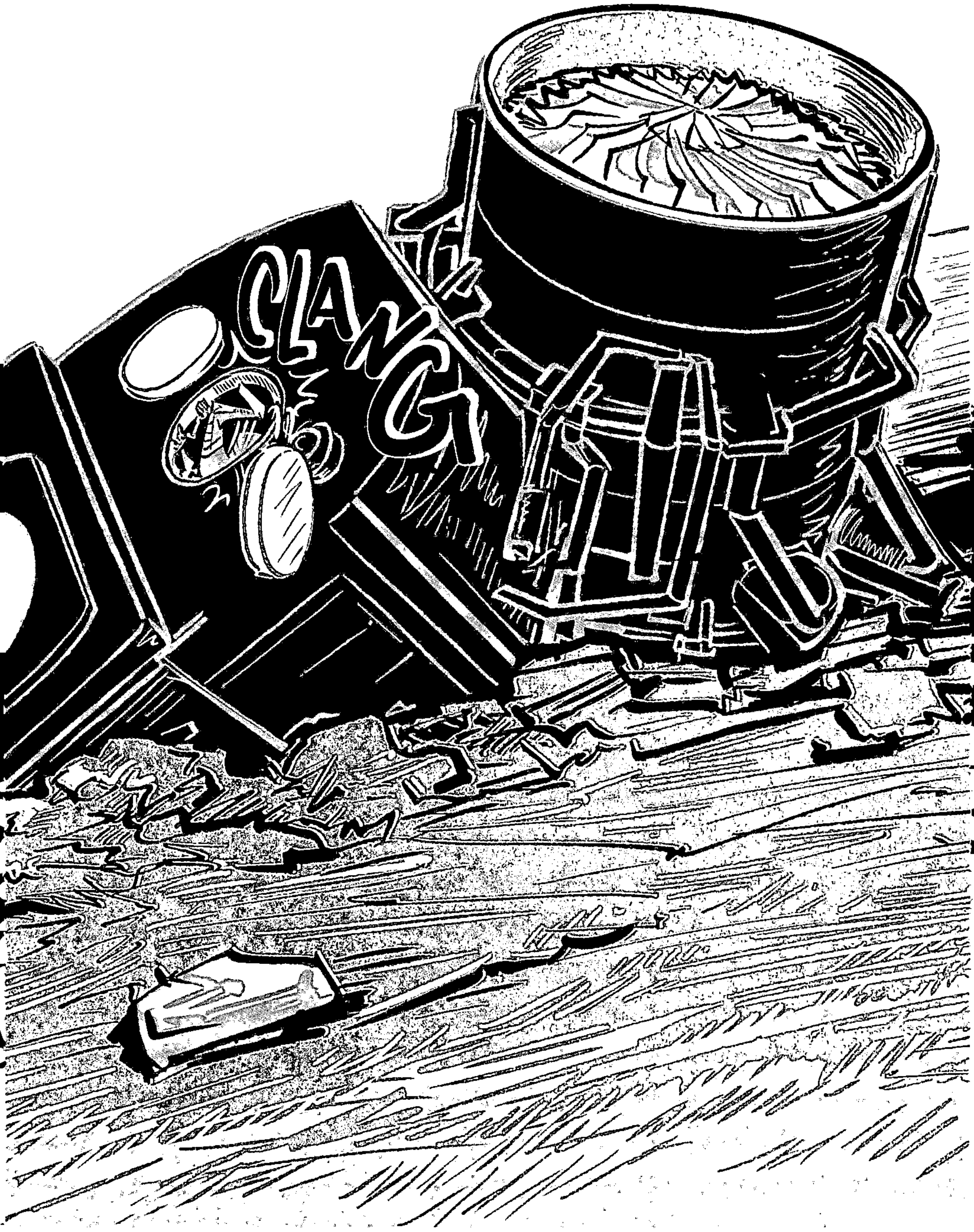
CLANG

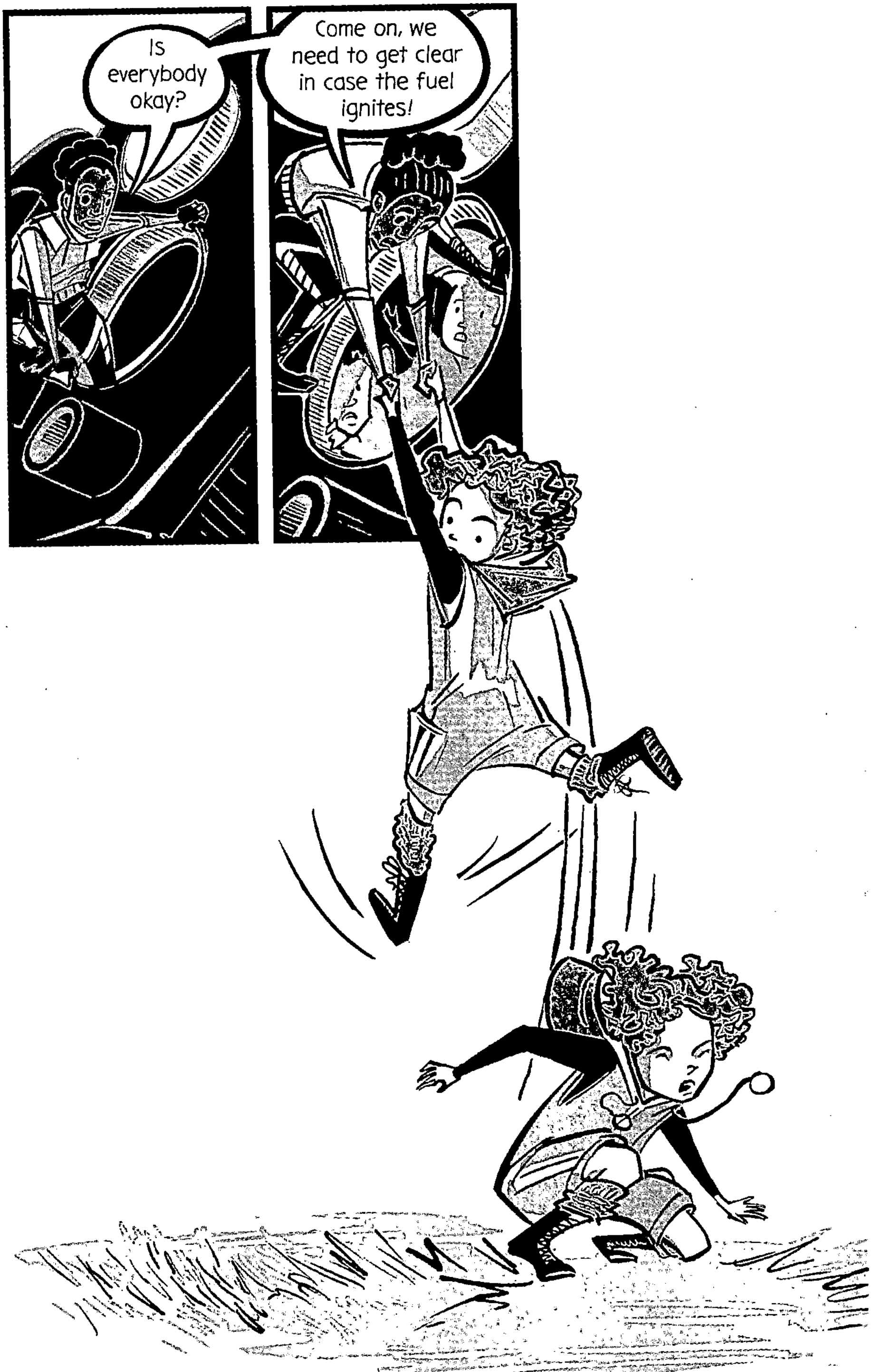
Is everybody okay?
Come on, we need to get clear in case the fuel ignites!

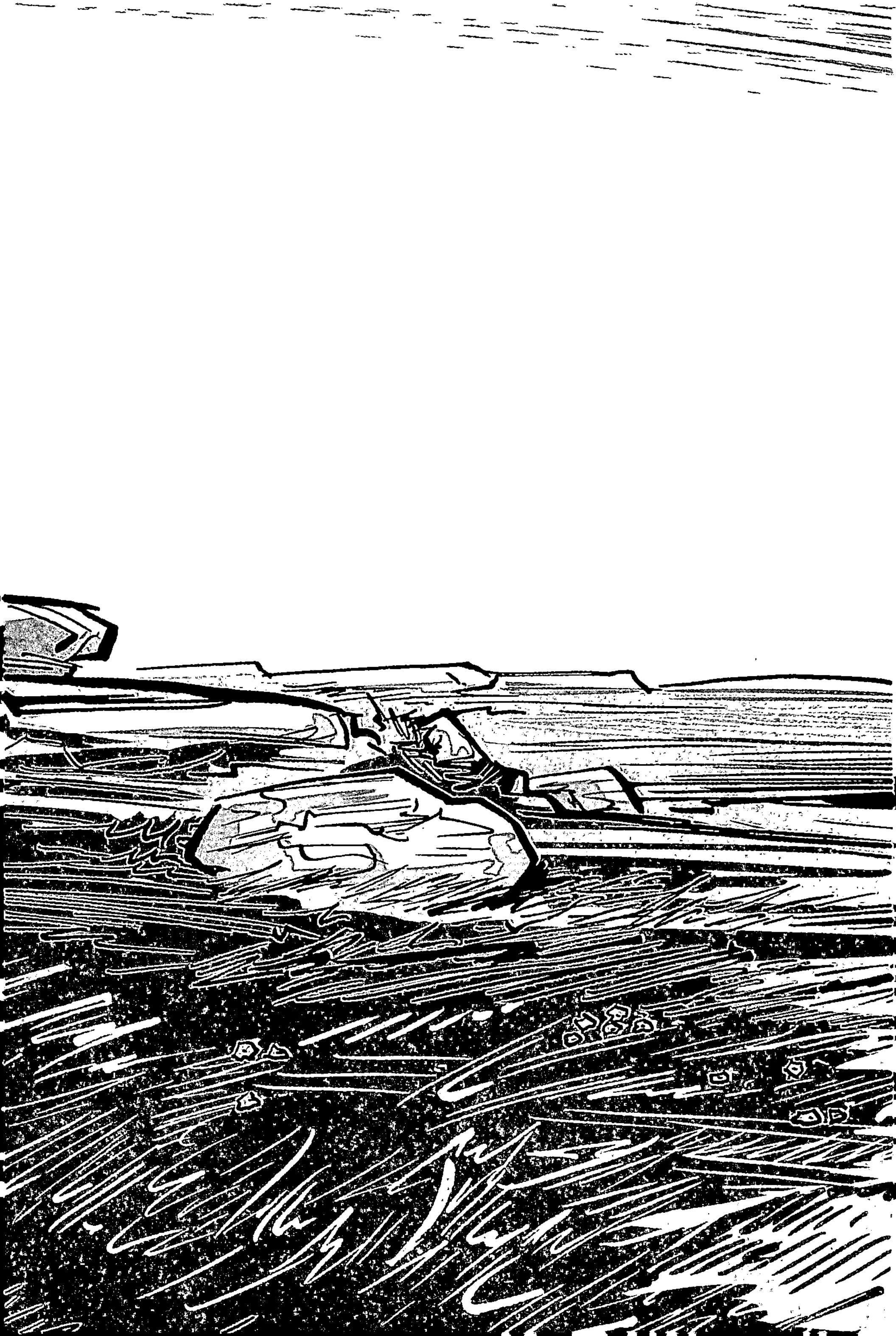

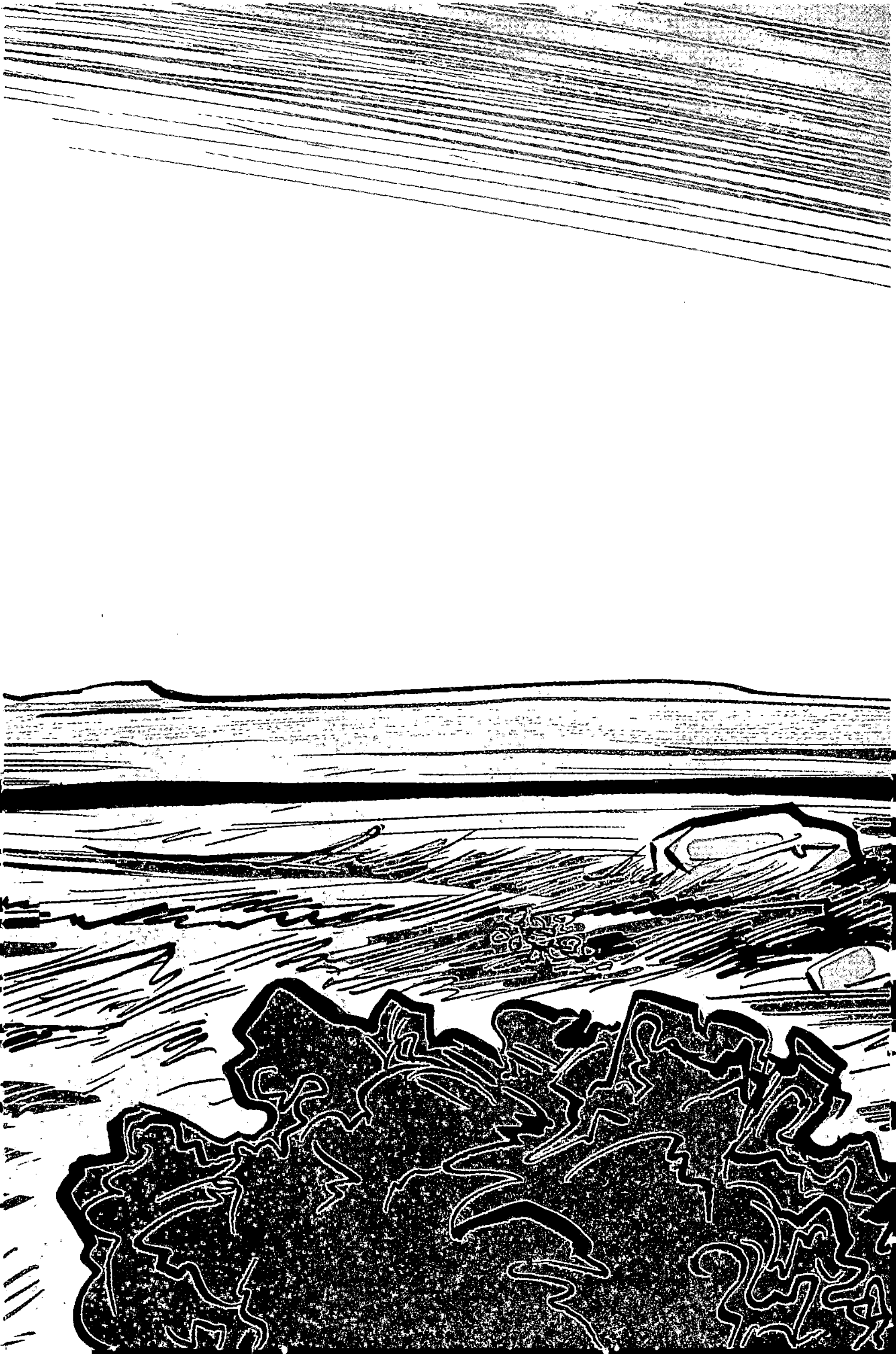

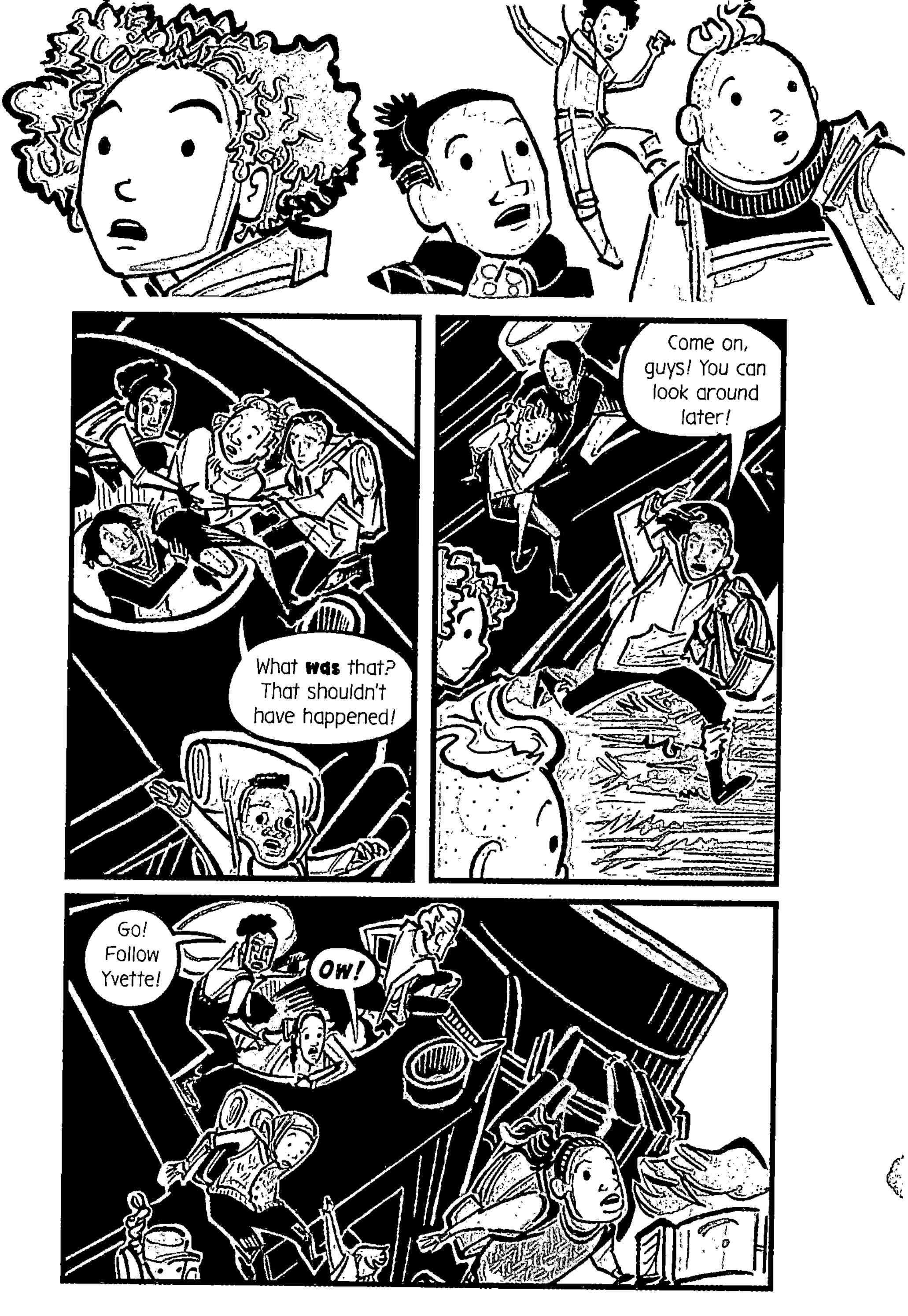
What **was** that? That shouldn't have happened!
Come on, guys! You can look around later!
Go! Follow Yvette!
OW!

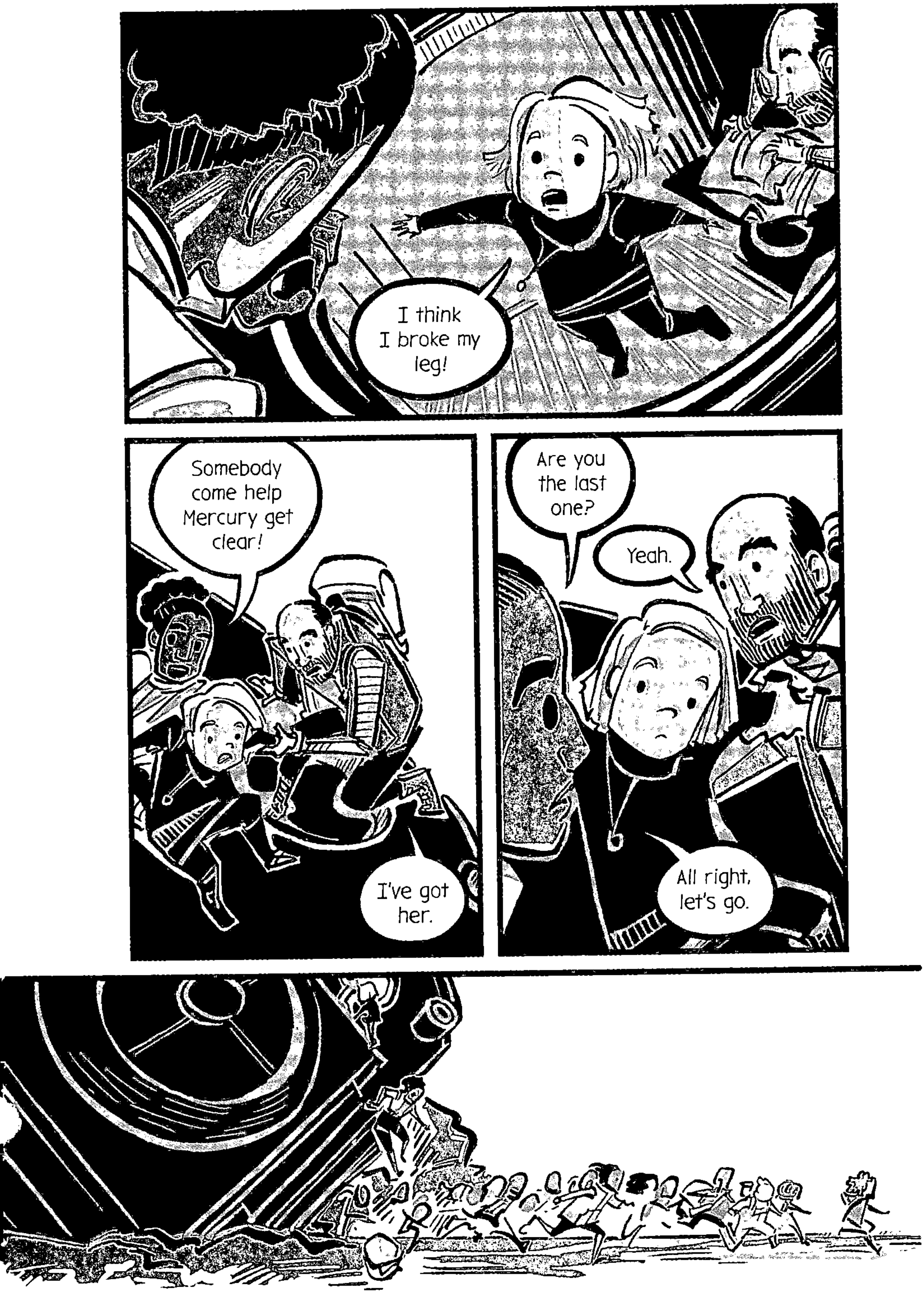
I think I broke my leg!
Somebody come help Mercury get clear!
I've got her.
Are you the last one?
Yeah.
All right, let's go.

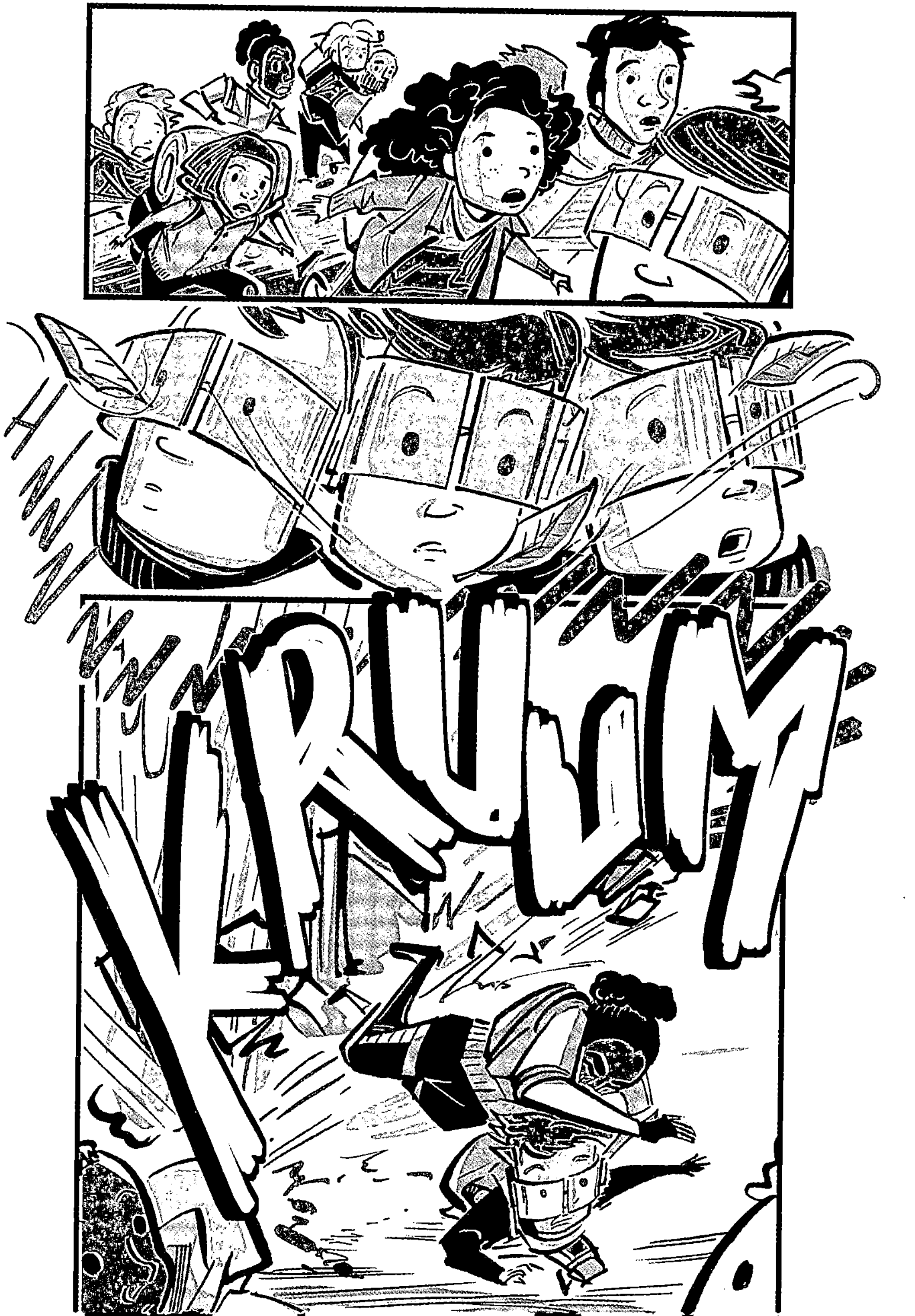
KRUUM

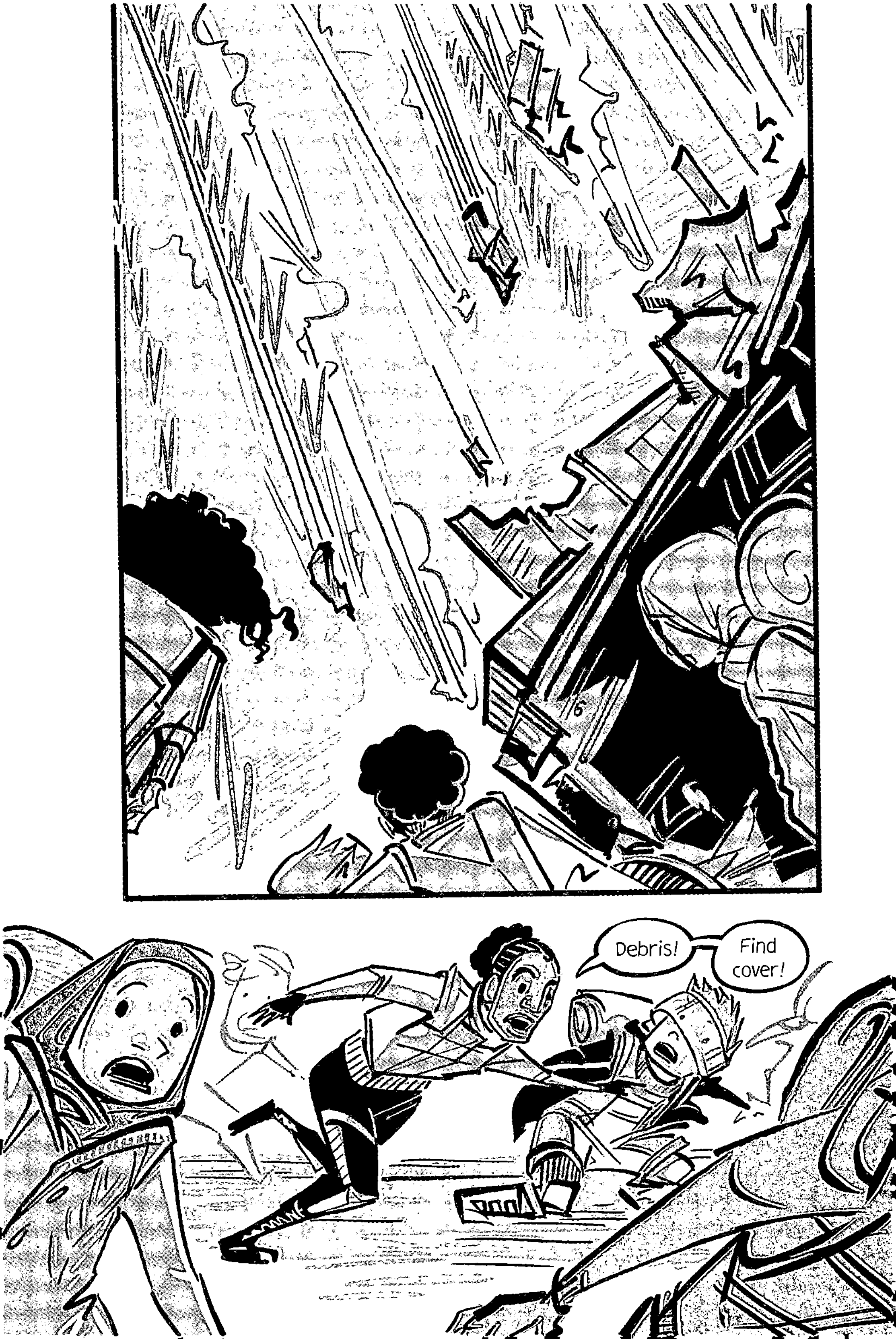
Debris!
Find cover!

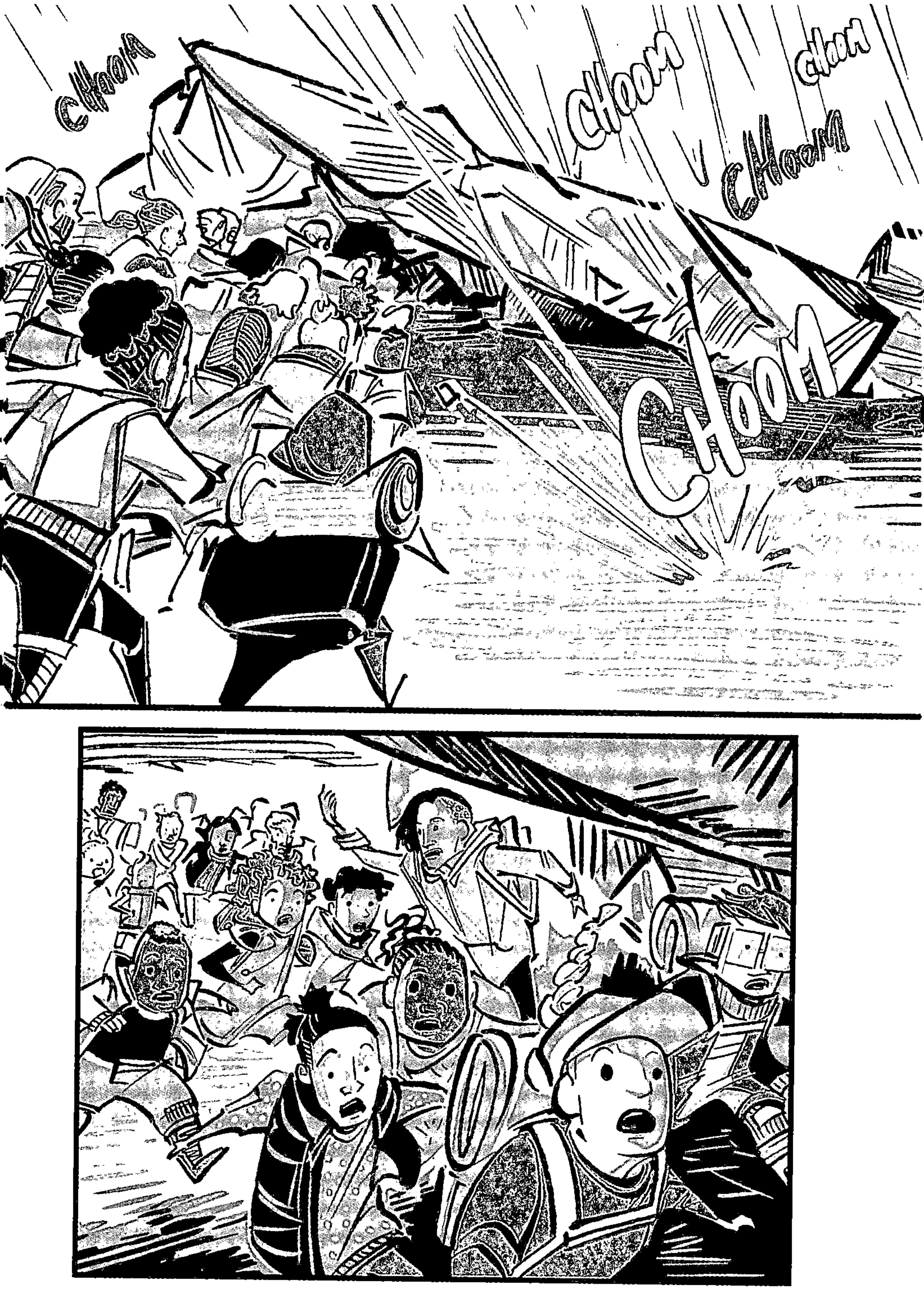
Choom
Choom
choom
Choom
Choom

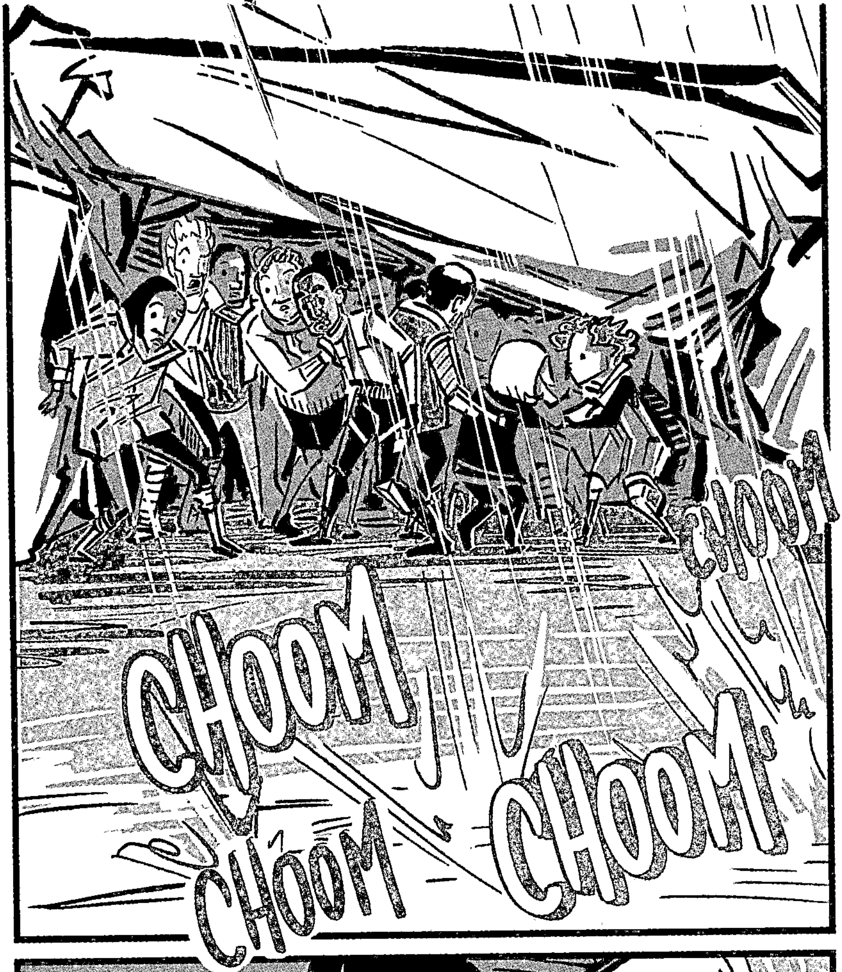
CHOOM
CHOOM
CHOOM
CHOOM

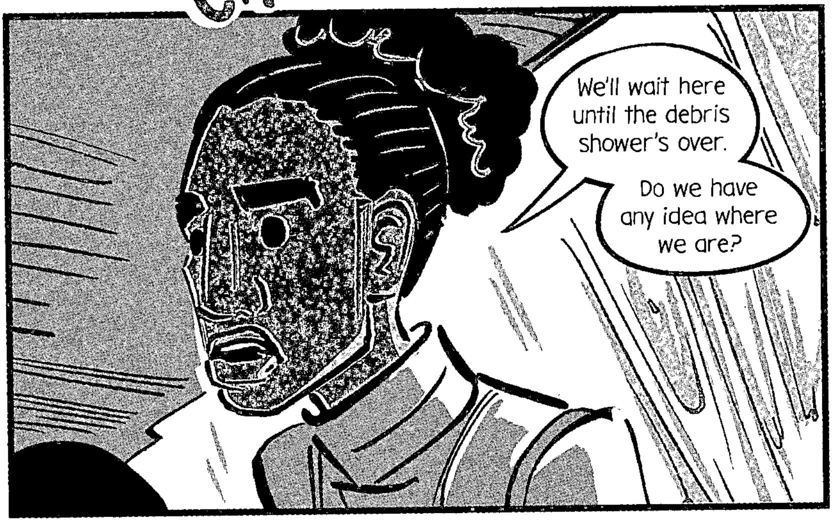
We'll wait here until the debris shower's over.
Do we have any idea where we are?

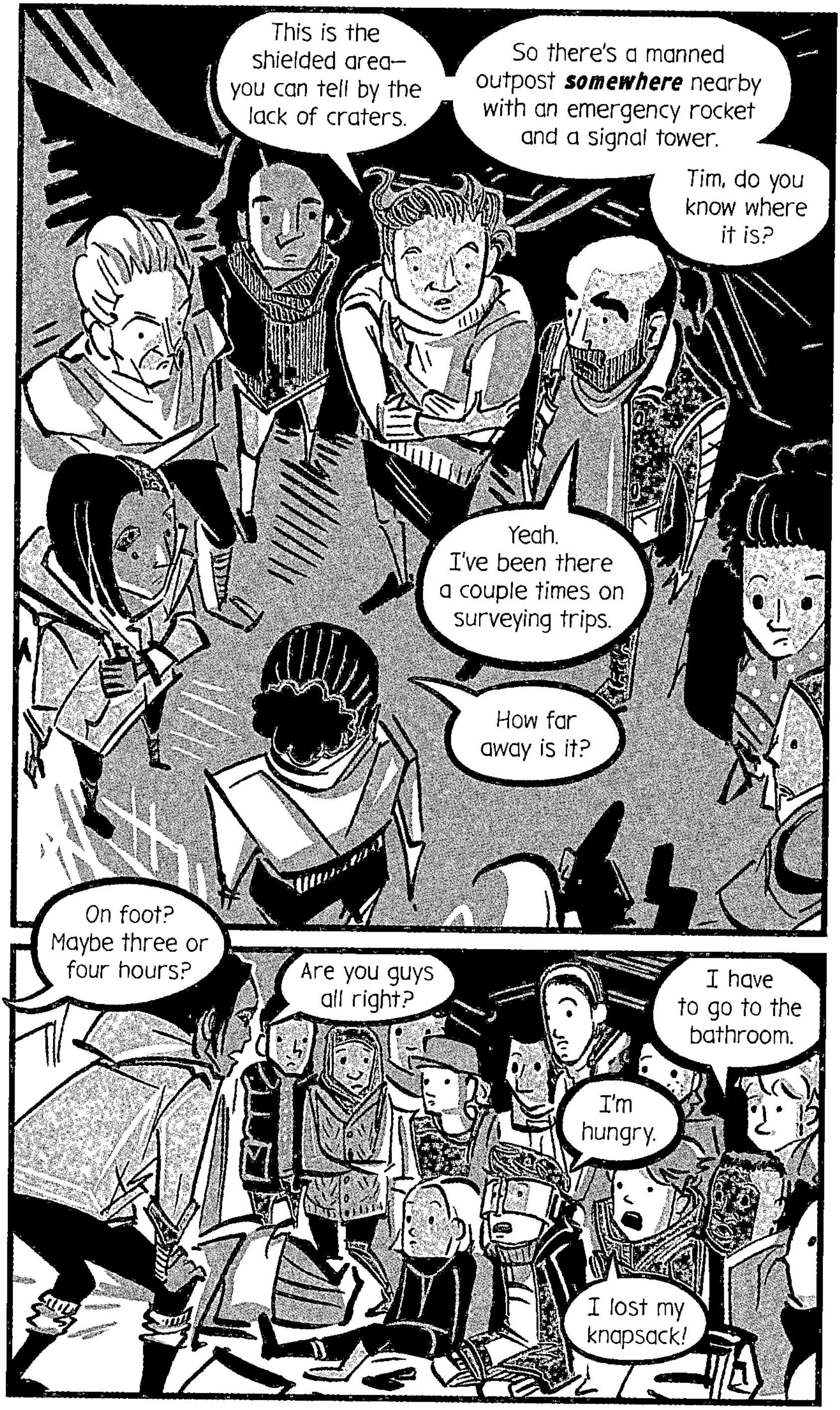
This is the shielded area—you can tell by the lack of craters.
So there's a manned outpost ***somewhere*** nearby with an emergency rocket and a signal tower.
Tim, do you know where it is?
Yeah. I've been there a couple times on surveying trips.
How far away is it?
On foot? Maybe three or four hours?
Are you guys all right?
I have to go to the bathroom.
I'm hungry.
I lost my knapsack!

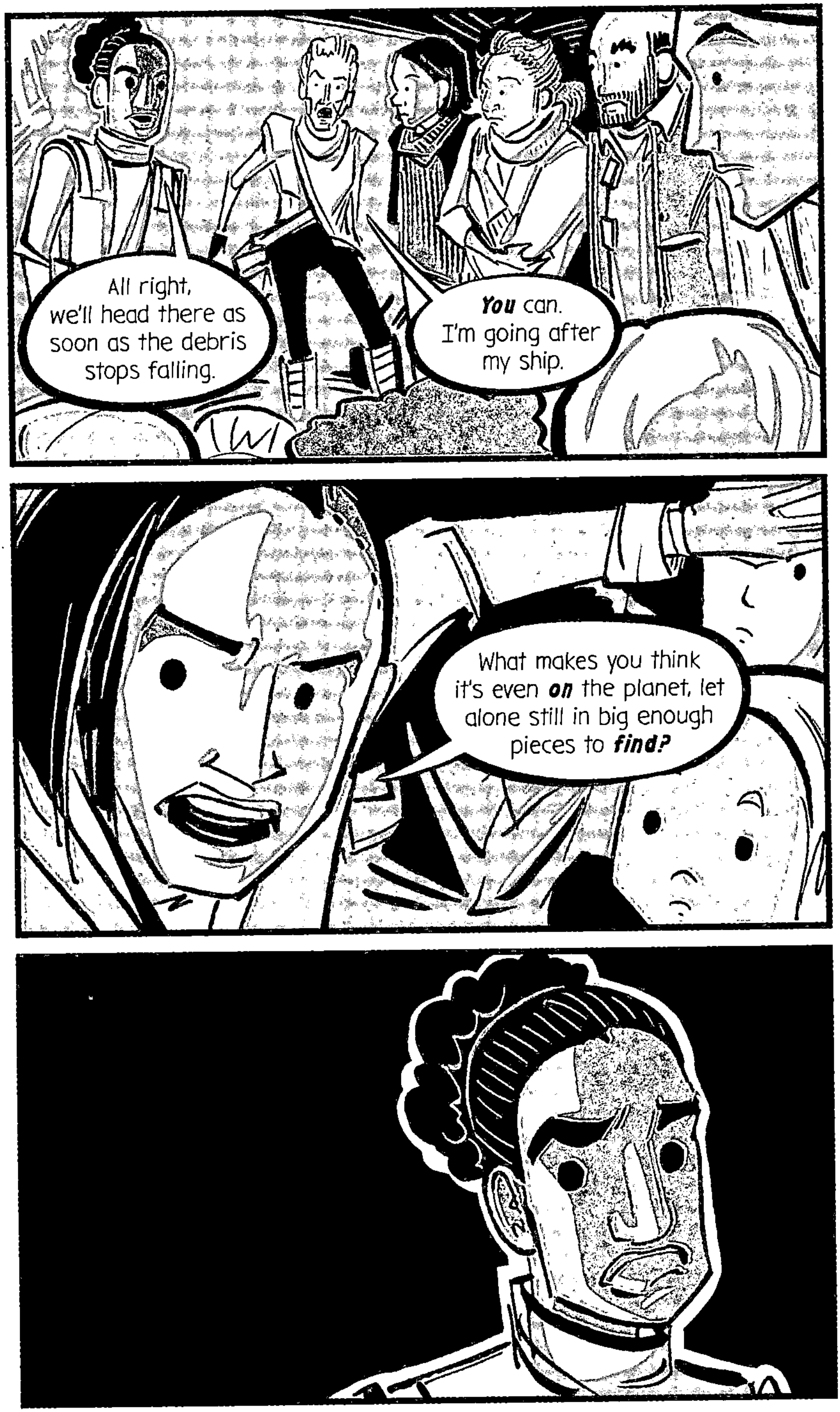
All right, we'll head there as soon as the debris stops falling.
You can. I'm going after my ship.
What makes you think it's even *on* the planet, let alone still in big enough pieces to *find?*

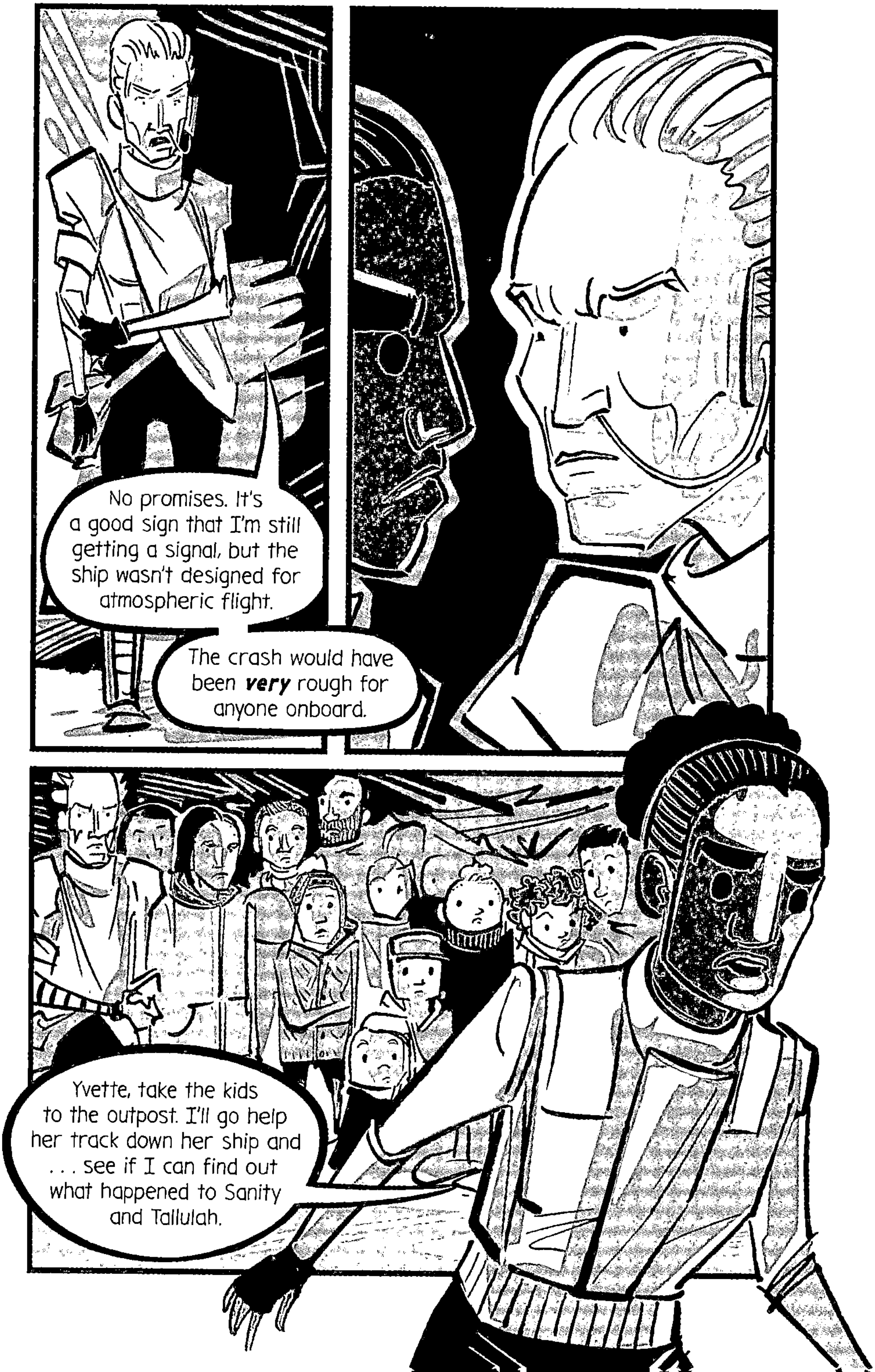
No promises. It's a good sign that I'm still getting a signal, but the ship wasn't designed for atmospheric flight.
The crash would have been **very** rough for anyone onboard.
Yvette, take the kids to the outpost. I'll go help her track down her ship and . . . see if I can find out what happened to Sanity and Tallulah.

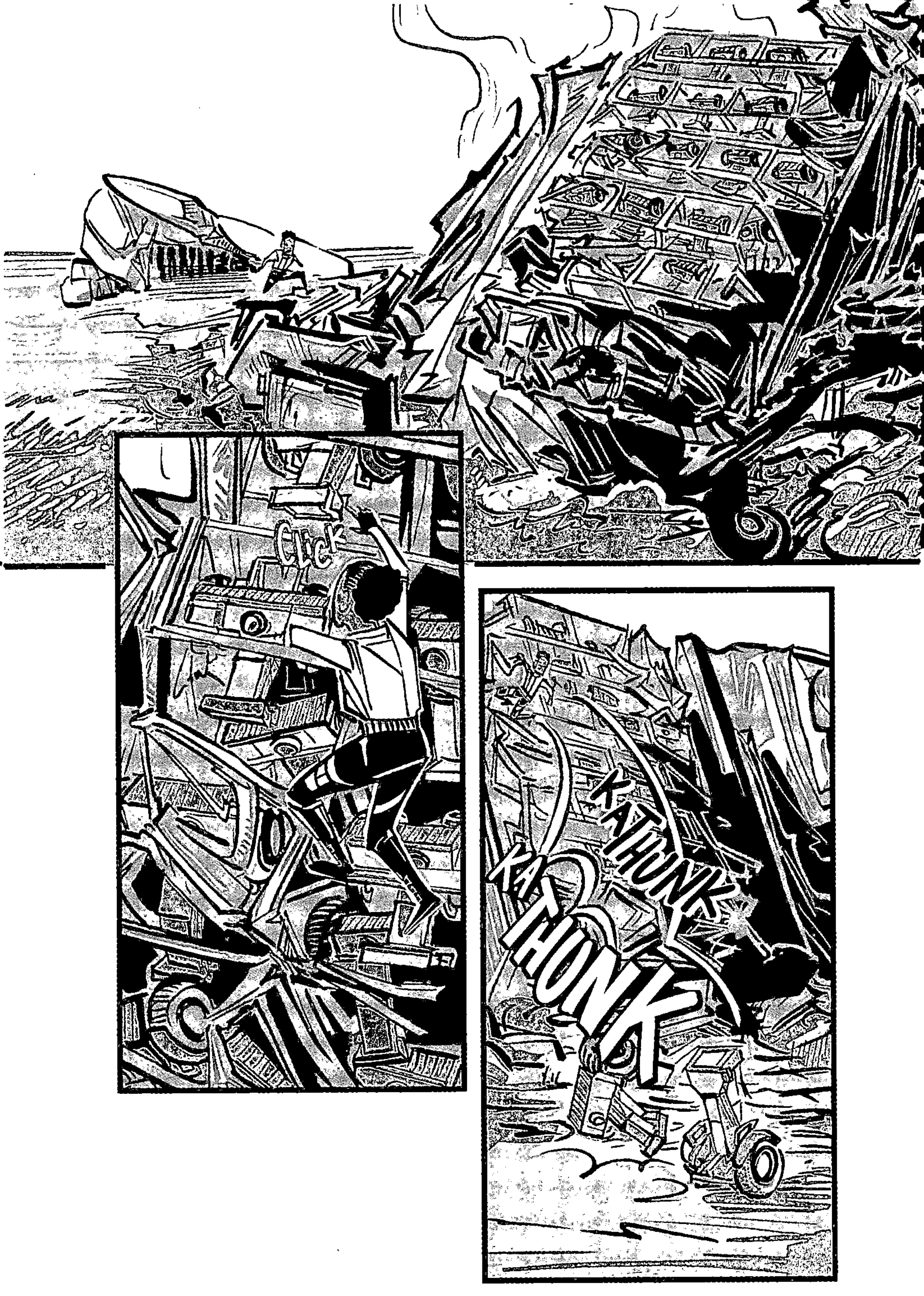
CLICK
KATHUNK
KA THUNK

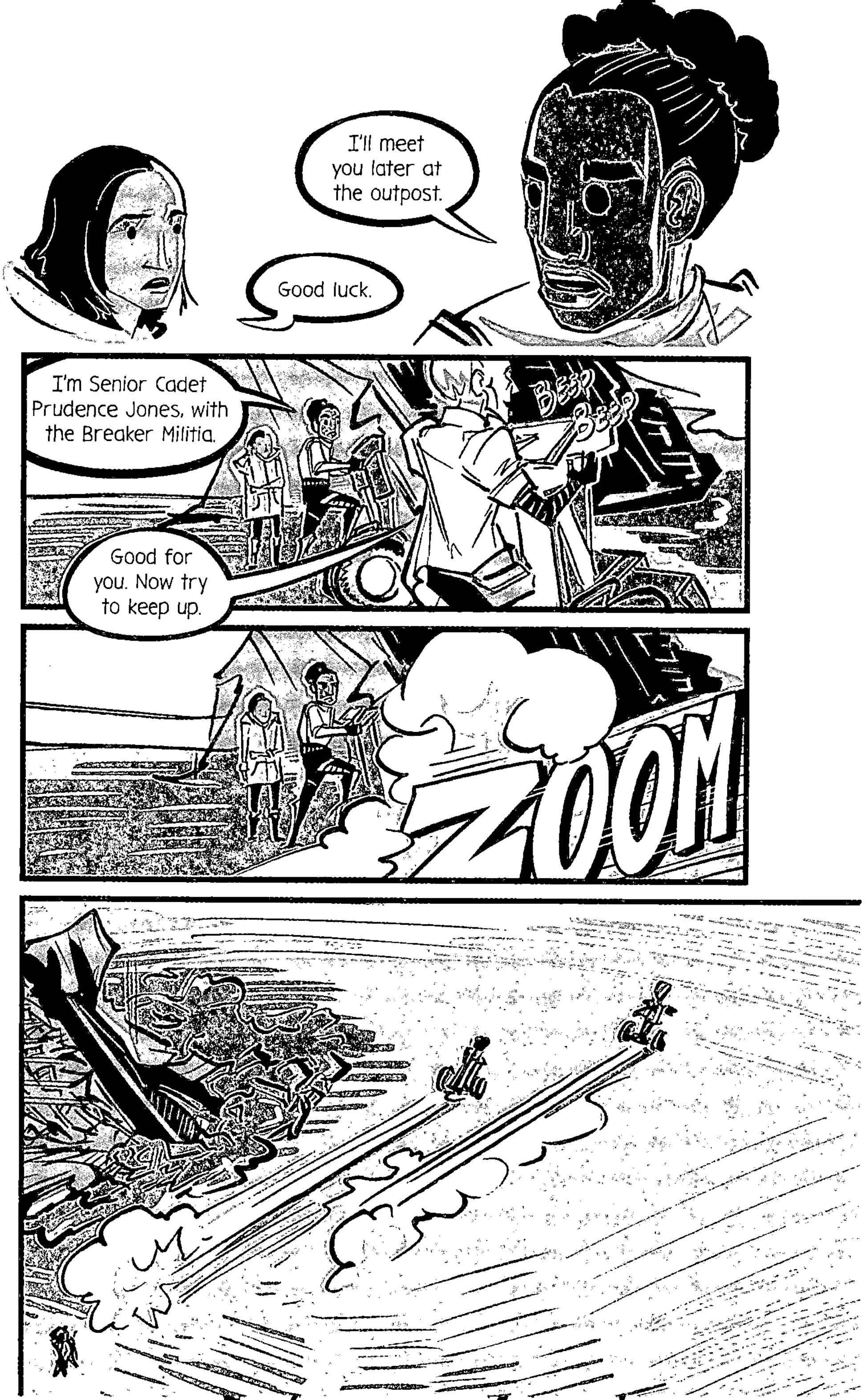
I'll meet you later at the outpost.
Good luck.
I'm Senior Cadet Prudence Jones, with the Breaker Militia.
BEEP BEEP
Good for you. Now try to keep up.
ZOOM

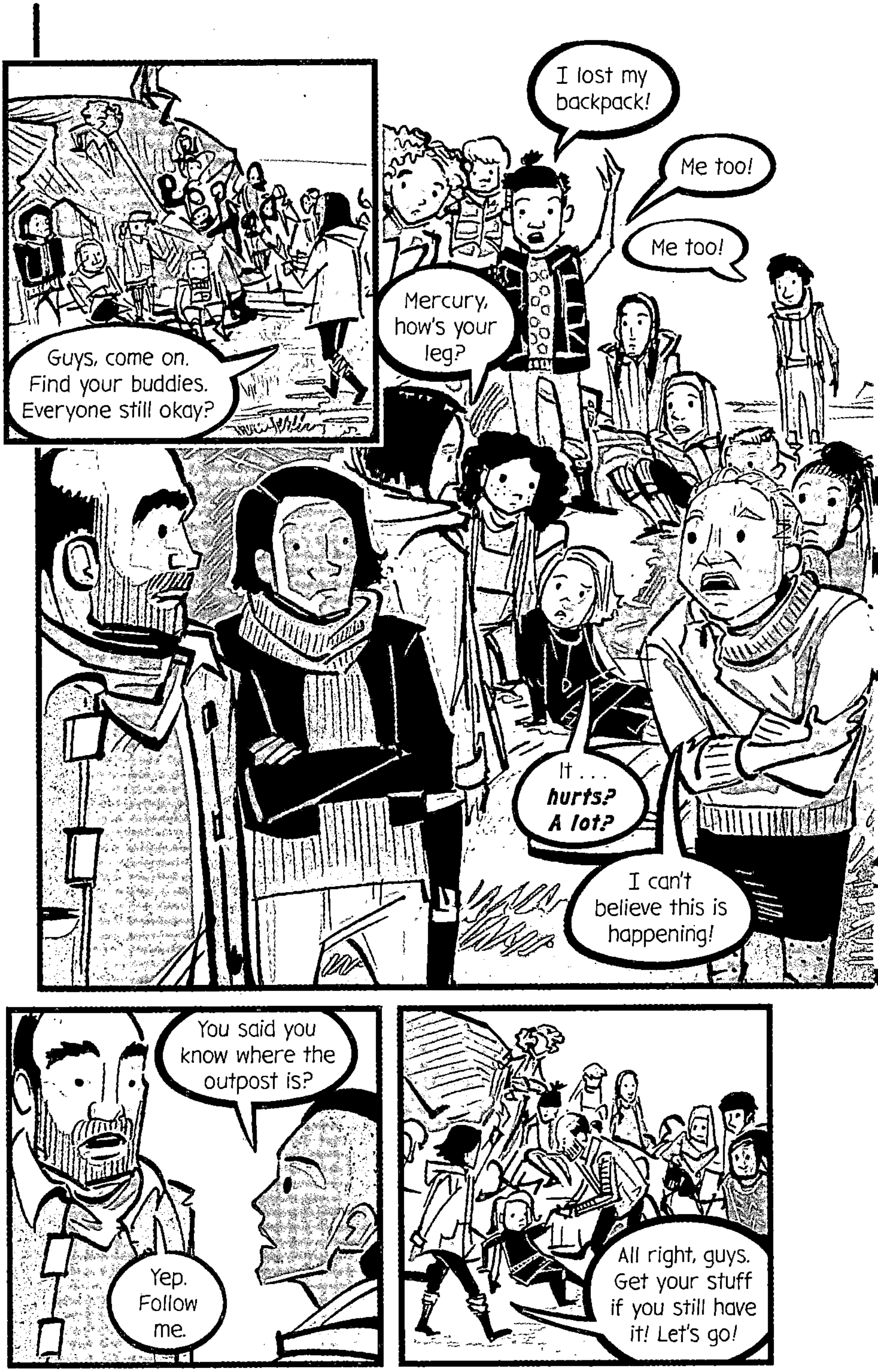
Guys, come on. Find your buddies. Everyone still okay?
I lost my backpack!
Me too!
Me too!
Mercury, how's your leg?
It . . . *hurts? A lot?*
I can't believe this is happening!
You said you know where the outpost is?
Yep. Follow me.
All right, guys. Get your stuff if you still have it! Let's go!

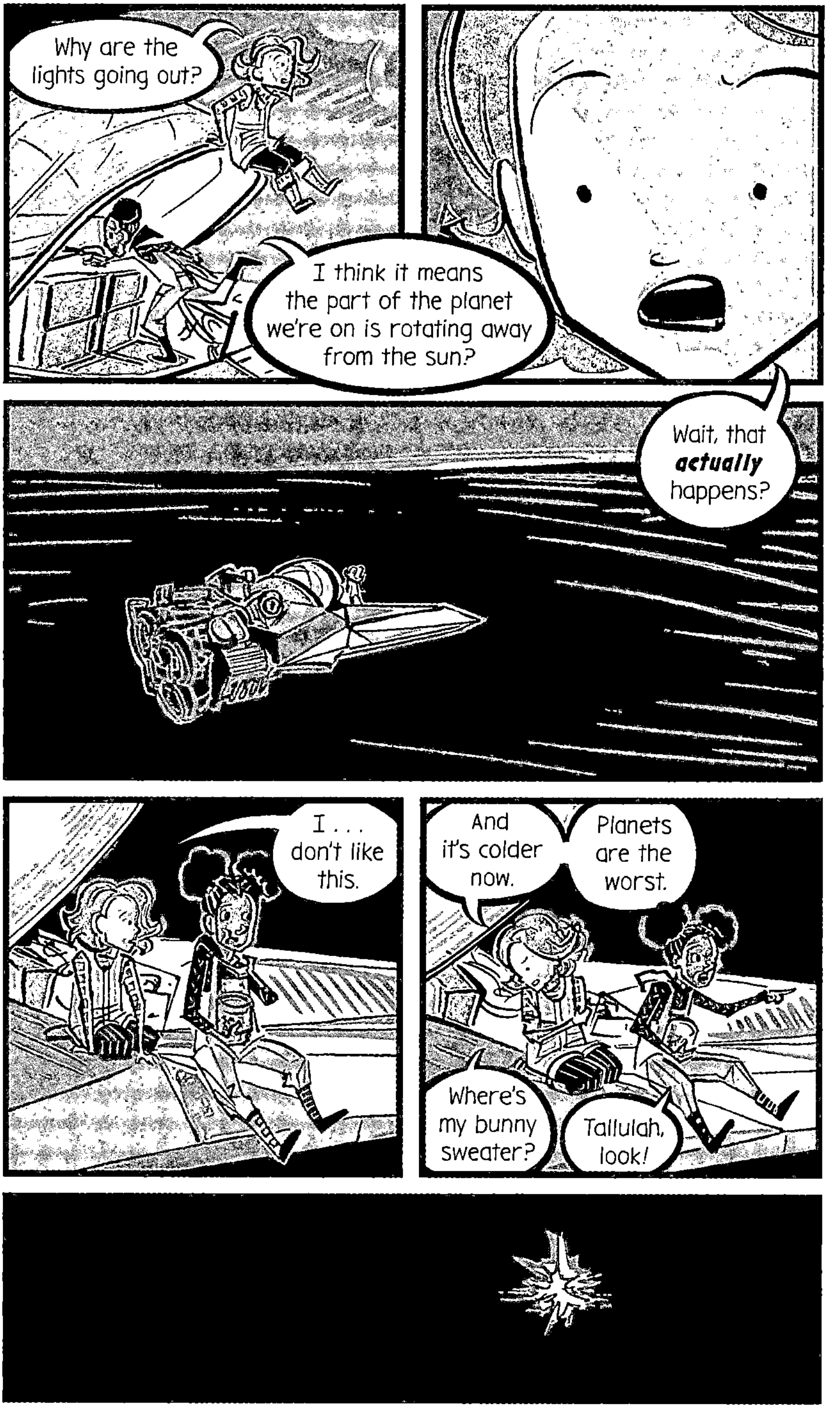
Why are the lights going out?
I think it means the part of the planet we're on is rotating away from the sun?
Wait, that **actually** happens?
I . . . don't like this.
And it's colder now.
Planets are the worst.
Where's my bunny sweater?
Tallulah, look!

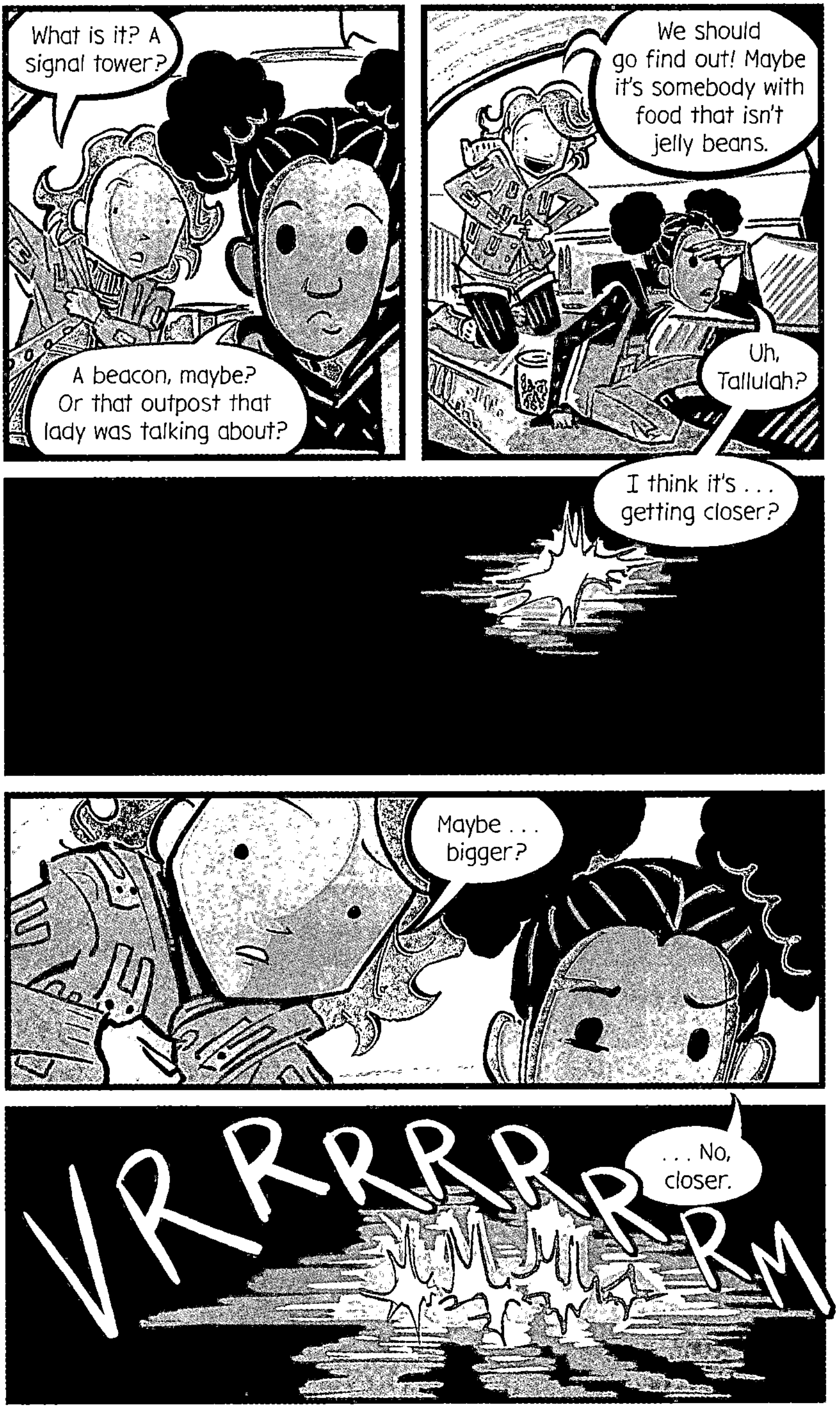
What is it? A signal tower?
A beacon, maybe? Or that outpost that lady was talking about?
We should go find out! Maybe it's somebody with food that isn't jelly beans.
Uh, Tallulah?
I think it's . . . getting closer?
Maybe . . . bigger?
VRRRRRRRM
. . . No, closer.

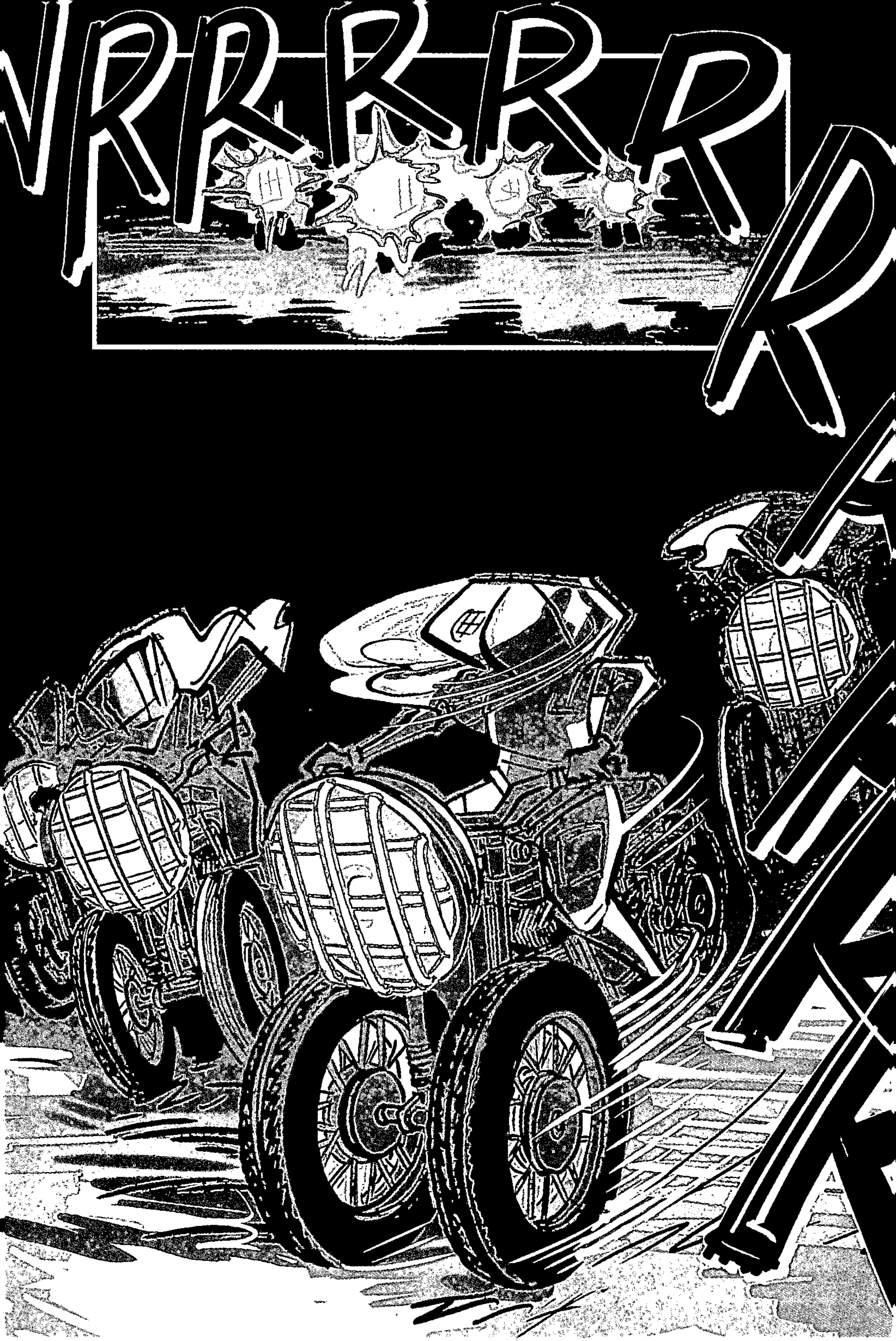
VRRRRRRRRRR

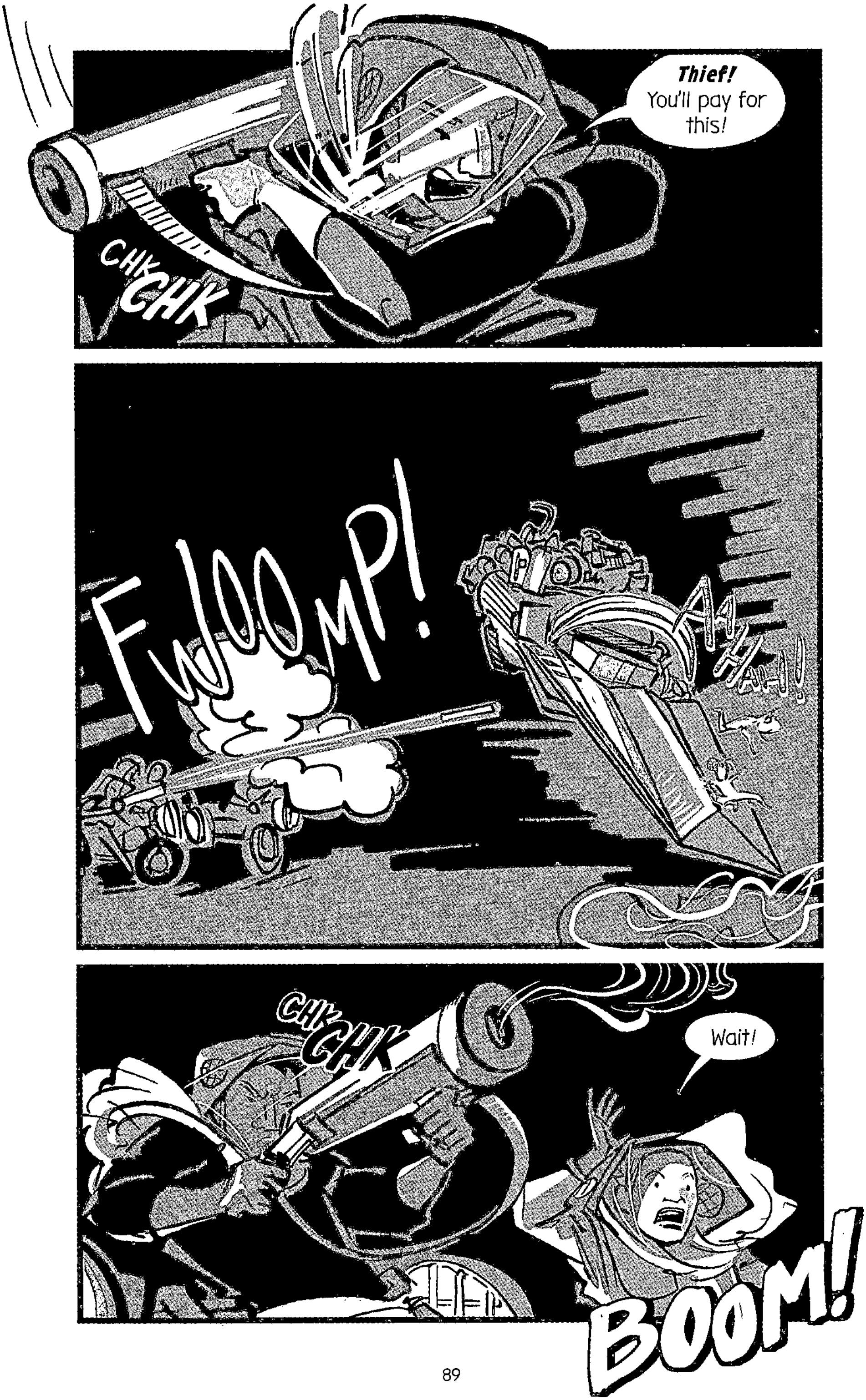
Thief! You'll pay for this!
CHK CHK
FWOOMP!
AAHHAH!!
CHK CHK
Wait!
BOOM!

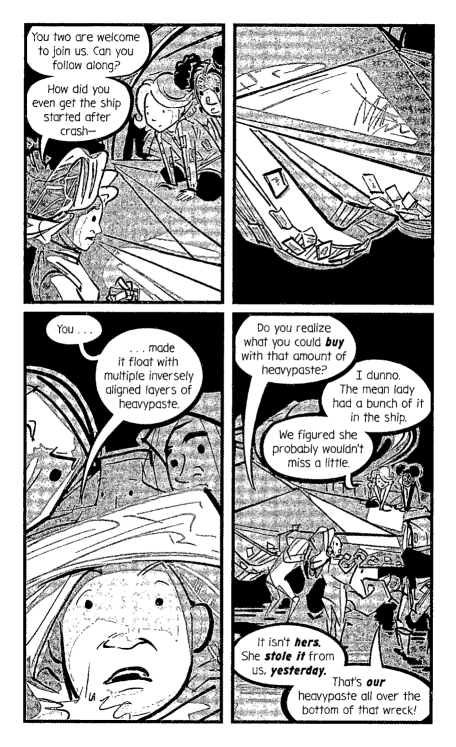

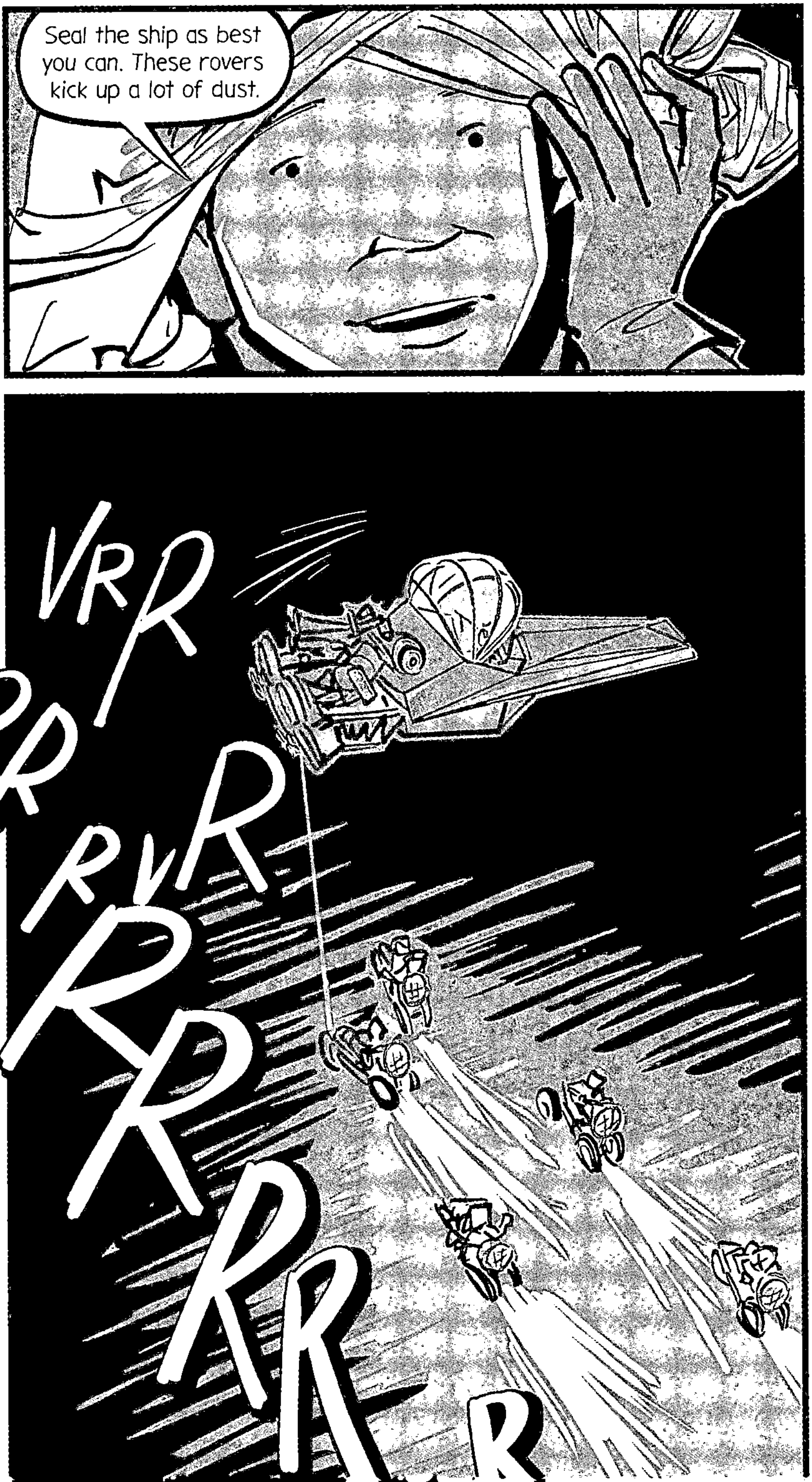
Seal the ship as best you can. These rovers kick up a lot of dust.
VRR
VRR
RVR
RRRRR

(MEANWHILE, AND ALSO ROTATING AWAY FROM THE SUN)

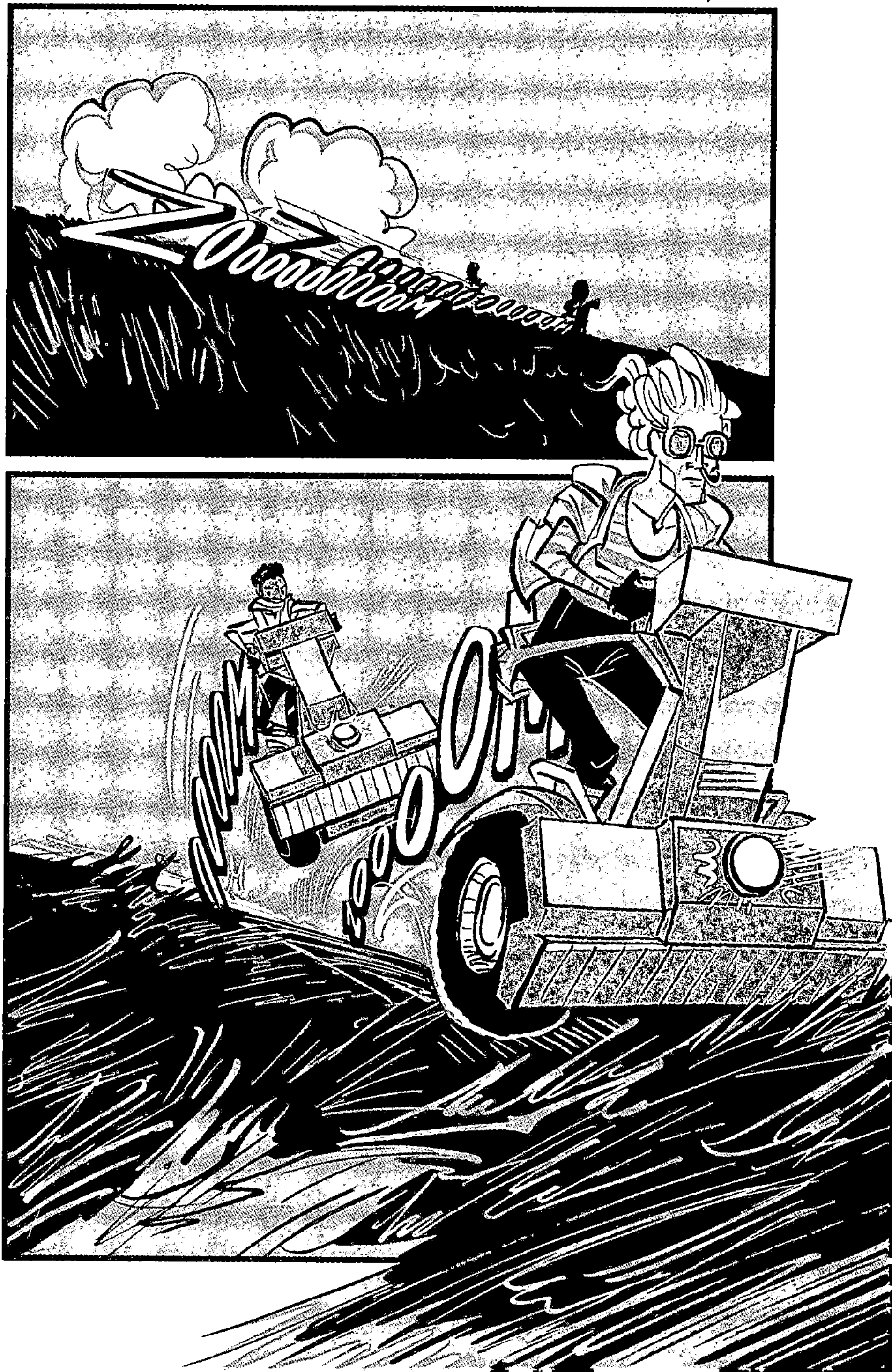

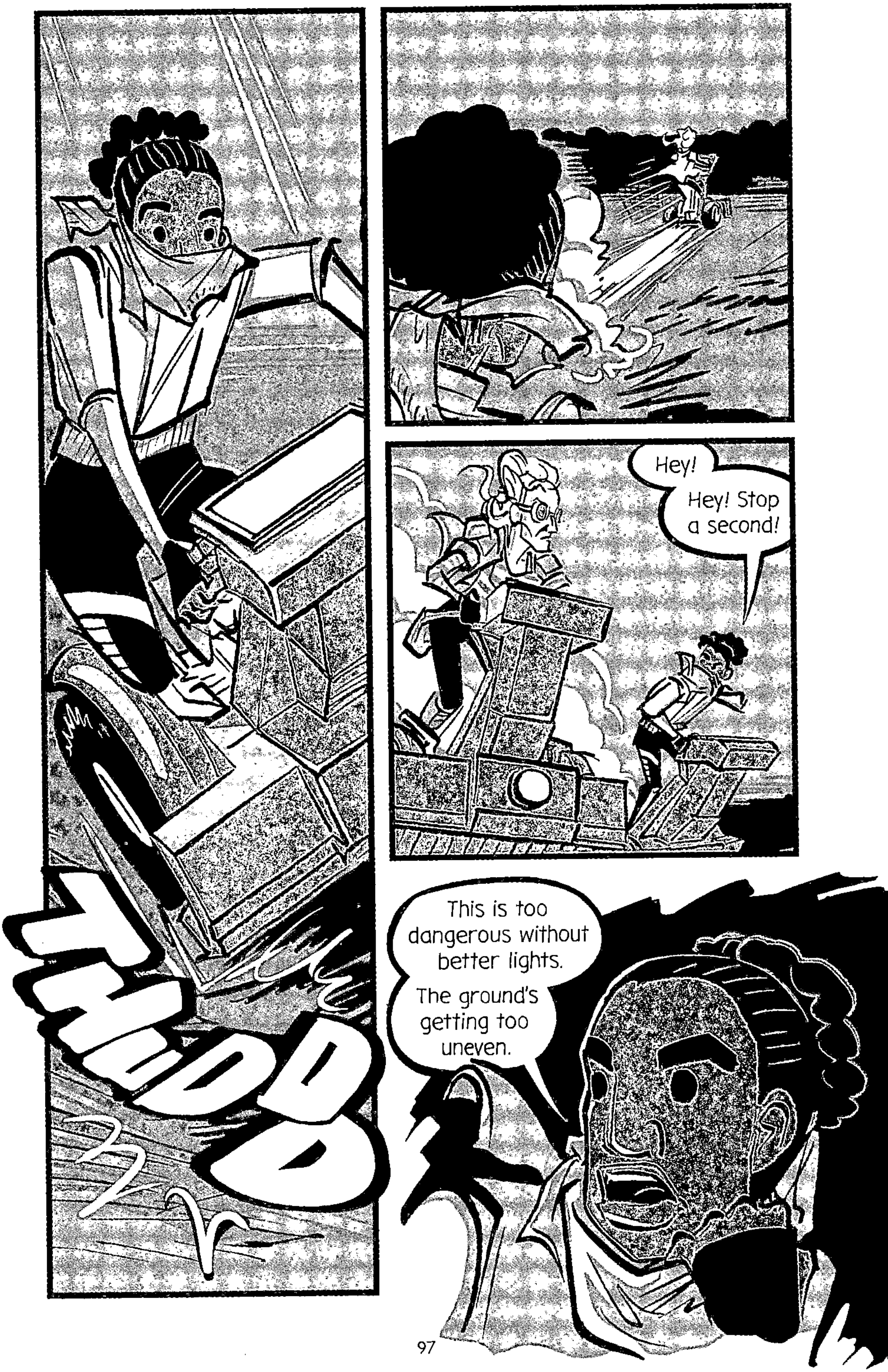
Hey!
Hey! Stop a second!
THUDD
This is too dangerous without better lights.
The ground's getting too uneven.

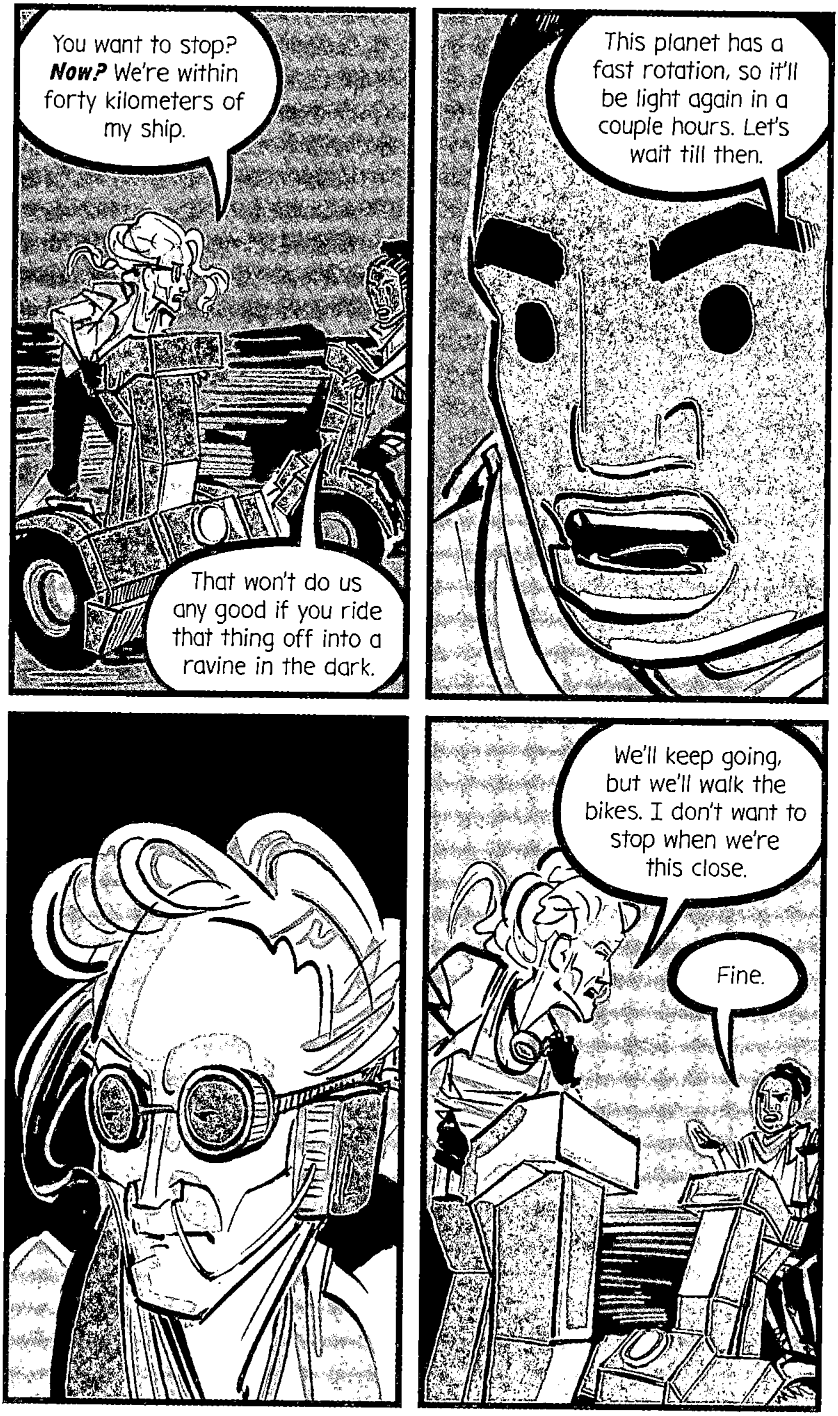
You want to stop? **Now?** We're within forty kilometers of my ship.
That won't do us any good if you ride that thing off into a ravine in the dark.
This planet has a fast rotation, so it'll be light again in a couple hours. Let's wait till then.
We'll keep going, but we'll walk the bikes. I don't want to stop when we're this close.
Fine.

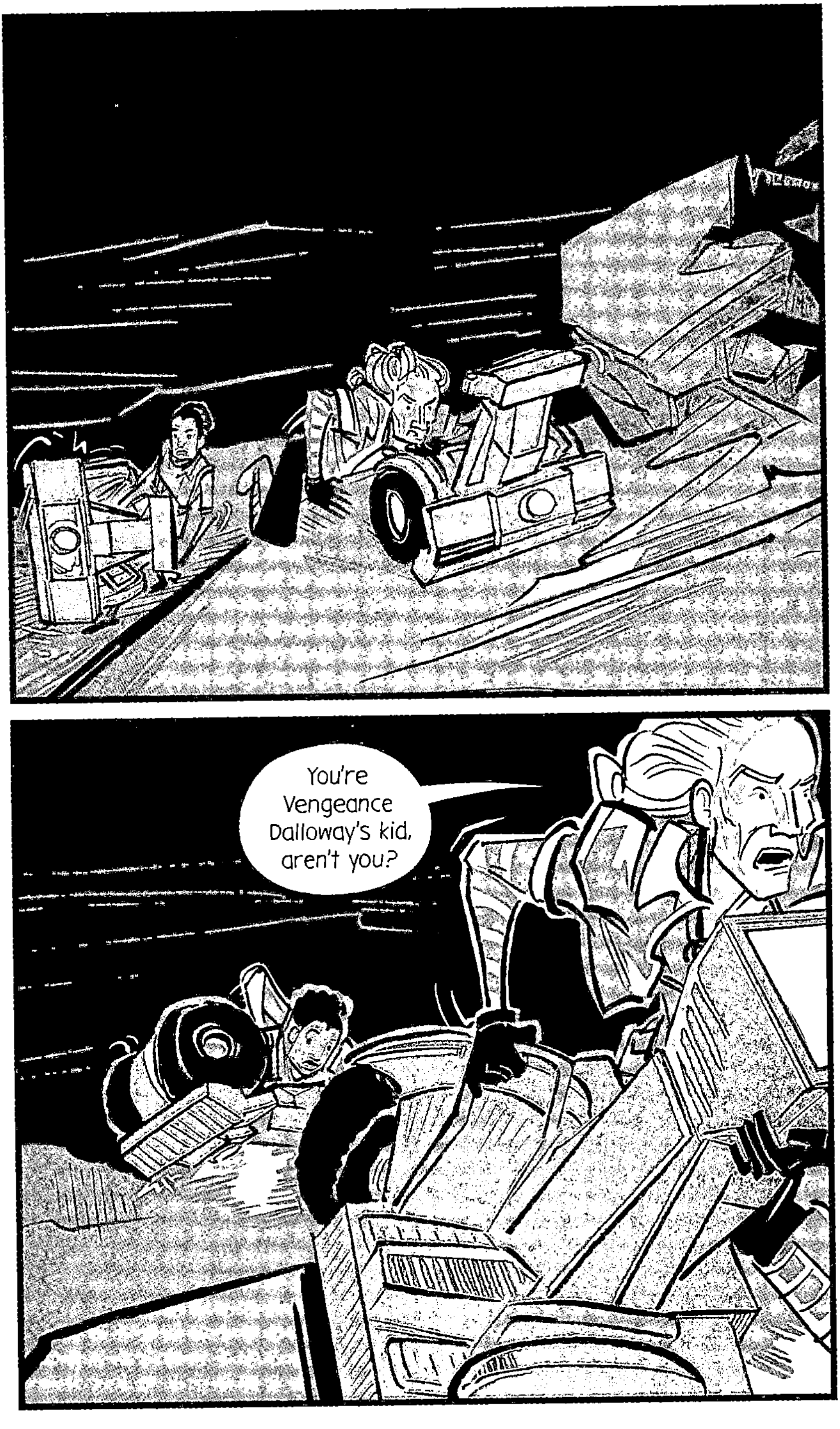
You're Vengeance Dalloway's kid, aren't you?

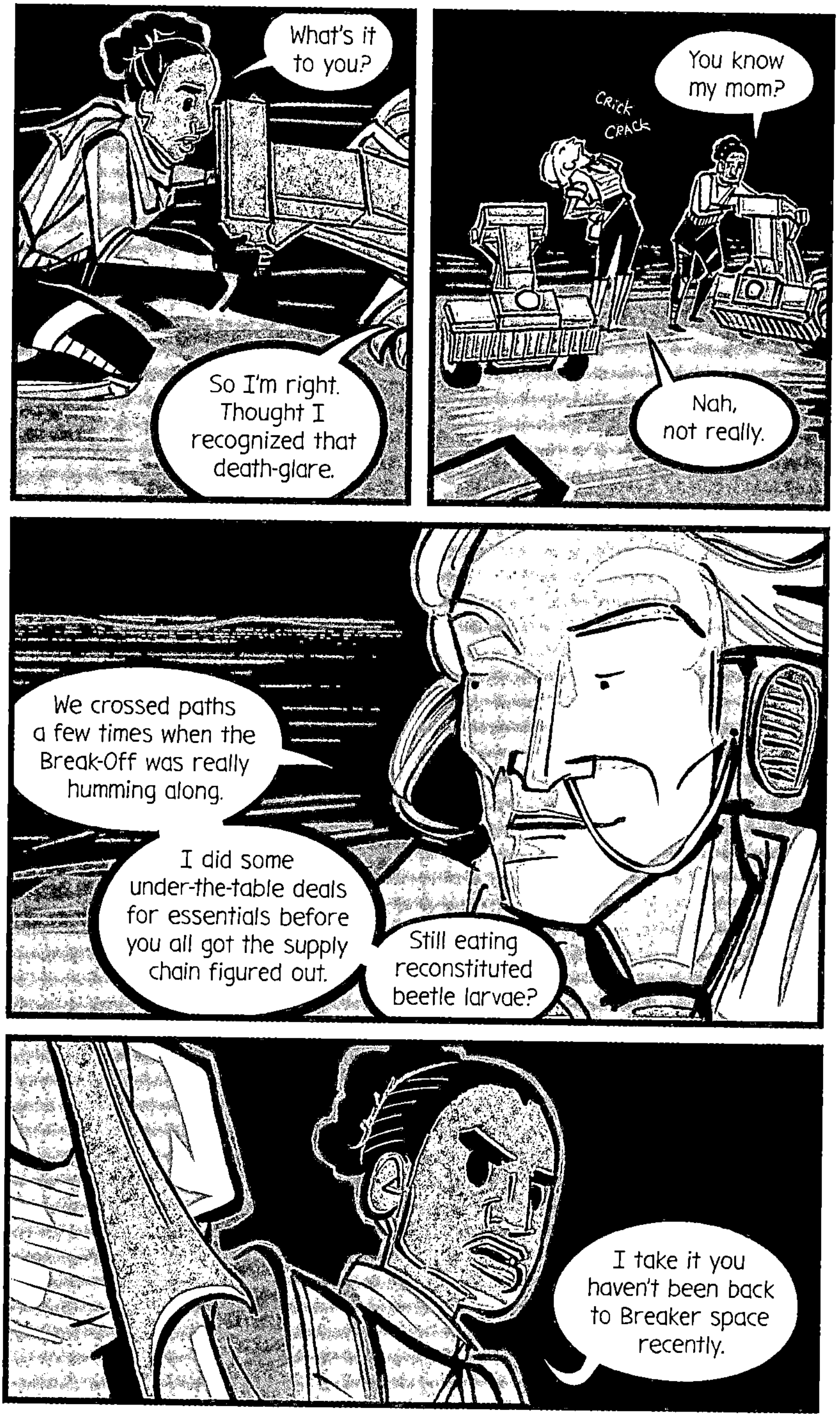
What's it to you?
So I'm right. Thought I recognized that death-glare.
You know my mom?
CRick
CRACK
Nah, not really.
We crossed paths a few times when the Break-Off was really humming along.
I did some under-the-table deals for essentials before you all got the supply chain figured out.
Still eating reconstituted beetle larvae?
I take it you haven't been back to Breaker space recently.

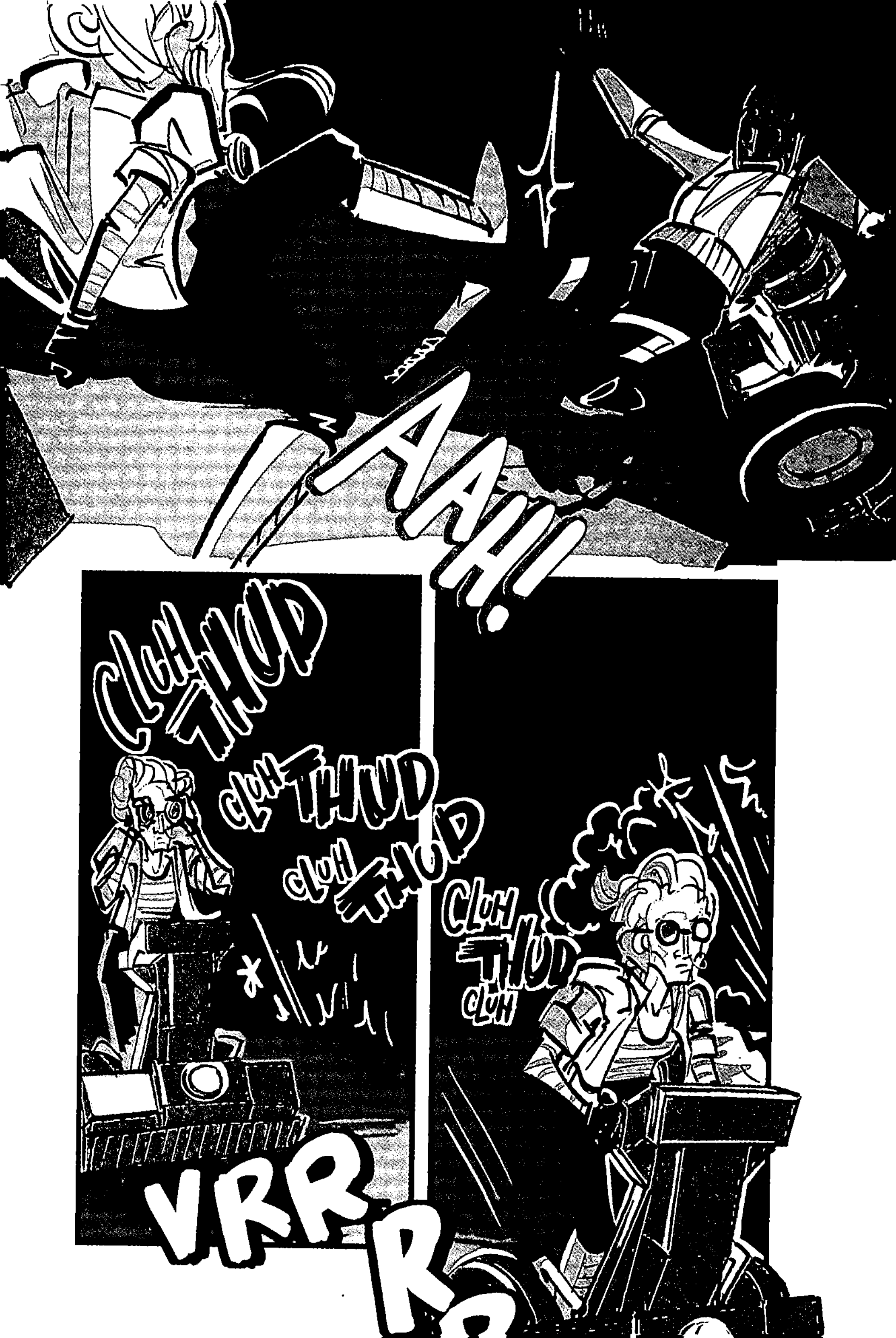
AAH!
CLUH THUD
CLUH THUD
CLUH THUD
CLUH THUD CLUH
VRRRR

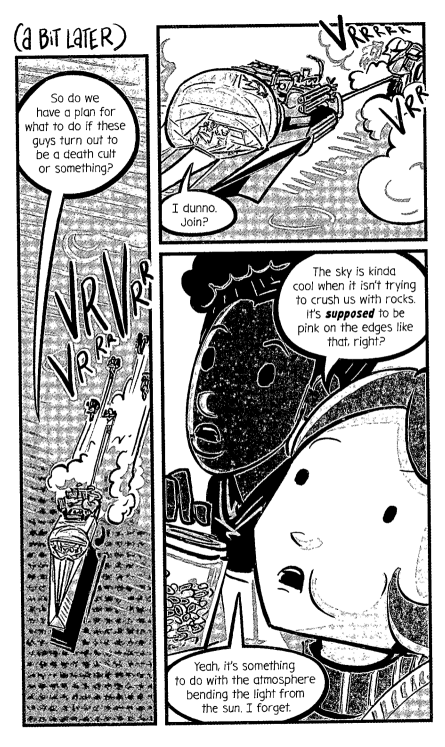

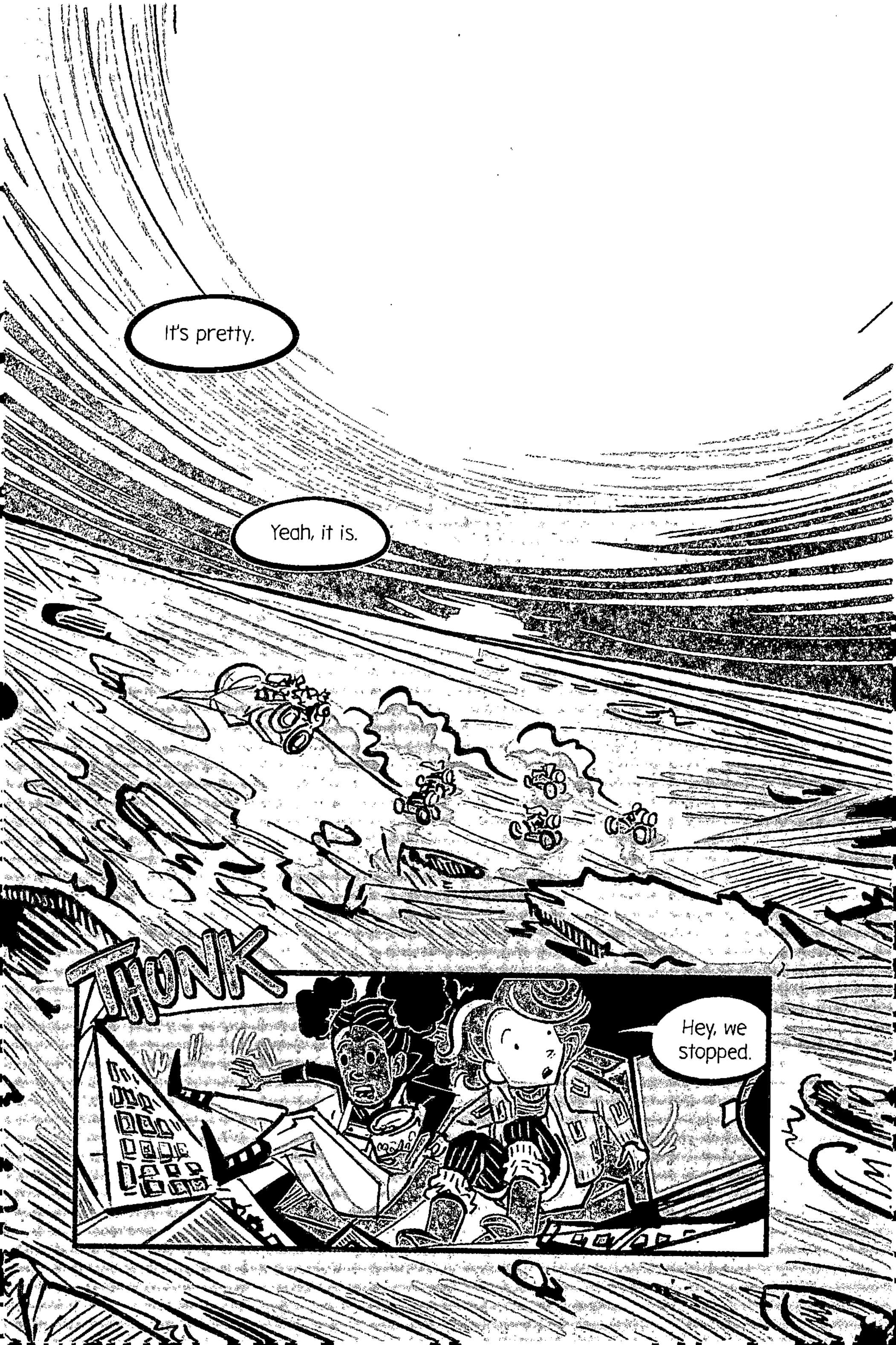
It's pretty.
Yeah, it is.
THUNK
Hey, we stopped.

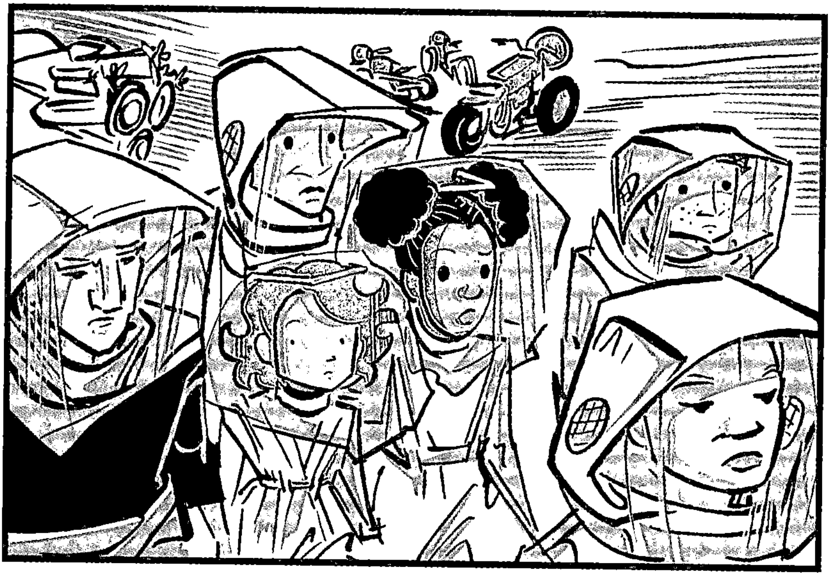

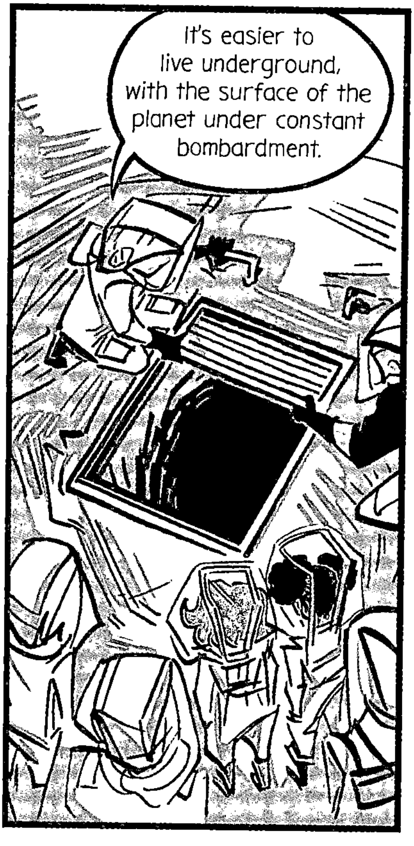
It's easier to live underground, with the surface of the planet under constant bombardment.

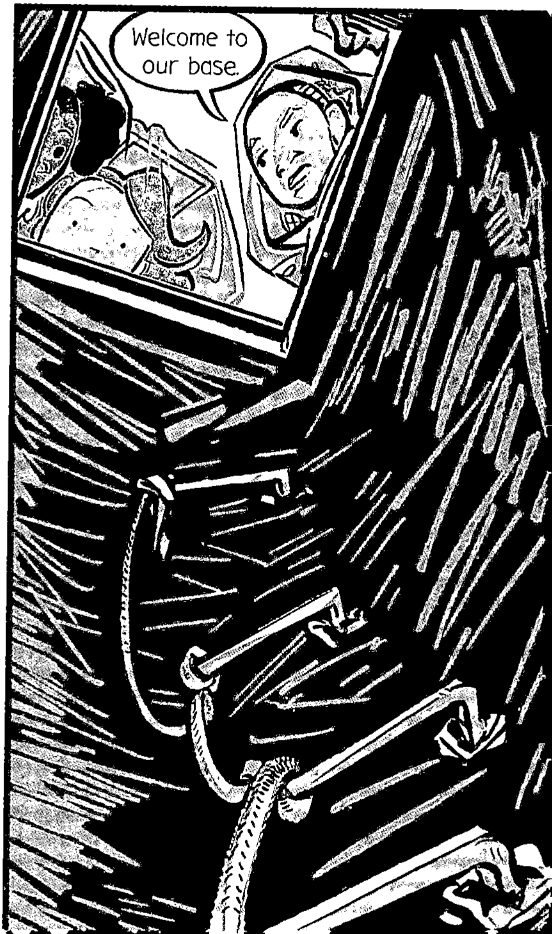
Welcome to our base.

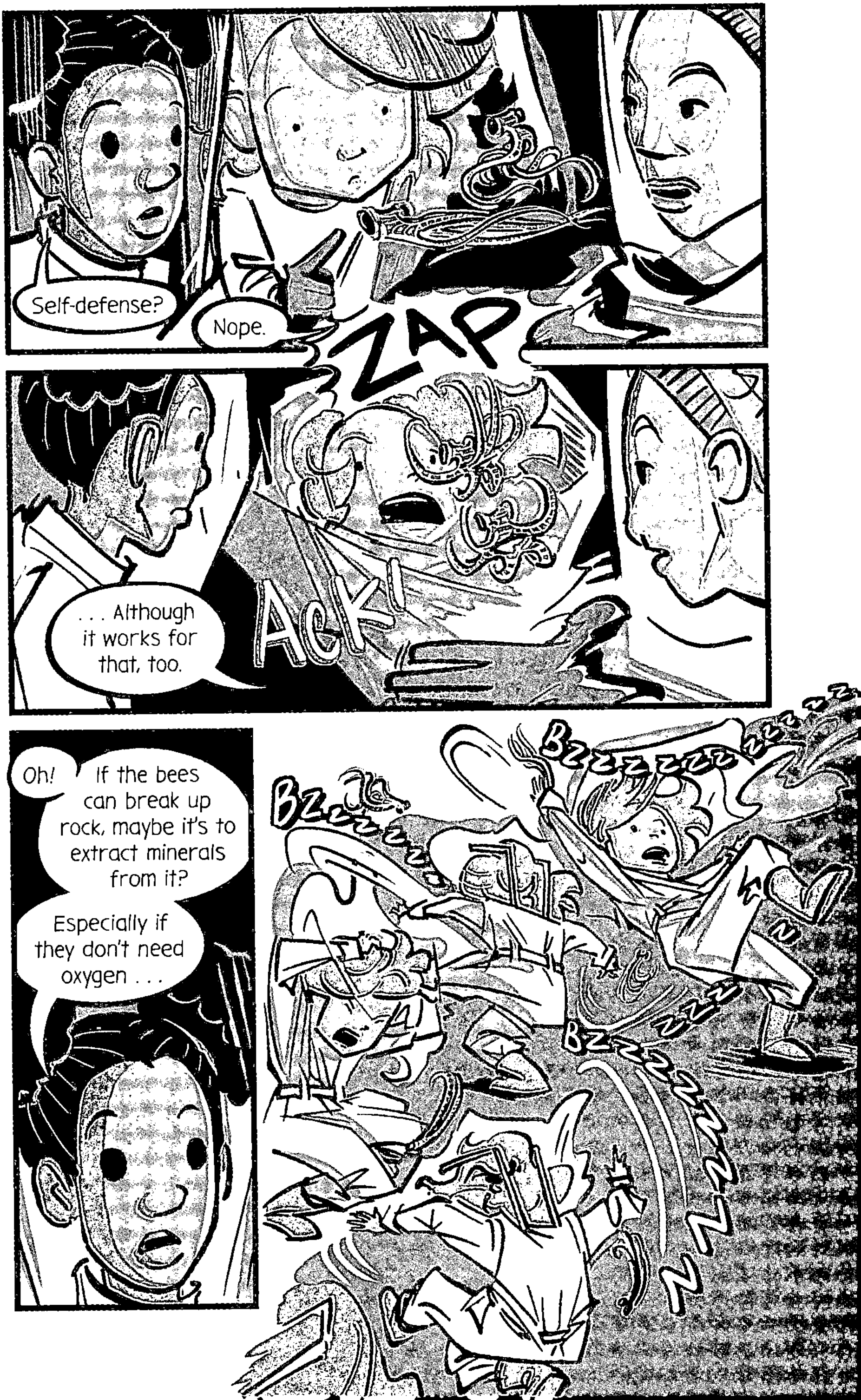
Self-defense?
Nope.
ZAP
. . . Although it works for that, too.
ACK!
Oh!
If the bees can break up rock, maybe it's to extract minerals from it?
Especially if they don't need oxygen . . .
Bzzzzzzzzzzzzz
Bzzzzz
Bzzzzzzzz

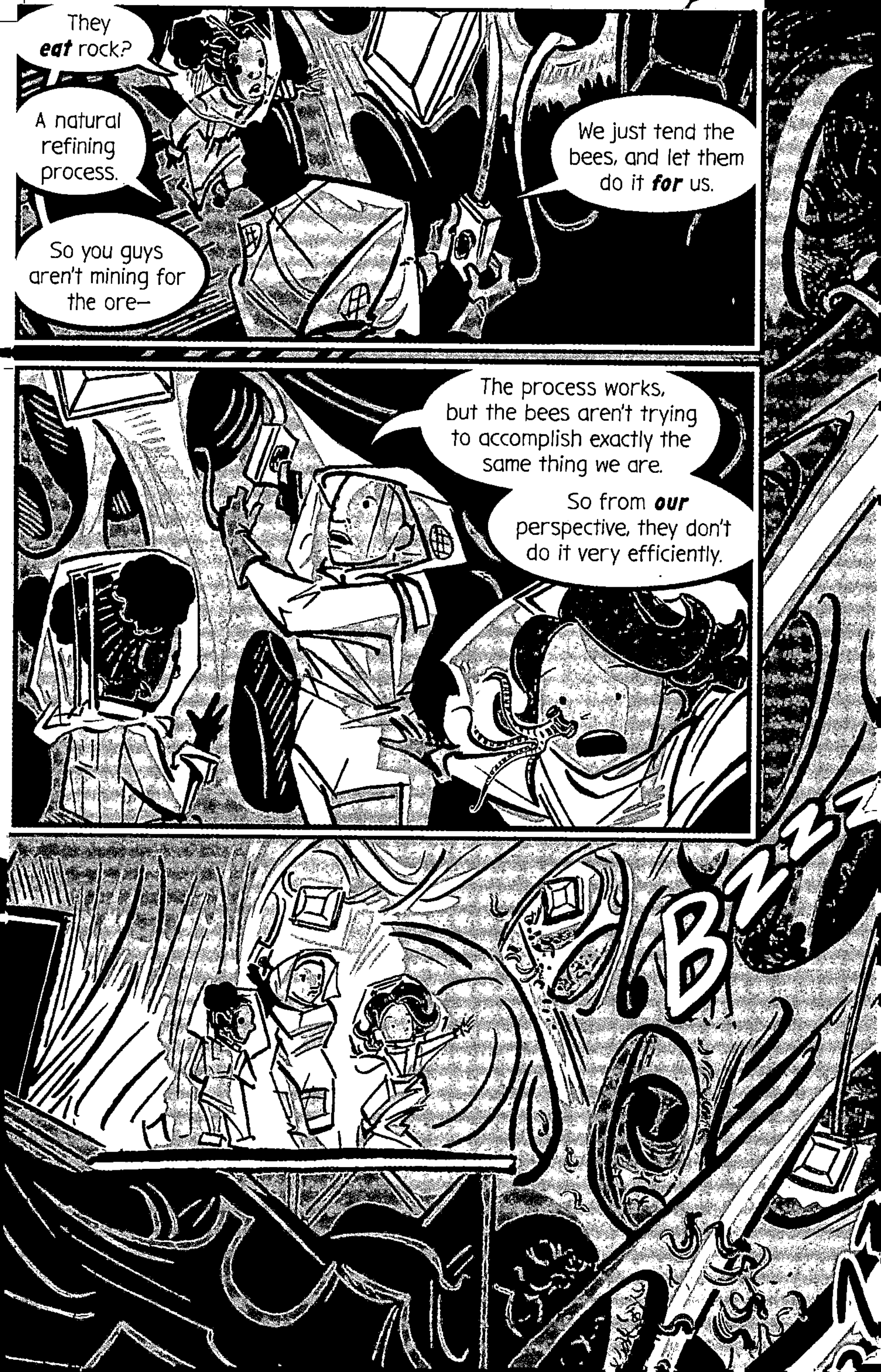
They **eat** rock?
A natural refining process.
So you guys aren't mining for the ore—
We just tend the bees, and let them do it **for** us.
The process works, but the bees aren't trying to accomplish exactly the same thing we are.
So from **our** perspective, they don't do it very efficiently.
BZZZ

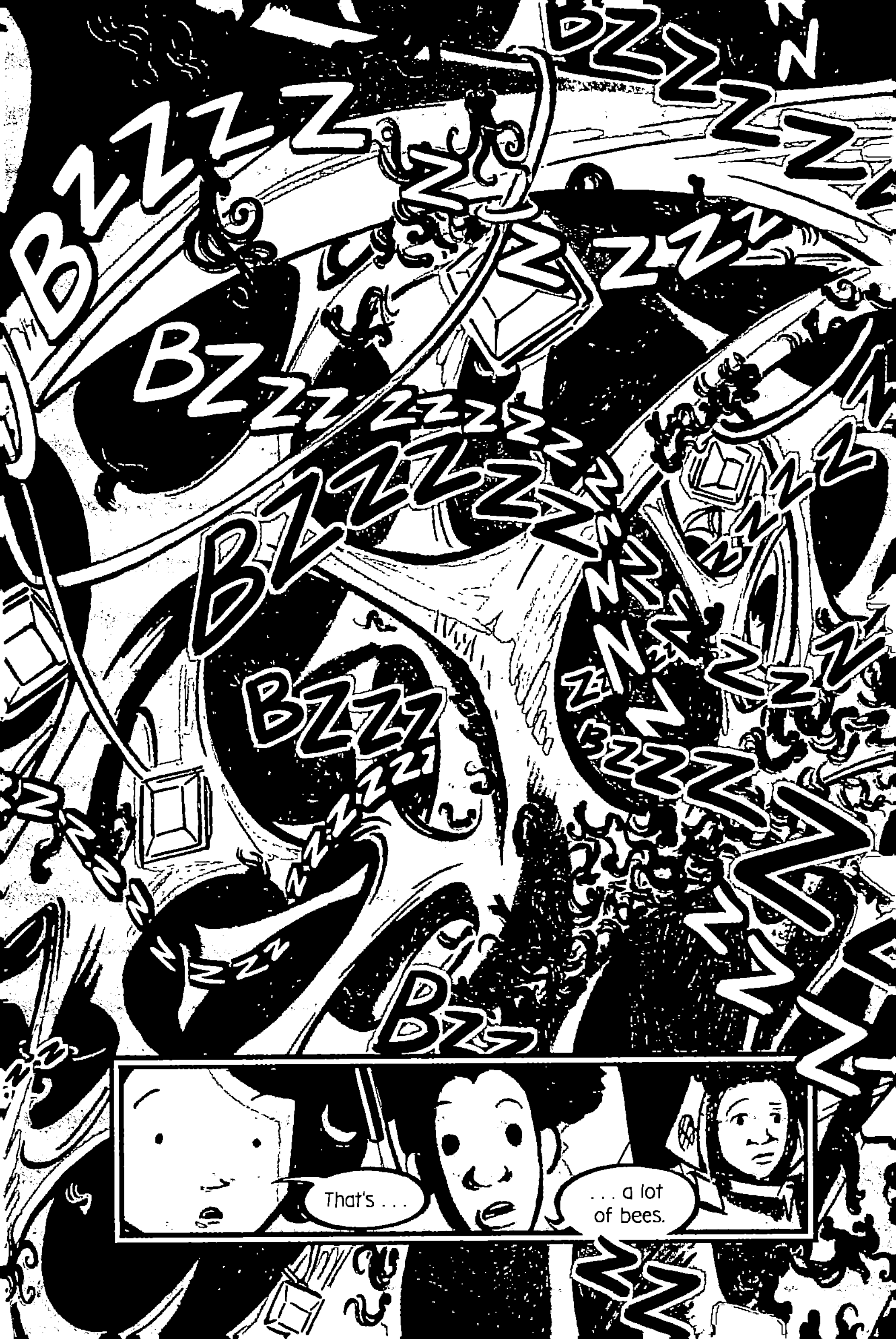
That's . . .
. . . a lot of bees.

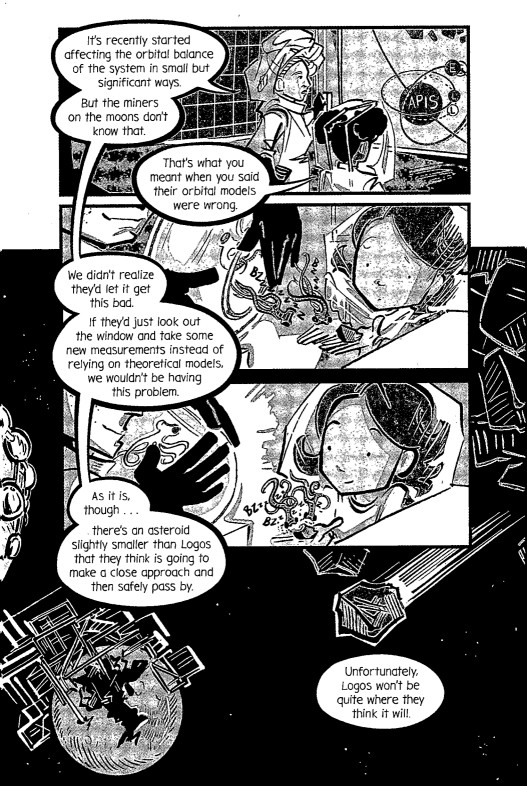

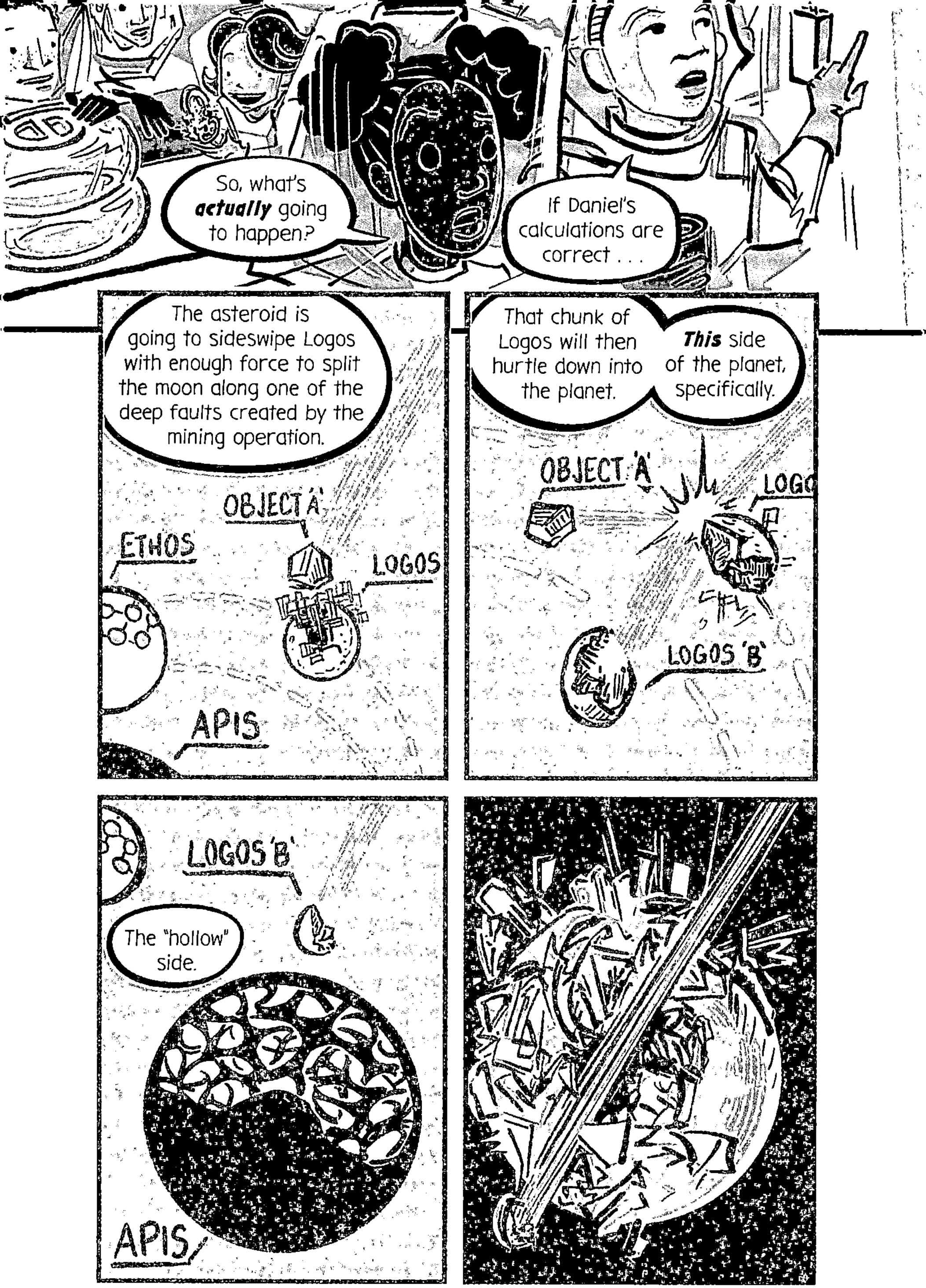
So, what's **actually** going to happen?
If Daniel's calculations are correct . . .
The asteroid is going to sideswipe Logos with enough force to split the moon along one of the deep faults created by the mining operation.
OBJECT 'A'
ETHOS
LOGOS
APIS
That chunk of Logos will then hurtle down into the planet.
This side of the planet, specifically.
OBJECT 'A'
LOGOS 'B'
LOGOS 'B'
The "hollow" side.
APIS

(THE FOOTHOLD OUTPOST)

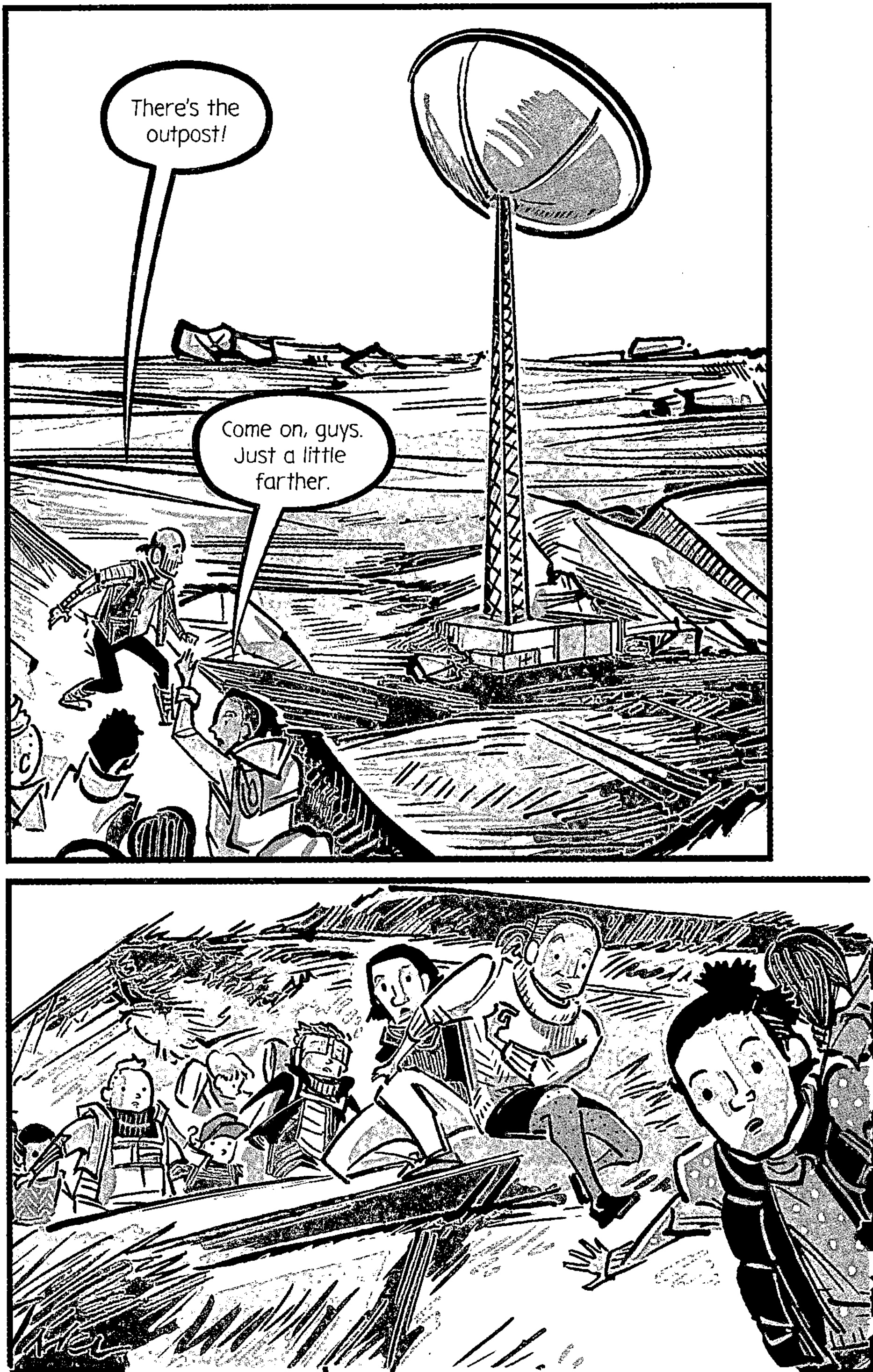
There's the outpost!
Come on, guys. Just a little farther.

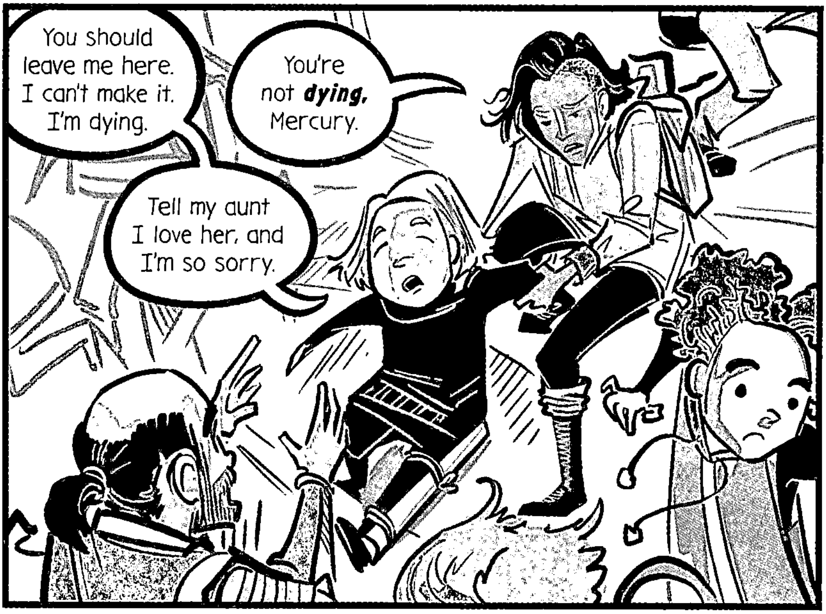
You should leave me here. I can't make it. I'm dying.
You're not **dying,** Mercury.
Tell my aunt I love her, and I'm so sorry.

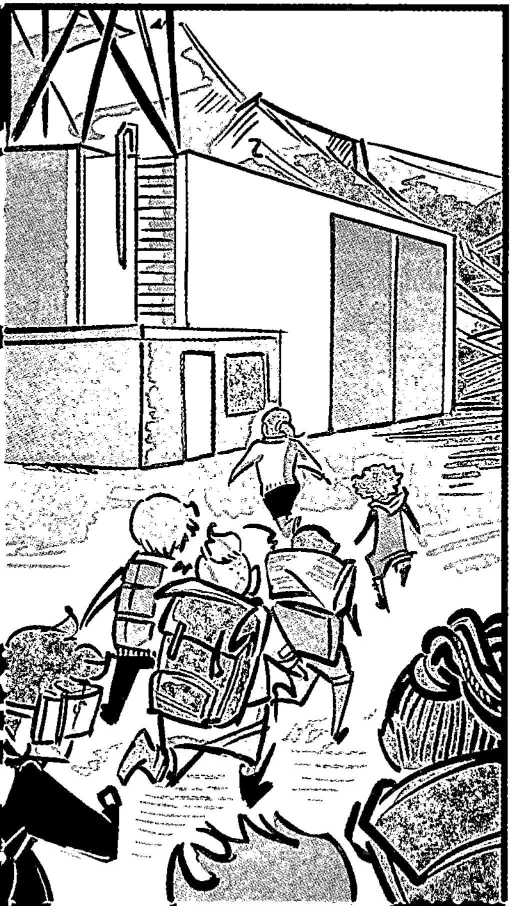

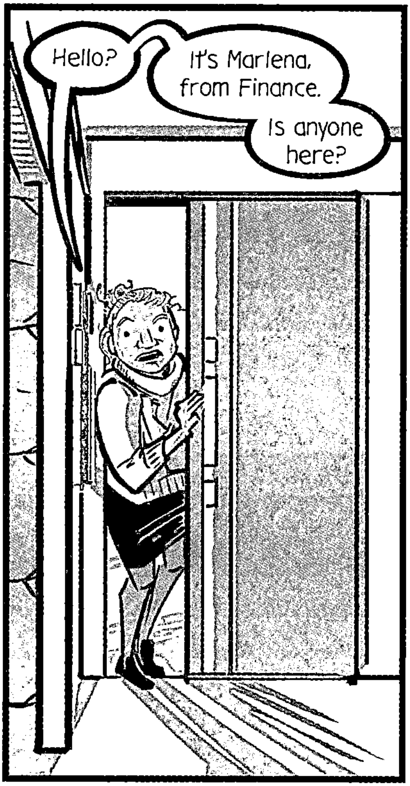
Hello?
It's Marlena, from Finance.
Is anyone here?

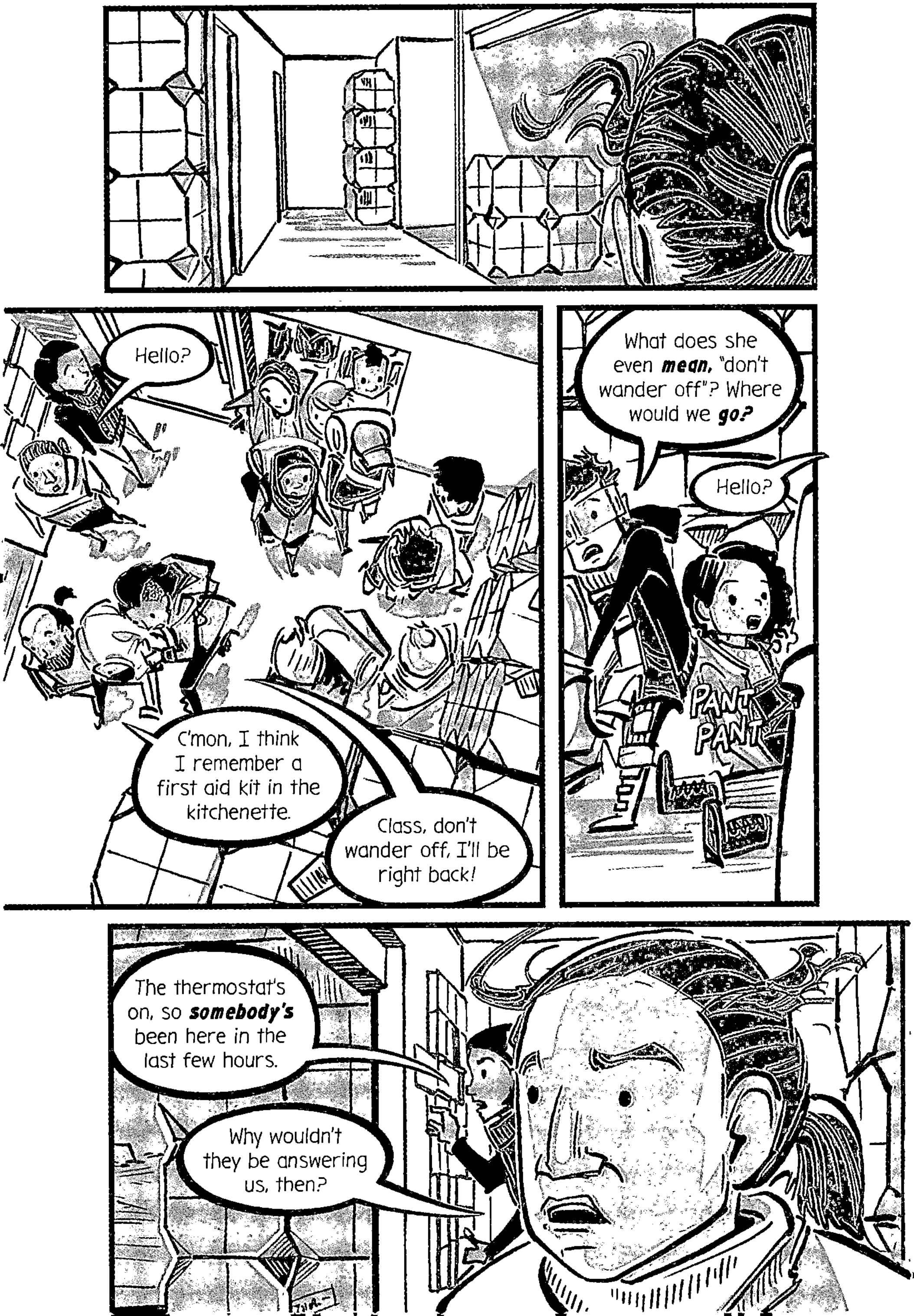
Hello?
C'mon, I think I remember a first aid kit in the kitchenette.
Class, don't wander off, I'll be right back!
What does she even **mean,** "don't wander off"? Where would we **go?**
Hello?
PANT PANT
The thermostat's on, so **somebody's** been here in the last few hours.
Why wouldn't they be answering us, then?

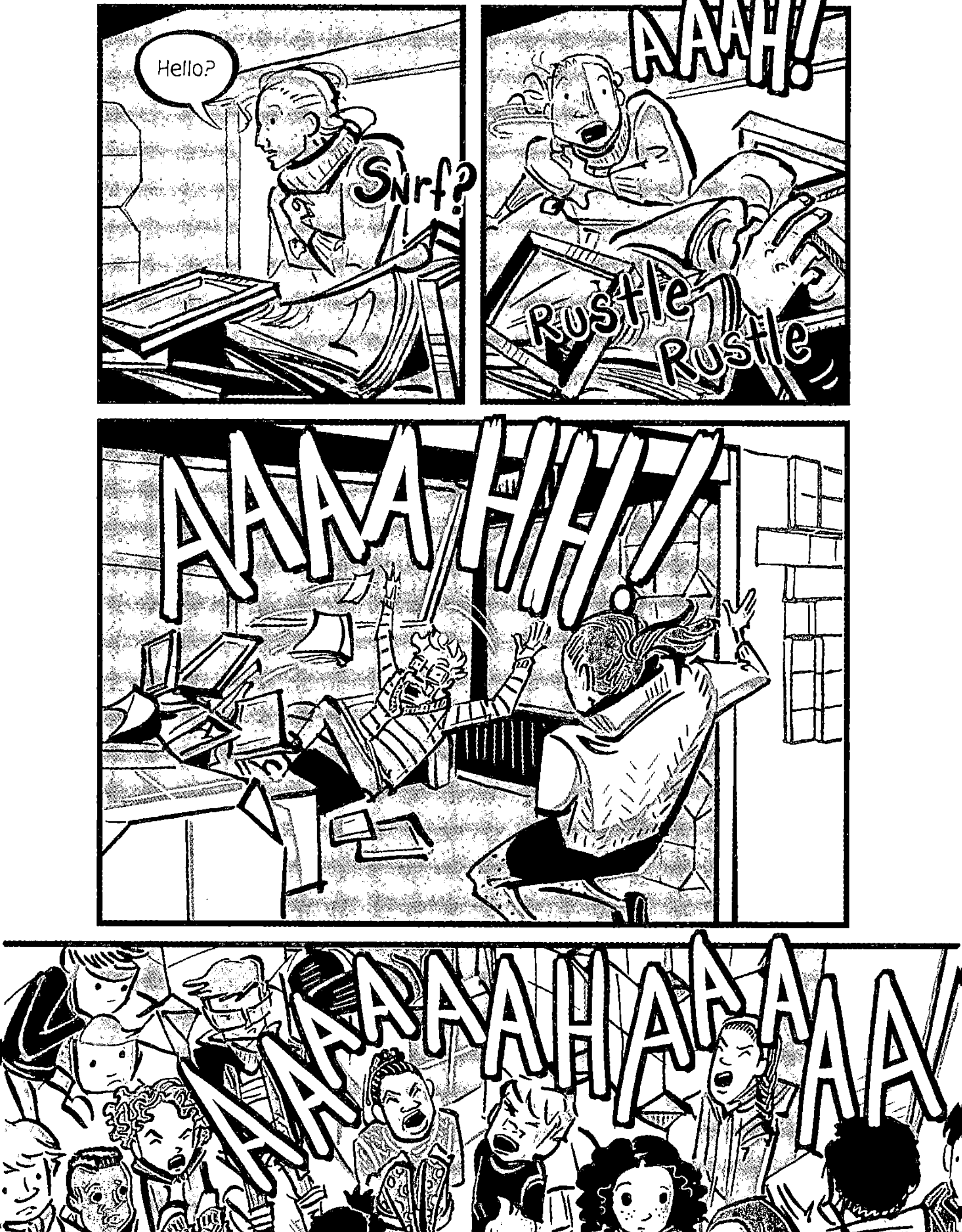
Hello?
Snrf?
AAAH!
Rustle
Rustle
AAAAHH!!
AAAAAAHAAAAA

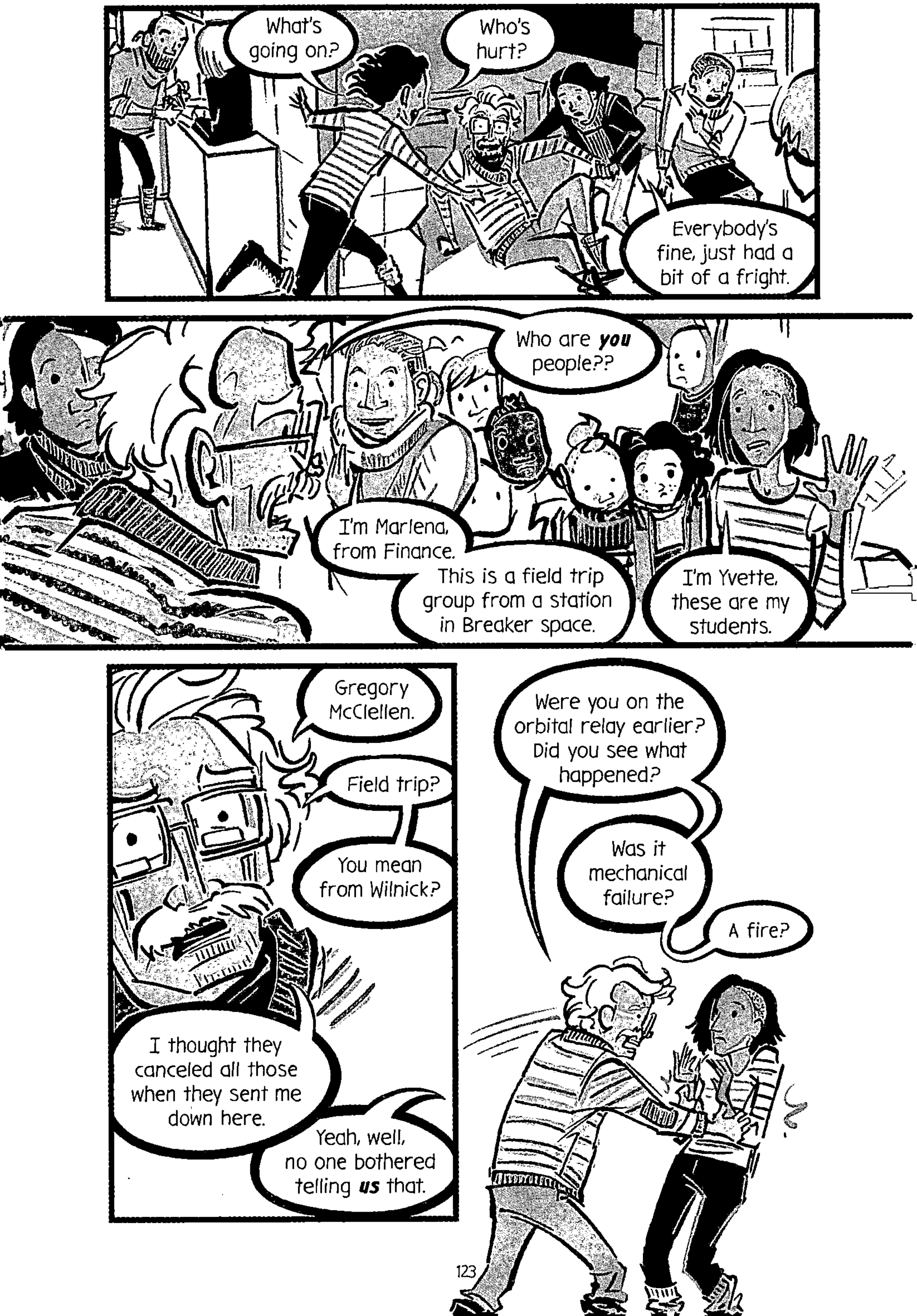
What's going on?
Who's hurt?
Everybody's fine, just had a bit of a fright.
Who are *you* people??
I'm Marlena, from Finance.
This is a field trip group from a station in Breaker space.
I'm Yvette, these are my students.
Gregory McClellen.
Field trip?
You mean from Wilnick?
I thought they canceled all those when they sent me down here.
Yeah, well, no one bothered telling *us* that.
Were you on the orbital relay earlier? Did you see what happened?
Was it mechanical failure?
A fire?

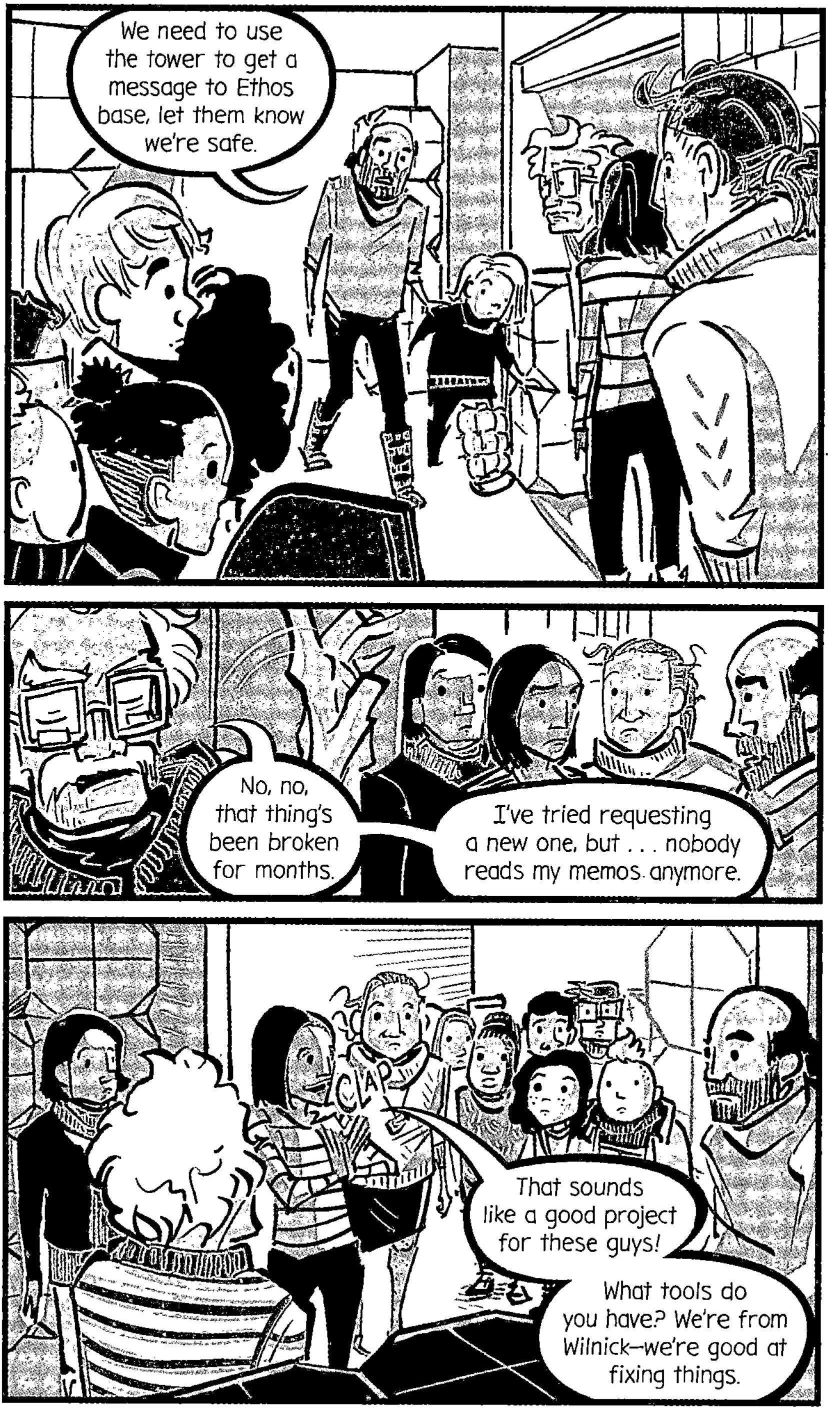
We need to use the tower to get a message to Ethos base, let them know we're safe.
No, no, that thing's been broken for months.
I've tried requesting a new one, but . . . nobody reads my memos anymore.
CLAP
That sounds like a good project for these guys!
What tools do you have? We're from Wilnick—we're good at fixing things.

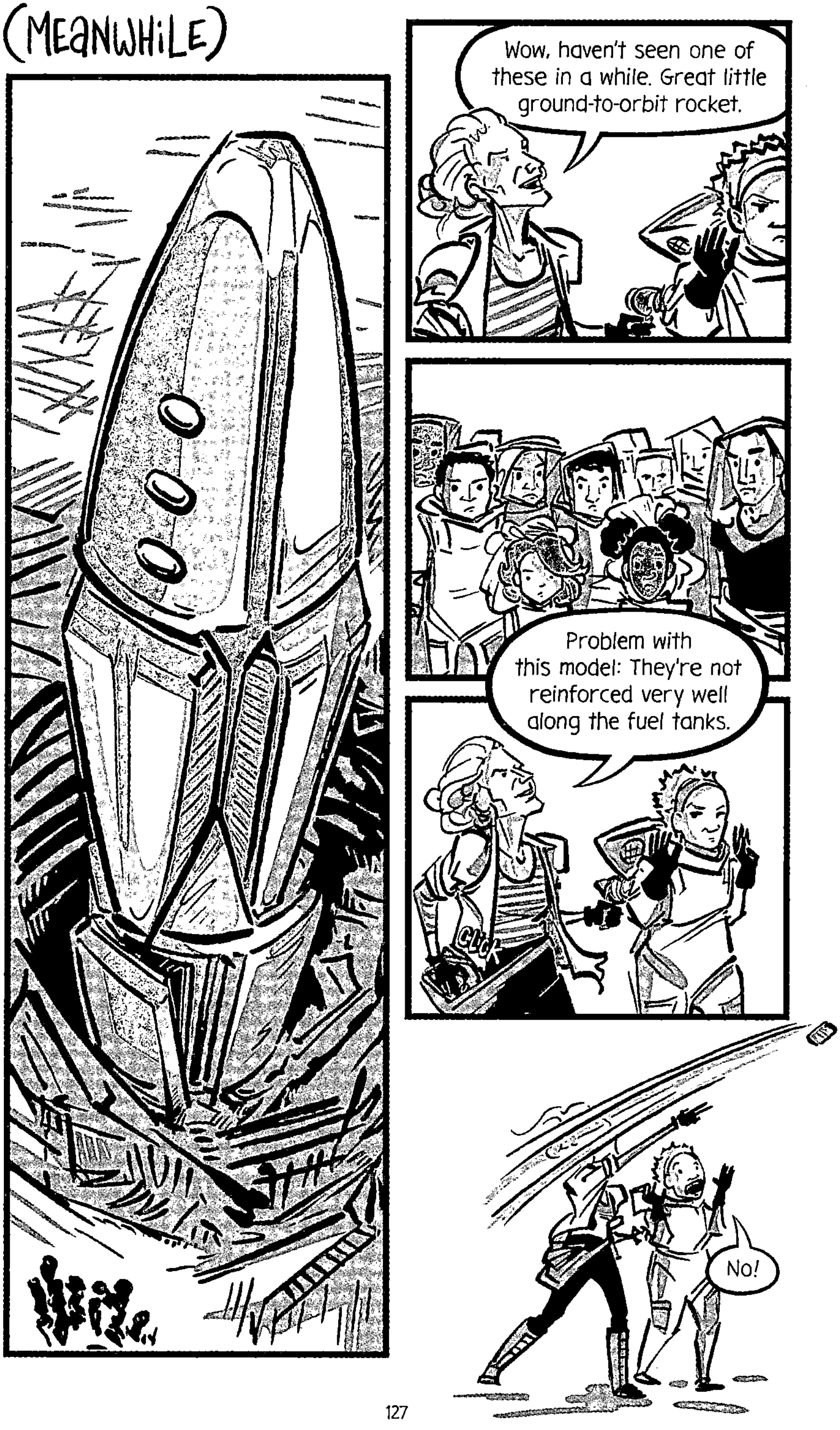
(MEANWHILE)
Wow, haven't seen one of these in a while. Great little ground-to-orbit rocket.
Problem with this model: They're not reinforced very well along the fuel tanks.
CLICK
No!

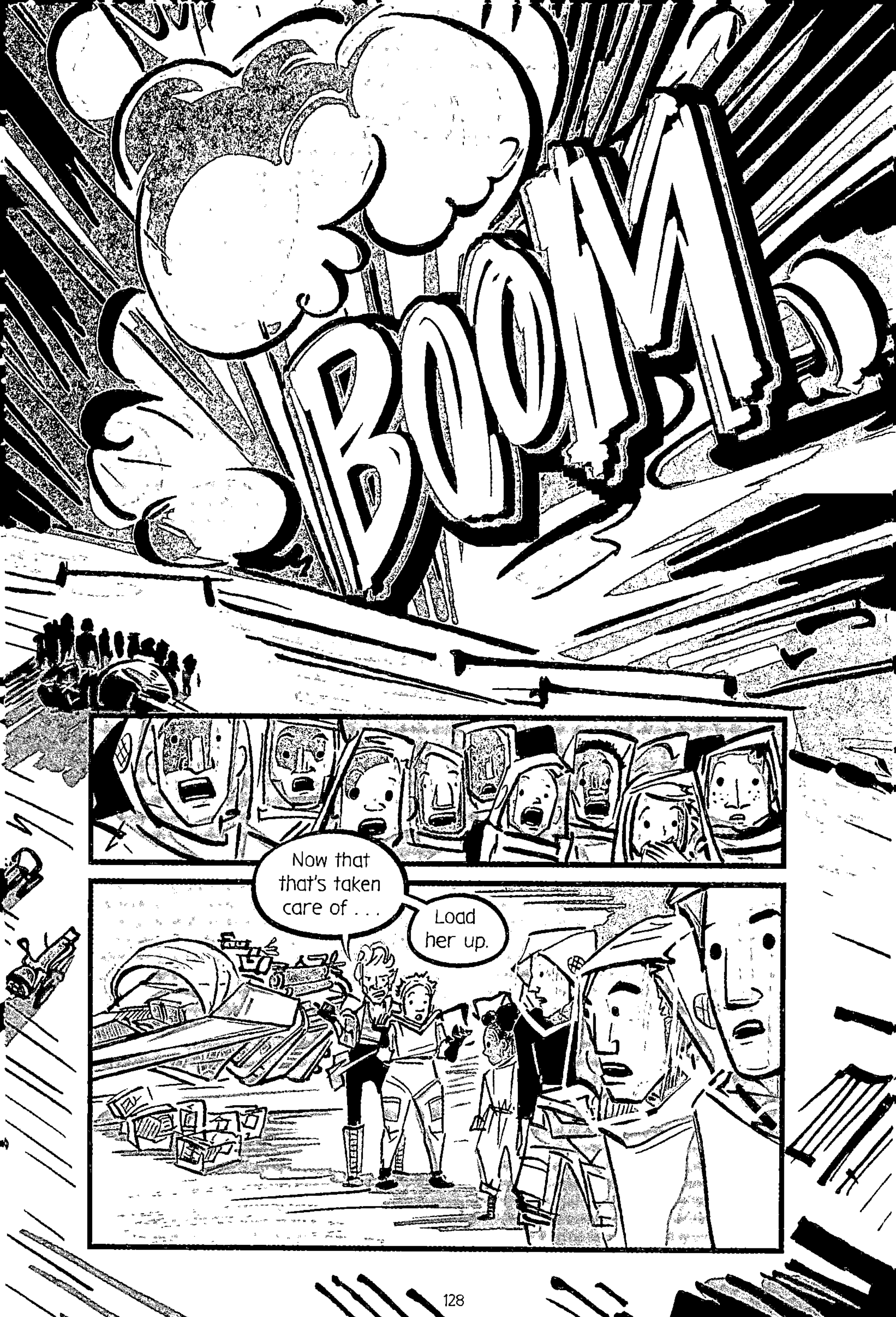
BOOM
Now that that's taken care of . . .
Load her up.

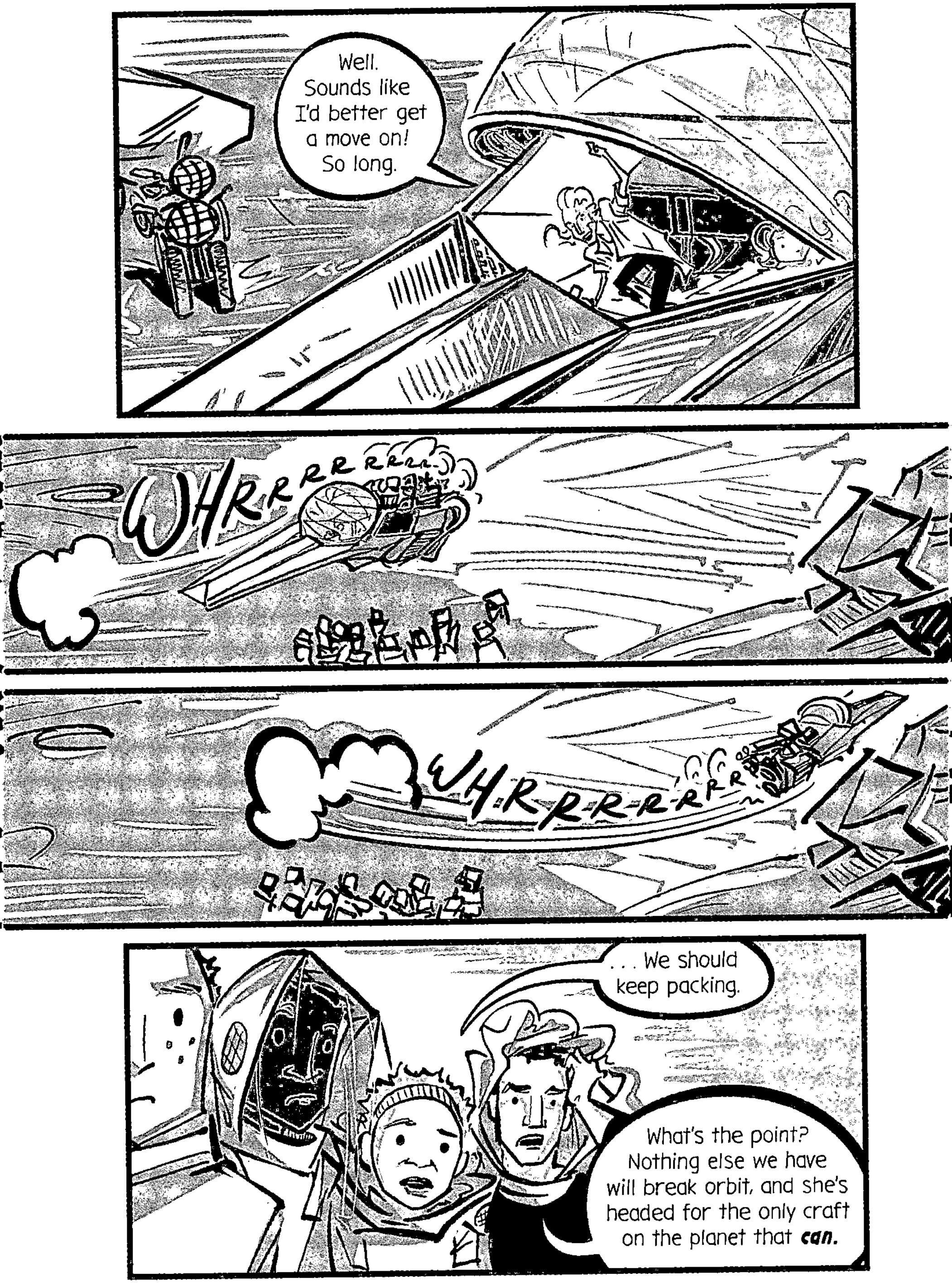
Well. Sounds like I'd better get a move on! So long.
WHRRRRRRRR
WHRRRRRRRRR
. . . We should keep packing.
What's the point? Nothing else we have will break orbit, and she's headed for the only craft on the planet that *can.*

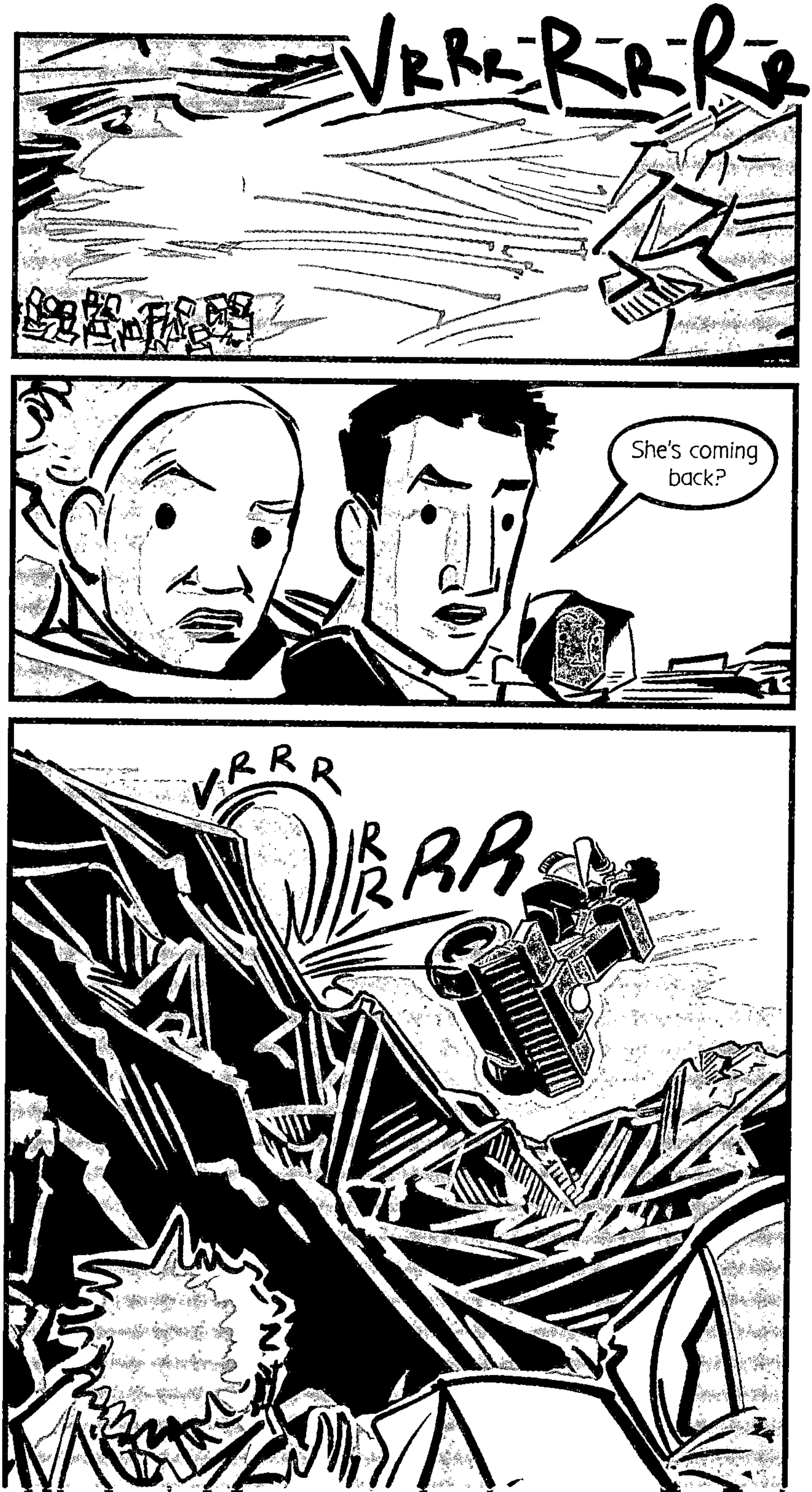
VRRR-R-R-R-R
She's coming back?
VRRR
RRRRR

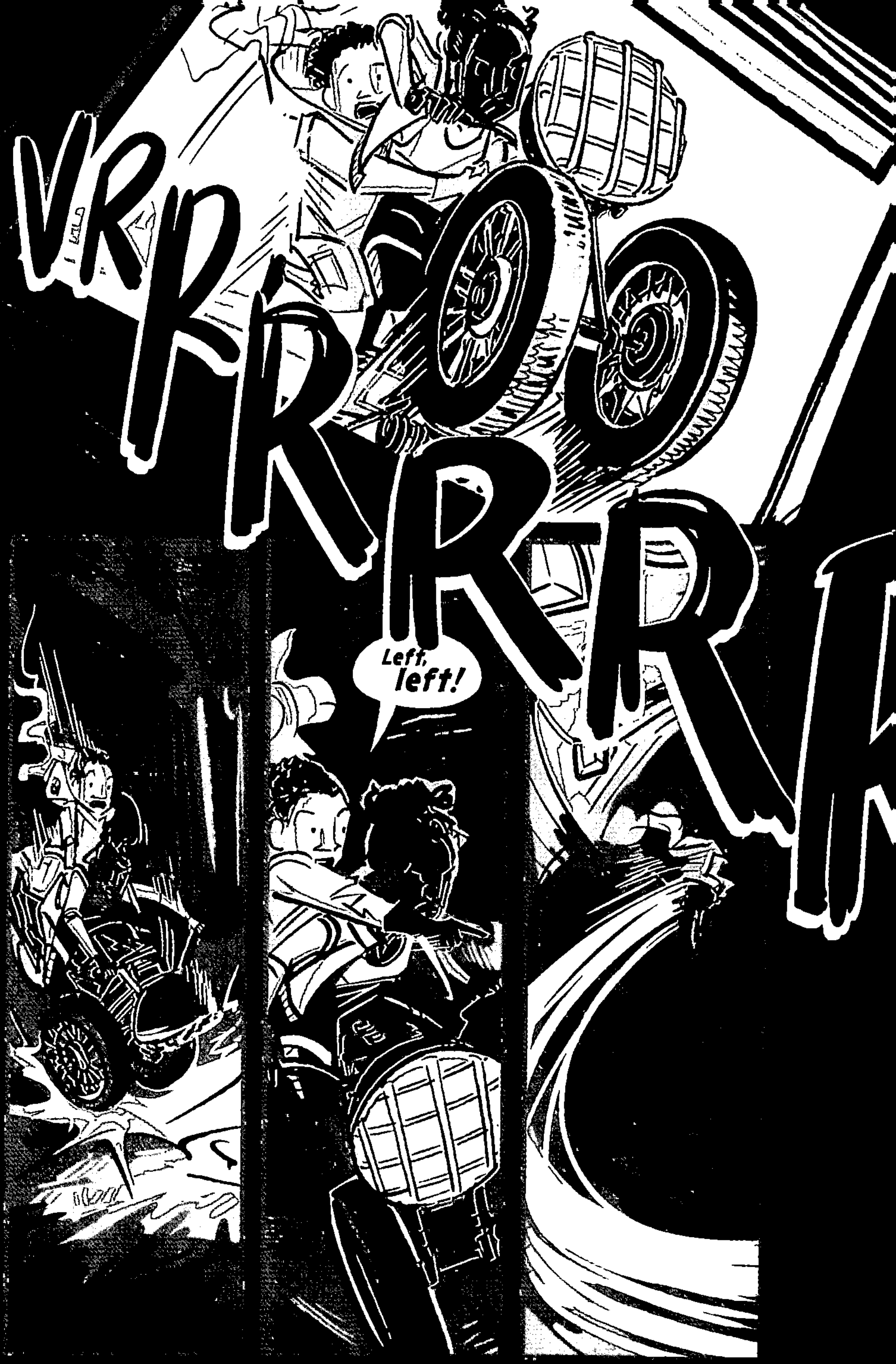
VRRRRRRR
Left, left!

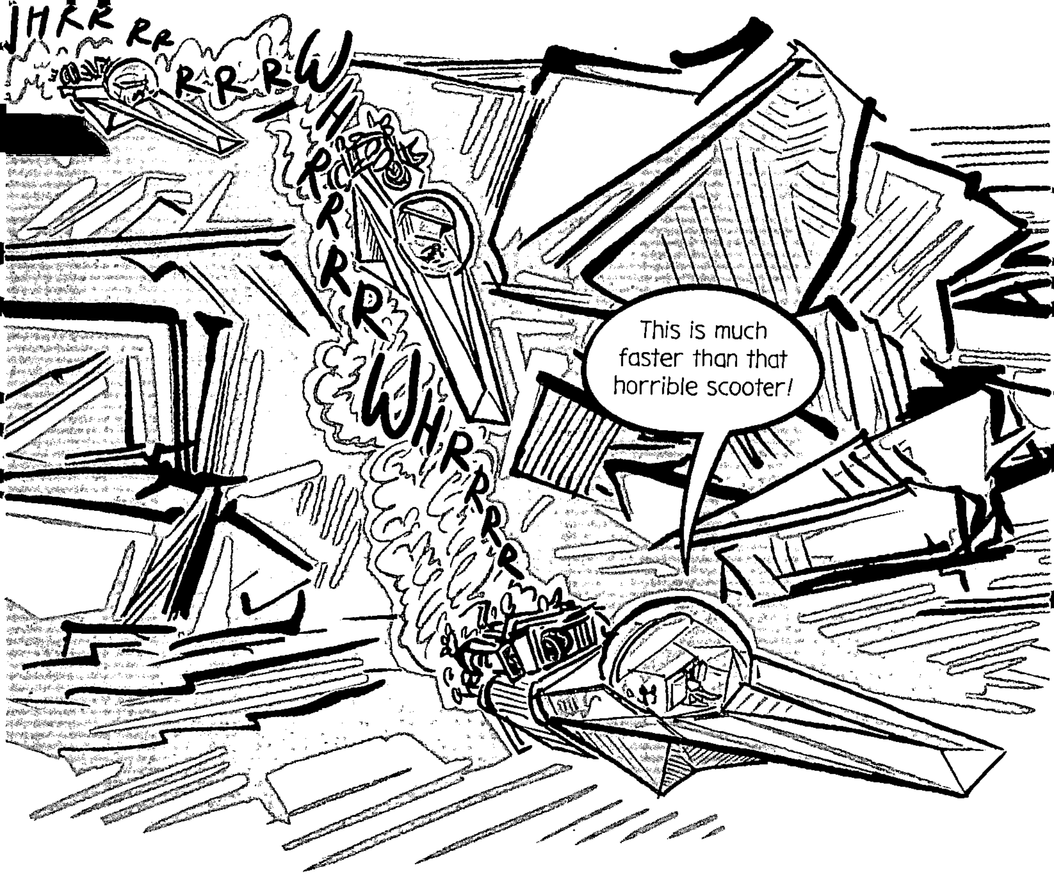
JHRRRRRRRRW
WHRRRRRRW
WHRRRRR
This is much faster than that horrible scooter!

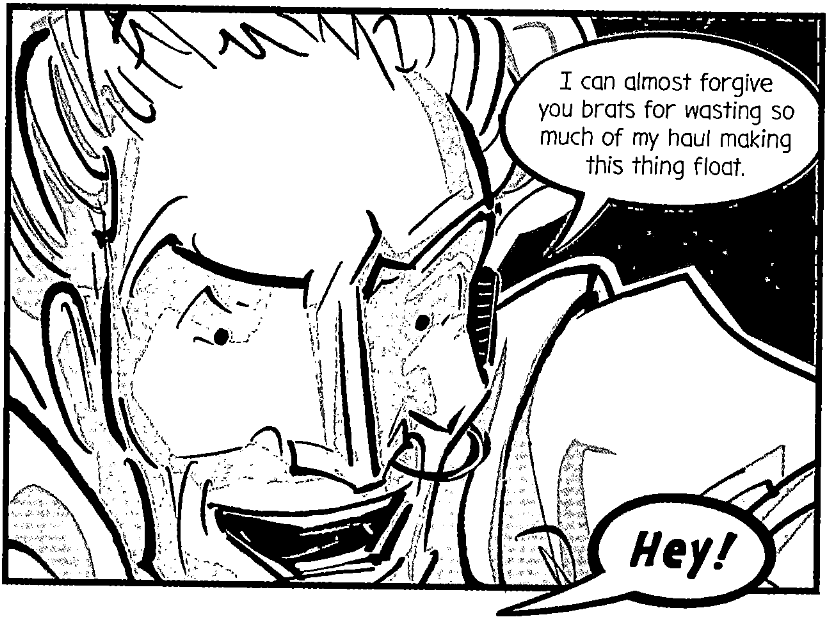
I can almost forgive you brats for wasting so much of my haul making this thing float.
Hey!

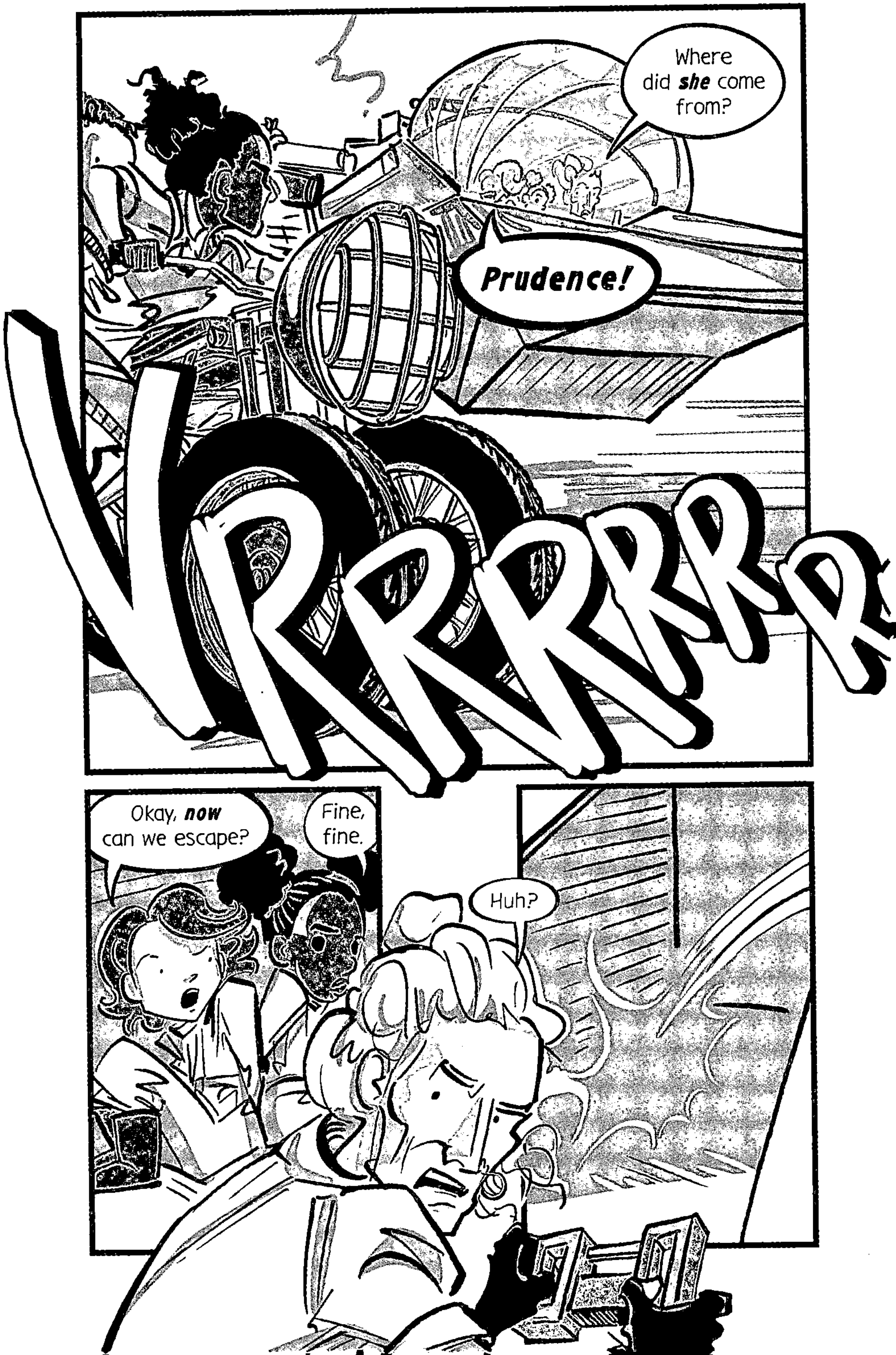
Where did *she* come from?
Prudence!
VRRRRRR
Okay, *now* can we escape?
Fine, fine.
Huh?

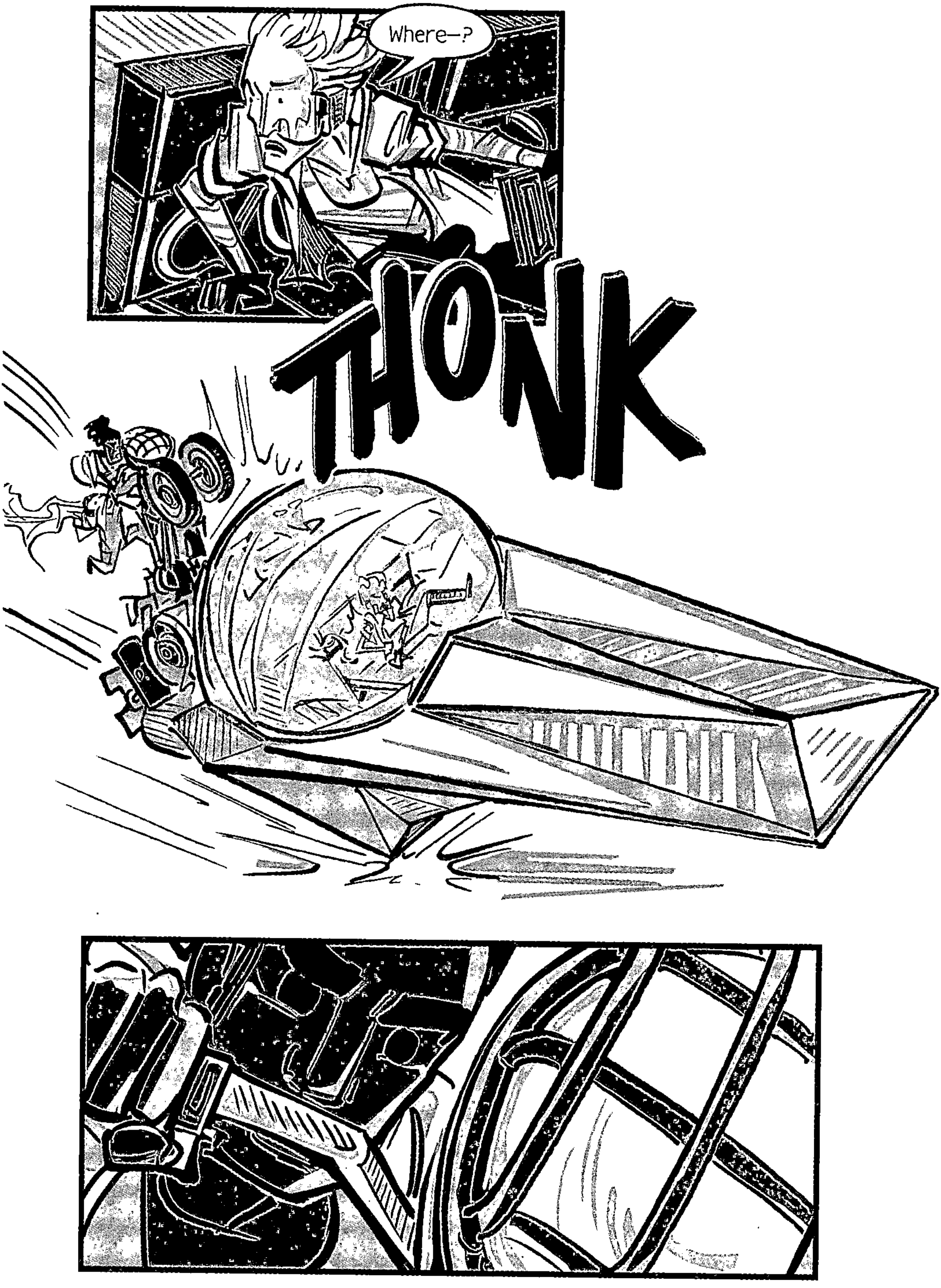
Where—?
THONK

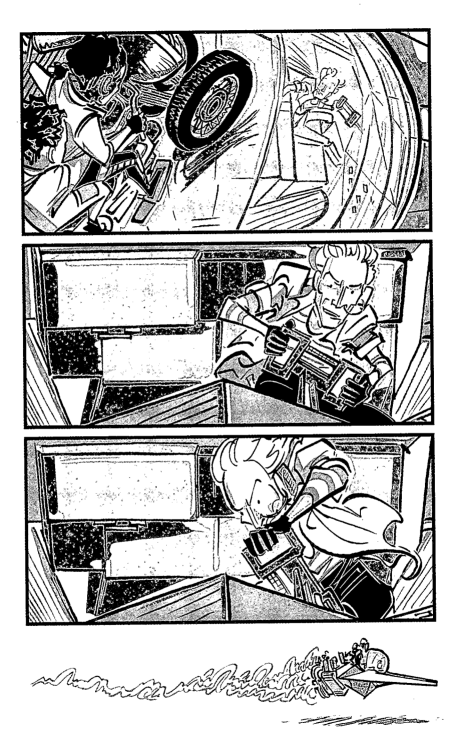

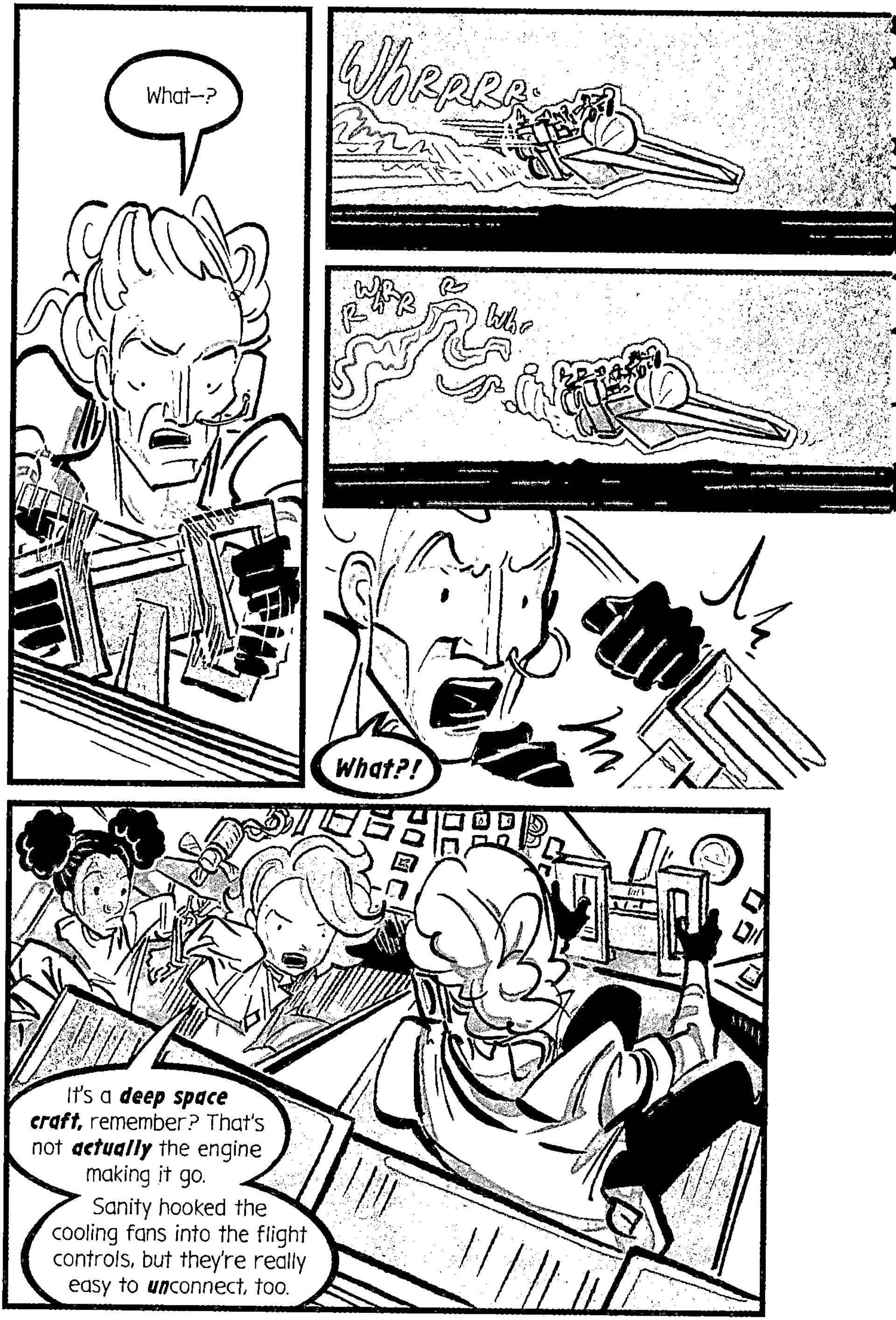
What–?
WHRRRR
What?!
It's a **deep space craft,** remember? That's not **actually** the engine making it go.
Sanity hooked the cooling fans into the flight controls, but they're really easy to ***un***connect, too.

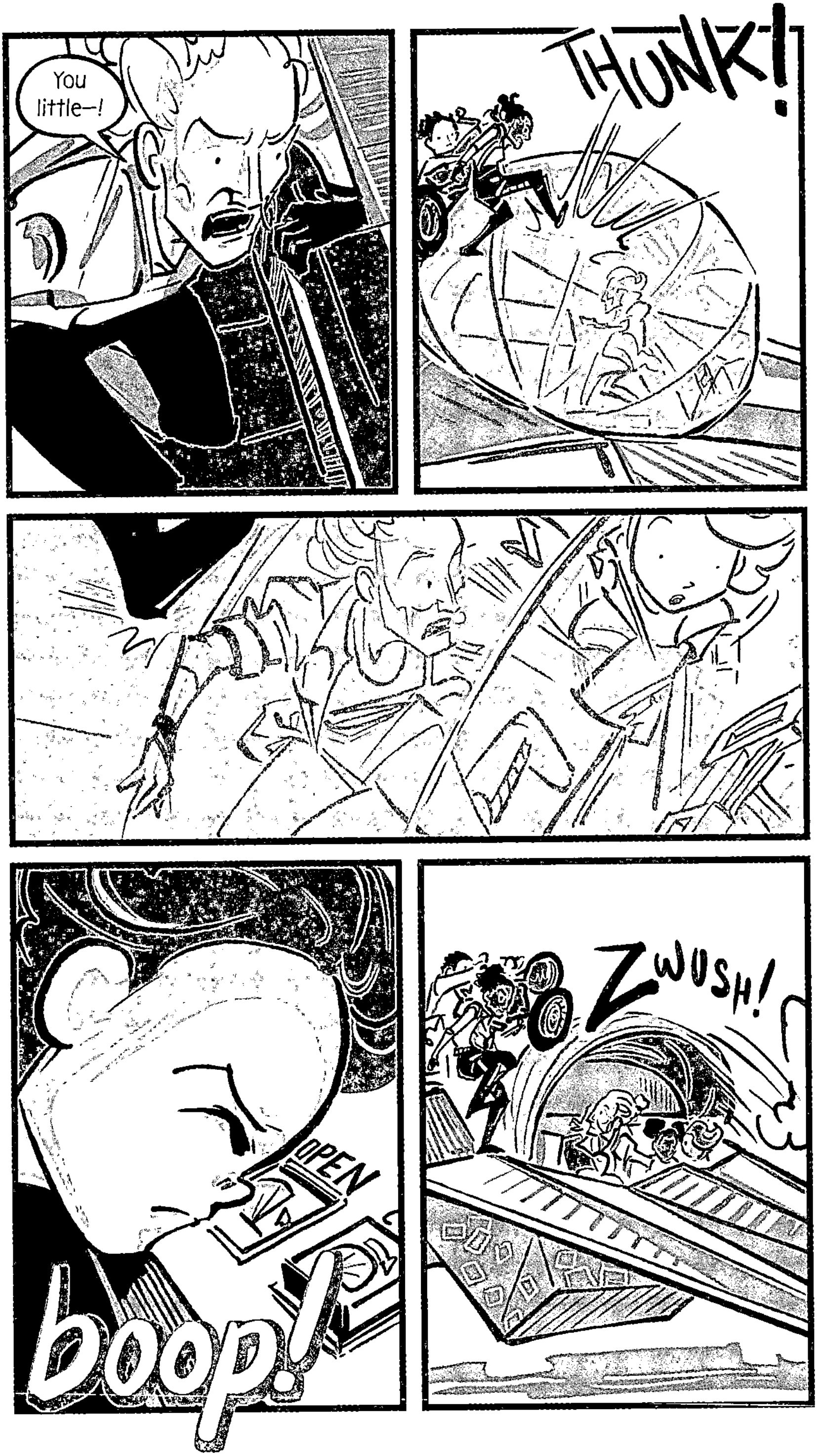
You little–!
THUNK!
OPEN
boop!
ZWUSH!

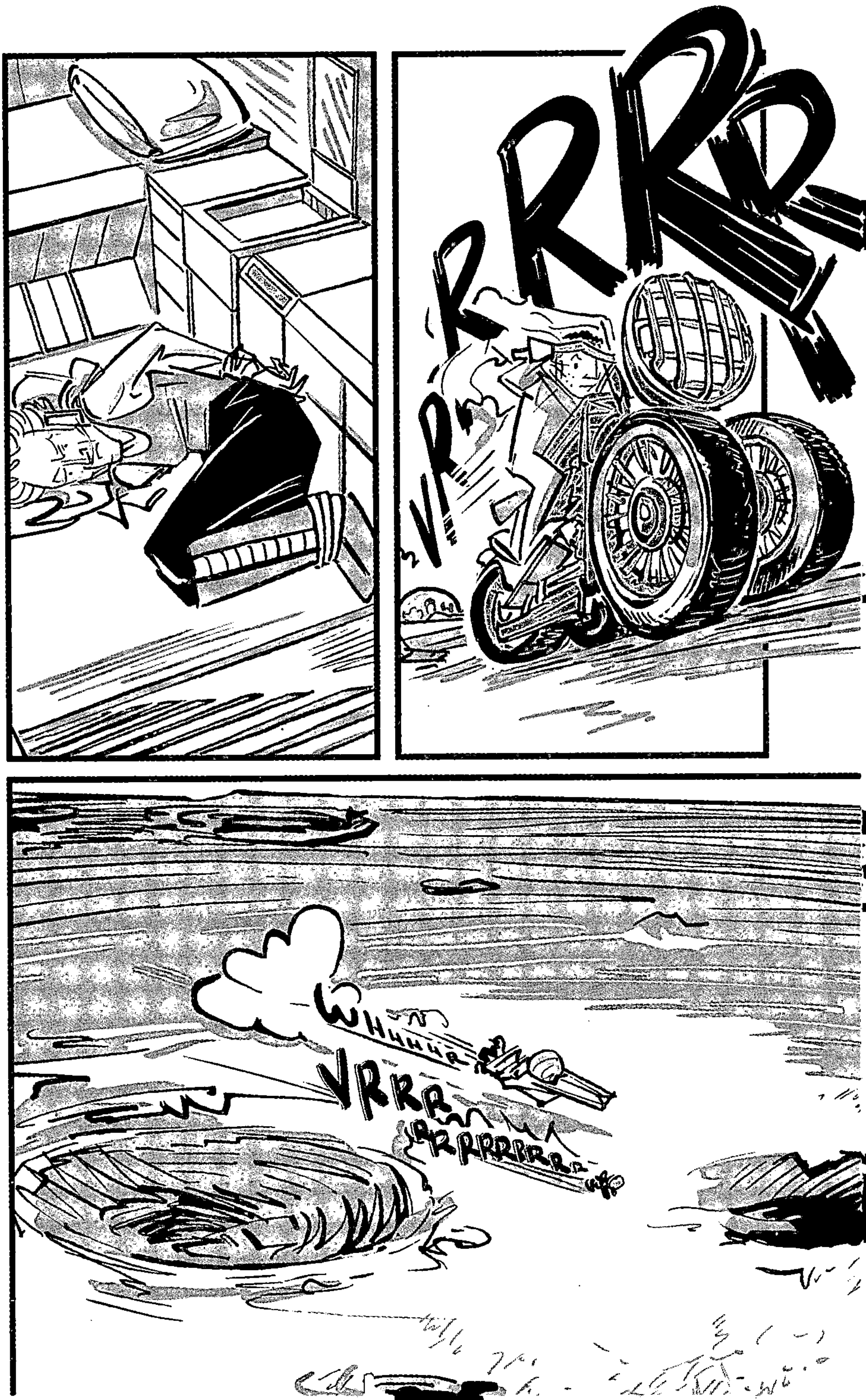
VRRRRR
WHHHHR
VRRRRRRRRRRRRR

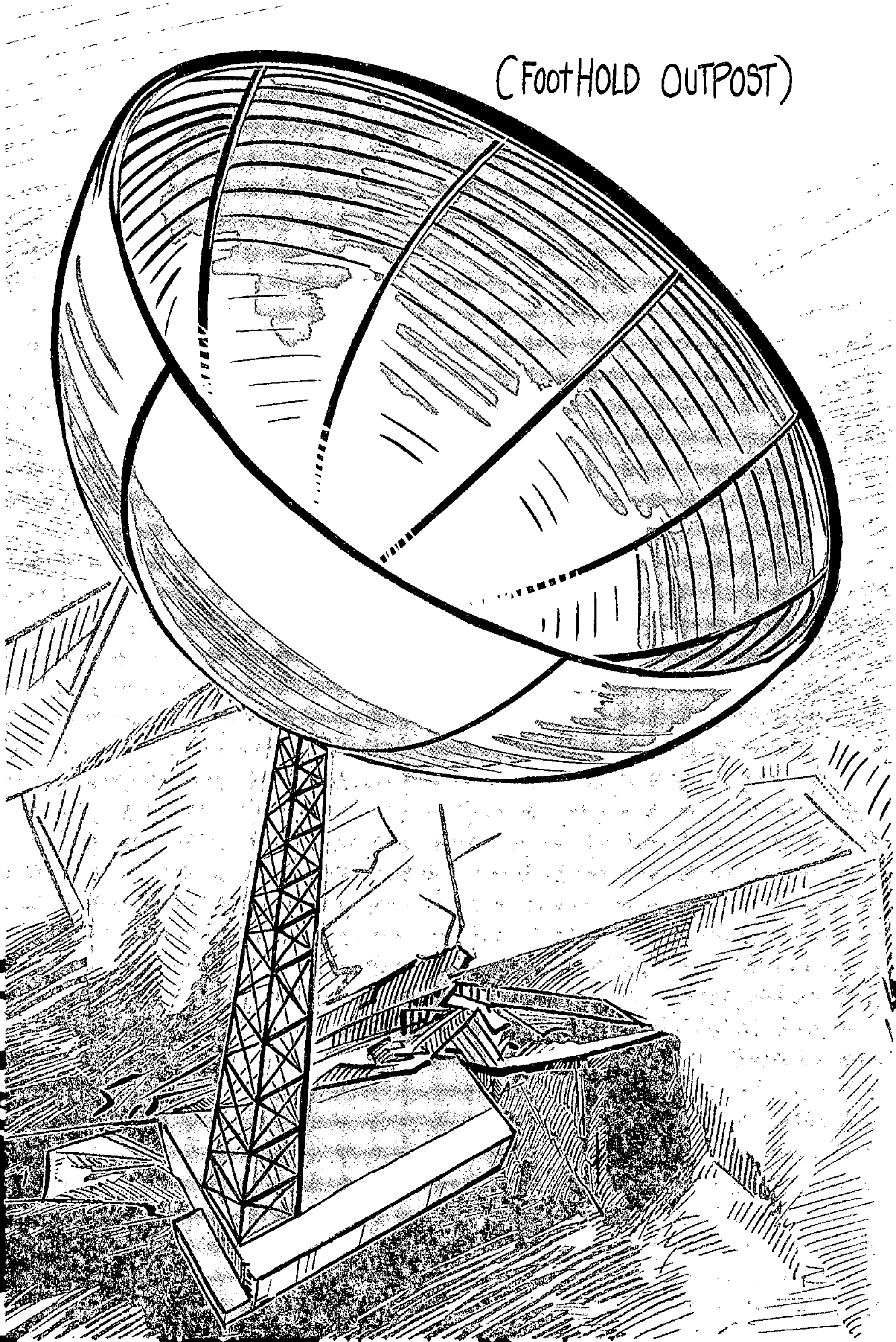
(FootHOLD OUTPOST)

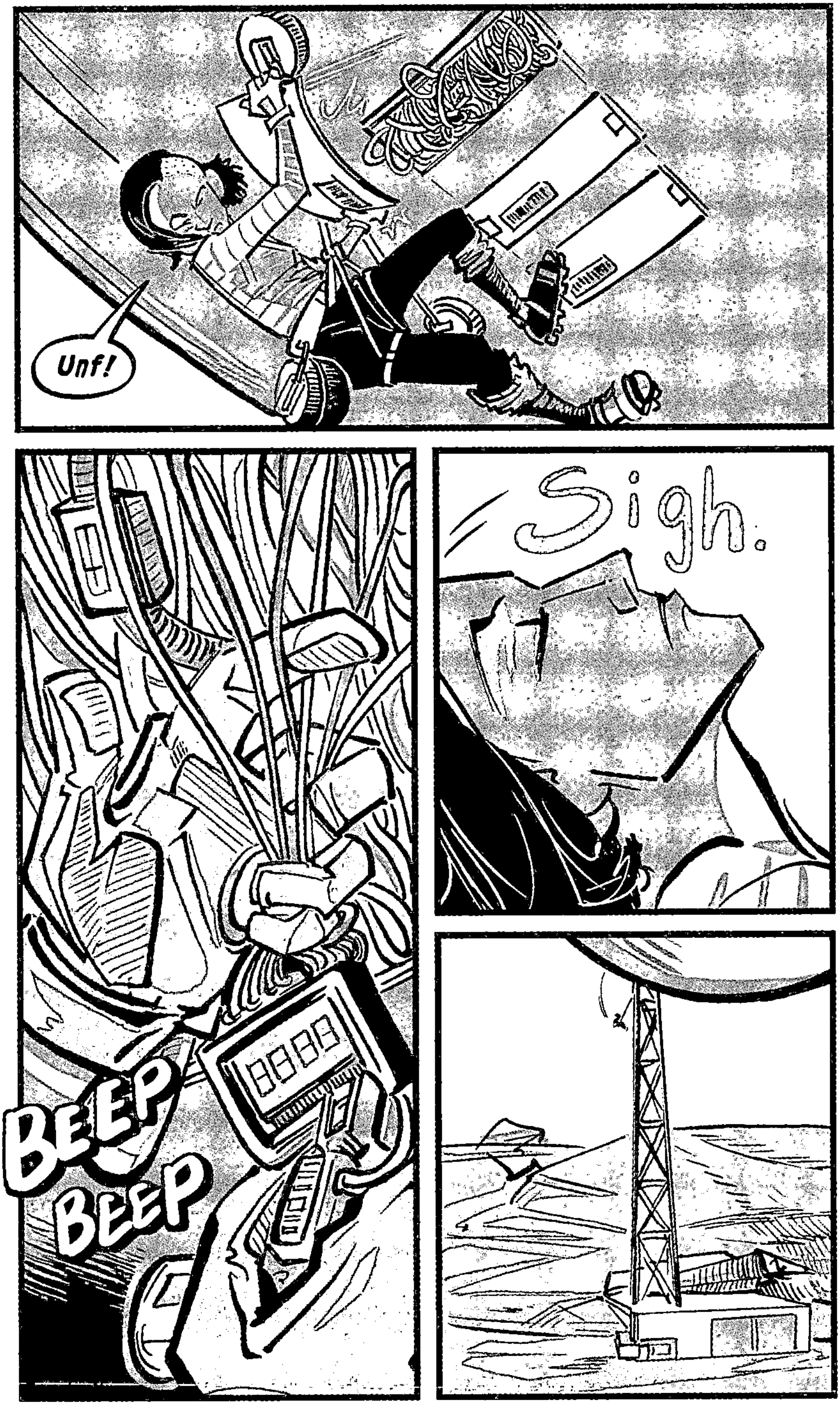
Unf!
Sigh.
BEEP
BEEP

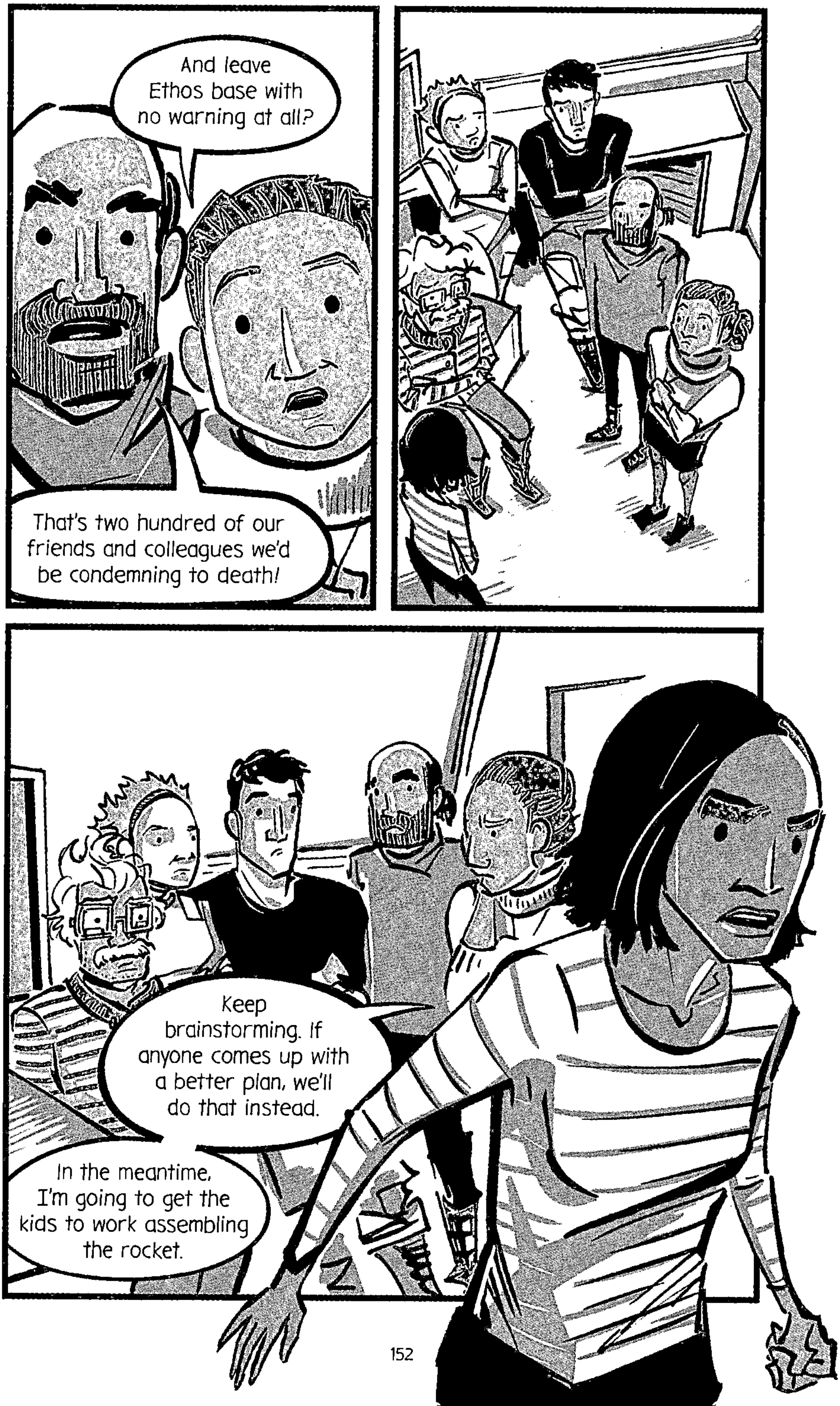
And leave Ethos base with no warning at all?
That's two hundred of our friends and colleagues we'd be condemning to death!
Keep brainstorming. If anyone comes up with a better plan, we'll do that instead.
In the meantime, I'm going to get the kids to work assembling the rocket.

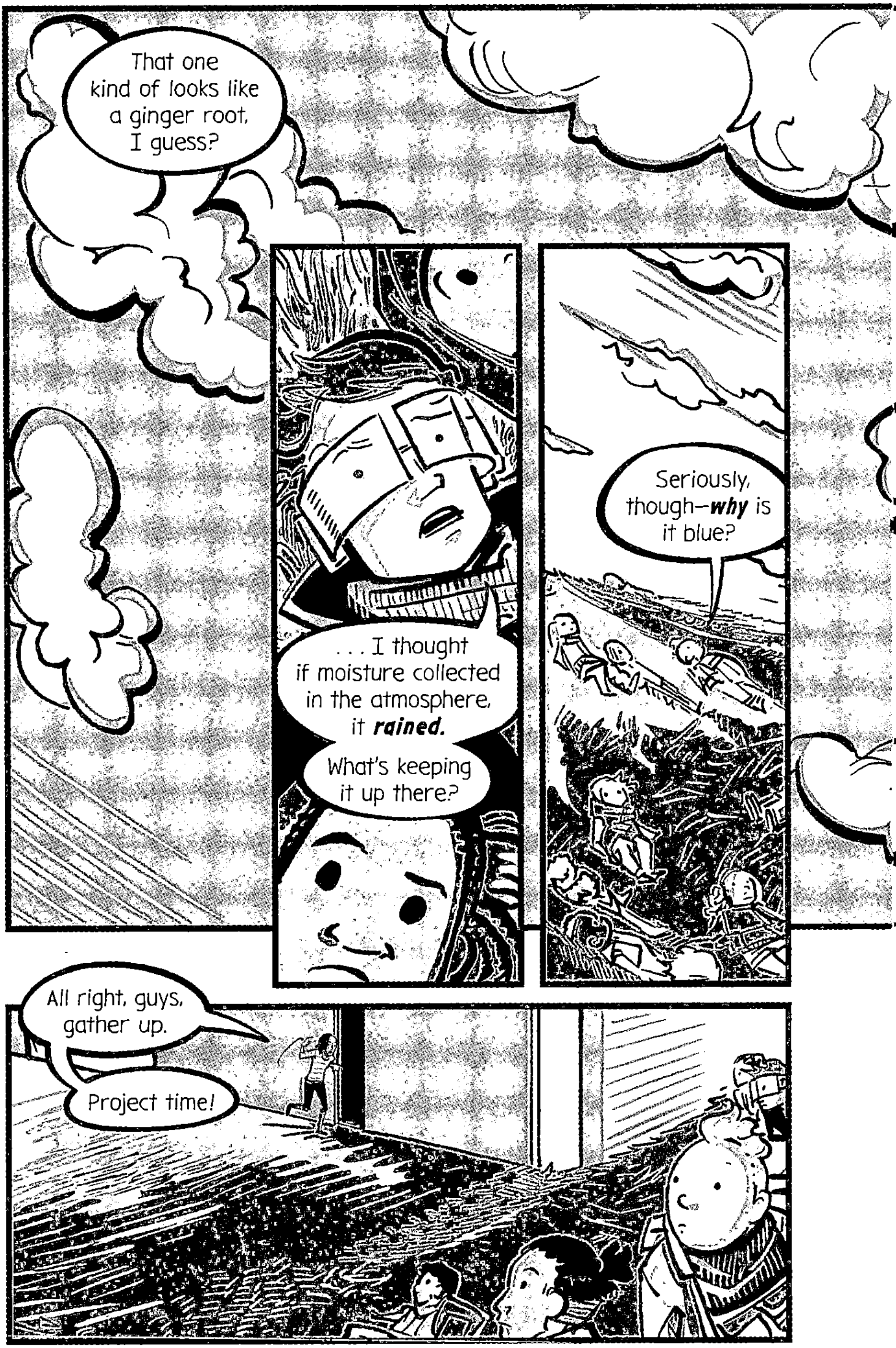
That one kind of looks like a ginger root, I guess?
. . . I thought if moisture collected in the atmosphere, it ***rained.***
What's keeping it up there?
Seriously, though—***why*** is it blue?
All right, guys, gather up.
Project time!

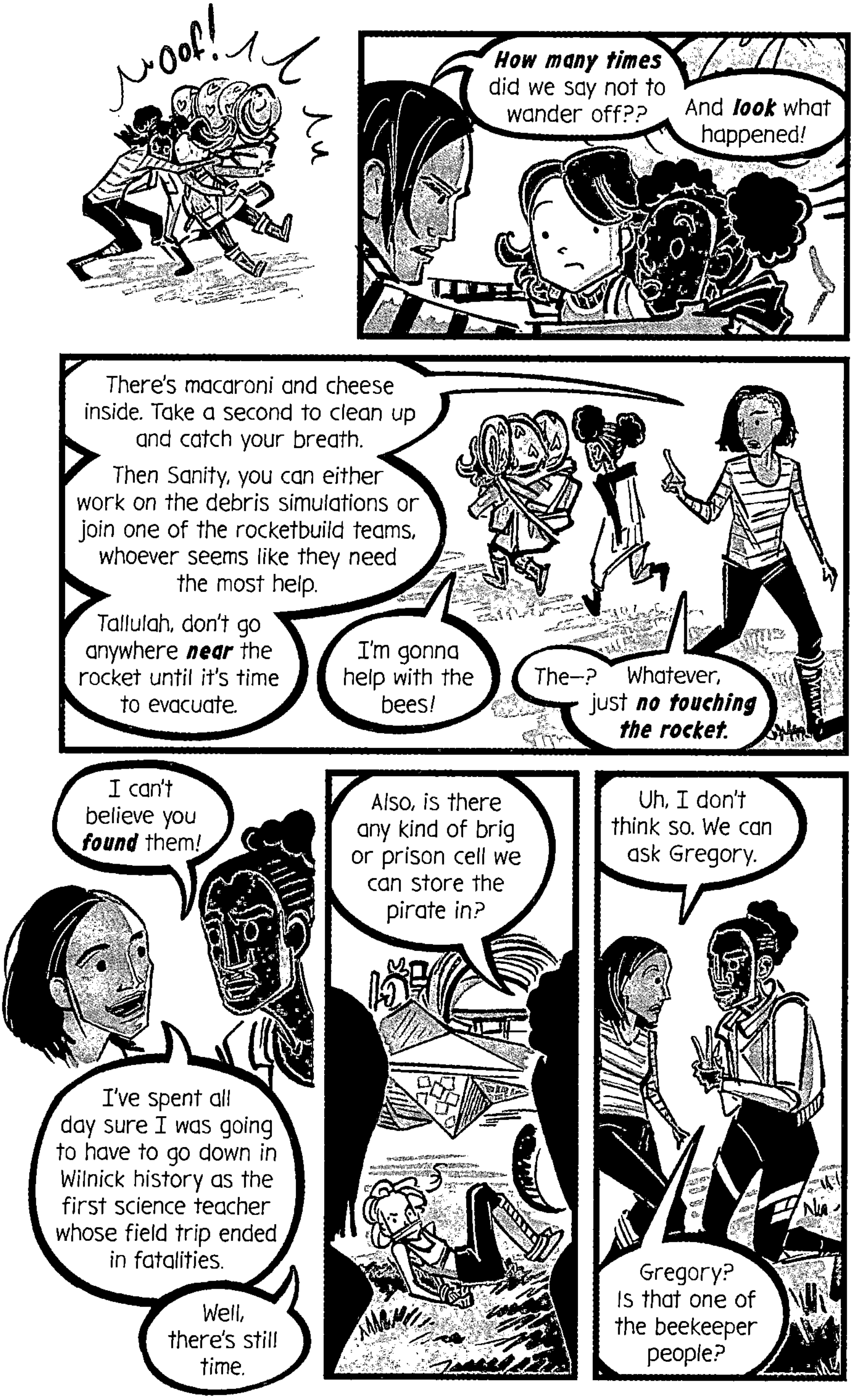
Oof!
How many times did we say not to wander off??
And look what happened!
There's macaroni and cheese inside. Take a second to clean up and catch your breath.
Then Sanity, you can either work on the debris simulations or join one of the rocketbuild teams, whoever seems like they need the most help.
Tallulah, don't go anywhere near the rocket until it's time to evacuate.
I'm gonna help with the bees!
The—? Whatever, just no touching the rocket.
I can't believe you found them!
I've spent all day sure I was going to have to go down in Wilnick history as the first science teacher whose field trip ended in fatalities.
Well, there's still time.
Also, is there any kind of brig or prison cell we can store the pirate in?
Uh, I don't think so. We can ask Gregory.
Gregory? Is that one of the beekeeper people?

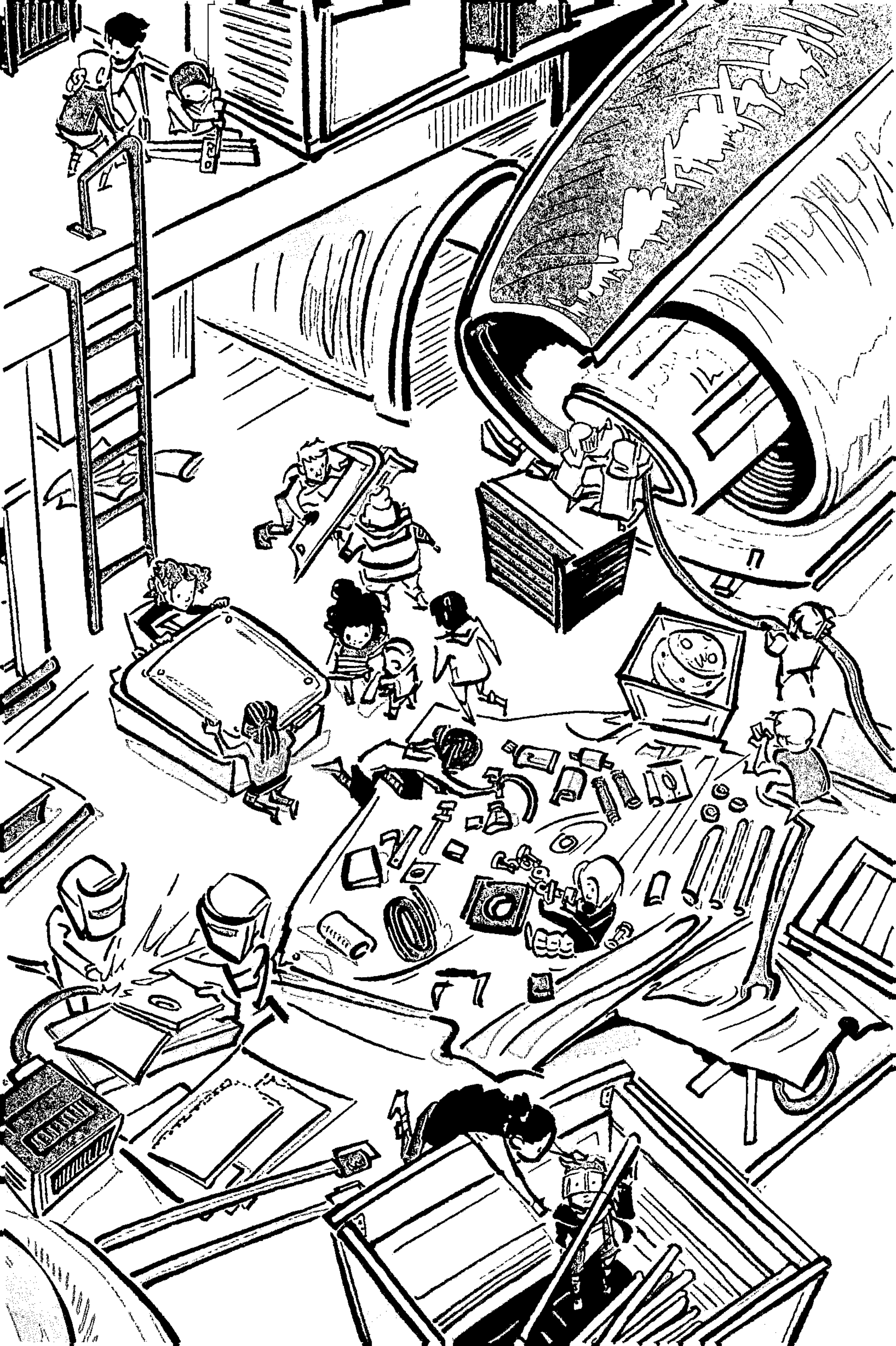

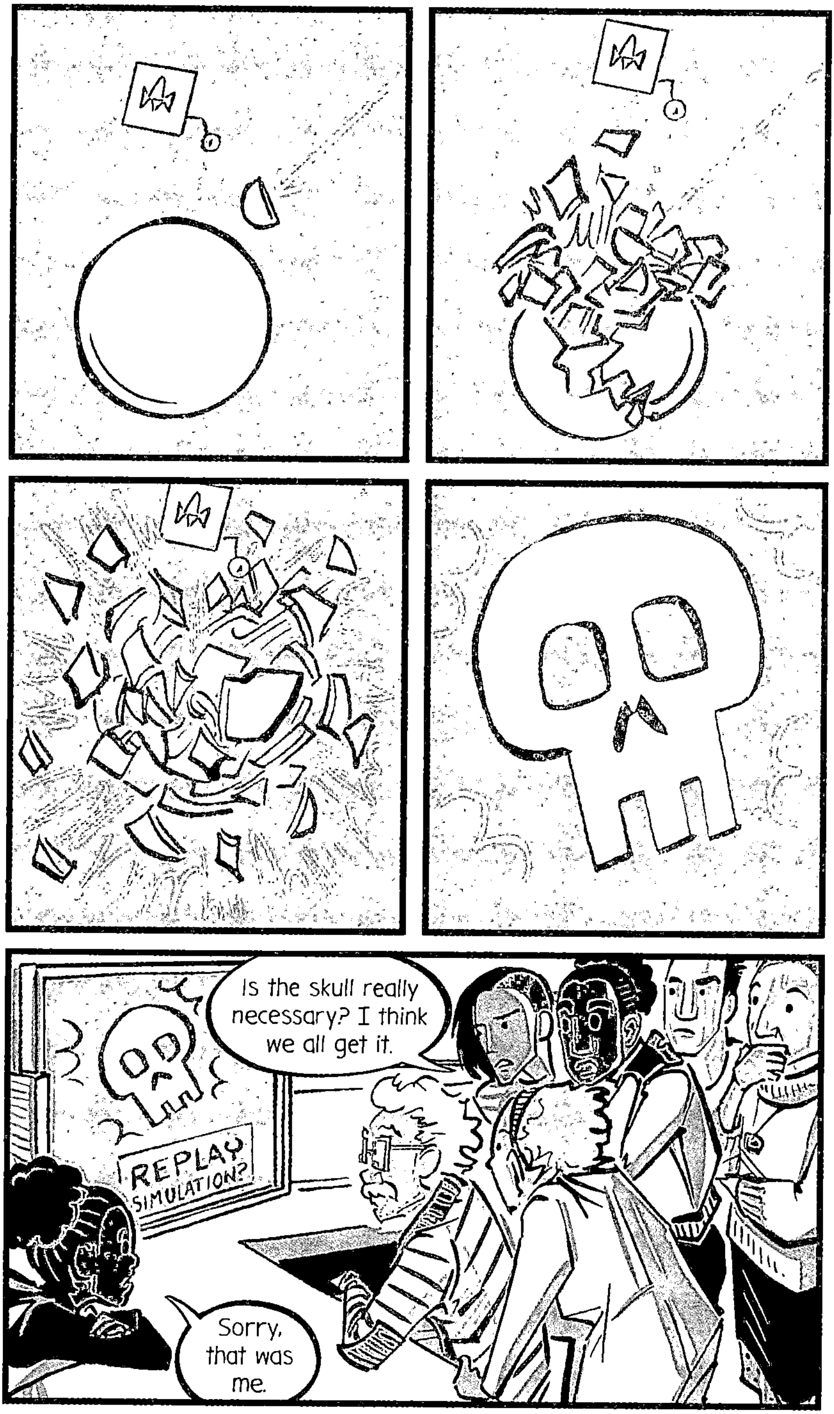

REPLAY SIMULATION?
Is the skull really necessary? I think we all get it.
Sorry, that was me.

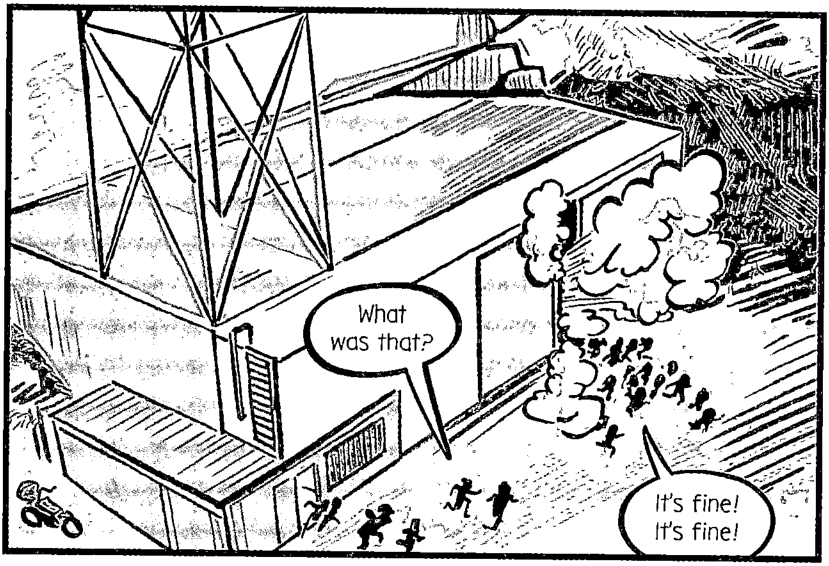
What was that?
It's fine! It's fine!

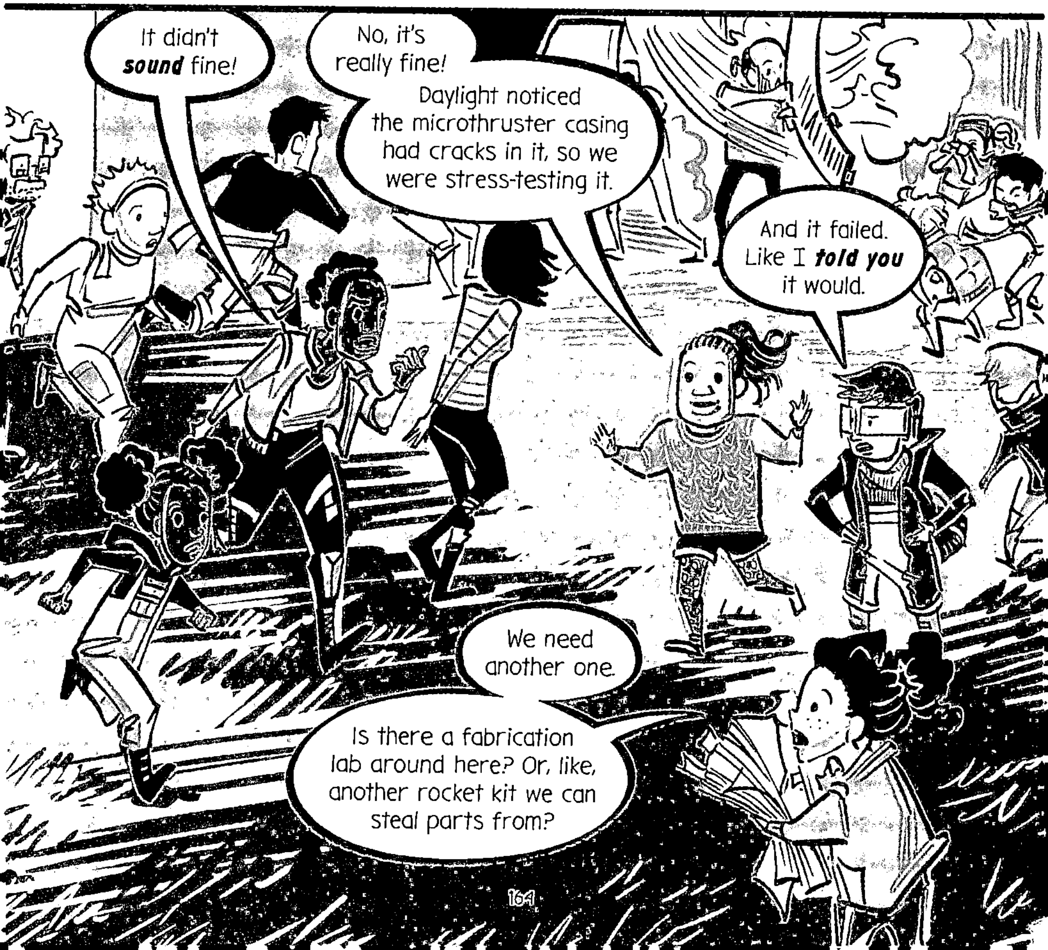
It didn't **sound** fine!
No, it's really fine!
Daylight noticed the microthruster casing had cracks in it, so we were stress-testing it.
And it failed. Like I **told you** it would.
We need another one.
Is there a fabrication lab around here? Or, like, another rocket kit we can steal parts from?

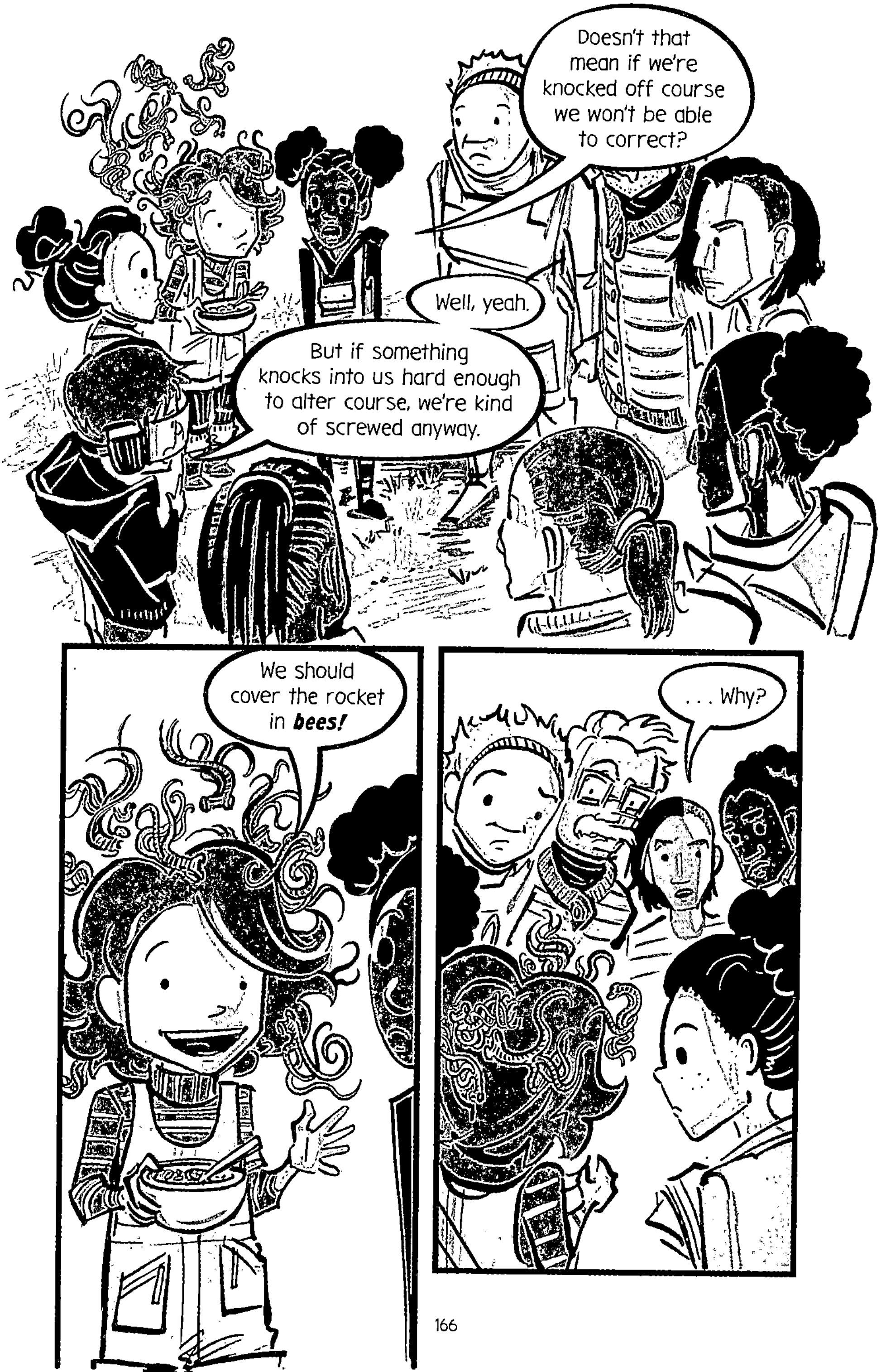

Doesn't that mean if we're knocked off course we won't be able to correct?
Well, yeah.
But if something knocks into us hard enough to alter course, we're kind of screwed anyway.
We should cover the rocket in ***bees!***
. . . Why?

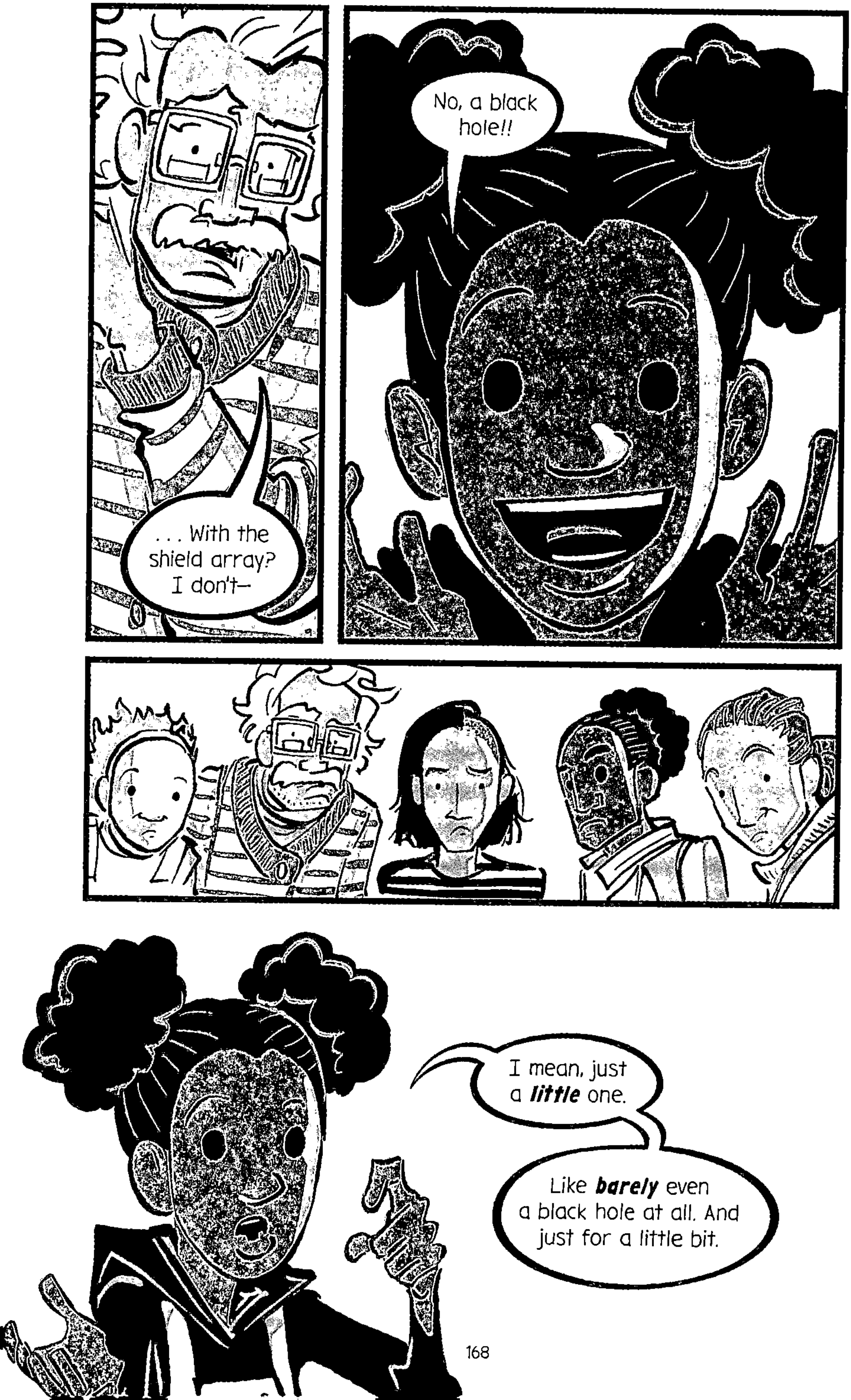
. . . With the shield array? I don't–
No, a black hole!!
I mean, just a ***little*** one.
Like ***barely*** even a black hole at all. And just for a little bit.

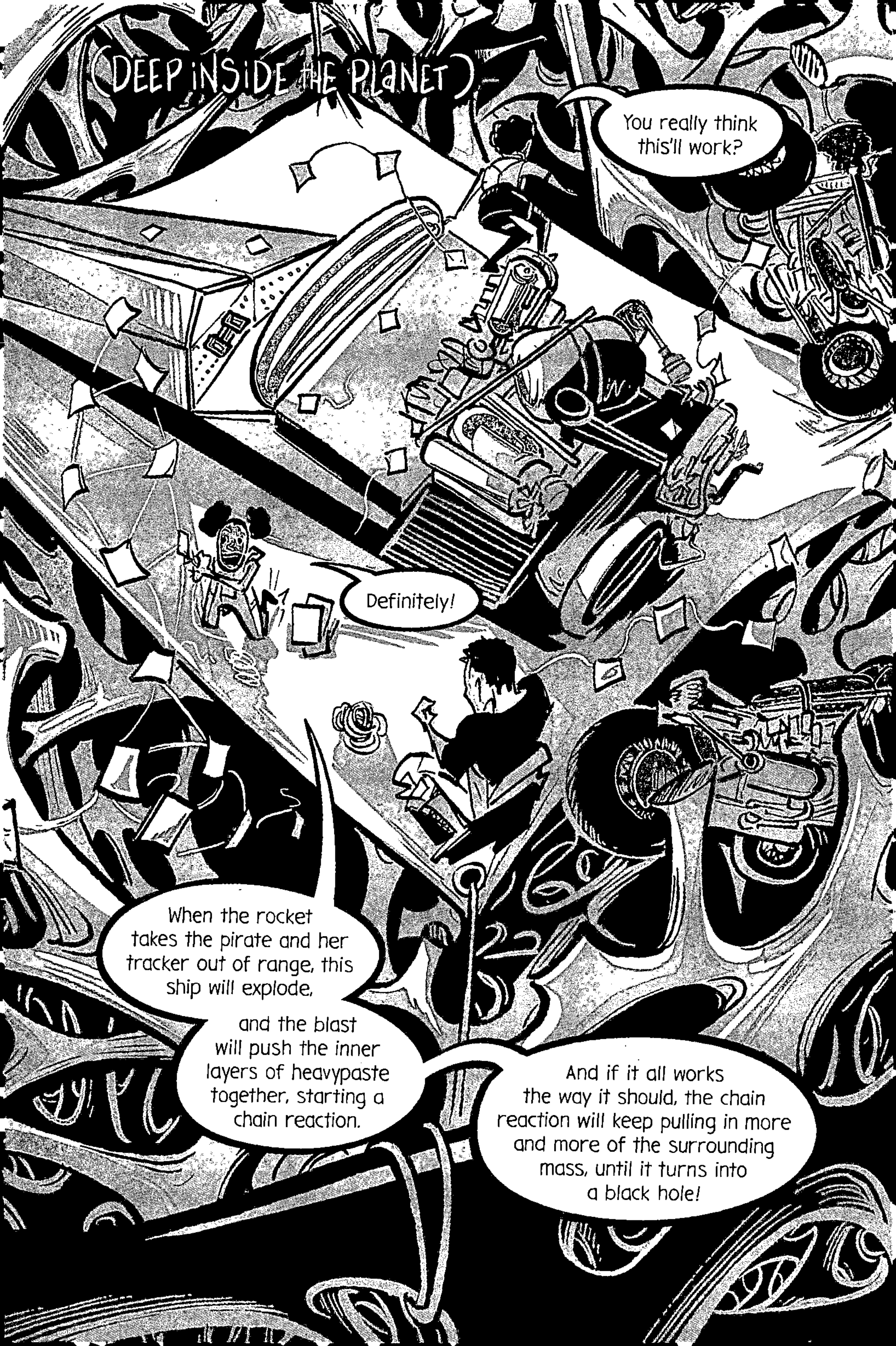
(DEEP INSIDE THE PLANET)
You really think this'll work?
Definitely!
When the rocket takes the pirate and her tracker out of range, this ship will explode,
and the blast will push the inner layers of heavypaste together, starting a chain reaction.
And if it all works the way it should, the chain reaction will keep pulling in more and more of the surrounding mass, until it turns into a black hole!

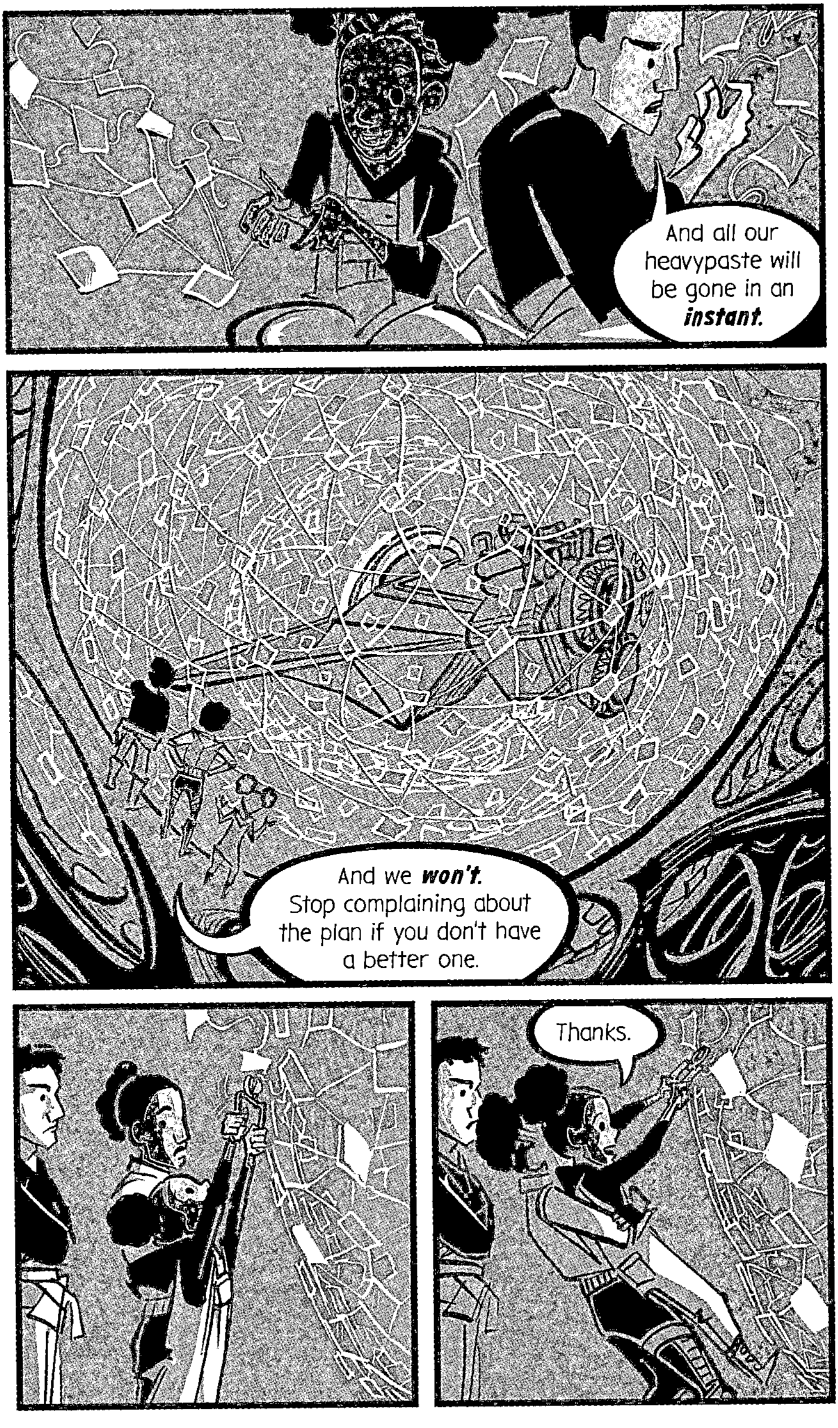
And all our heavypaste will be gone in an ***instant.***
And we ***won't.*** Stop complaining about the plan if you don't have a better one.
Thanks.

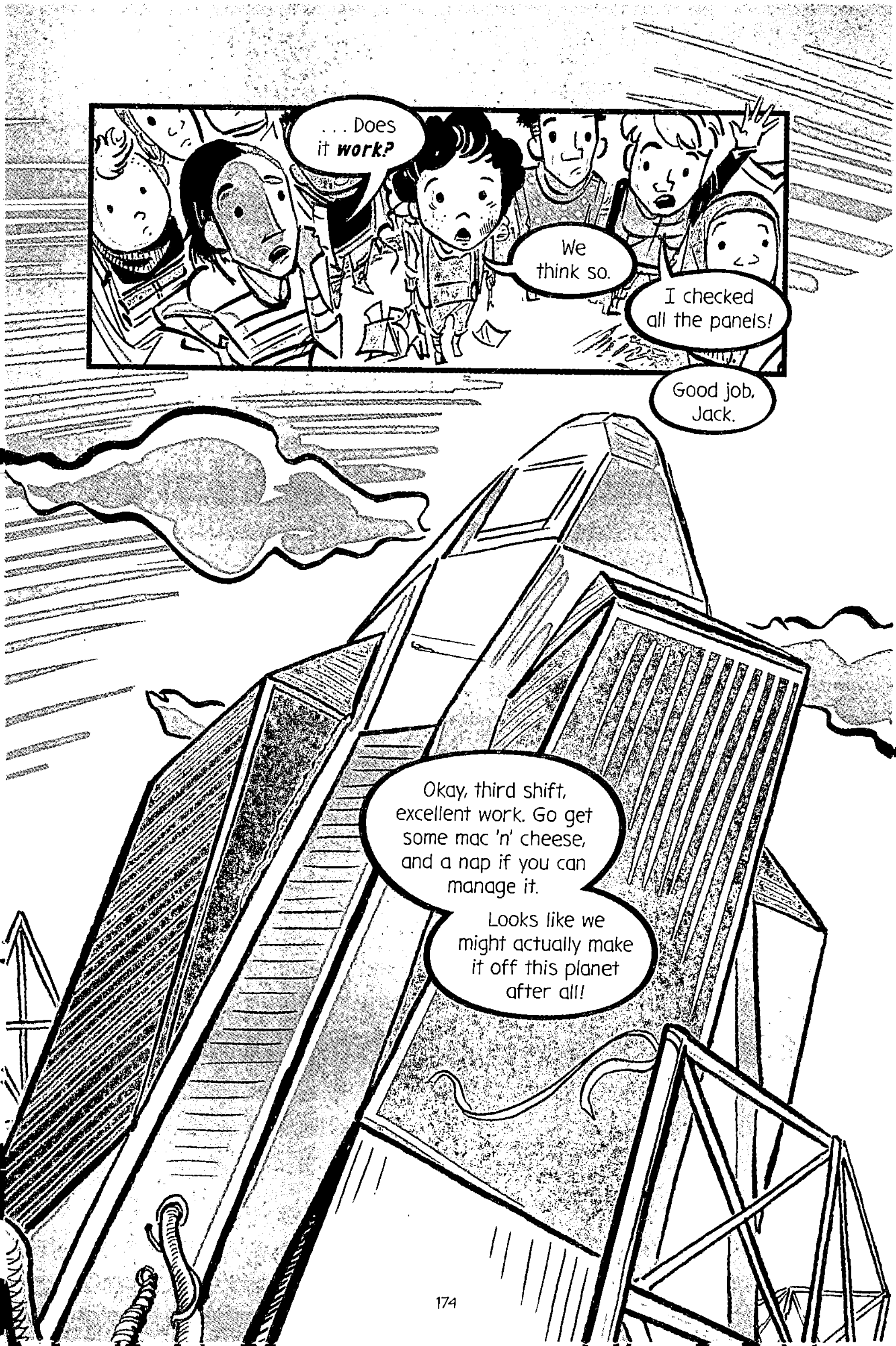
. . . Does it work?
We think so.
I checked all the panels!
Good job, Jack.
Okay, third shift, excellent work. Go get some mac 'n' cheese, and a nap if you can manage it.
Looks like we might actually make it off this planet after all!

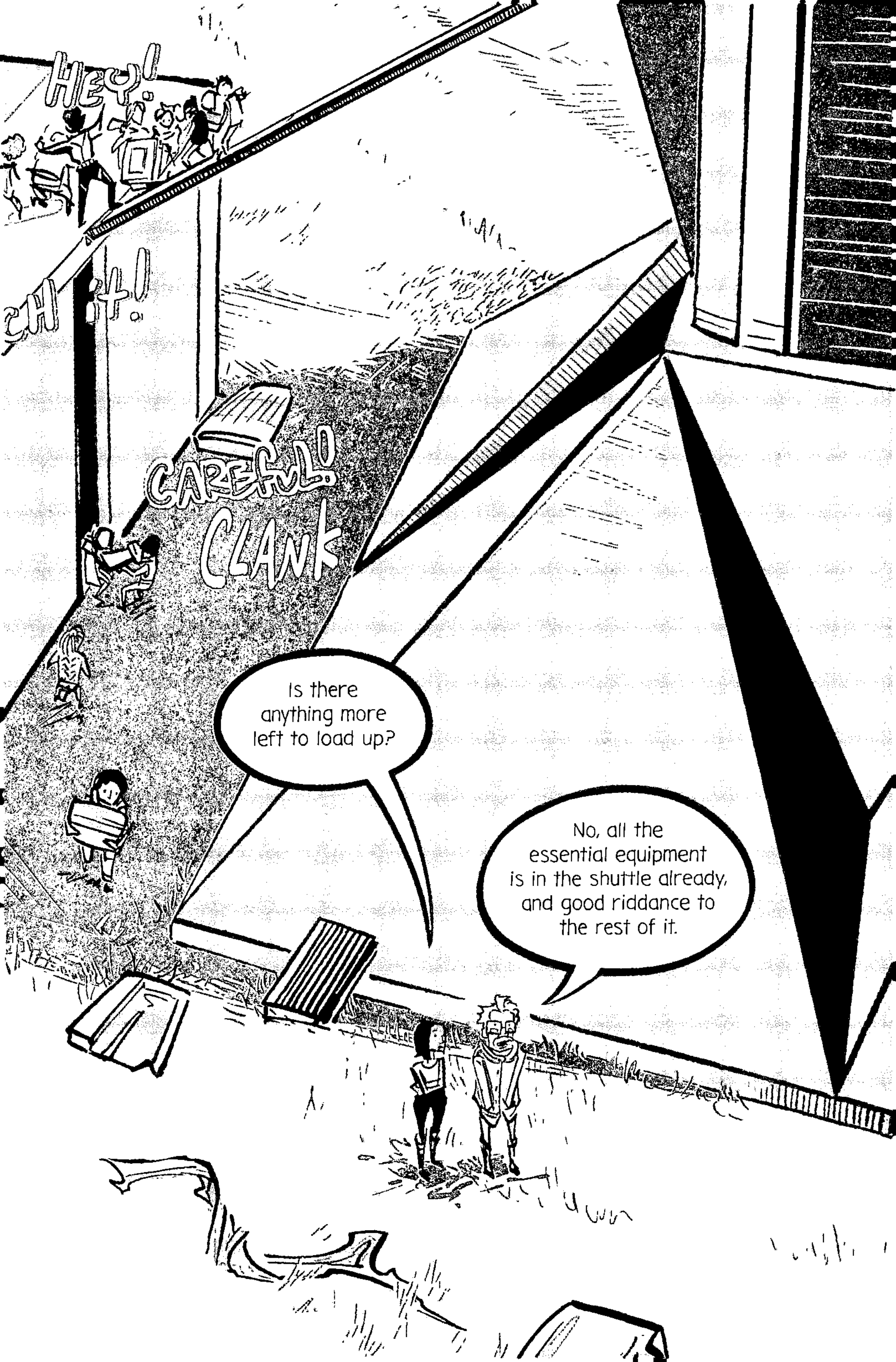
HEY!
CAREFUL!
CLANK
Is there anything more left to load up?
No, all the essential equipment is in the shuttle already, and good riddance to the rest of it.

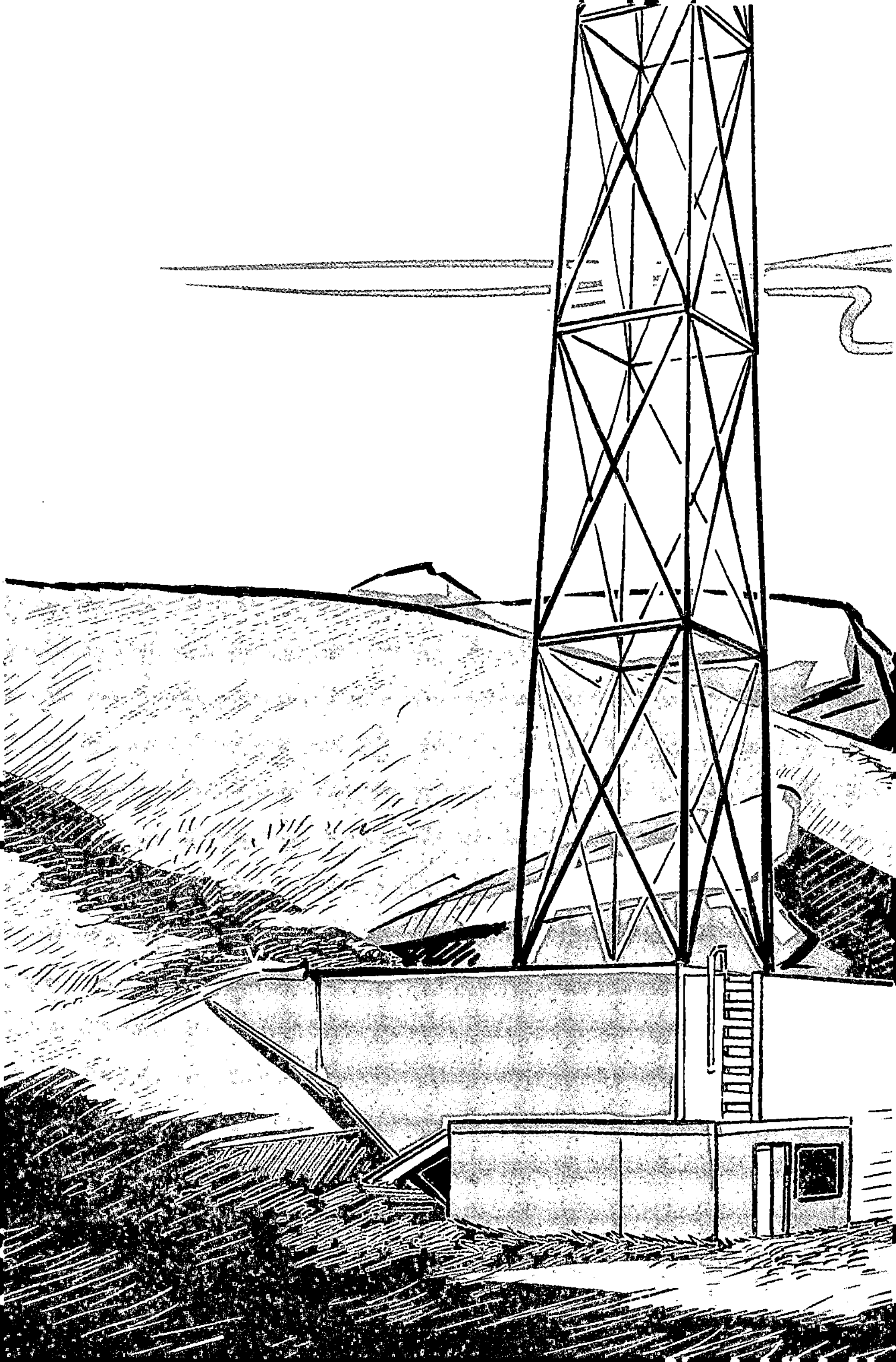

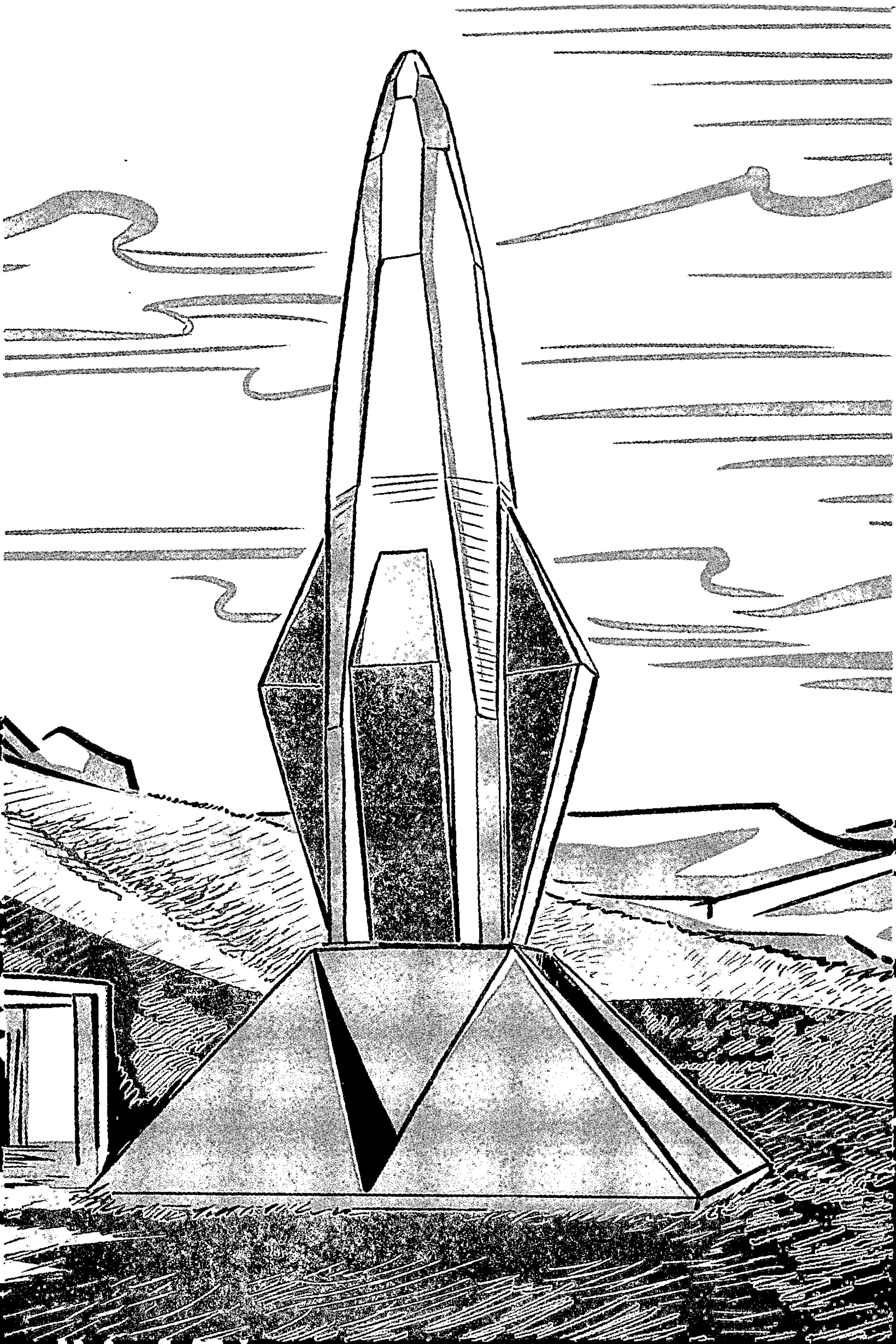

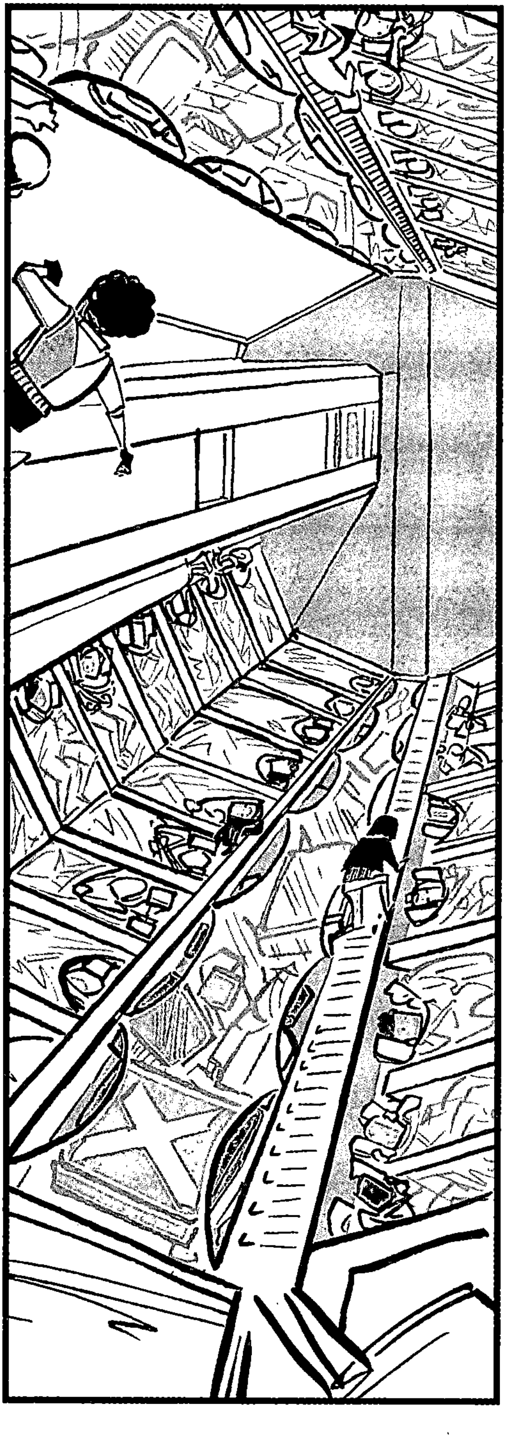

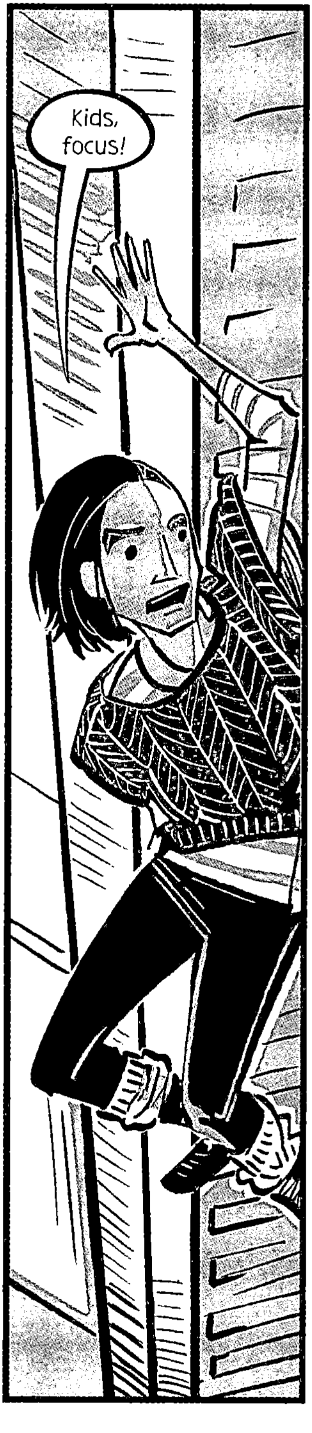
Kids, focus!

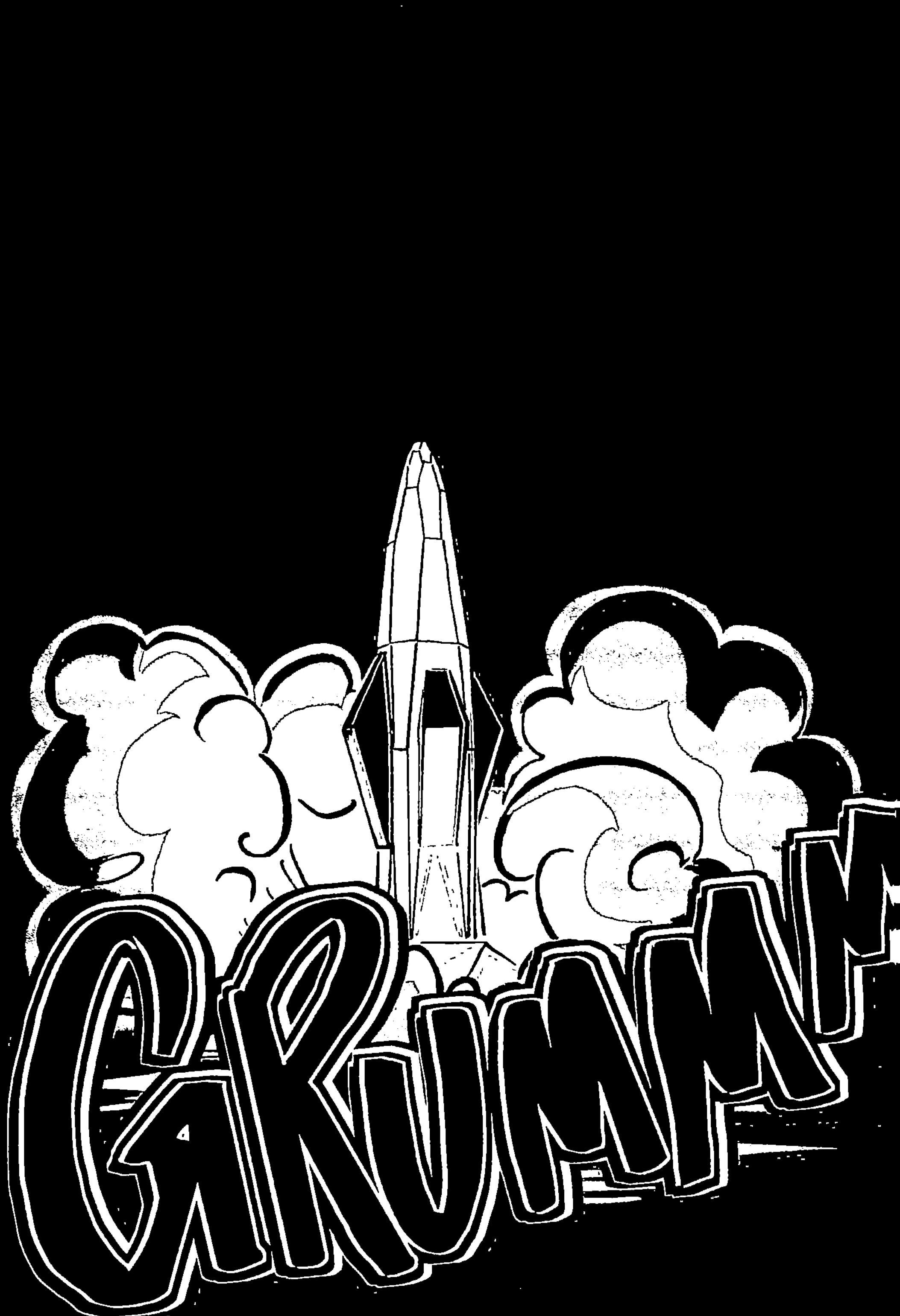
GRUMMM

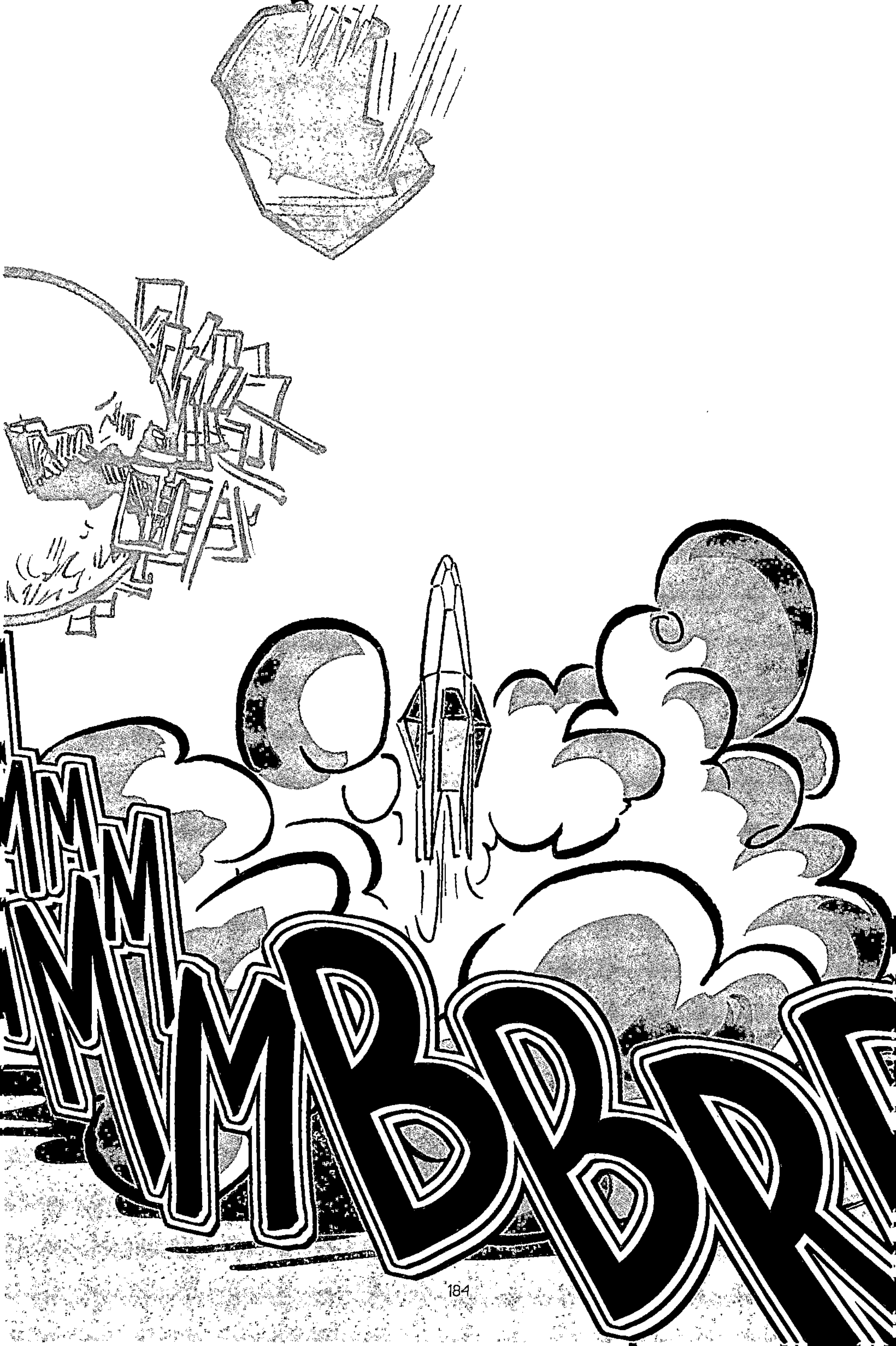

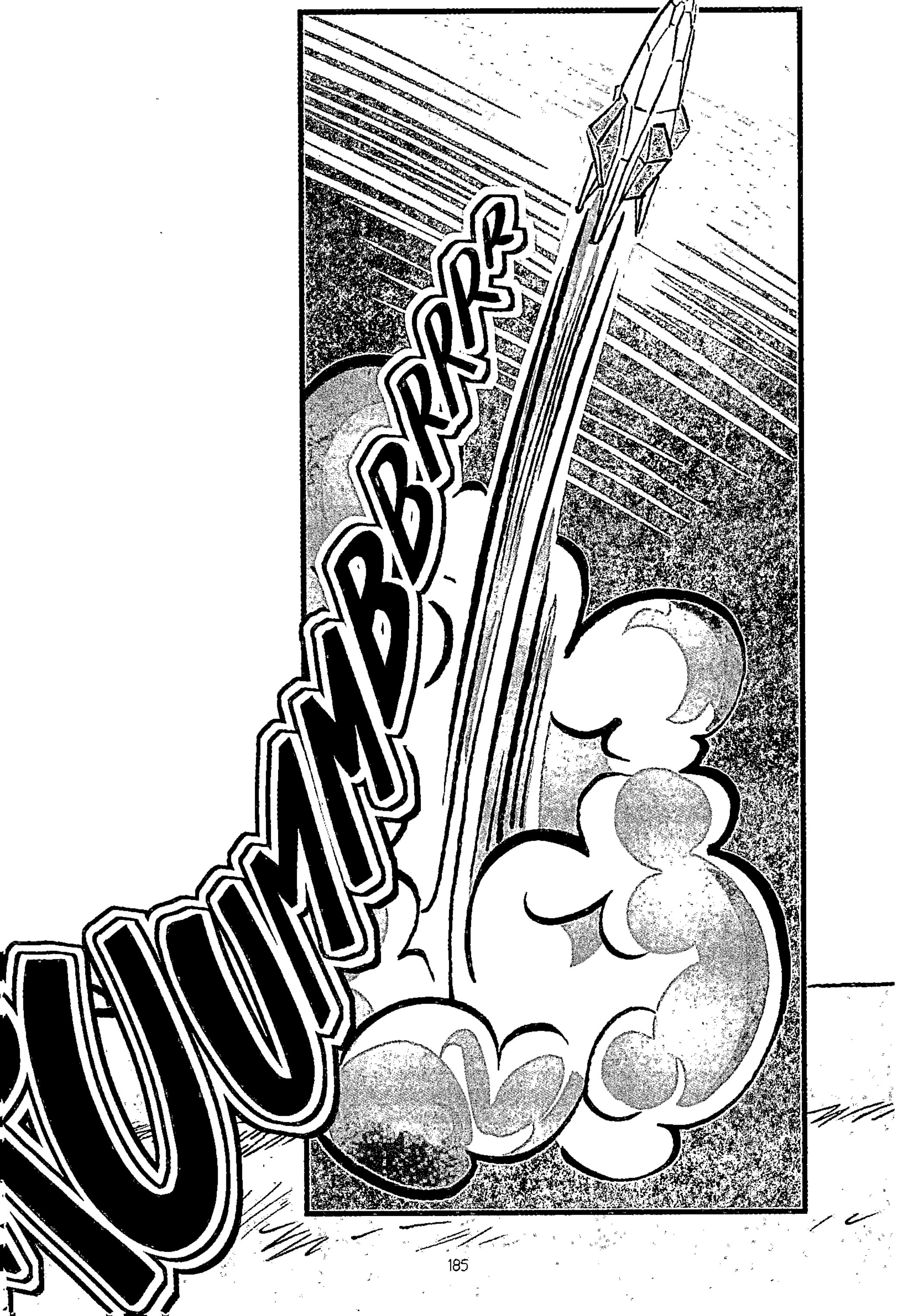

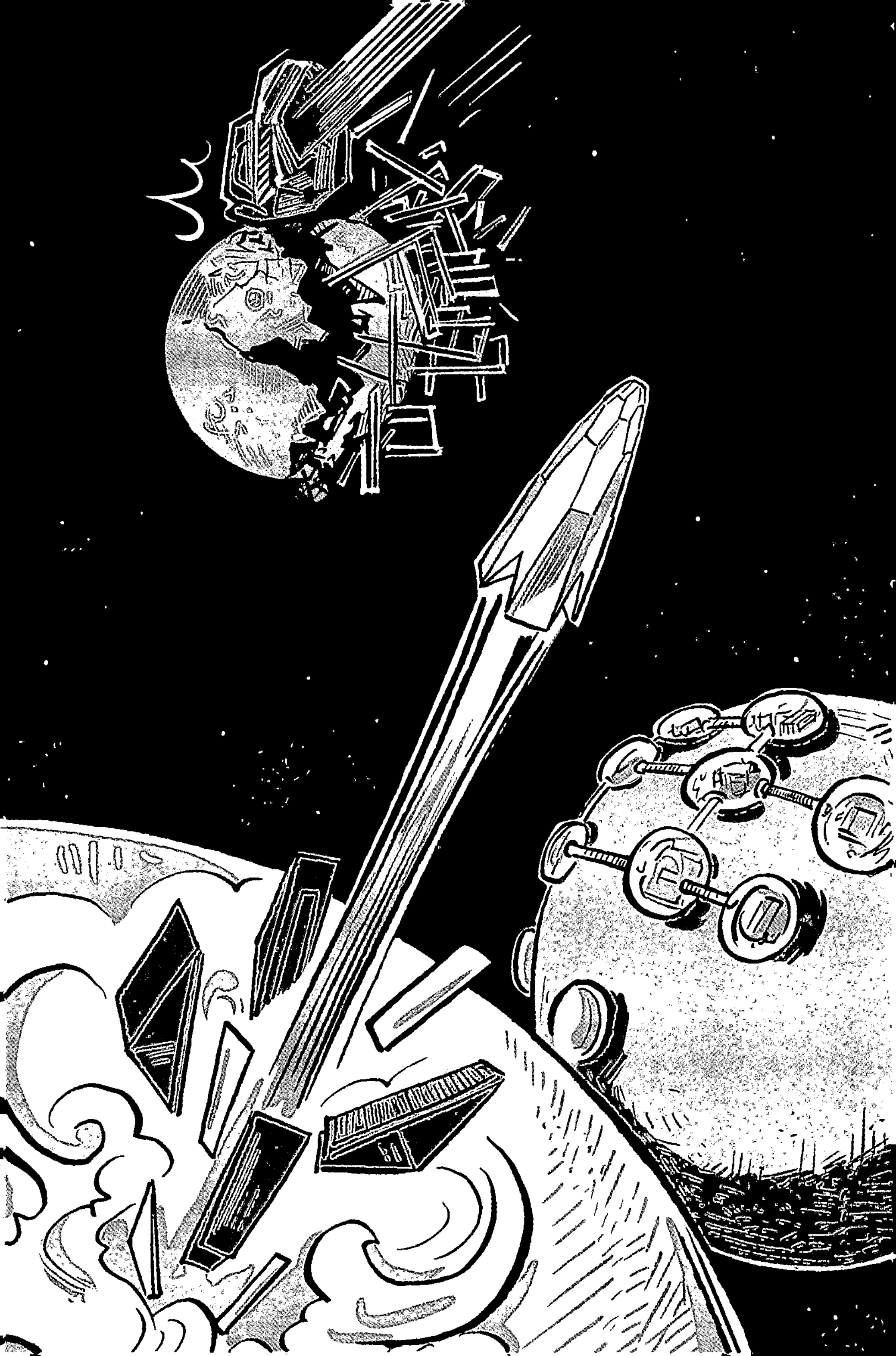

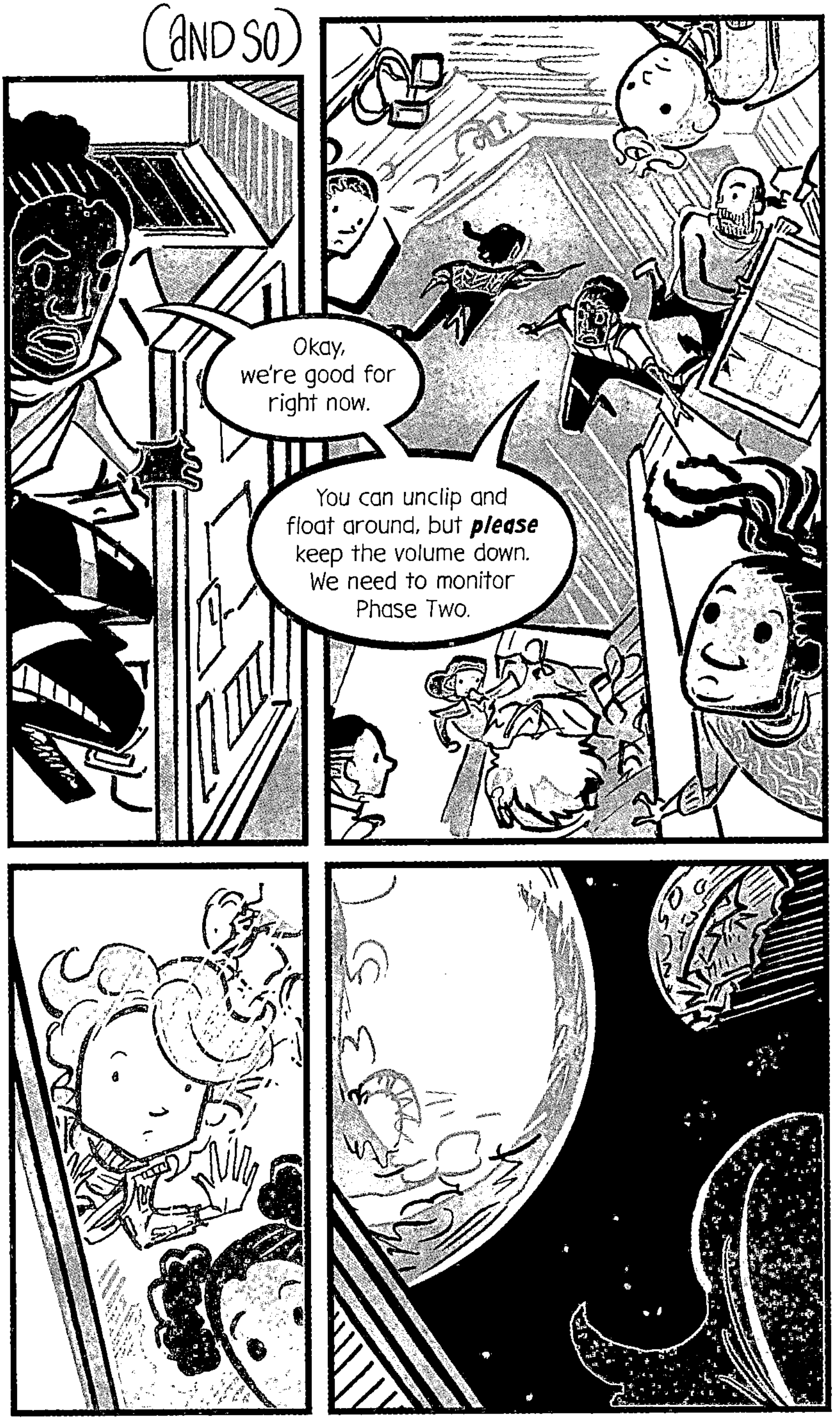
(AND SO)
Okay, we're good for right now.
You can unclip and float around, but ***please*** keep the volume down. We need to monitor Phase Two.

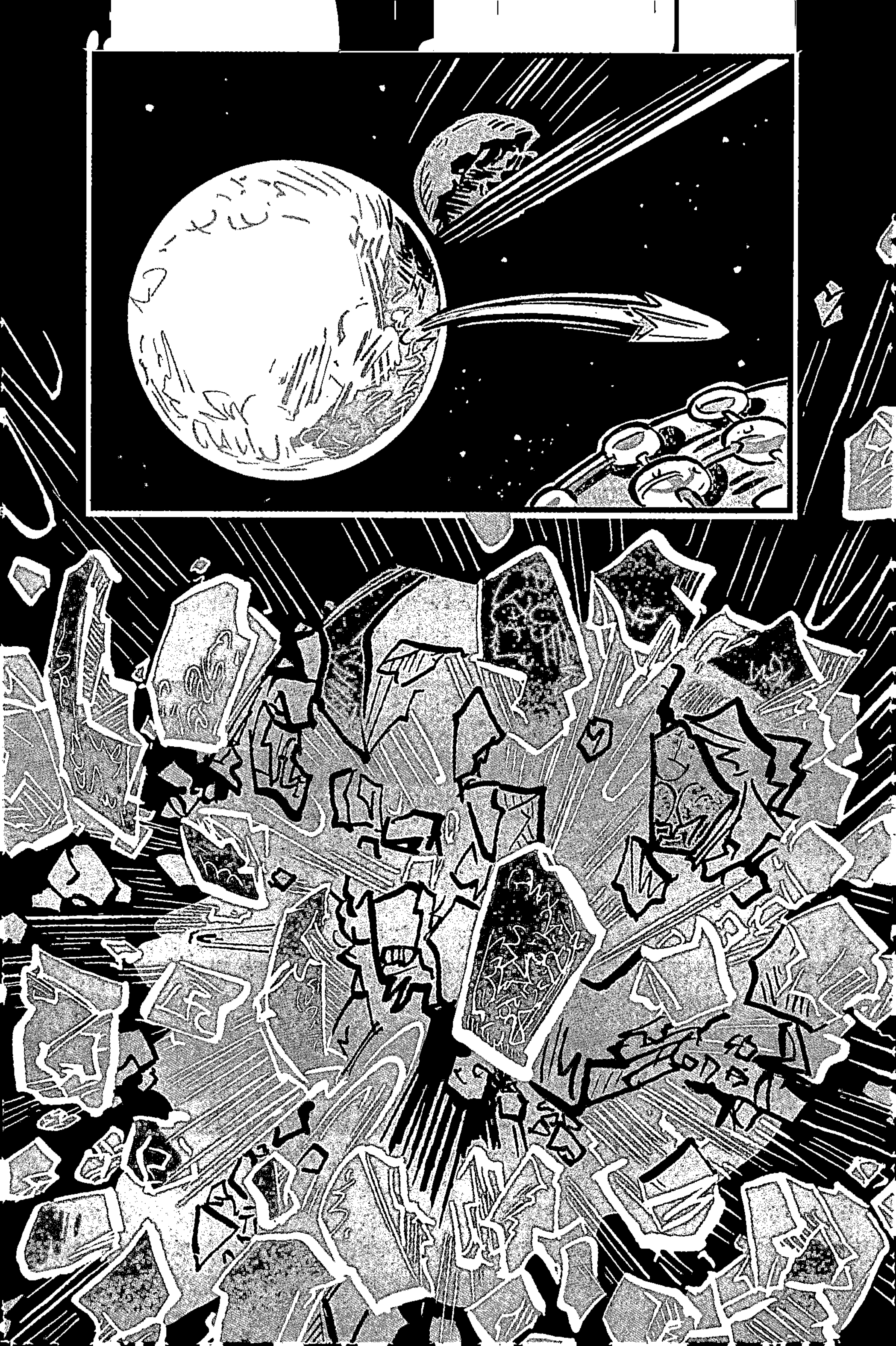

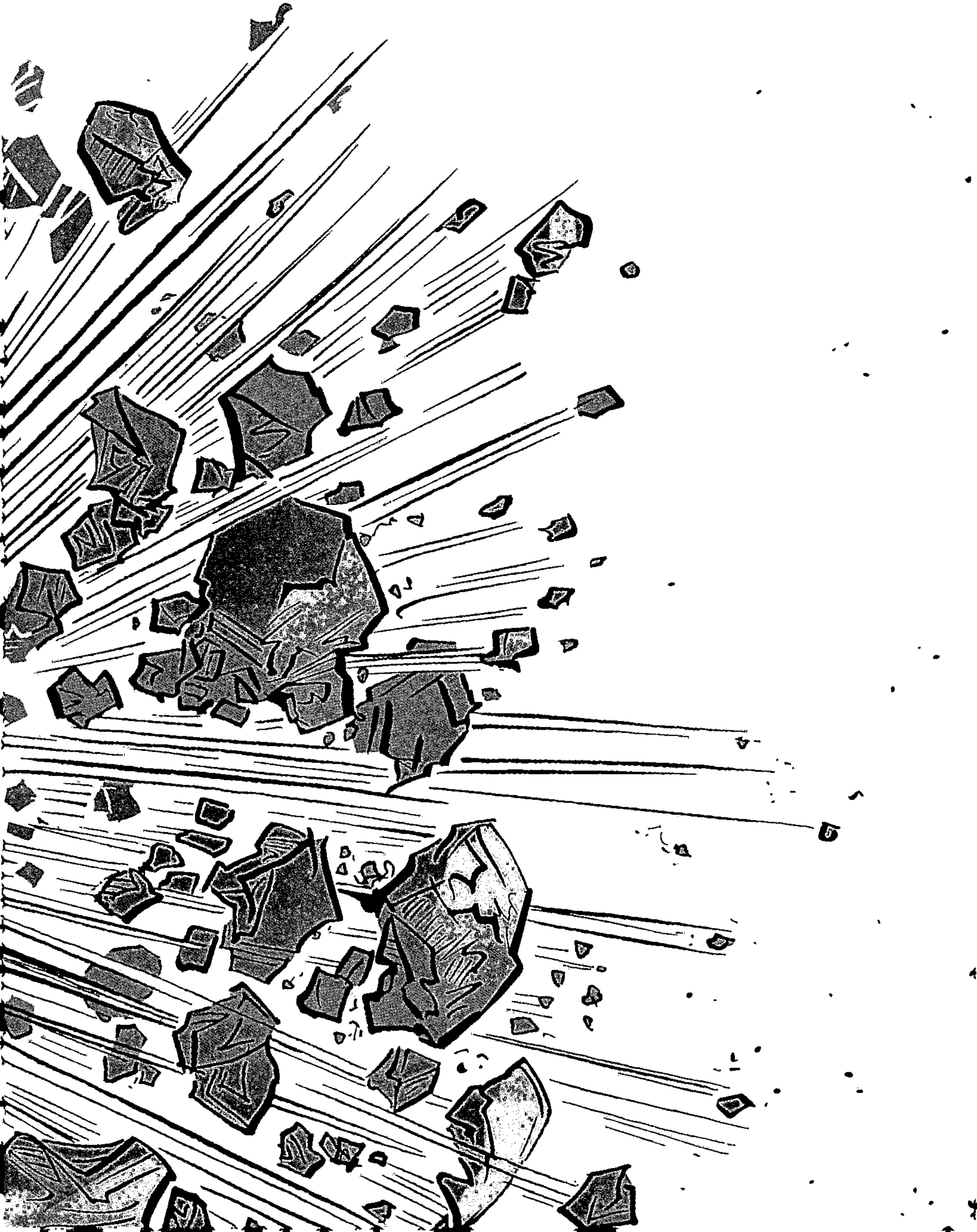

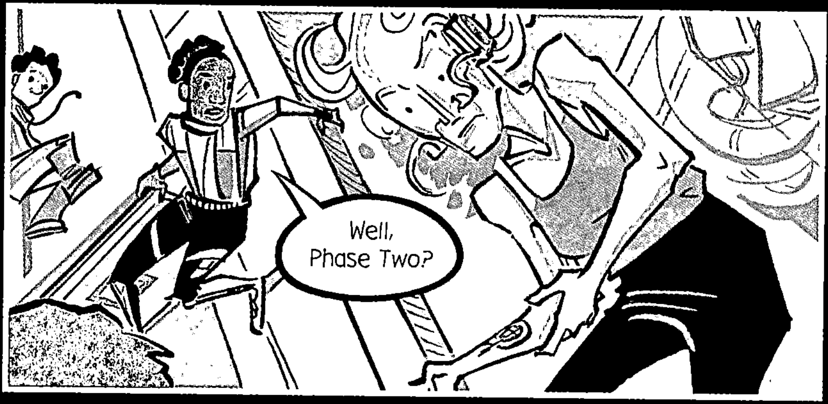
Well,
Phase Two?

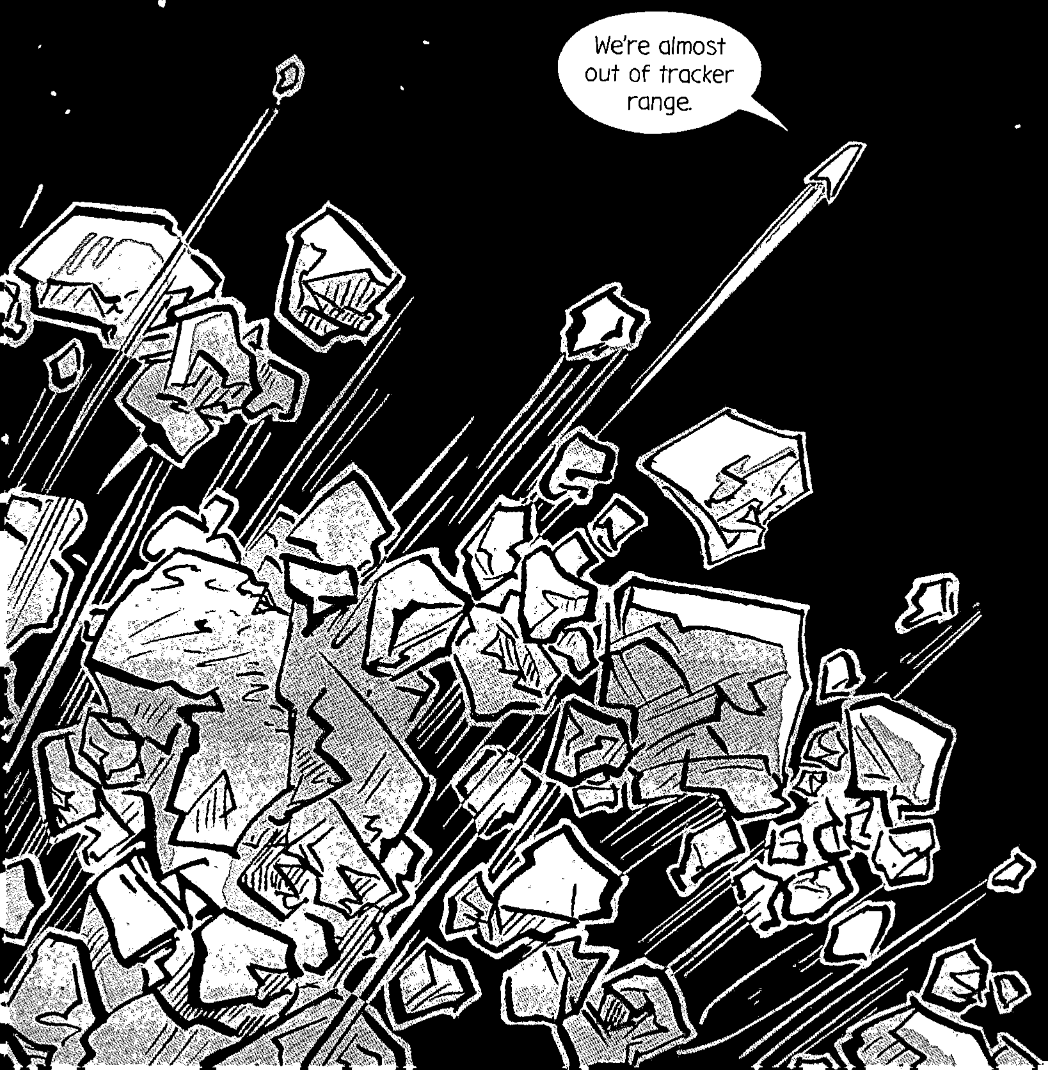
We're almost
out of tracker
range.

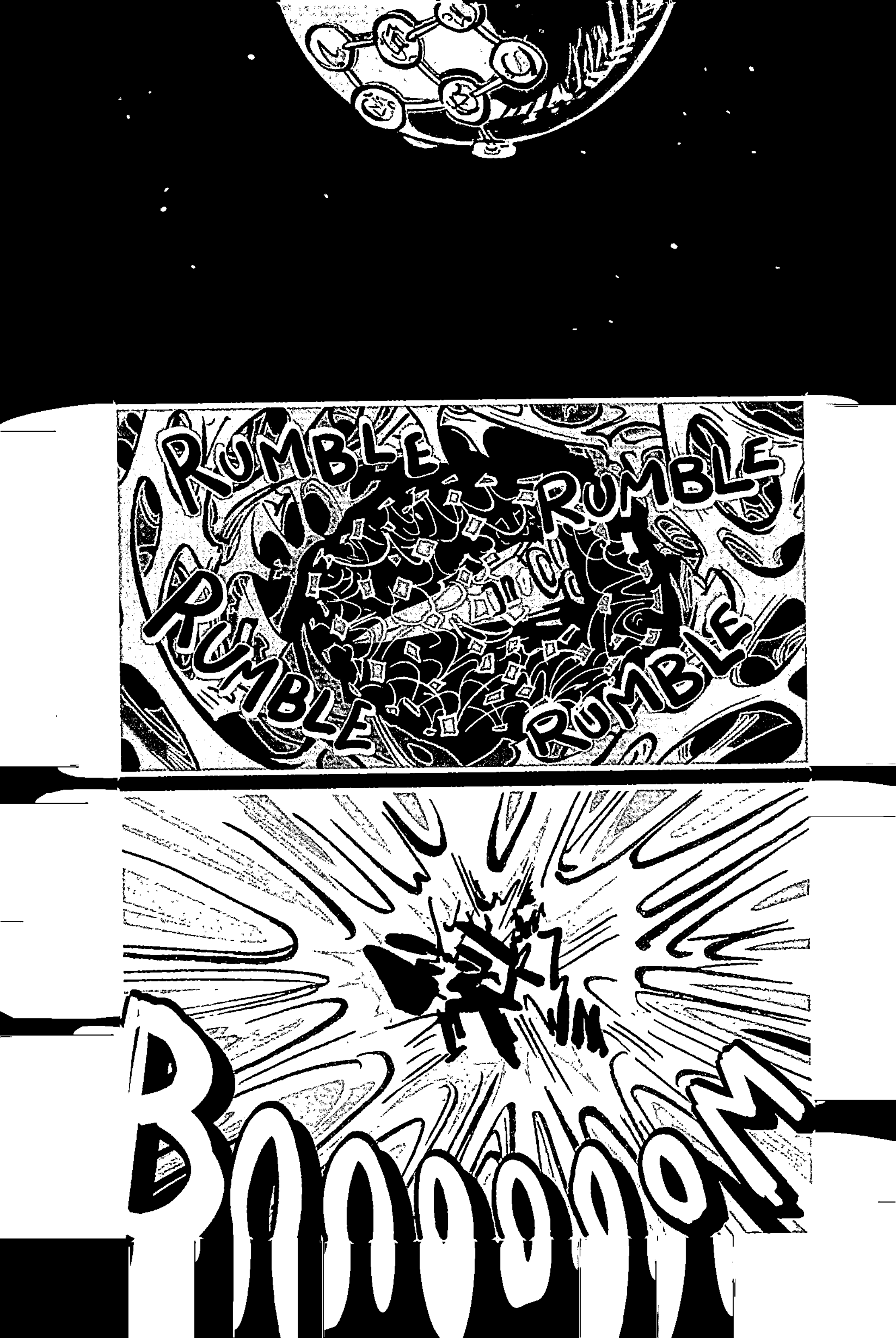
RUMBLE
RUMBLE
RUMBLE
RUMBLE
BOOOOOOM

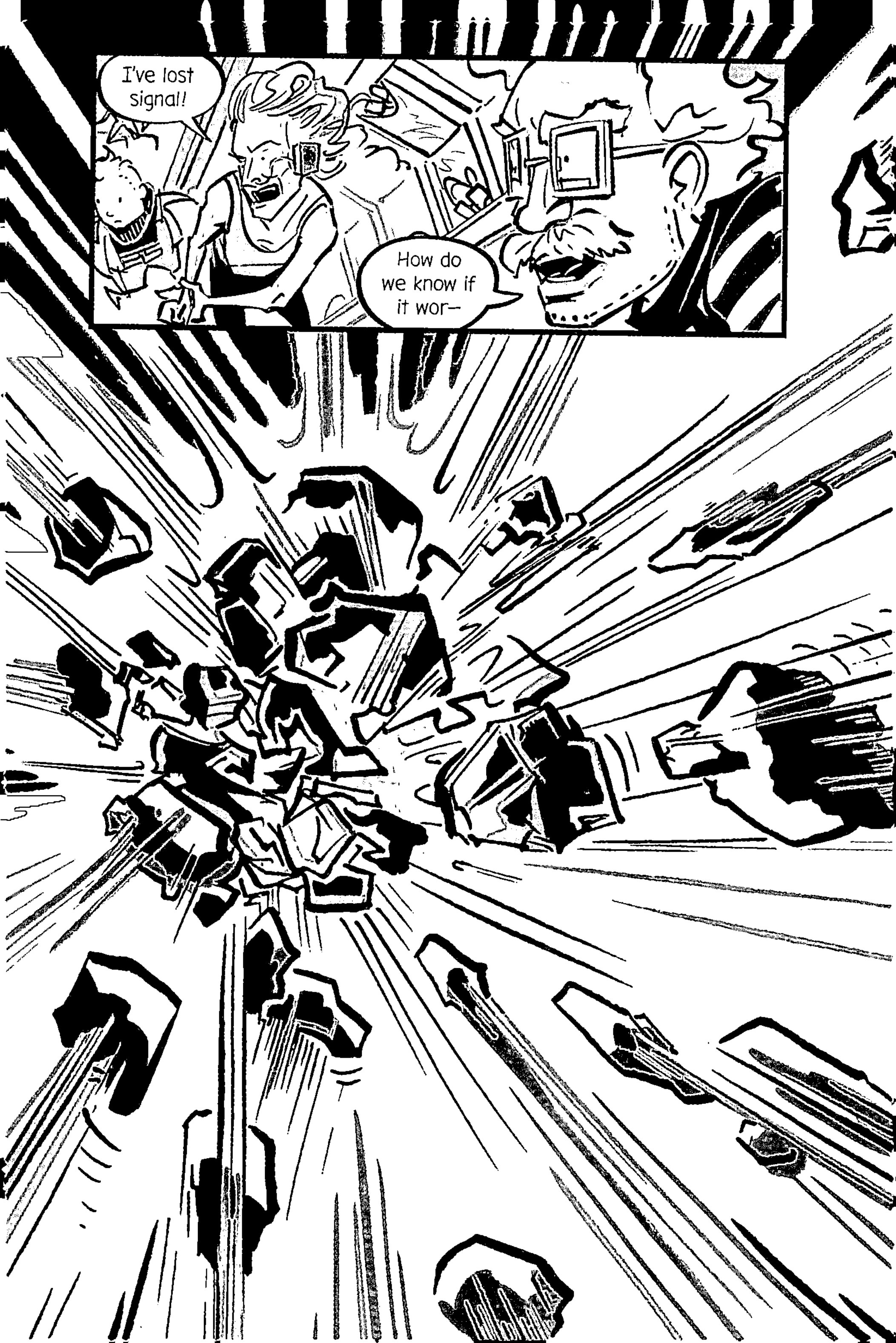
I've lost signal!
How do we know if it wor—

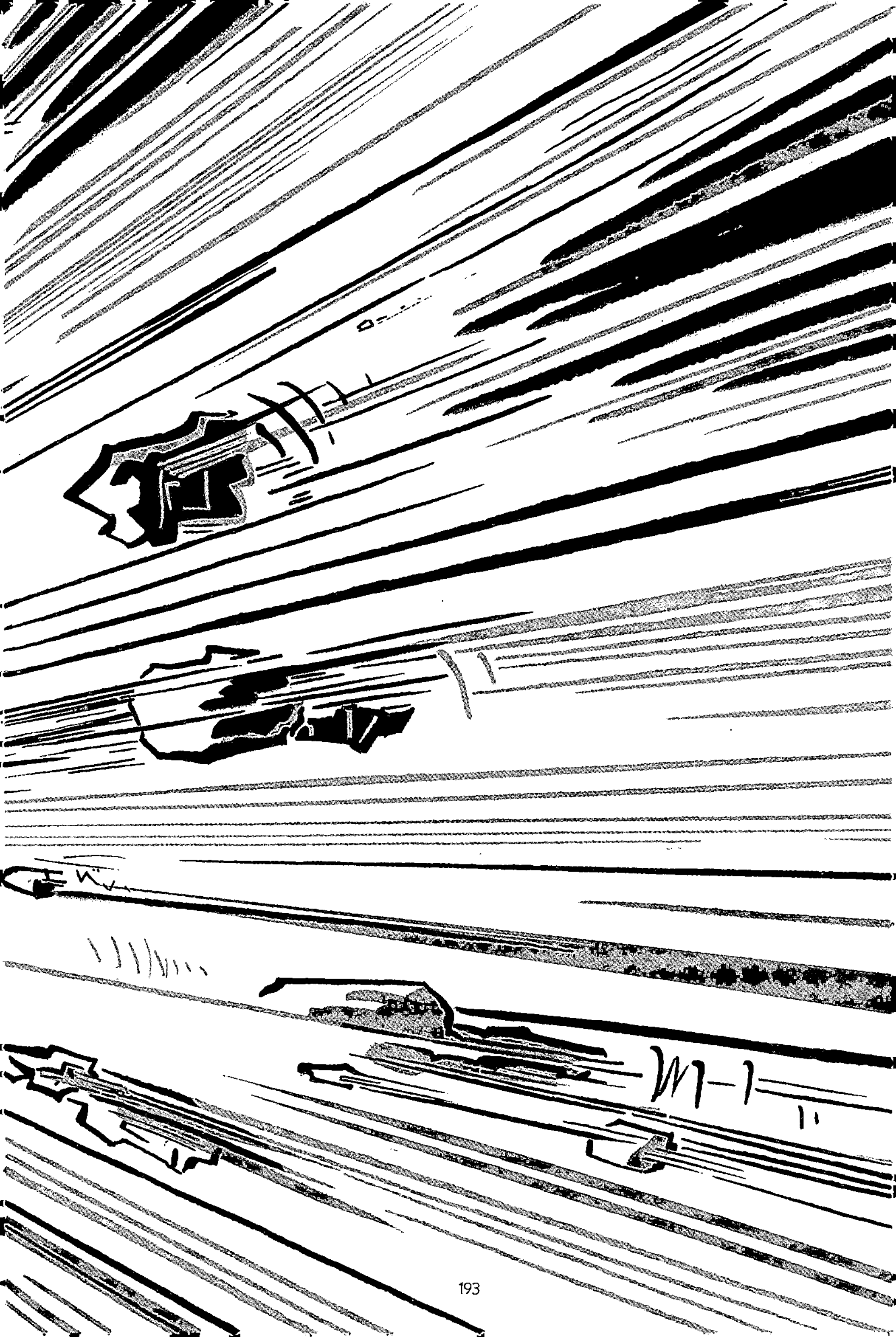

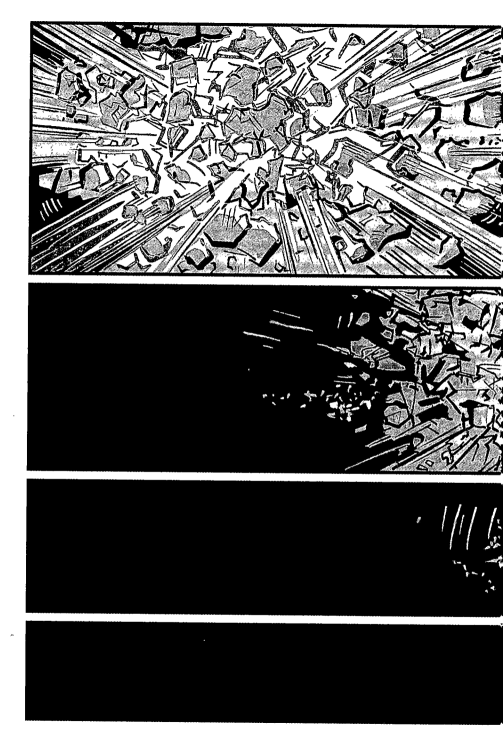

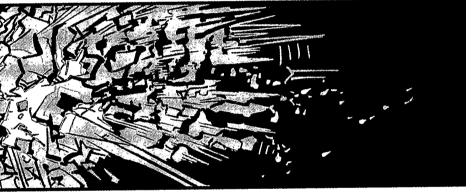

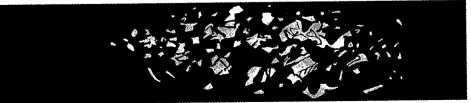

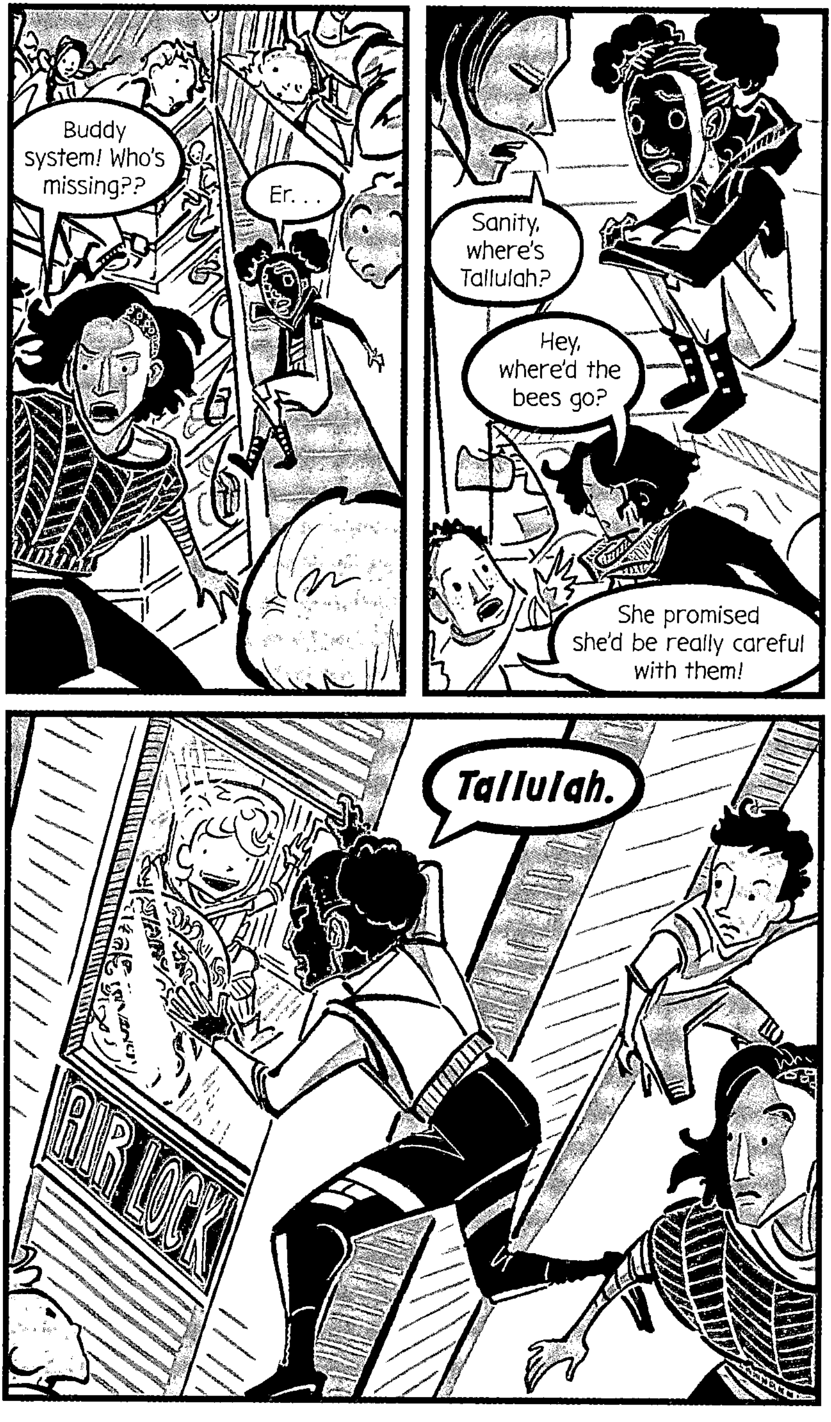
Buddy system! Who's missing??
Er. . .
Sanity, where's Tallulah?
Hey, where'd the bees go?
She promised she'd be really careful with them!
Tallulah.
AIR LOCK

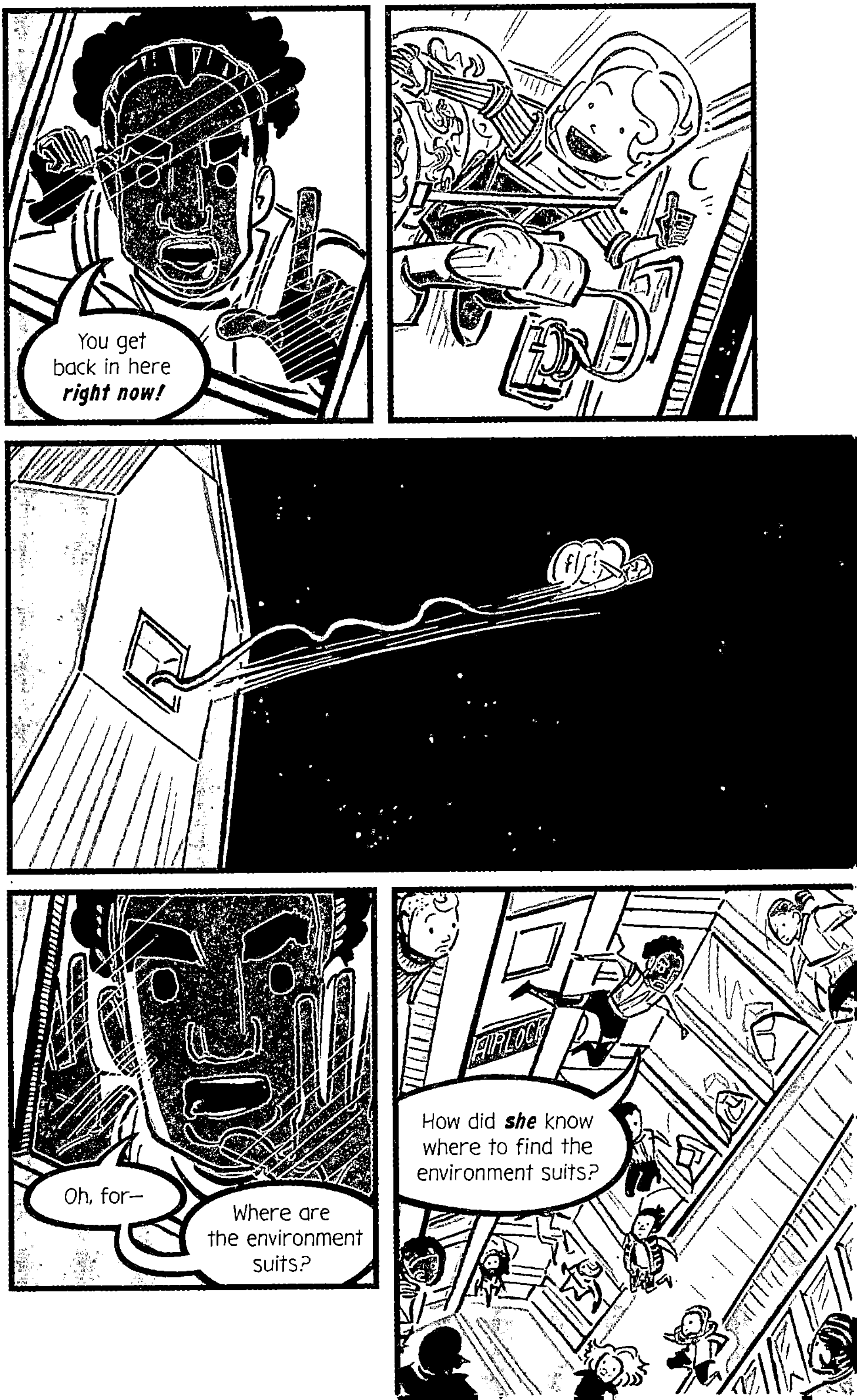
You get back in here ***right now!***
Oh, for—
Where are the environment suits?
How did ***she*** know where to find the environment suits?
AIRLOCK

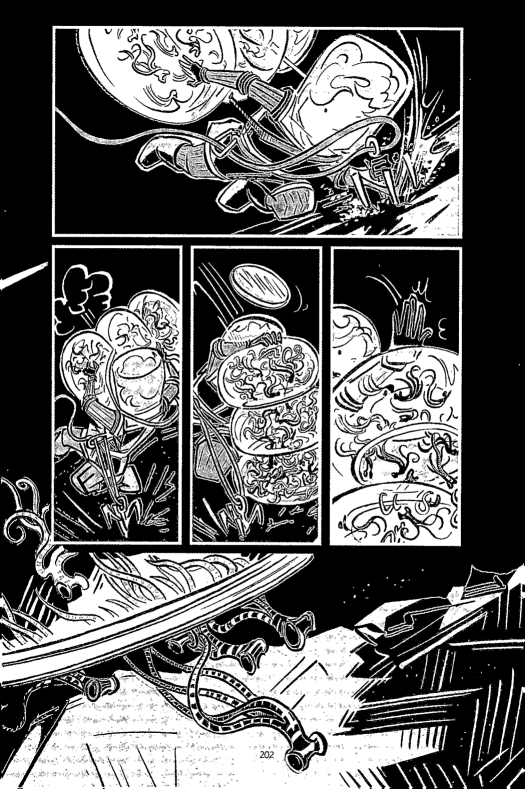

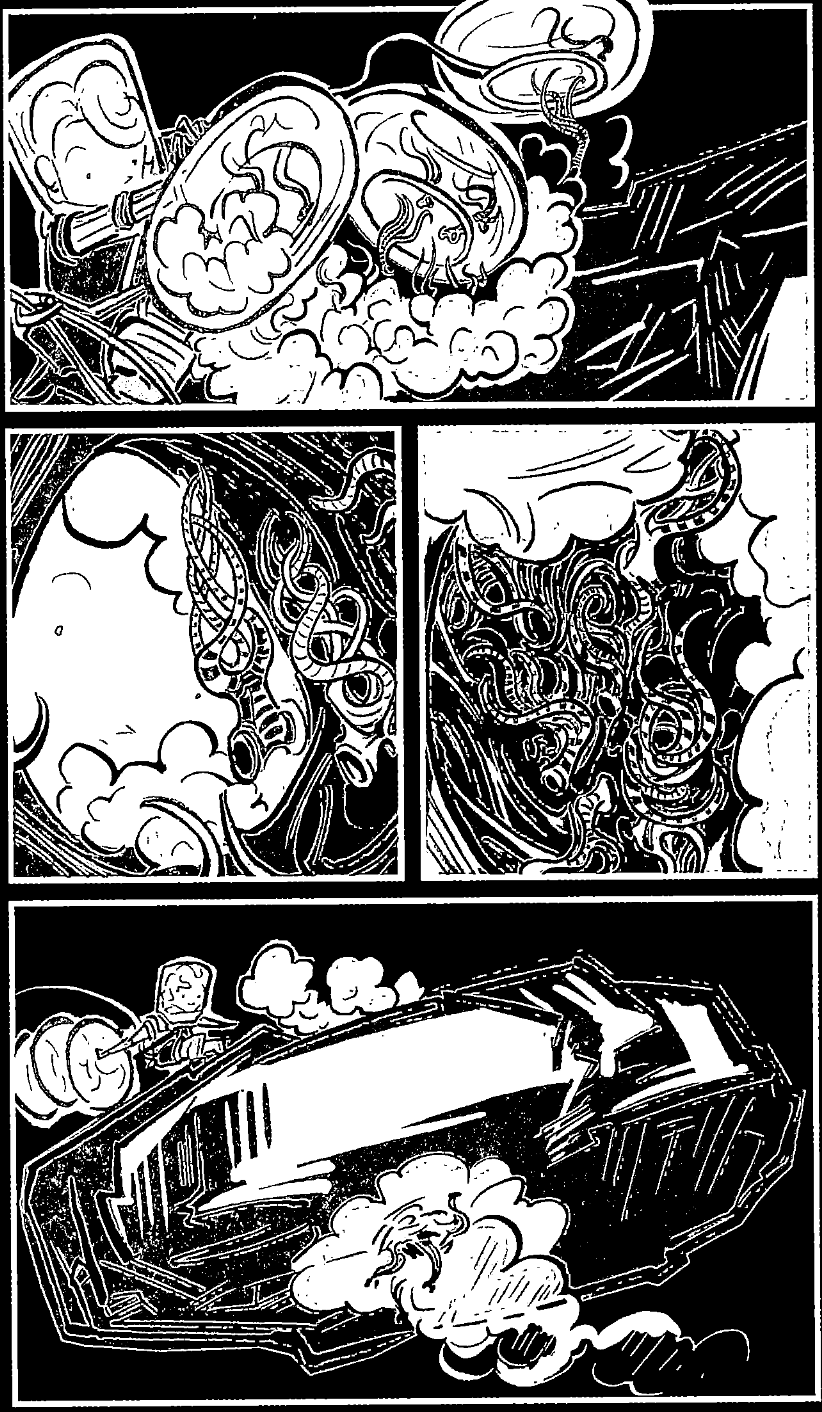

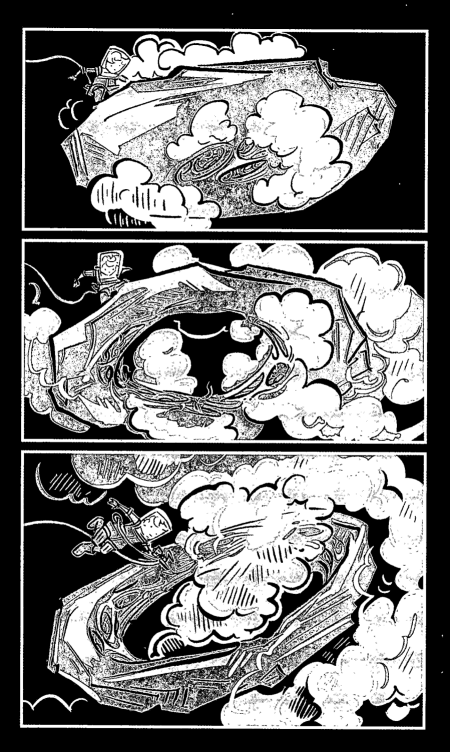

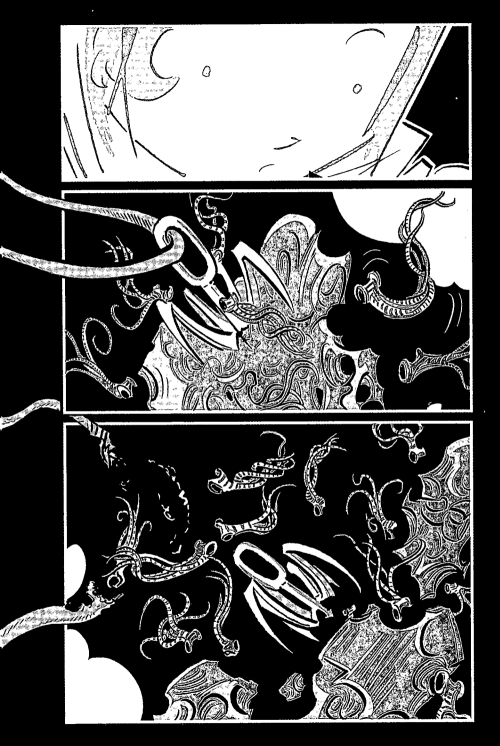

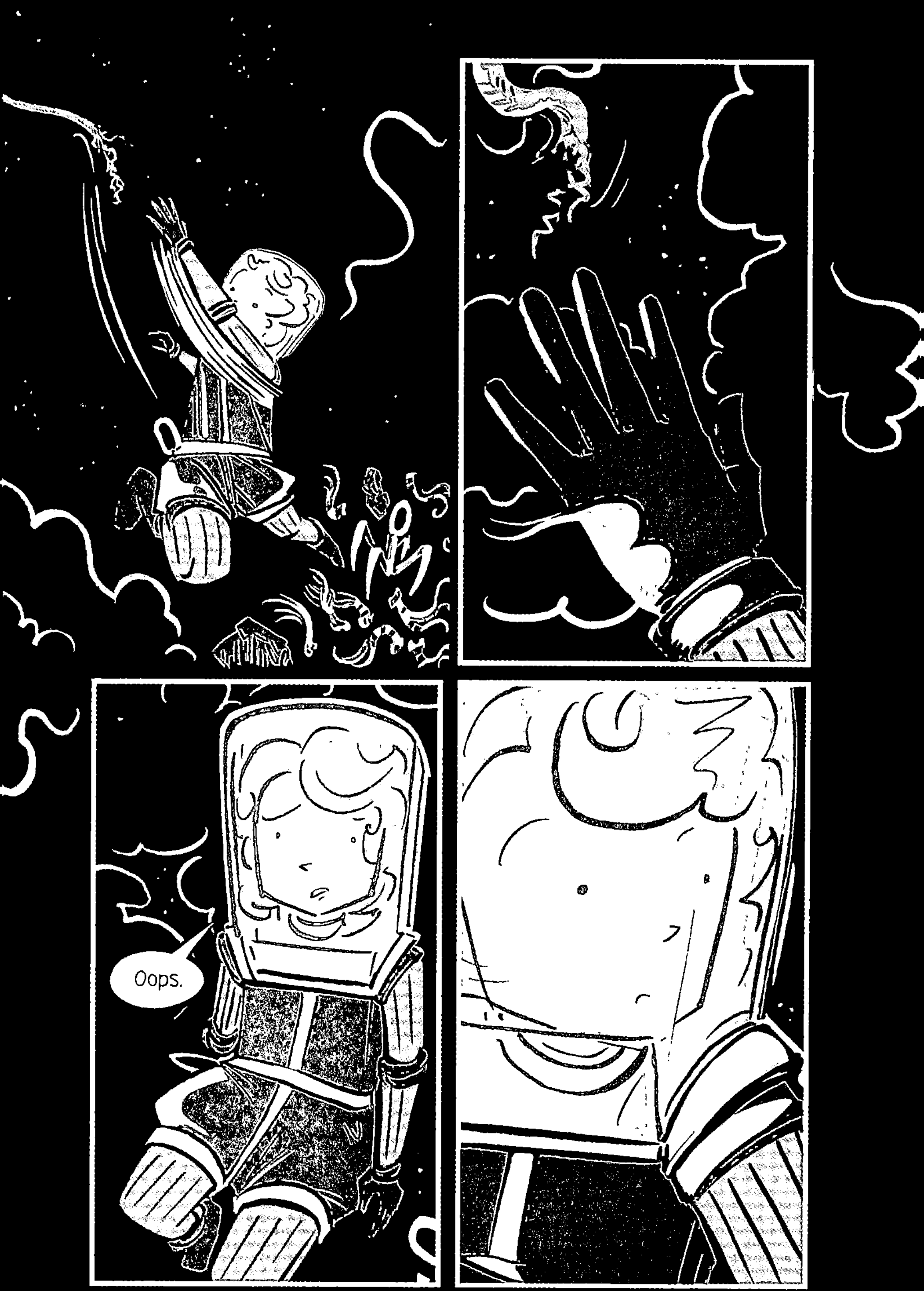
Oops.

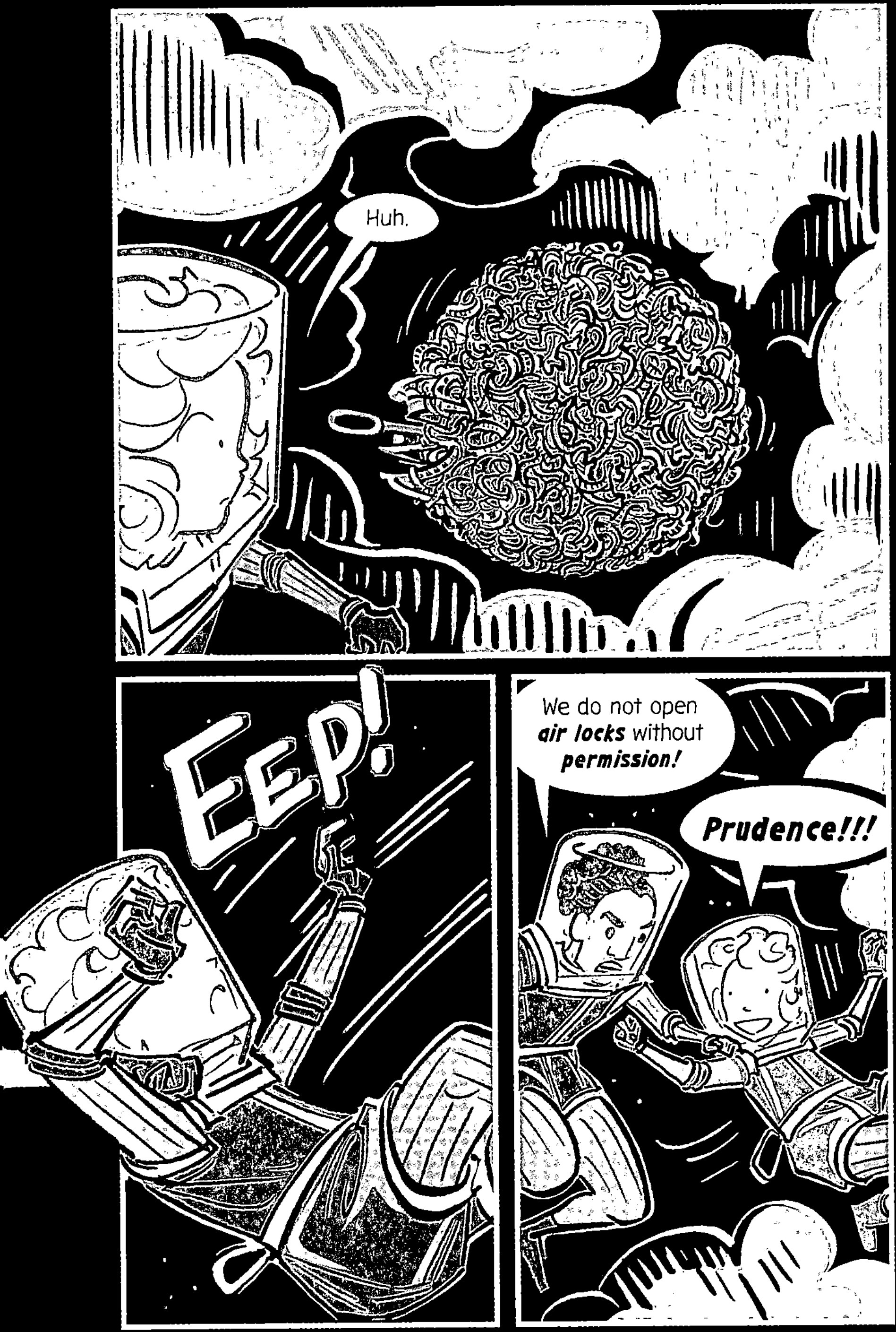
Huh.
EEP!
We do not open air locks without permission!
Prudence!!!

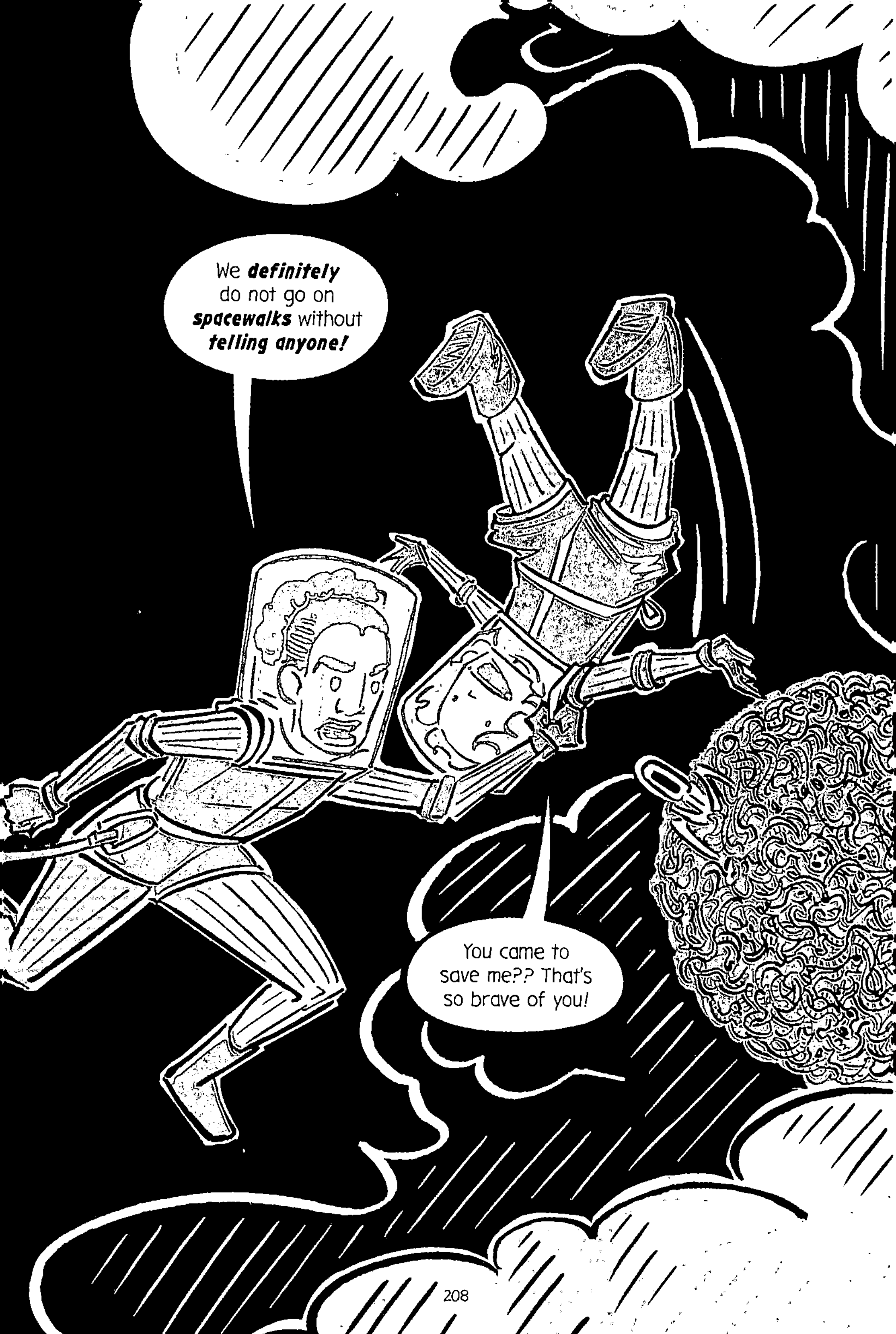
We **definitely** do not go on **spacewalks** without **telling anyone!**
You came to save me?? That's so brave of you!

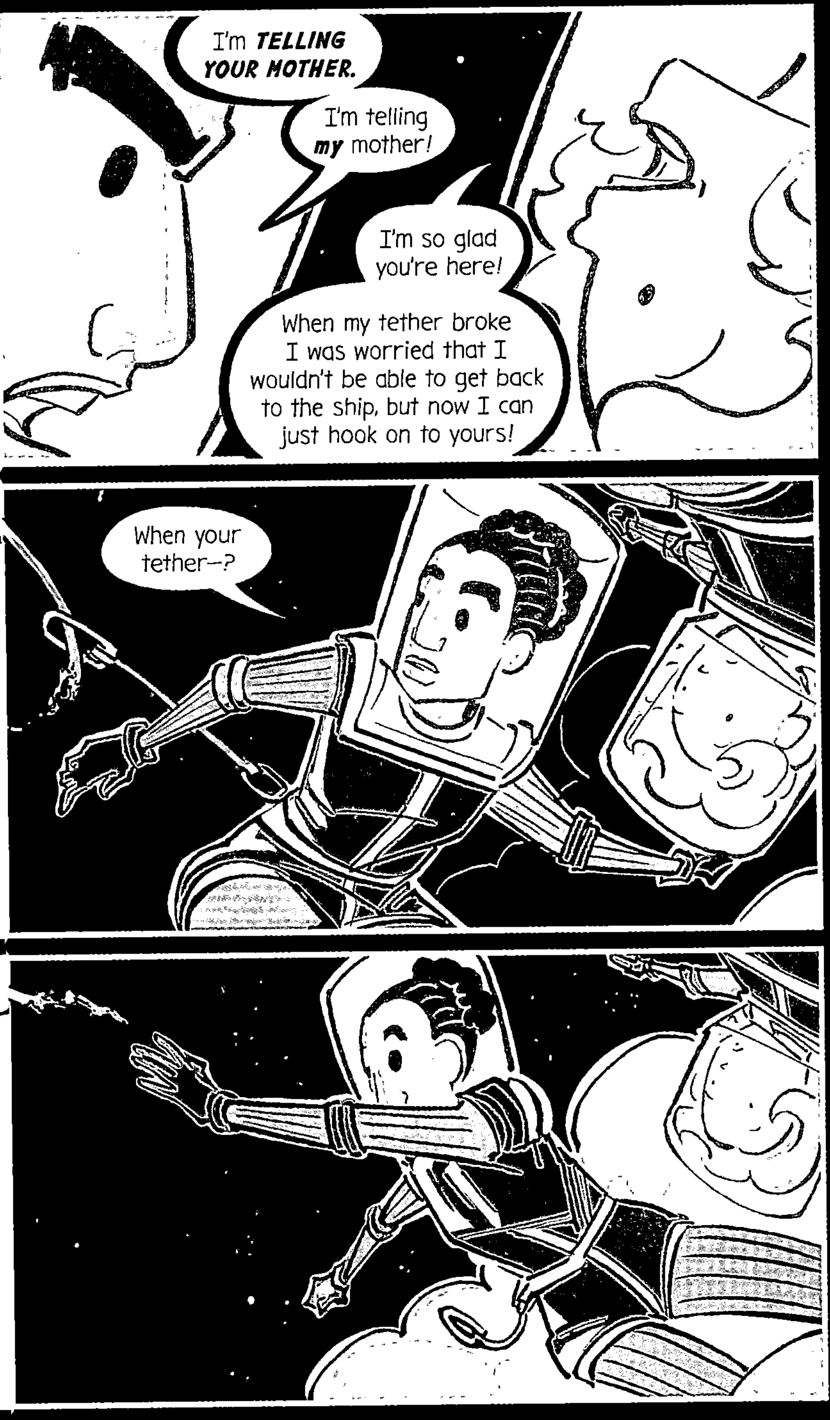
I'm **TELLING YOUR MOTHER.**
I'm telling ***my*** mother!
I'm so glad you're here!
When my tether broke I was worried that I wouldn't be able to get back to the ship, but now I can just hook on to yours!
When your tether—?

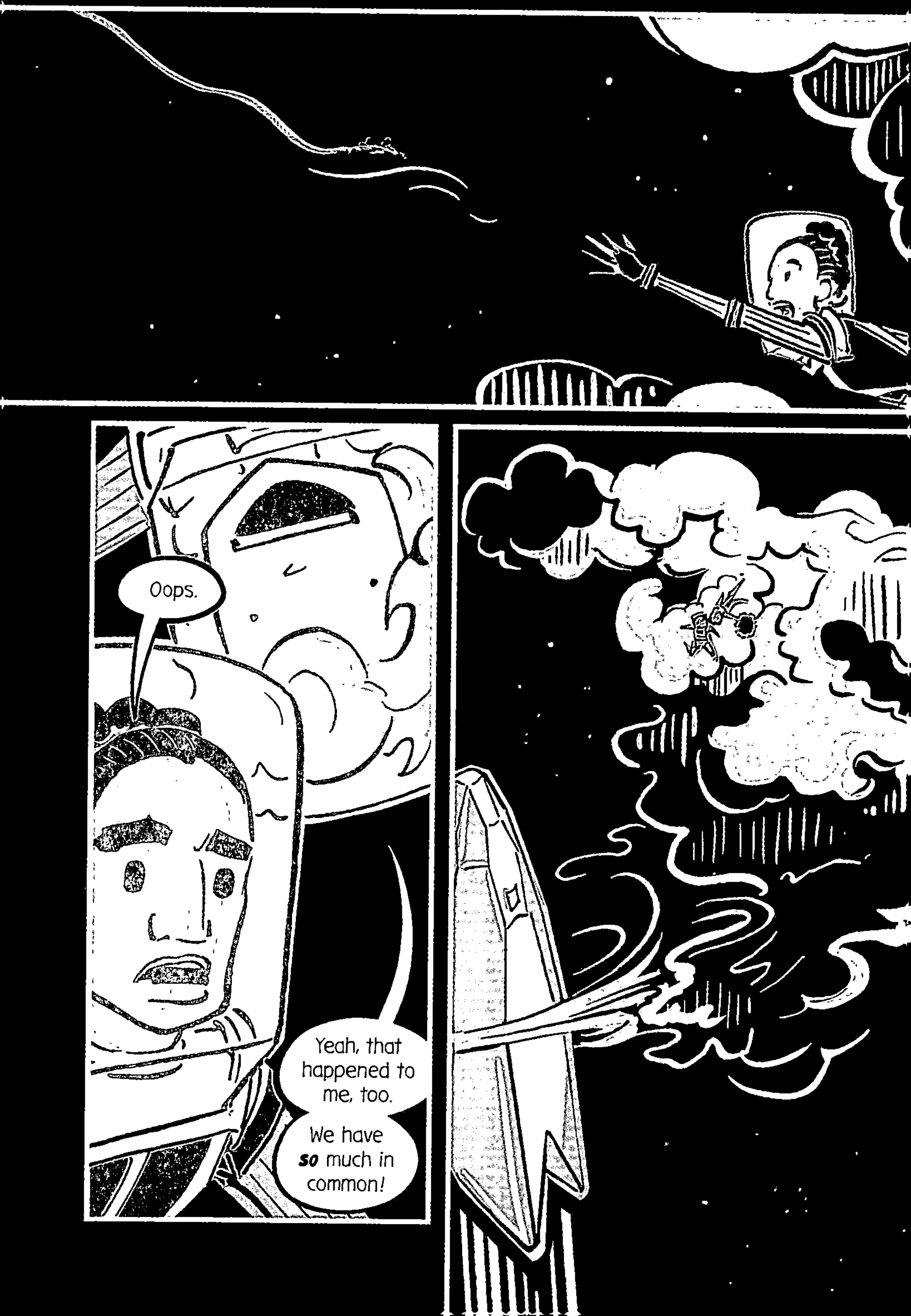
Oops.
Yeah, that happened to me, too.
We have **so** much in common!

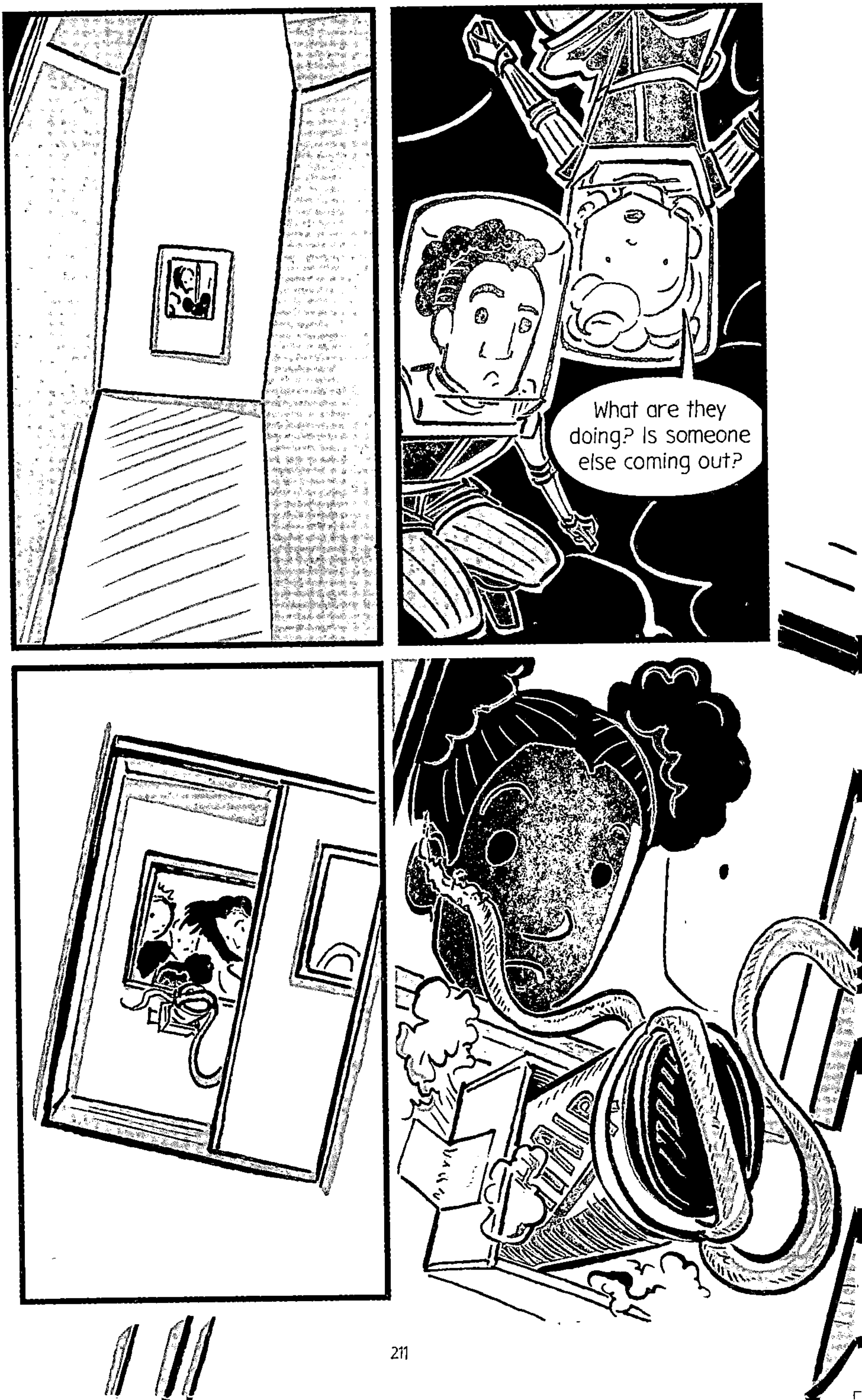
What are they doing? Is someone else coming out?

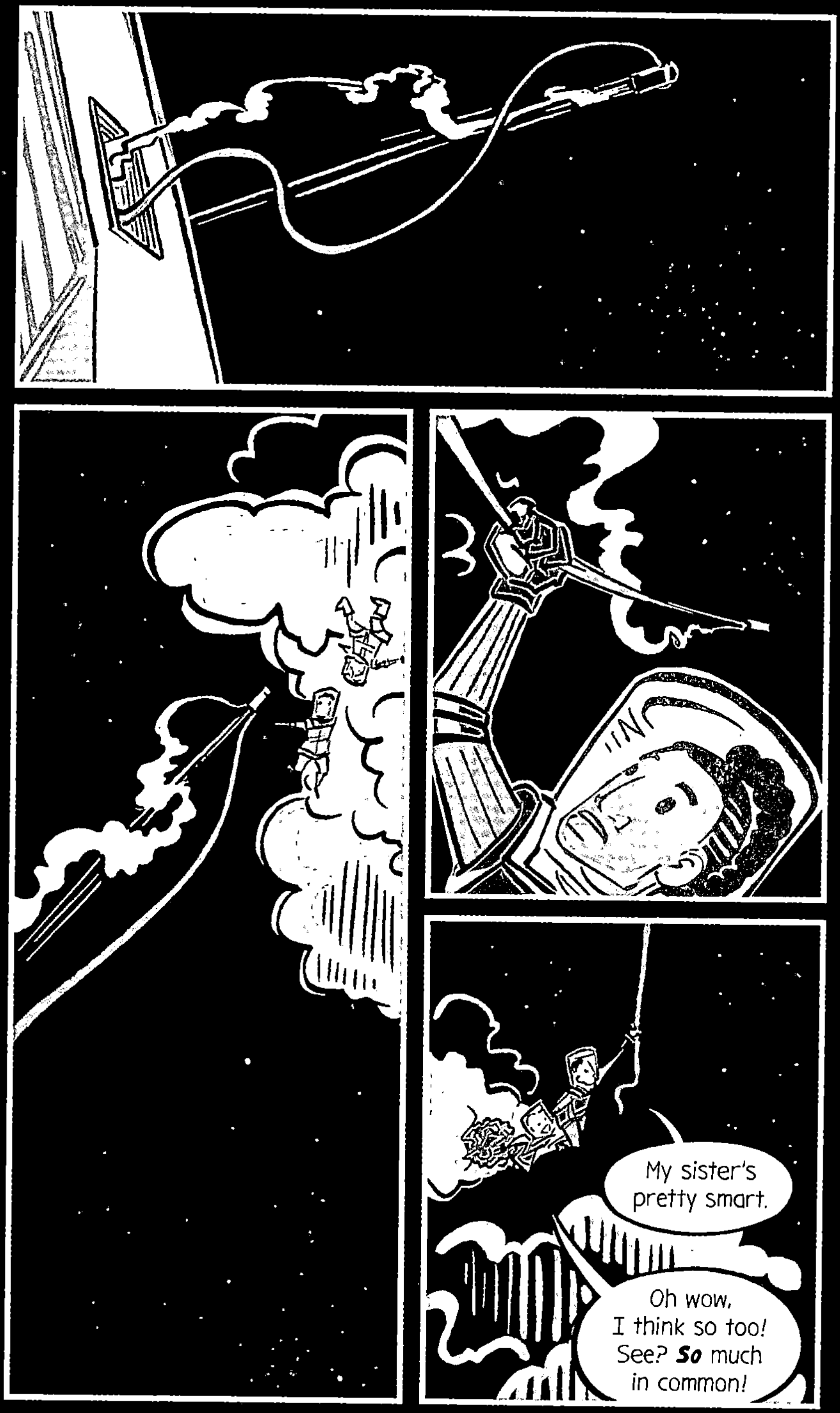
My sister's pretty smart.
Oh wow, I think so too! See? **So** much in common!

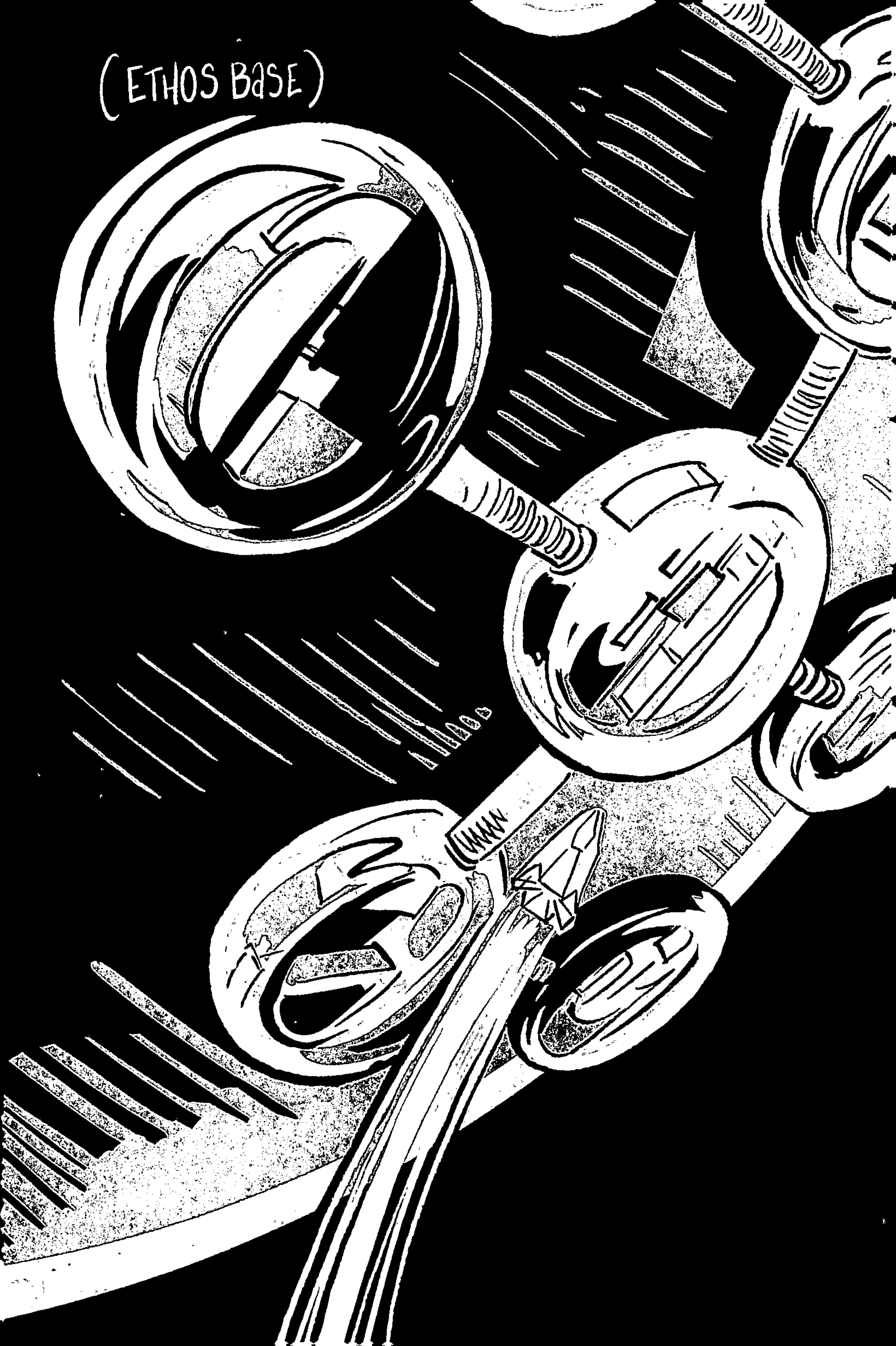
(ETHOS BASE)

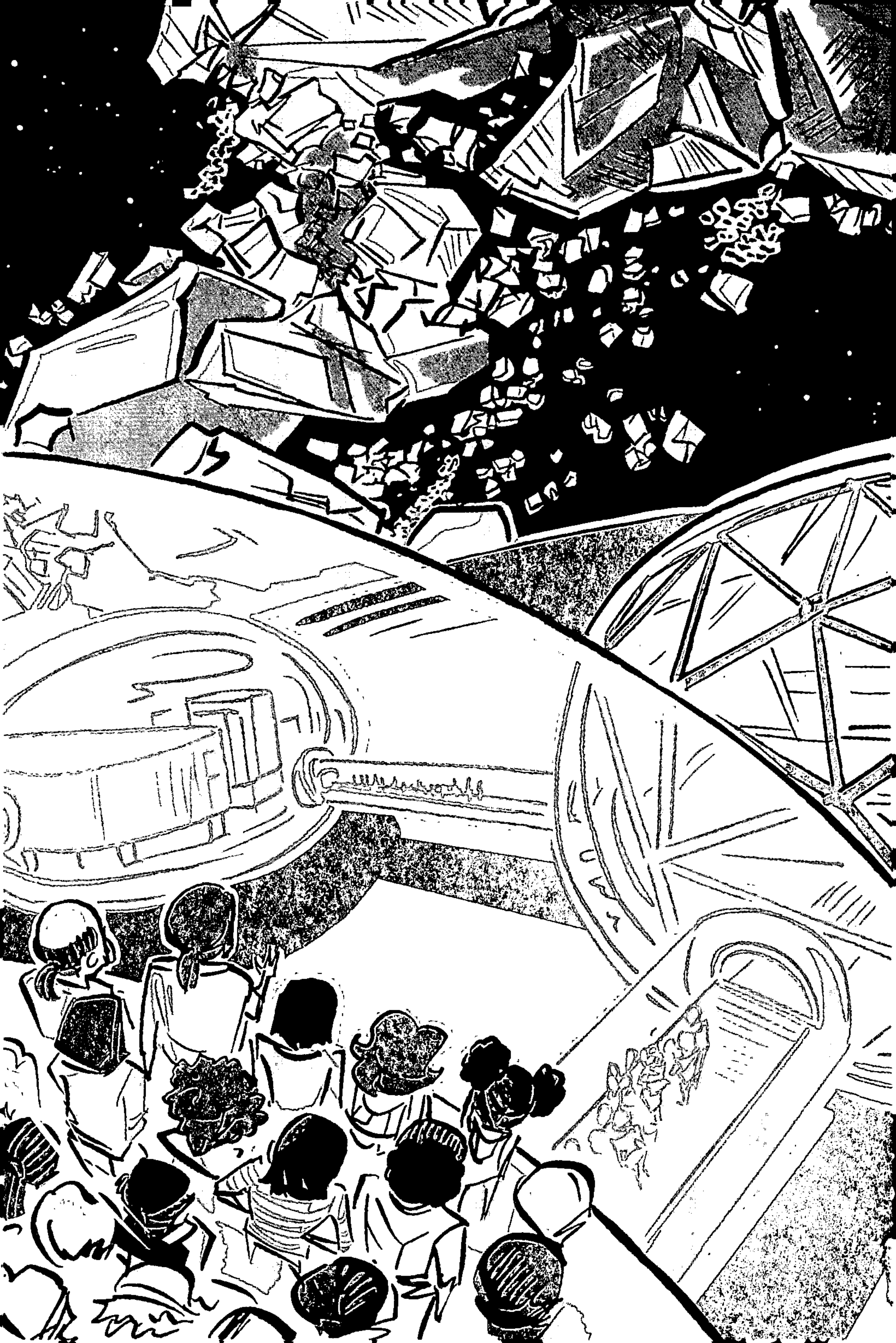

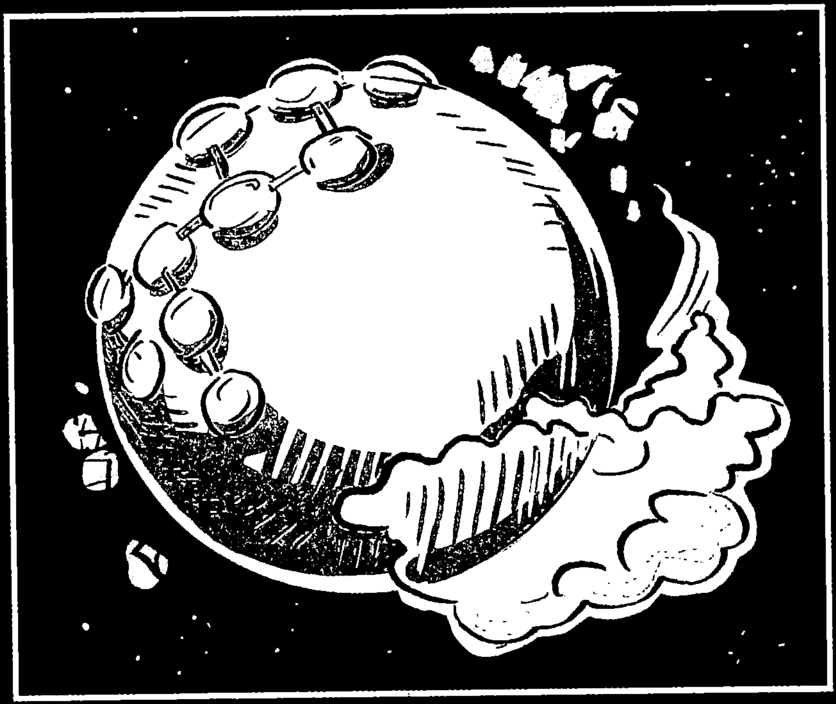

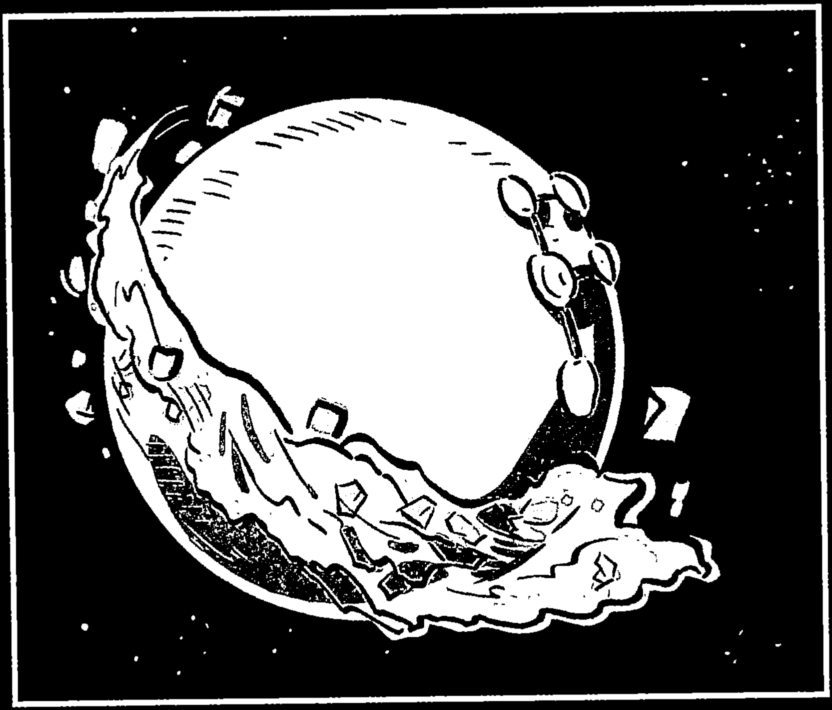

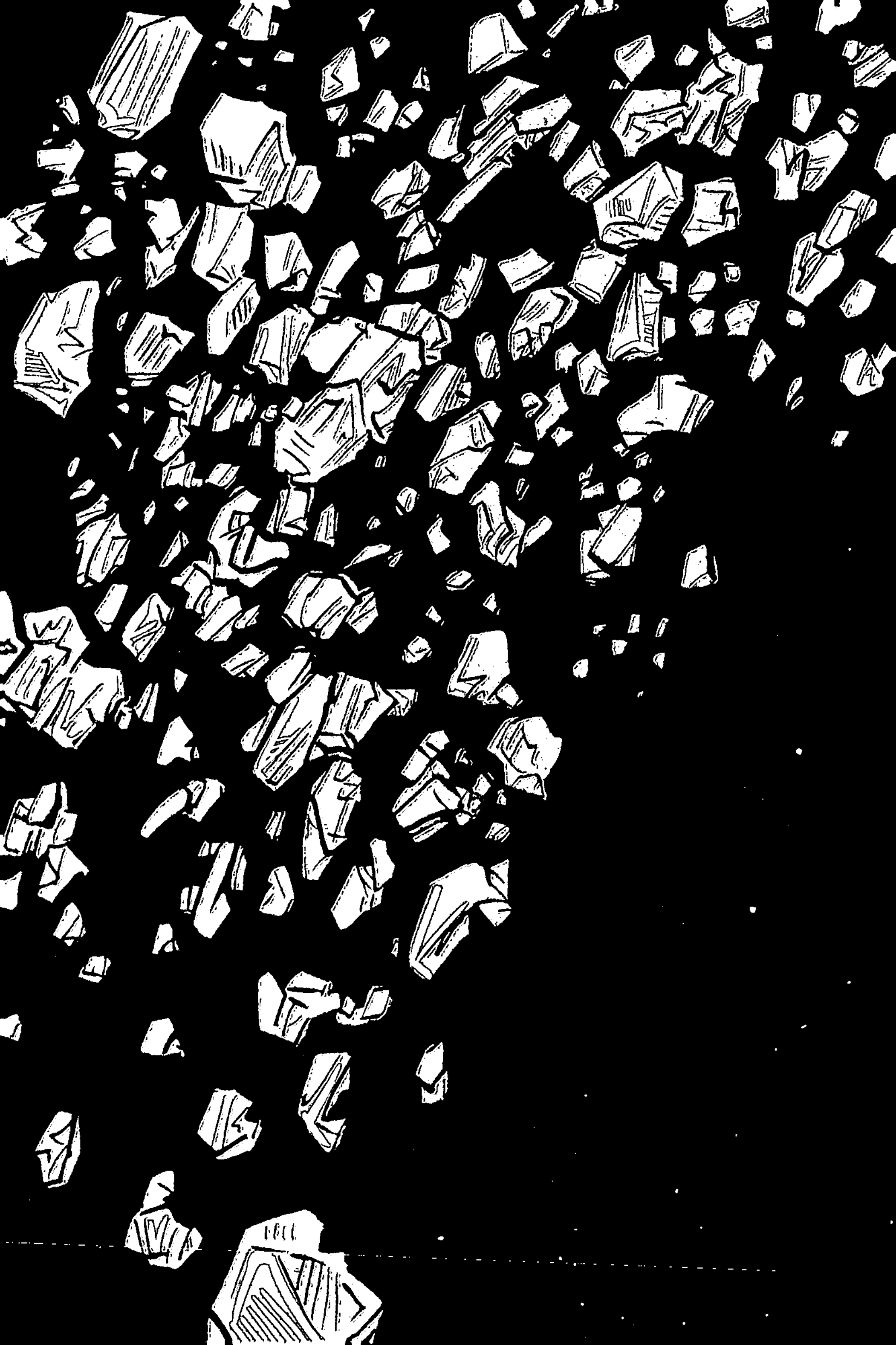

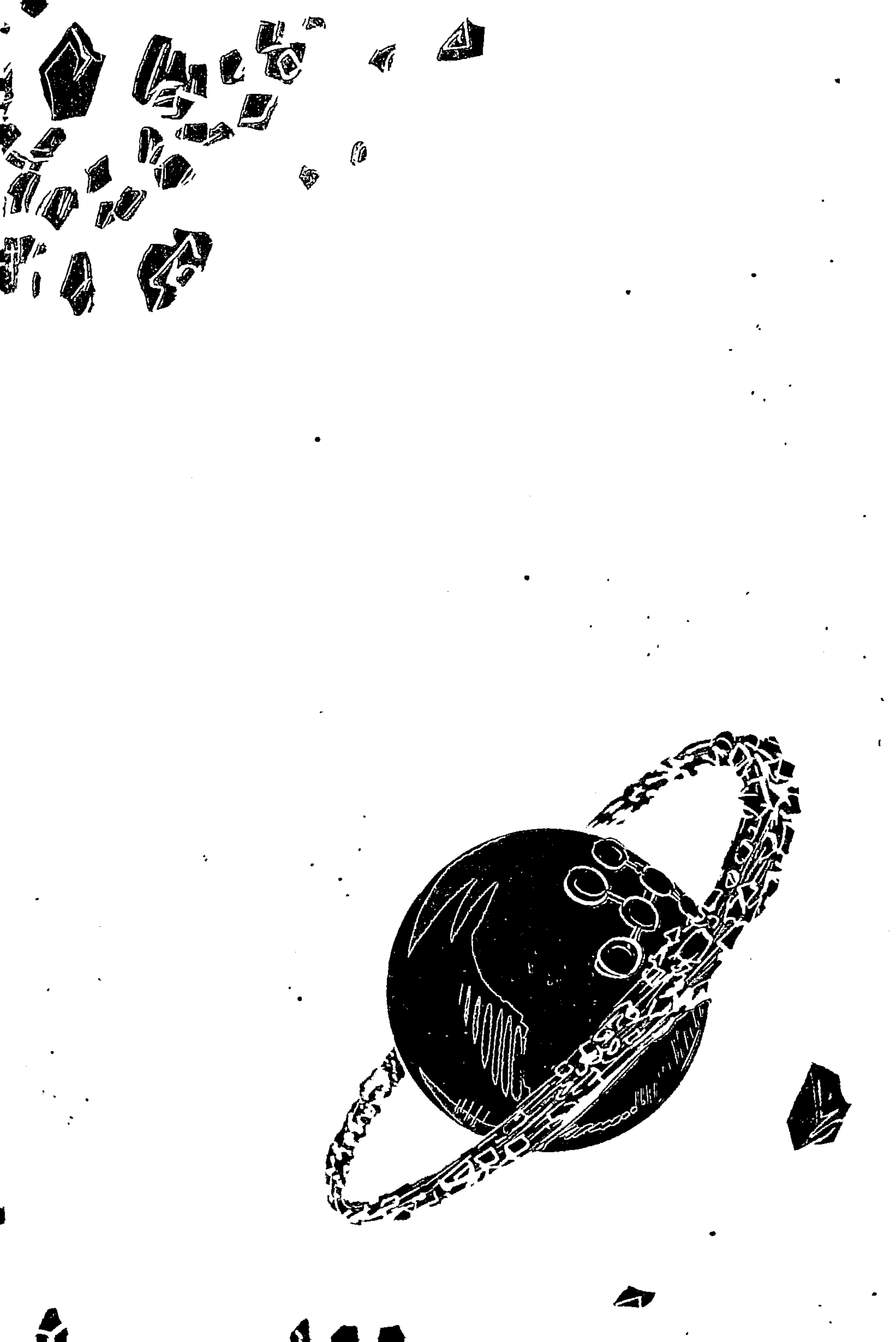

(BACK ON WILNICK)

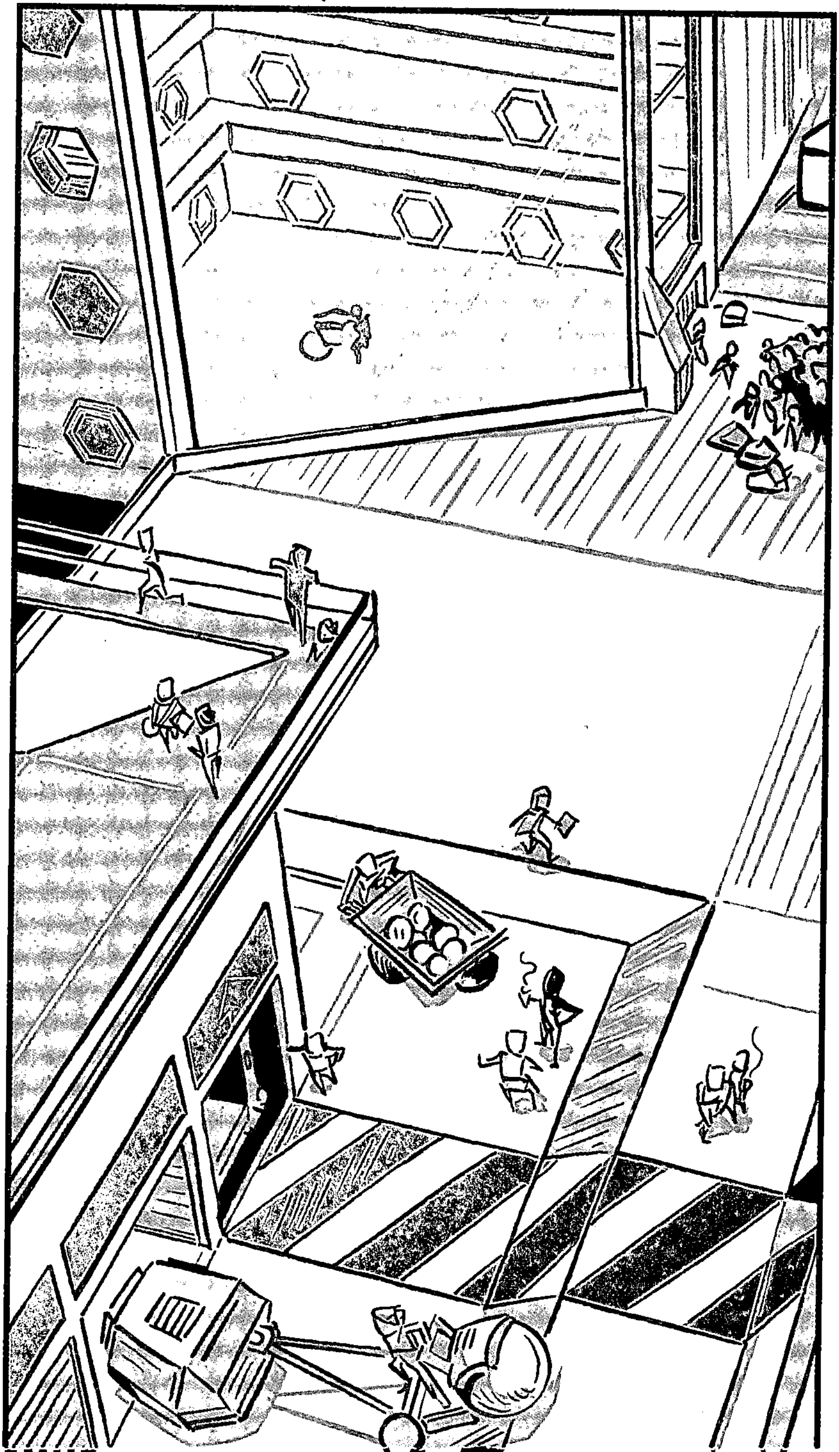

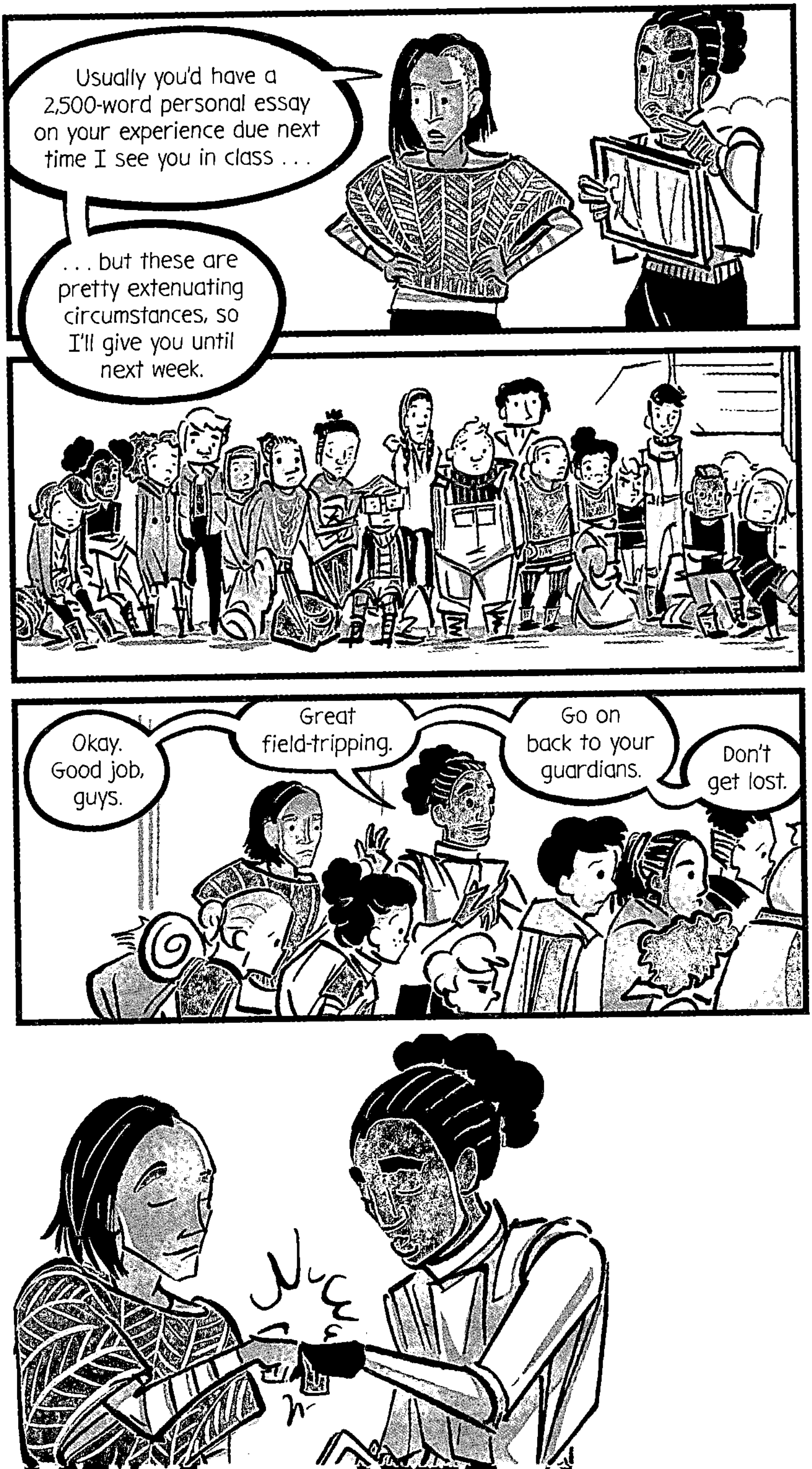
Usually you'd have a 2,500-word personal essay on your experience due next time I see you in class . . .
. . . but these are pretty extenuating circumstances, so I'll give you until next week.
Okay. Good job, guys.
Great field-tripping.
Go on back to your guardians.
Don't get lost.

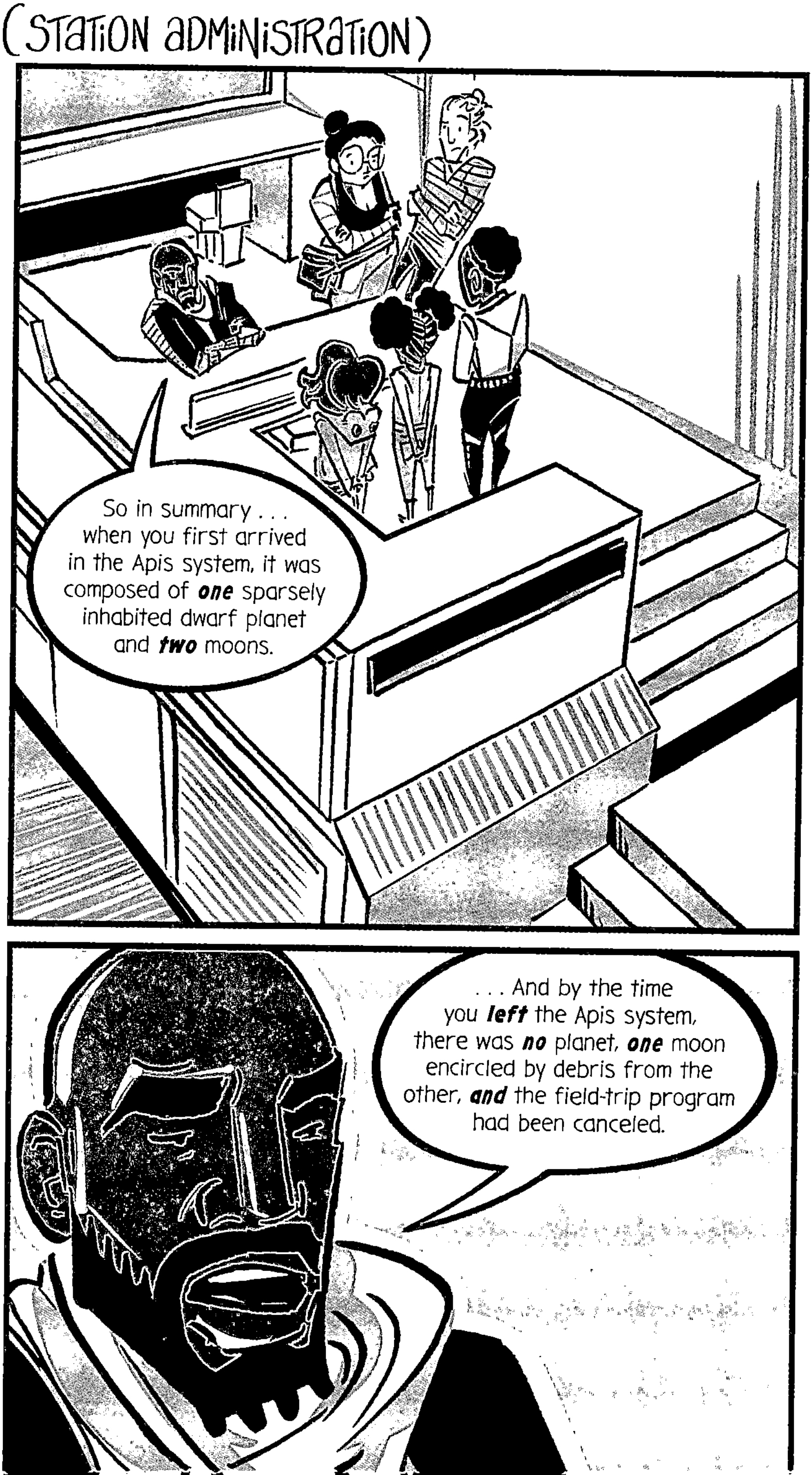
(Station Administration)
So in summary . . . when you first arrived in the Apis system, it was composed of ***one*** sparsely inhabited dwarf planet and ***two*** moons.
. . . And by the time you ***left*** the Apis system, there was ***no*** planet, ***one*** moon encircled by debris from the other, ***and*** the field-trip program had been canceled.

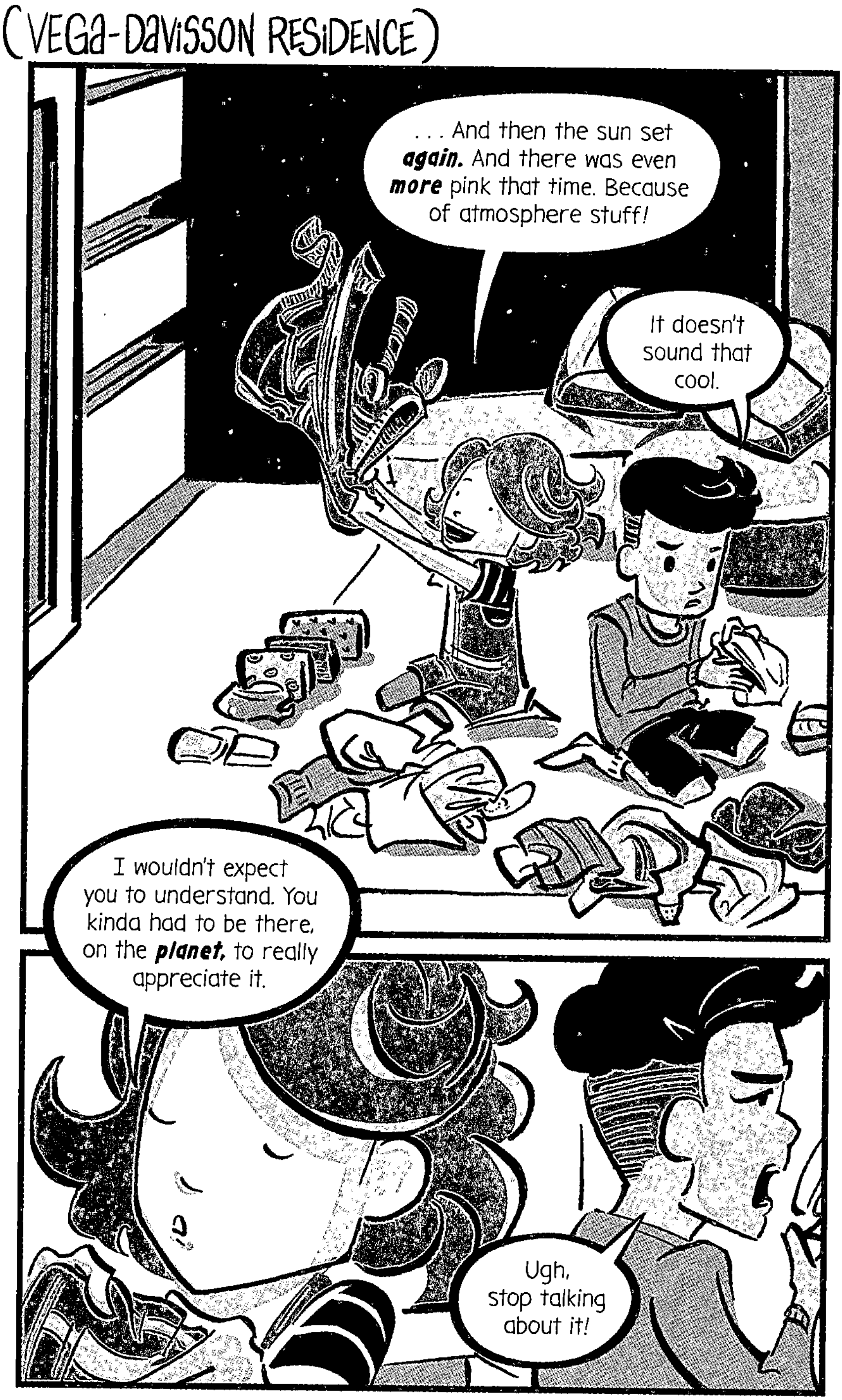
(VEGA-DAVISSON RESIDENCE)
. . . And then the sun set **again.** And there was even **more** pink that time. Because of atmosphere stuff!
It doesn't sound that cool.
I wouldn't expect you to understand. You kinda had to be there, on the **planet,** to really appreciate it.
Ugh, stop talking about it!

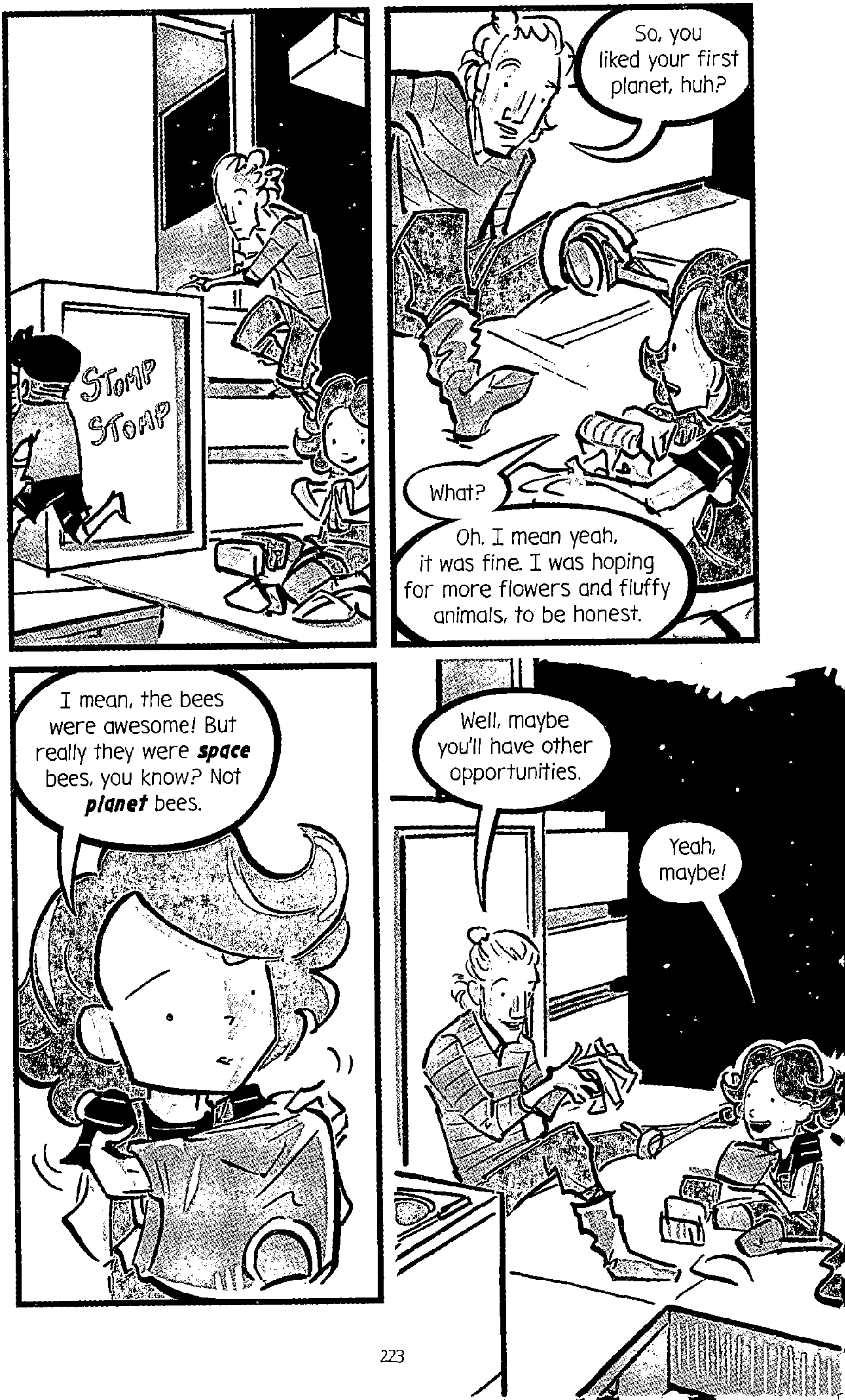
STOMP
STOMP
So, you liked your first planet, huh?
What?
Oh. I mean yeah, it was fine. I was hoping for more flowers and fluffy animals, to be honest.
I mean, the bees were awesome! But really they were **space** bees, you know? Not **planet** bees.
Well, maybe you'll have other opportunities.
Yeah, maybe!

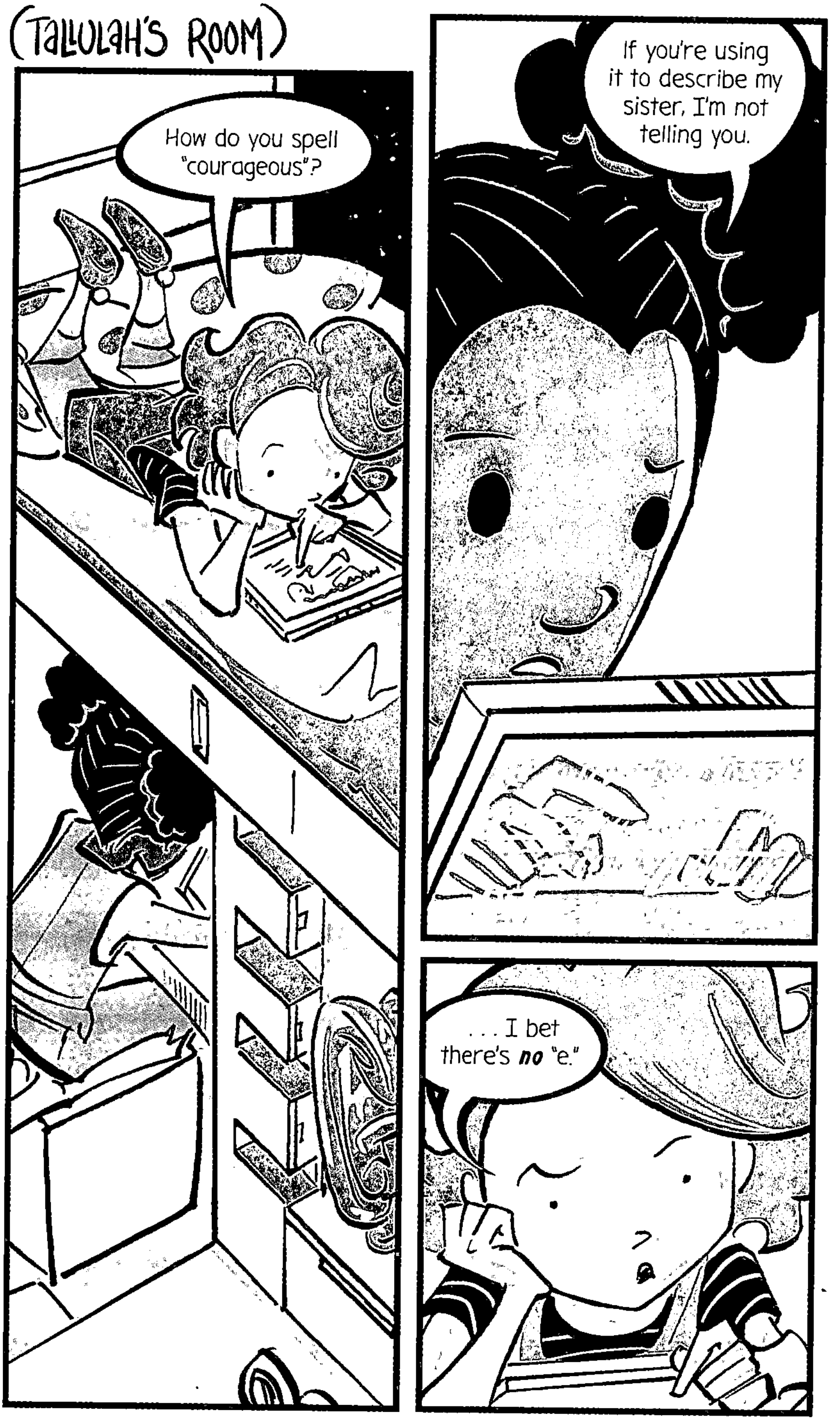
(Tallulah's Room)
How do you spell "courageous"?
If you're using it to describe my sister, I'm not telling you.
. . . I bet there's ***no*** "e."

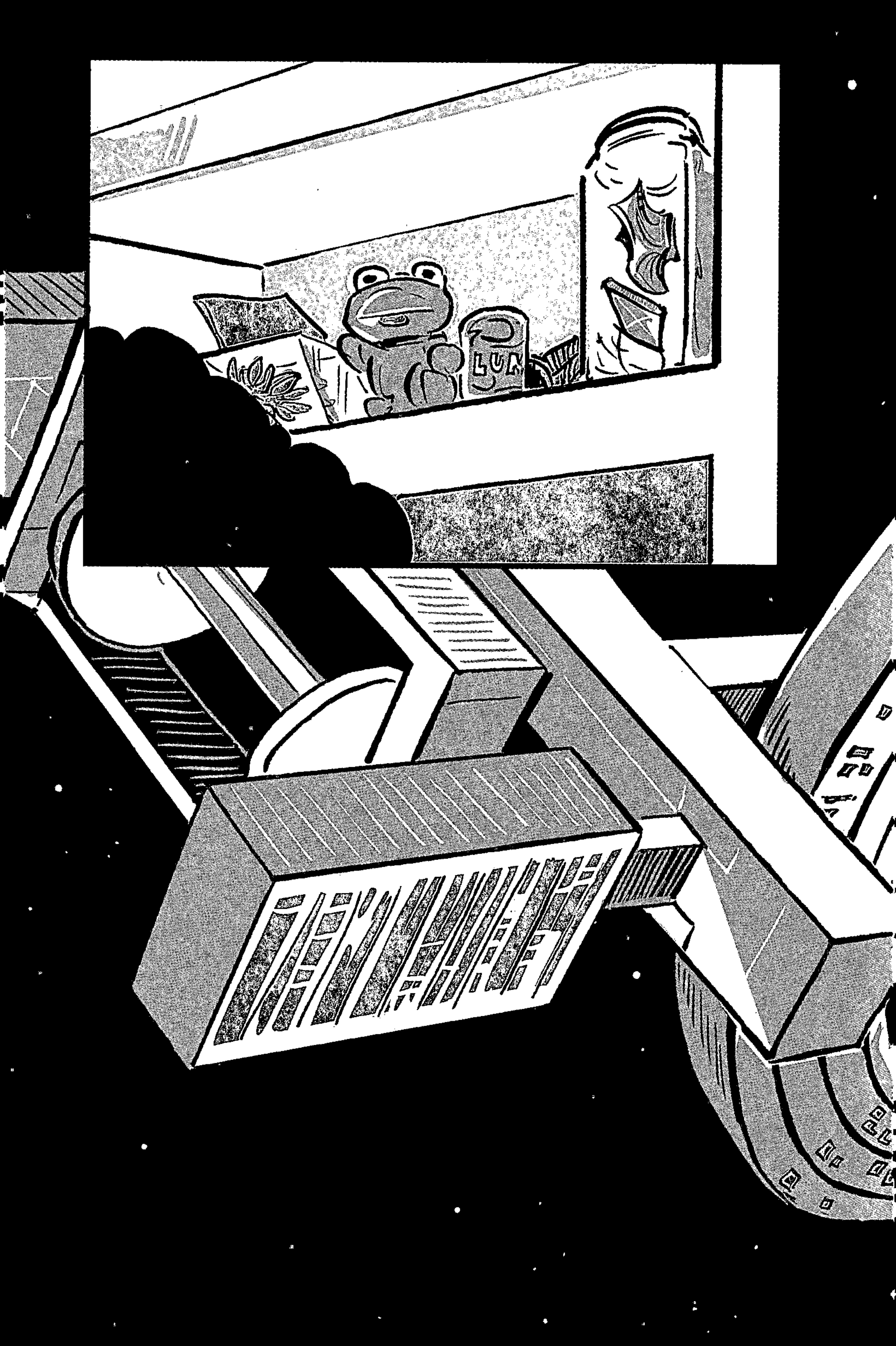

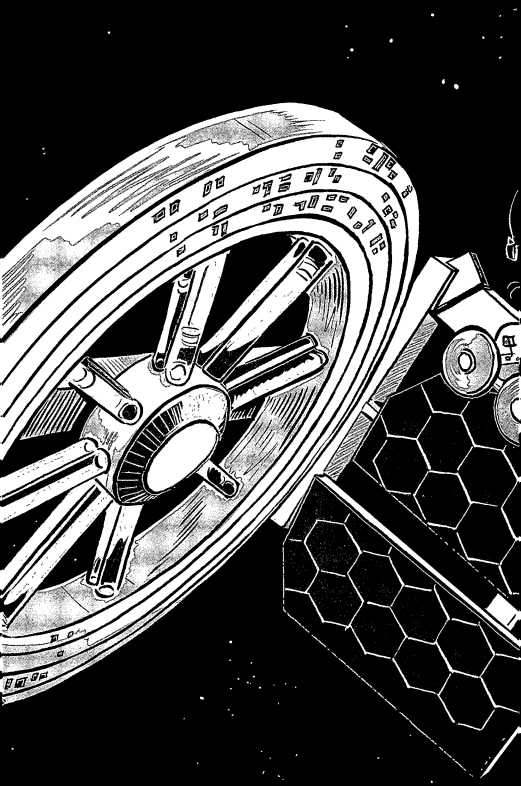

MOLLY BROOKS wrote and illustrated *Sanity & Tallulah,* and is the illustrator of *Flying Machines: How the Wright Brothers Soared* by Alison Wilgus, as well as many short comics. Her work has appeared in the *Guardian,* the *Boston Globe,* the *Nashville Scene, BUST* magazine, ESPN social, *Sports Illustrated* online, and others. Molly lives and works in Brooklyn, where she spends her spare time watching vintage buddy-cop shows and documenting her cats.

mollybrooks.com

Stay tuned for
more adventures with

Sanity &

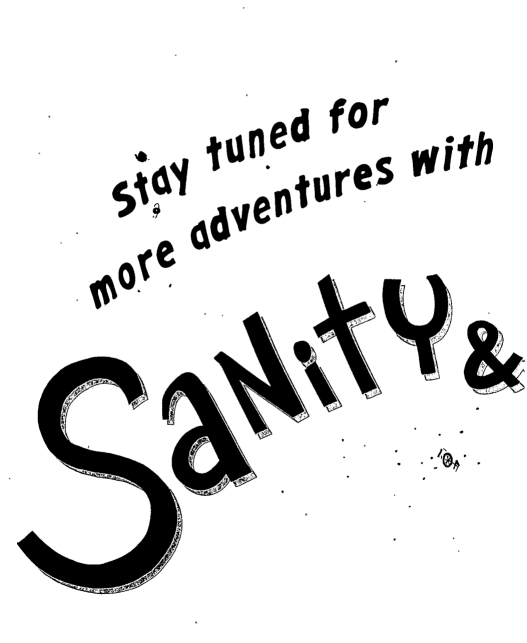

TALLULAH

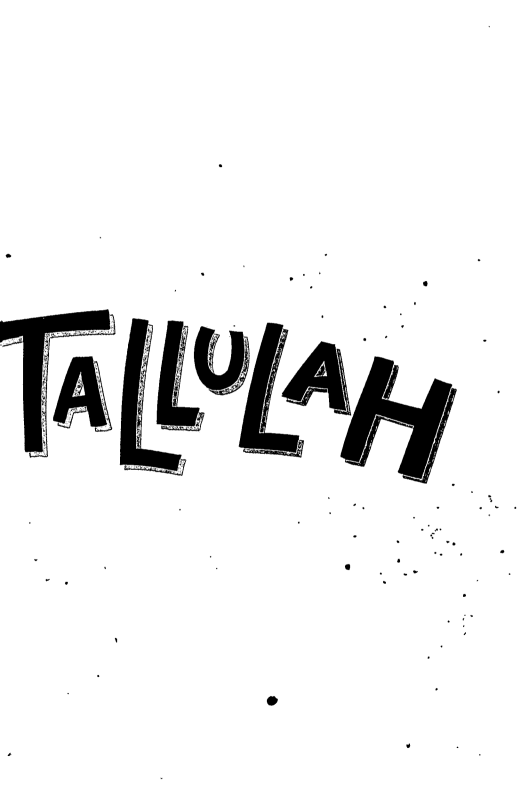

Don't Miss

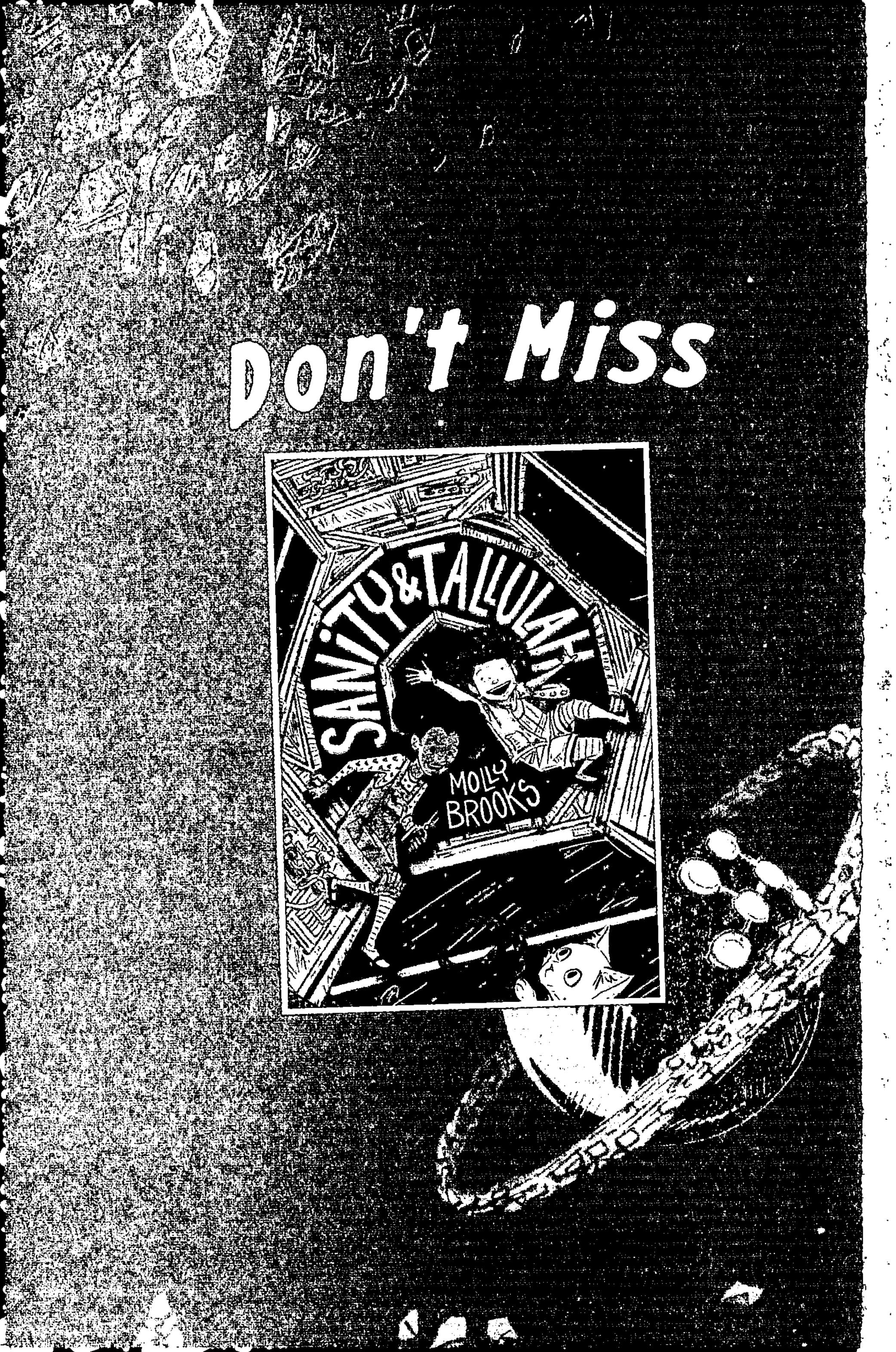
SANITY & TALLULAH
MOLLY BROOKS